OF ANGLES
&
SAXONS

OF ANGLES & SAXONS

Marc Cohen

Great Work Pub.
Toms River, NJ

Typography by Sasha Raught
Cover design by Donald Leitch

ISBN 978-0-692-67205-1

Printed in the United States of America

3 5 7 9 10 8 6 4 2

Third Edition 2016
Great Work Pub.
Toms River, NJ

Library of Congress Control Number:

2016917540

www.hitlersrockets.com

Acknowledgments

Special thanks go out to the following people: Ray Eales, a great man; and, even more rare, a good one; Karen Hahn, for believing in me even at my worst; Joshua Zintel, who taught me to strive for excellence; Israel Doyle, a brother from another mother; Rick Reid, whose wisdom and friendship have helped me to navigate many a darksome night; Lisa Fugard, bestselling author, for her invaluable critique; Donald Leitch, a brilliant designer, friend, and plot-whisperer; Denise Frame-Leitch, a great friend and heavy metal screamer; Nancy Condardo, a wonderful painter of words, who taught me the art of *story*; Sasha Raught, a master painter and terrific writer, whose talent will surely some day be appreciated; Michael Courter, another brilliant and prolific novelist, who, together with Sasha, played good-cop/bad-cop while teaching me how to write; MaryBeth Colosi, *nee* Mulhall, writer and master technician, whose critiquing skills border the præternatural; Marilyn Kralik, penner of the most mellifluous prose, whose critiques I have saved due to their puissance; Stephen Kahofer, an action writer with the character to speak his mind; Laura Lifshitz, a real-life *Carrie Bradshaw*, whose indefatigable spirit is truly inspiring; Stephen Phillips, a dedicated writer, whose breadth of knowledge has helped to uncover many things that otherwise would have been missed; David Stein, friend for twenty-odd years, who has driven thousands of miles in order to lend a hand;

Dominic Catusco, a wonderful artist, friend and pillar of his community; Timo Knopf, a great musician and friend from across the pond; Sebastian Antonin, another brother from another mother, who helped steer me through a dark point in my life; Monica D. Rocha, a great writer, artist, and woman, an important translator of almost-forgotten works; the late Gregory von Seewald, whose stern advice has, many years later, proved to have been the greatest kindness; Marcus Wendel, and the Axis History Forum, for providing a scholarly means for research; Pete, at the Toms River Diner, for always making me feel at home; and all the writers, magi and musicians, which space has prohibited me from naming, for sharing the pursuits of the path.

Finally, I wish to thank my mother, Sue; my father, Joe; my brother Phil and his family; plus, all the aunts and uncles, cousins and grandparents: you have taught me how supportive, and friendly, people can actually be; and, especially, Michele Clark Peace, a wonderful writer, and great friend over the past few years.

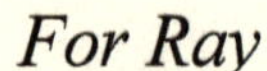

For Ray

PART I
THE LAST FÜHRER ADJUTANT

Prologue
Berlin, 1945

The Russians will be here any minute, and I know I'm about to die. In the next room is the Führer, a shadow of his former self. The once spellbinding charm which moved millions? Gone, incinerated just like our cities. Yet worse still is the fact that the Führer must now meet his fate, not deep in the snows of Russia, fighting the good fight, rather; but stabbed in the back, through the banal machinations of cowards and traitors. The things the Führer's been made to suffer! *Mein Gott*; they've broken him on the wheel.

Slowly do we suffocate under this soulless mass of concrete filled with despair. Daily does one struggle to maintain any sanity; for this is the last battle that we must face. Siren-like calls elude the defenses, coruscating the walls of this vestibule howling their paean to loneliness. The mad onrush it comes promenading into my mind, and I like the rest fear all to be lost. Life it recedes, and the memories come rushing through, paralyzing their prey.

I bite my tongue, that the pain thereof might snap me from this vision, and call the men to arms. "The Fatherland it calls," I say, bidding them do their final duty in this the last battle of the Reich. Yet they've abandoned all hope; *as have I.* But what is one to do? Well, first, the carrot. "We must hold on, so the Führer can find a way out —just like he always has." Then, as ever, the stick. "Else the Russians will exterminate us."[1]

---

[1] [Editor's Note: These are the memoirs of one Windemeer Hossbach, the last Führer Adjutant, whose verdict in the Nuremberg trial they say is about to come through any moment. I've taken his record, parts of which were written on toilet paper, and tried to convey a comprehensible narrative.] [Late Note: The final chapter is now in my possession: Thus this present translation. As for its authenticity, however, I'm sure the General will vouch for it: That is, if they let him.—Jack Suffler, 1 Oct. '46.] {Pub. Note: Friedrich Hossbach, the accused's cousin, bears no relation to this work.—Legal Dept., G.W. Pub.}

Chapter 1: Nuremberg

Prison Behind the Palace of Justice
September 2, 1946[2]

I keep reliving the scene, over and over in my mind. I mean, it's like I'm still there: trapped in the hallowed halls of the Führerbunker; yet truth is I've traded but one prison for another. Ach for the swine you see they simply shunted me off in the middle of the night, what with the rest of the so-called 'war criminals'.[3] And who calls us this rather than the very butchers themselves: the midget, the drunk, and a cripple;[4] the authors of the holocaust upon Hiroshima.[5] I just thank my lucky stars the Führer didn't live to see it.

I know what year it is too, because Hess[6] here once passed me a newspaper during inspection. And, on it, I saw the date: March 6, 1946; and now that must be weeks, if not months ago. It's so hard to tell time, what since the beatings I received at the well-practiced hands of the Americans. Sonsofwhores, why they'd written this bogus confession, expecting me to sign it. When I refused, they marched me straight to Dachau; *the punishment bunker.*

Now I fester here, what just like some common criminal. What, and Göring? Oh, he's here, too. Yes for the Fat One still thinks he can lord it up on me. Only, for once, *I have it up on the swine*; ach, for they've taken his Emmy and Edda—pah, and his morphine, too! Yes, Colonel Andrus—our dear, dear warden here—confiscated two suitcases of the stuff. Only, now he's been weaned, Fatty looks better than ever. Why he was the star of the trial; no doubt they'll save the last rope for him.

---

2 [Actual date affixed by me.—J.S., hereafter referred to as 'N.B.']

3 [They 'shunted' him from a POW camp, in the American zone.—N.B.]

4 [Stalin, Churchill, and Roosevelt respectively.—N.B.]

5 ['The authors of the holocaust upon Hiroshima': One may forgive the General his confinement, for getting his facts wrong. Hiroshima was destroyed under the watch of Truman. Meantime, in England, Attlee had already usurped Churchill from power.—N.B.]

6 ['The Deputy Führer,' likewise awaiting the verdict to his trial.—N.B.]

Yet most maddening's the fact that the Führer's prophecies are starting to come true. No, you can't fool me: for I know all about your Winston's secret speech. Yes an 'Iron Curtain's descended across Europe' indeed now, has it, Mr. Churchill?[7] Fools; for at least *my* Führer realized this all along. Only, now, what some hundred million too late, finally you've come to your senses—backed the wrong horse, did you? Well then I feel no pity for you. It's like I said in court, if Europe's going to survive—*you're going to need men like me.*

Oh, just come out and say it, alright: *the Jews.* There's no need to shirk it; *my conscience is clear.* Now I swear on my honor I'd no idea of any plan to exterminate Europe's Jews the way they said we did. Oh, sure, things may have gotten a bit rough; especially in Russia. But, dammit, *war's war*; besides, there you see we had no choice but to combat them. You know, *combat the Jews.* Ach, for they fomented these gangs, called 'partisans'. And, what had begun as an orderly occupation soon gave rise to these criminals running around, shooting my men in the back. I mean it was obvious who was behind it: didn't Weizmann[8] declare war on the Reich, on behalf of every nations' Jews? Hell—six years before Poland! Well, then why should we have treated them any differently from any other combatant? What, did they expect us to just turn the other cheek? No, a thousand years of Christianity is enough, thank you.

Now you see, when a terrorist strikes, the only thing there is is to shoot say a hundred Jews; for everybody knows they organize the stuff. What, the Russian? The

---

7 ['secret speech': There was nothing secret about it. The actual words run: "From Stettin in the Baltic to Trieste in the Adriatic, an iron curtain has descended across the Continent."—N.B.]

8 [Weizmann, Chaim, *Ph.D.*: Zionist leader; and, incidentally, a brilliant chemist.—N.B.]

swine's totally incapable of thinking for himself; let alone raise an uprising.[9]

So you see, our anti-Semitic measures were really but *prophylactic* events; compelled by the soundest military reason. We bore them no malice; at least, I didn't. We were impelled by the noblest of motives. By our love for the Fatherland. We, the cream of Europe; the masters of the world who keep burning the sacred fire of the race...

But the atrocity films; why, I just can't wrap my head around them. I mean it's impossible to believe a *German* could have done such a thing. All our achievements—victories the likes of which songs should be sung for a thousand years—yet all anyone wants to talk about's a few miserable Jews. Really, it's not my fault; I had nothing to do with it.

Still, women... *children?* Why I don't know what Himmler must have been thinking. I mean, it all seems so *ungentlemanly.* No, whenever I had to conduct an execution, everything was done in a strictly military manner. Yes it's 'One Bullet for Every Man,' that's what I'd always say.

Now it was the SS's job to comb through the rear. Well, what did their stance on the Jewish Question have to do with me? I had my own troops to worry about. Oh, only some civilian could have thought up such a scheme—a Himmler maybe, he could have done it; *but not the Führer.* Now I won't hear it any other way—please respect a man's memory!

---

[9] Until the Summer of '43, by which time the Russian had learned to mimic the tactics of our great *Panzers*. And almost overnight, there arose an entire class of artful—and, therefore, *dangerous*—men; men from whom only *we* can save you. Hang us if you will; *but tarry not take down the gallows.* For, rest assured: your time too will come.[—W.H.] [Scribble atop this sheaf has been turned into a footnote here by me. The procedure has been adopted, wherever such addendums abound. Brackets, unless otherwise indicated, are strictly the work of the editor. Prisoner's desiderata remain un-bracketed, save I have 'signed' them "[—W.H.]"—N.B.]

(A guard has just turned in to drop me a note: my attorney.[10] He says, 'The Tribunal's just begun deliberating.')

Why, where did everybody go? I mean, everything's so black. And it's hard, so hard to breathe. And so, I write; I write you see lest I should die. Oh—this is not how it was supposed to be! But when did the world go mad? Why I remember a time when the English were our friends; but then that damned woman had to come into my life, and ruin it all. I was in England, with my best friend, Jack Suffler.

It was the summer of 1914.[11]

---

10 [Seidl, Alfred, *Ph.D.*: Defendant's Counsel.—N.B.]

11 I shall write while in trance, as taught by Rosenberg; a trick Socrates himself once employed. Yea I leave this world, even as I write. For like Wells you see I've a time-machine, too. Only, mine's in my head; *for memories are all we've got.* I close my eyes, and the walls this prison dissolve. When I open them—*I will be young.* [—W.H.]

Chapter 2: The Summer of 1914

Leceister, England[12]

I wakes up on me couch, after a dream. Coming to, I takes in the sights—and smells—of Twenty-nine Chancery Lane. For as Sheila, one of the working girls has it, "Yours's definitely all-boy; especially seeing it ain't got no sense of orn'ment. That is, unless you counts the fundament 'dirty undies building up in the sink—pah, students!"

I've got to pee really bad, right but, owing to the dilemma of ages don't wants to get up. And so, stumbling off me couch, I falls upon the water-closet—which just so happens to be the best part of the flat. For it can make the unique claim to being the only pisser in all England open up on the balcony. And, down the sides run rickety-red (and, sometimes, yellow) stairs leading into the courtyard. Such contraption, a travesty 'pon taste, at least serves so's to warn passersby's to which side of the tracks they truly are on.

As the graffiti: 'Down with the King'; 'Up with the Worker'; and as ever the inimitable, 'Piss off!'

---

12 [As translator, I caught a break: All but the end of the chapter is in English. As editor though I had to scream, resisting the impulse to amend the Cockney (essentially limited to this chapter) that he had acquired. Also, certain idiosyncrasies had better here be mentioned. First is the omission of articles and prepositions (much more frequently than those of us who have also spent time in England.) In addition, he breaks off dialogue, mid-sentence, then continues via a new fragment. Only with the rarest exception have I remedied this with a comma. As for the original, much of it adorns the countless reams of toilet paper hitherto mentioned. For, the old war conference journal had been confiscated: The beginning of this record with it. I have since had the good fortune to obtain it. Moreover, certain chapters were written while in the dock: Hence the 'court apportioned paper,' to which the General later alludes. It appears he had been working on this memoir, in lieu of his defense, throughout the course of the trial.—N.B.]

I've been living here almost a year, what since me step-mum you see dug her claws into the old boy. Then, soon's I turned eighteen I enrolled in uni.[13] Of course, it was only a matter of weeks before I pissed away all me pounds. And I laughs; cynically, I laughs, not carelessly as better befits me. For almost it seems some future self's speaking right now. Whether to mock at or preach, that I do not know; *I ignores it.*

Pub-lic Ed

Raleigh's, that rustic pub, devoted to the fine art of collegiate excess; a home away from home. Only, not for me Jack. Why, he's always so busy with these *books.*[14] But not tonight. "We've been invited to this gath'ring," I says, shoveling some gruel. "For God's sakes, it's the weekend." *Besides—I could use me a companion.*[15] Well, so I lets into him. "Is that why we're here—*books*?"

"I, I wouldn't know what to wear. I—"

And ah; *I can smells blood...*

"Come," I says. "It'll do you some good for once to go on a bender. You know, meet a few ladies[16]—why, I'll introduce you to Sheila; it'll be a laugh!"

The Jacker less agrees, so much as follows me down the path to the pub.

Raleigh's

Decrepit stucco walls, drenched with what a rot of paint, mixes with the stink of sulfur so's to greet us.

---

13 [At the *Leceister* (read, 'Lester') *Municipal Technical and Art School*, currently known as the *Leceister Colleges of Art and Technology.*—N.B.]

14 [Where he has employed underlines for emphases, I have treated these as italics.—N.B.]

15 [re, internal mentation: Further have I italicized any such apparently *originary* utterance, as opposed to simply entranced addendum. The convention is strictly arbitrary, representing merely my best effort to tease out what the General originally meant.—N.B.]

16 [ladies: *i.e.*, 'of the streets.'—N.B.]

Saddling up to the pub, I light this tart a fag. "A toast," I says, in honor her 'fession. "To red light and to liquor!"

And everybody laughs. For, at Raleigh's, *I am a God.* A bit largish for me age, I've thinned out, owing what to this 'fine cuisine' in England. Ah, but the wenches simply loves me six-foot frame; *that is, when I've the quid for it.*

The Jacker's busy telling me how he likes to transport himself to the "World of the inner vision, open to both scientist and dreamer alike."

The wretch, but I could've told him: *it's open to drunkards as well.*

Only, something's wrong with me Jack; why he ain't list'nin to a word I says. So, I follows his eyes, right, and so comes to the source: *Monique Gabell*, the only amateur here. Well, so I warns him: "You best be careful with *that*; for Monique you see's the only stupid slut dumb enough to bethink herself she should go to school." No, I points him a more fruitful direction; for thank God at least Raleigh's never lacks that other sort[17]; the likes of which without life in England would truly be impossible...

An indeterminate time later I awakes, banging me 'ed on the table. Then I remembers: *it was awful.* I mean, I seen them... *kissing.*

So, I filibusters me drink as though it's me last. Eventually, the Jacker passes out; and now *I* moves in for the kill...

The stupid slut; why, she swatted me like I'm some fly. I feels woozy; I feels ill; why I feels I's the center o' 'tention. But then I realize: 'I've just ridiculed that wily slut in front of the whole place—I made that hussy flee!'[18]

Again the world it goes black.

***

17 ['other sort': Again, courtesans.—N.B.]

18 [Here Hossbach uses single quotes, apparently to indicate internal mentation.—N.B.]

Coming to, I helps the Jacker gets home. For you see he ain't yet 'dept in the fine art of the pub crawl; whereas I've long acquired me sea-legs...

Morning hits.

'Humph,' I says to meself. 'I'm getting too old for this'; knowing full-well I'll be back at it tomorrow. You know, the growing resolution, and what the headache that goes with it which says, 'I'm never drinking again!'

The Girl

Monique Gabell did not mean to fall in love with Jack Suffler. Why the lascivious little slut you see wouldn't go for a real man. So she flirts with this harmless boy; *only, I has to watch.*

But you should hear what passes his lips: 'Oh Monique, me darling of ages.' Or, 'Honeybun I do think I's the lost Earl o' Leicester.' And, worse still, 'When I looks in your eyes I sees why God made the Rainbow...'[19]

Still, she found him cute. What with the ruffled brown locks; and that impudent, self-effacing smile. *And the eyes*; good God, *eyes*: 'Russet, brown, riveting; why Raphael himself never an once suspected the depths, the which such brilliance could lend.'[20]

But I'll be: the Jacker's just come in with his foal. I looks up from me couch; she eyes me up and down; and God I wants to fuck her...

So I goes to the pub; and returns; and good God they're still at it. Eyes half-closed, yet still, I can sees nothing but her.

Time begins to pass; and Monique to take the hint. Only too well, rather. For, they're gone. Day after day, gone; *leaving me all alone...*

---

19 [re, single quotes: Here he uses them in introducing a quotation predating the 'present.'—N.B.]

20 [Saying attributed to Aloysious Hossbach: Family album, ca. 1896. —N.B.]

At the end of the month, our rent is due. And so, alone amidst all the bedlam and the bunk, I begins to brood: *England has nothing more for me.*

Unable to obtain passage I sequesters meself inside the coaling station on-board some merchant vessel; trick one of the working girls taught me. And so, covered in blankets, and boosted by all the confidence of the naivete of youth, I steels meself for the journey; bottle of schnapps don't hurt, neither.

North German Coast

'Pon reaching port, I jumps ship, heading south. It's dark, yet still I can make out some *Wandervogel*[21] hiking the way to Bremen; and, mixing among them, desperately tries to recall mein *Deutsch.* I smiles, pretending me toothache; another trick of the working girls. Oh—P'pa'll be so glad to see me!

At the first rail-head however I'm accosted by the constable and made so as to stop. Having no papers with which to prove *mein*[22] identity, he throws me in back his truck. Swine—took away me bottle! Oh, but ach, the prospect of being sent back to England's upset me no end...

After a night in jail—with my[23] best meal in weeks —I'm taken to a barracks outside Oldenburg where, much to my incomprehension, I'm forcibly repatriated and enlisted in the German Army.

Some silly git's before me. Confused, and what so stumbling with the subtleties of my native tongue I say, "Why, what the devil you want with some bloke like me?"

The Sergeant he smiles. "Haven't you heard? The Serbs have rejected the Austrians' terms—you're going to war, boy!"

---

[21] [*Wandervogel*: Youth movement committed to cross country travel, and oft given to strange, bohemian tastes.—N.B.]

[22] [A mishmash of Gutter German, and Potpourri English.—N.B.]

[23] ['my': *mein* in the original, which, this point on, reverts to German for the duration; whence continues this present translation.—N.B.]

Chapter 3: The Birth of the Bomb

Somewhere in Belgium: August 5, 1914[24]

We march seven hours empty of stomach, on a caricature of sleep. Yes for ours you see's an historic mission: to smash the perfidious French; then, God willing, enter Paris.[25] To me it seems a whole lot of marching over nothing. Still the *Zeitung* thinks our plan to be 'bold, meticulous; yea nigh-infallible'—whatever that means.

Still you see there's a kink in their logic; and now it's arisen to block our path in the form this Lilliputian[26] Army. Why no less than the Kaiser himself only recently'd offered an alliance.

'I'm so sorry,' they say. 'We're sitting this one out.' Then, to cover up the deceit, they act as any scoundrel would act—why they've gone and declared themselves neutral. Swine say they'll fire on anyone who so dares cross 'their' soil; pah, as if some pimple on the arse of Europe could have its own soil.

Ach, but the Belgian's insane with pride, owing what to his mad king: 'History's greatest criminal,' the Zeitung has it. 'Has allowed himself be led astray,' owing what to the 'venomous vituperation of pacifists and Jews'; and now he's gone and declared war on us, even as we march through his shitty little country...

At length we're conducted into this ditch, whereupon each man lays claim to his own piece of dirt. I fashion my own little hovel just a few inches from the man to the left and to the right. Schmidtie, my new neighbor here, thinks they haven't a clue what they're up to, and that, "That's why they've stuck us here."

I bid him be quiet, then feed him the sum of my wisdom: "If we take fire—*duck.*"

---

24 [While, typically, the German soldier was subjected to four months of the most rigorous training, a group of students had been allowed to pass after a mere six weeks. Our memoirist had all of six *days*. Whether a misunderstanding, or some sergeant's idea of a joke, he, along with said students, had been made to accompany a fully trained unit, already on its way to the front. As for the 'students,' it seems Hossbach was the only one to have survived.—N.B.]

25 ['Paris': *Pr.* 'Pah'ree,' with a slight *roll* of the 'r.'—N.B.]

26 ['Lilliputian': He means Belgian.—N.B.]

We break camp, headed destination unknown. The long dusty road,what the howling wind kicking up midst the groans of sleepless men still—*but we march.*

Hossbach's Cell

Verdict Day, 1946,[27] *the guard says Zero two-hundred*

The light'd come on in the hall. With it, this wave of oppression washed over. Panic mixed with fear ran wallowing up to my head to the pitter-pat-pat of boots; and, oh good God, I'm awake; and, blast, an old man once more. Worse, my stomach seems to be taking revenge. The Americans. Haven't fed me for days: 'punishment' for concealing Jodl's knife during inspection. That's alright: Speer[28] *snuck me some potatoes from the mess. Plus, I killed a rat last night: I'm full.*

Somebody's coming [...][29]

03.00

The swine simply tore my cell apart, rending me from the vision. Ach, for the Fat One[30] *you see'd carved the Amis*[31] *a new one. True, that was weeks ago; still, it's all the papers wish to talk about. And, now, it's payback—*

27 [The General's non trance, *i.e.*, imprisoned present, narration is indicated in italics. What he refers to as 'Verdict Day' was September 2. Hossbach had been under the impression—rightly—that the Justices had just met to decide Jerry's fate. As for the immanence of any such results, he was badly mistaken. The verdicts are expected any minute today, 1 Oct. '46.—N.B.]

28 [Speer, Albert: Minister of Armaments. Pity poor Hossbach; or, at least, the eyes of his editor. For, Speer, who sung like a canary during the course of the trial, has not only been allowed to continue *his* memoir—but even granted use of a typewriter!—N.B.]

29 [Brackets: Again, mine, unless otherwise indicated.—N.B.]

30 [*Reich Marshal* Göring, Hermann: Head of the Luftwaffe; *Shitler*'s chosen successor.—N.B.]

31 [*i.e.*, Americans.—N.B.]

Dachau Mark Two! *Save, instead of being beaten, these motherless plutocrats have caused my record to simply 'disappear'.*[32]

Now I'm reduced to documenting such ill-treatment here on bum-fodder. I'll keep it with my toiletries, in case of another search: for you cannot deny me my memories. *Let no one tell me 1914's not so real as now; for my thoughts you see are more vivid than your miserable existence. What with your family; your church; why your whole nation in hock to the Jew. Really, how dare such swine presume pass judgment on me...*

Thus, pen in hand, I try to get back to the vision. Eyes half-closed, and ah—I can but smell *grapeshot. Dust it kicks out from under—then, pffah! Like that my limp is gone; and the eyes, those golden eyes of youth appear once more:* awake, alert, alust they come into focus. *Full of wonder my mind moves quicker than it has in years. And, though this toilet paper's still a bit clumpy, I make the adjustment: and give myself up to the vision...*

The Road to Paris: August 5, 1914

Dust it kicks out from under; *I am beginning to choke.* Still I can make out that we're on the march, owing what to the fact of my feet moving under; *God knows where.* Still, if my senses don't deceive me there's this voice, this disembodied voice; yielding memorics of things gone by.

As if in answer to my question it says we're on the march against the delightful little town of Liege. Delightful you see because it's the last fortress before Paris. Really, I hope we shan't have to destroy it; for Liege has the best drinking houses in all Europe...

---

[32] [Through a sympathetic gaoler, I have managed to procure the confiscated record: It's an eight by ten inch hardbound. A carryover from the last days of Hitler's Reich.—N.B.]

Oh—donnerwetter, nochmal![33] Glancing at my insignia I see: *I am only a Private*; and yet, somehow, somehow I'd thought myself more. Yes for there's this 'Sergeant Hossbach', you see, this character I've built in my head; I suppose we all have one. Must be he who told me of Liege.

Schmidtie he doubts any such prescience, saying I must've overheard some officers during my sleep. Still, like any man, *I cling to my delusion...*

As Above

Bullocks; for our commander it seems's a dirty Jew. Why the swine you see sent me here along with Schmidtie —the only friend I have in this godforsaken place—to reconnoiter the enemy. At least we can drink. Still, what good's a drink without a wench? Still, *we drink.*

Squinting through the spyglass Schmidtie sees, "Maybe a battalion, judging from the proliferation of campfire some five-hundred meters north."

We radio *HQ*, then descend to the swamp, whereupon we're joined by the rest of the regiment. And, well what do you know? It turns out that Winckelmann[34] really isn't such a bad chap after all. Says there's an 'Iron Cross' in it for me when we get back.

He's in a good mood—then again, aren't we all? I mean, fancy a battalion taking on a regiment! No, next stop —*Paris...*

So Below

We occupy this series of trenches, which just a few days ago'd belonged to the enemy. Alas one of the Waffle

33 [*donnerwetter, nochmal*: fig., 'Blast!'—N.B.]

34 [*Captain* Winckelmann, Mordecai: Hossbach's Battalion Commander.—N.B.]

Eaters arrives, bearing a message: request to retreat, no doubt. Fine—let them all go home!

Yet still, what does that race-traitor do, that mad king? Why he pulls a stunt you see the likes of which no one's ever seen. Gathering at Battalion,[35] Winckelmann reads us his message: 'Neither peace, *nor* war.'

That degenerate inbred[36]—who shouldn't be allowed to speak—adds some silly canard about 'defending Belgium's honor'; huh, since when did the Belgian have any honor?

We're conducted back to the trenches, whereupon, a voice, this manly voice it booms out: 'A man must be willing to see villages burn, rather than give way to such swine.'

But then I realize: *I have just said this to Schmidtie.*

Unable to restrain myself I continue: "These degenerate race-mixers are always busy running around, what with all the inferior races—egged on by the Jew no doubt who, of course, keeps to his own. Why just look at America, a country he's only recently infested: they too've declared themselves neutral. The American—bother the American! *He'll* never amount to anything."

Schmidtie does not reply. At least now he's his rifle facing the other way. All this time I've been busy cleaning mine, or playing look-out for the Belgian; yet he's his face stuck in some book. I'd say he's the trench fever; *save he reminds me of someone.*

---

35 [After their amalgamation at the swamp, it appears the two, perhaps three battalions constituting Hossbach's regiment, now dispersed once more. Upon instruction at battalion, the regiment presumably would have been re-formed along a broad based front. I lay this all out, lest there be any confusion, being the Belgians that had opposed them are said to have constituted that of a 'mere battalion.'—N.B.]

36 ['degenerate inbred': Albert, King of the Belgians, a man to whom history perhaps has been more kind.—N.B.]

And, while I don't own any books, through the press you see I've managed find myself somewhat an education; unlike—oh, donnerwetter, nochmal! Why they've gone and blown the only bridge leading over the Meuse; now we'll have to build another...

It's hard work, but eventually we succeed in fashioning enough ships so's to constitute a bridge over which to cross. Still, our timetable's a shambles. The Captain's beside himself. Discipline's meted out like we're all in some prison: newspapers, books, all the diversions of trench-life are made to simply disappear. It's fortification by day; and drill at night. Personal time comes to naught. And, though no one says it, still it's on everybody's mind: *Liege must pay...*

20.00 Hours

Torches extinguished, I make myself one with the muck. Now, as a rule you see I like to sleep in battle dress; especially in the trenches. For, there's simply not enough time to (a.) take off one's boots (and, if they're a Corporal, shine them); upon (b.) adhering to infinitesimal quantities of sleep; all while (c.) still being able to function; that (d.) one may give battle in the morning. That is, should we ever actually have to leave the trenches...

Night falls. Fires are put out, then Winckelmann gathers us round to read us our orders. What all bemedalled and shiny, his chest like an ornament on somebody's hood, he unravels this great big scroll; then, stentorian, reads: "By order of the High Command, the Fifty-first Regiment shall go over to the offensive, commencing Zero Eight-hundred."

We laugh. I mean everyone knows they'll run first sign of battle. Still, we're ordered to get a few hours sleep; which, of course, nobody does.

08.00

Zero eight-hundred arrives; and what the whistle along with it. In a daze, owing to a lack of sleep, I go over the top.

Bullets they fly. Why, we're supposed to be making for the hill; and yet, somehow it seems, I'm headed for the woods. And then, a voice, this manly voice it booms out: 'Just where do you think *you're* going?'[37]

I try to ignore it, thinking my feet to be shuffling me away from the sound of fire. But then, something inside takes over, something more ancient within and says: 'Sergeant Hossbach must look out for his men'; and, shouting hurrah, I realize: *I've come back to join them...*

Metallic clamoring rends the air, midst the onrushing echo of discordant gears; must be some farmer. He's fucking his wife, you see; forgot to turn off the tractor. I turn to Schmidtie, who it seems's accompanied me into this ditch. "Look," I say. "A shed, Schmidtie, a shed! Like this tart you see I was shagging once back in Br—"

Blood it pours out the side of my head; like a tire shredded through steel. What red-marrowed hues darken my countenance, painting me some savage Ingun-red. And, though I cannot see, I can but smell the stench of phosphorus; lingering with the scent of haemorrhage and death. Pulsations they growl deep from within when, releasing my hand, I note this funnel piercing the side of my skull. Something it grabs me, a hand; *no, it's my hand, you see, and I am going to die...*

"Now," I say. "*Jump!*"

---

[37] [Single quotes in the original, ostensibly to indicate *internal* mentation. Yet such scruples seem evidence of an epiphany strictly contemporary in origin. I have nonetheless chosen to retain the device, in order to indicate their (supposedly) internal provenance. —N.B.]

Flopping in the lake, I bark at that fucking farmer, so's to have something on which to concentrate; *why the pain's excruciating.*

A bullet whizzes past, seeking finish me off when, lungs half-full, I realize: 'I am underwater.' Spasmodically, a lone figure washes up beside; bubbles they proliferate. Why, it seems we've come up for air.

"*The bridge*," Schmidtie huffs, dragging me onto shore where, amidst the confusion, nearly do I fall back.

And, grabbing about half-blind, I reach for my weapon—or, at least, somebody's—off the pile of men slowly building about; then go over the side. On purpose, I think; yes for, it seems I've spotted one of our rafts adrift.

Now, some men jump; others still swim. And yet, somehow, one by one they all come to my boat like it's some fucking floating trench; surely we all must sink.

I turn, facing the sound of fire, desperately trying to recall the drill: 'Point, aim, and shoot; lock, reload, then duck; point, aim and—oh shit, I forgot to shoot; point, *aim...*'

The Colonel arrives, some crazy sonofabitch up on a horse. He orders us mount the bridge; thence over the hill to the dock where the enemy lay.

Paddling something fierce, our fucking floating trench's reconnected to the bridge, rather more boat than hole; bullets they expedite our exit.

I run, and then fall; leap, and then limp. Ten, no less twenty boots they pounce upon me, eliciting a murderous scream from within; *life it begins to fade...*

An indeterminate time later I awake: *my ribs*; why, my ribs they seem to have been crushed; and I think someone must have stepped on my nose. The dizziness begins to fade, and I can feel my legs come under. Yet every ounce of pain is magnified a thousand-fold, each time I'm buried under one more wounded or dead; the only question being, 'Which am I?'

Lifting my head, I witness the slaughter: row upon row of previously animate men; *gunned down by a few filthy Frogs in a trench.* I scream with a mad spasm; and, oh good God, it seems, I've ejected my insides; a twitch; then, nothing.

August 6, 1914[38]

The Fifty-first Regiment really did succeed in taking that hill; at least, that's what they say, *these voices here which surround me.* Eery we lay, propped not by dirt, rather, but beds; then so at last we've taken the approach to Liege. At least, I hope; I mean, I'd hate to have been taken prisoner.

An orderly arrives—speaking German, thank God—saying, “Headquarters found out what happened back at the bridge; and then the word came: '*Liege must be destroyed...*'”

The doctors encourage the more ambulatory among us look outside, so's to witness the slaughter. Seconds they pass,minutes perchance; *we await transfixed...*

Fire it pours from on high; why the very heavens seem to open. Zeppelins come hurling bombs upon their unsuspecting victims; these sons of Adam who've sinned against the race. The earth it opens as if to swallow them; the people they pray; Armageddon is here...

***

The truth however is somewhat different. For, the death toll they say inside the doomed city proved to be all of nine people.

Well, one thing's for sure: the bomber's[39] no use in war.

---

38 [Thirty-one years to the day preceding the atomic destruction of Hiroshima—N.B.]

39 [*Ohr-boxen*: lit. 'ear boxing;' fig. 'to inflict aerial bombardment.' 'Bomber' is more than adequate for the English speaking reader, provided he keep in mind that, at the time, 'bomb' would have meant 'grenade.' Aviation soon altered this fact.—N.B.]

Chapter 4: My Awakening

Hospitals give you time to think; yet think you see's the last thing I want to do right now. And, through the morphia, I begin to feel the pain of a world gone to smash. This laminate it cuts with morgue-like sterility, in quietude conspiring me to turn philosophical. For, hitherto I've been concerned only with my belly, and my bed; with my old man, and Jack. Yet slowly comes creeping some nameless fear, imaginary phantasms come wringing out my mind taking aim at me; *and I it.*

Shapes which seemingly inhabit the ward come into focus, and I recognize the scent: like an insane mist, it wraps itself about. And, opening my eyes I see: *a woman bearing down upon me...*

"He's awake. No, he was up before, but—"

Bespectacled, bald, the doctor he booms: "Why was I not informed!"

Hands on thighs, she sneers: "You were too busy riling them up for the bombing; well, you sure succeeded with *this*. Ech, we had him all safe and sound; a *coma*. But you—yes you, doctor—you woke him, alright. It's just," she glares, staring self-righteous. "He couldn't take it; collapsed during the bombardment. Poor sot: been in and out ever since."

White light inundates my eyes when, tracing the scent, I come to; *why, she's simply stunning.* I pat my cot; only, daren't ask if she should sit. Rather I say, "Any bloody English?"

Apparently my question's a sign I'm better; *she moves on.*

The manly nurse (for, there's always one) brings me my meal: egg rolls, parsley, and pork; *hmm, fattening us like calves for the slaughter.* And, fiddling with what must be yesterday's corn, I muse: 'Good God, Jack—where *are* you? In the grave, what down by some river? Or perchance in bed the other side this wall?' This question it torments me no end.[40]

Why, I feel so *ill*; almost I give up the ghost. Not before recalling this story P'pa used to tell, concerning the which, in this feverish state, I figure must be true. Eyes half-closed, I envision my doppelgänger[41] leaving my body; and, piercing the wall, cause it to say, 'Any bloody English?'

There is no reply.

A noise it causes me to stir. Sweat runs down the side of my face: *it's my fever; why, it's beginning to break.*

The return of my double heightens hallucination, and the world comes crashing down; alas I return to the world of the senses.

I feel I'm going to burst, and so focus upon something familiar; lest my soul not simply float off. And my attention is riveted to this man berating the nurse in front of me. I can't quite make out what it is he's trying to say.

'Who *am* I?' says this voice; this *different* voice within. 'A Jerry? A Brit? And just what do their squabbles have to do with me? Why if I'd been caught stowing off, I should have been taken for a spy and made an end of.' "And yet, I'm good enough to fight—and, if need-be, die? Oh—what's this war about?"

"This war is about leading a meaningful life," says the man upon whom I've been fixing. Some grim-faced Corporal; what with such exquisite mustaches.

---

40 [Scribble atop the sheaf reads: "Of course, my thoughts were with Schmidtie, too."—N.B.]

41 [*Doppelgänger:* A 'double,' or 'imaginary body,' common in popular lore.—N.B.]

And, woozy from the morphia, plus all the stink of anti-septic, I fixate on those royal whiskers. He's on crutches he is. Must be a leg injury, or a foot; I try not to stare. Now, in civilian life, one would find him gaunt, even sickly; and yet, he's the staunchest one here.

"You've gone delirious my boy. Whether from the pain, or the morphia, that I do not know; my intention was not to startle you. But you were wool-gathering out loud, and so in need of the answer."

"A *meaningful life*," I say, trying to wrap my head around it. And, finding those royal whiskers once-more, his face it comes into focus; this helps drive off some of the wooziness.

"Yes," he says. "*A meaningful life.* Oh, I know you: I know the type. You young people—generation of swine, I say; *of swine who like concrete weigh down the nation.* Of 'men' who live but to feed their own bellies; of 'men' with bourgeois wants; and hen-pecked needs. An entire generation only longing for sleep; or to but just drown itself with drink; *anything, anything lest consciousness not return.* Oh, sure, you'll find some meaningless job, stripping you of all vitality. Then, then you'll tie the knot with some ridiculous Hausfrau, who'll proceed to rob you of all zest for life: *thieves, scalawags, crooks*—the Undermen[42] who oppose this war! The born submissive; as opposed to the bold adventurer. The 'Family Man'; as opposed to the Man of Vision. Yes, I know you: I know the type. Now, *hear me,*" he prates, recalling me what from my stupor. "*Private*," he squints, trying to make out my name. "*Hoss-bach*: for a *Volk* cannot eternally evade the calling of the blood; *it cannot hide from destiny.*"

The apparition he vanishes; or, more likely, has merely moved beyond the field of my vision. Then, a voice, this ex-ternal voice continues: "This war shall teach man the virtue of Frank and of Gaul; of Angle and of Saxon.

---

[42] ['undermen': *Untermenschen*, i.e., 'subhumans.'—N.B.]

We, the creator of culture; we, the conqueror of Rome. Only, some forty years of decadent peace have sapped Man of that alone by which he is made truly great."

Now, I don't know whether it's the morphia or the message but, somewhere, something inside breaks; and, like a flower to the rain, *I give myself to this man...*

"The war," he proceeds. "Alas this great war's upon us! For, finally, a theater wherein Man might truly test his virtue. Oh, I thank God every day, for behold—behold this glorious war!"

He paces, stomping from another's cot to mine; until presently his leg gives out. Dispensing Nurse Manly's assistance, he hefts himself up then continues. "A war so colossal it shall impose selection for the next thousand years. *True meaning*: the meaning of blood; *the meaning of soil.*"

Why, something's been stirring in me all this while; the feeling of a fire within. Like when P'pa used to tell stories out by the woods; *oh, but then Stepm'ma would inevitably intervene, enchanting him what with her witcheries...*

Hmm; must be the scent this nurse's brought me back. And yet, his words, this Corporal's words somehow manage drown out her profundity. Like an opera he wails, his voice like unto some stringed-instrument; giving rise to a sea of hate. Hate for all the injustice; a hate buried deep within. And, verily, the voices of the ancestors arise, seeking their revenge...

And yet all this time you see my eyes they shift from grate to grate, as if in search of something. Moreover I seek reasons behind such wrongs he enumerates. Looking within I see: *nothing.* Next to God; and nothing still. Then in a flash the revelation is revealed unto me like some savior amidst the sea of senselessness. And, open-mouthed I reel, "Who *are* you"; half wonder, half rage.

Extending a hand he says, "You may call me Wolf.[43] Here, this is my landlady's address; should you be discharged, please pay her a call."

Like a vision he comes near, as though God himself approaching; then sticks this piece of paper in my hand. "Give this to Frau Zachreys: she will let you my room; for *I* shall no longer be needing it."

Why, who *is* this heaven-sent man?

And, weighing me what with these cold, magnetic eyes, he drones: "All I ask is that you should write. Write, and tell her your stories; for she has no one. Well, good-bye. Perhaps we shall meet again; perhaps not—long live Eternal Germany!"

And, almost against myself I say, "Long live the Greater German Reich!" Yet once more he's moved beyond my field of vision.

"*Wait*," I say, making an effort to turn my head when, finding those royal whiskers once more, his face it comes into focus. "Why are you being so kind? Why I'm just some poor swine such as yourself—doomed to die a meaningless death in a meaningless world—*bother* your meaningful—"

"*Silence.*"

This word it cuts, it stings; why, *stings* like P'pa's old whip...

"Show some respect; if not for me, then, at least for yourself." He props himself against the bedpost, careful lest his hands should touch any bedding. "Life indeed could turn out to be a series of disconnected incidents: a shell could land this instant—blowing you, me, and all our ideas to smithereens. So tell me—what have you done with your miserable life? Was it mere chance which brought me here; or perhaps something more? *I cannot answer this question.* One thing I do know is—such things are never trivial."

---

43 [In German, the *W* is pronounced like our 'V,' the *V*, 'F.'—N.B.]

Nurse Manly appears, proffering some papers, the which he dutifully signs. "*Private*," he prates, his discharge[44] apparently procured. "See you in Paris!"

And, with that, he's gone, faded from memory, that web of eternally-fleeting moment; forever grasping at the passage of sand through the fingers of fate. Which, try's one might, one cannot help but lose. The trick they say's not to think about how much you've lost, rather, than what you still have.

Therefore, if I am going to die, let it at least be for some cause; *you know, like all this 'blood and soil'.* I mean, otherwise, it's just slaughter: men mowing down men in one senseless assault after another; what with my number only waiting to come up...

After a snooze of inestimable duration, I recall what I was doing when this Wolf fellow'd chanced appear. During what few waking moments allotted, I'd been engaged in a mission of a very different sort; *alas my eyes they drift to the grate once-more.* I'm convinced it must lead to the laundrette. Well—what better place to literally change into a civilian?

Oh, but ach, this pressure's exerting itself in back of my skull; and events are more than I can take. Somewhere, something inside me screams: *this is your last chance.* The premonition it tightens like a vice upon my soul, and I know that I must choose: *I'm coming home...*

And yet, somehow, somehow my heart just isn't in it; why, all I want's a good night's sleep. And so, closing my eyes, I think of the Austrian chap I met before; and fall asleep.

August 19, 1914

Sonofabitch; why, they've sent me to Liege: same mud, different hole. Only, now, now this sensation's built up inside. If I had to give it a name I think I'd call it a 'fear

44 [re, 'discharge': Apparently from hospital.—N.B.]

of death'. Oh, I was scared before; the whole time. It's just, before I met this Wolf, I cared not whether I lived or died; *mine was only not that I should suffer.* Given the alternative —a life on the run, a life without *meaning*—the benefits of the soldierly life unfold before me; what with the championing of excess.

The NCOs[45] note my morale's improved almost overnight. Why even our Captain, the Jew, says he sees my potential, commending me for my work with the Shed.[46] Straight-faced and sober, he encourages me apply for officer's school.

Well... so I do.

45 [*NCO*: Non-commissioned officer; *i.e.*, a corporal or sergeant.—N.B.]

46 ['The Shed': Hossbach's name for the supply hut.—N.B.]

Chapter 5: Letters to the Enemy

January 01, 1915

I'd forgotten where I was. Life it comes crashing down, and I awake in this hell-hole, tied through a series of trenches stretching all the way to the Channel. Somehow, we've gotten bogged down in the north. So, we wait, albeit in such primitive quarters.

The same dream keeps repeating itself what, going on a week: *I am back at the General Staff in Berlin, raising my hand in map-class: time and again the first with the answer.*

Then, in the first waking moments, it's impossible to tell where I really am. Oh, I'm not so sure it has anything to do with some 'new found belief', rather, than three months from the front; but officer's school appealed to me. What's more, it's caused me to look at these men in a new light. No, no more of that 'Sergeant Hossbach' stuff. No, from now on, these men really are my responsibility; *for fate you see's allotted me see that they should die well...*

Moreover, now I'm a Leutnant, Winckelmann's a new-found respect for me. And so I'm not surprised he's invited me to quarters, which's really a field-tent the size of the eastern end of our trench. He talks a lot of nonsense before sending me off. Only, not before handing me my mail; really, how nice.

Returning to our trench, I make myself one with the muck; and, propping a few sandbags beneath my head, proceed to open my mail: *Jack, thank God*; the old b's[47] in England. Ach, for Monique's crazy uncle you see's taught

---

[47] ['bugger': *Br. colloq.* A more prosaic explanation was deleted by the Censor.—N.B.]

him to make this gas stuff everyone's talking about but, like God, no one's ever seen. Oh, but I know Jack: *war's not his thing.* For him, gas is but a chimera; a construct allowing Man to lift Isis' skirt, and so peer beyond into the secret of matter...

Still, a scientist needs patronage to fund his experiments; something concerning the origins of life. And so, like Da Vinci—nay, like every scientist—the Jacker's been forced to pander his genius to the expediency of the age; i.e., *to a military patron.*

The *Zeitung* it screams: 'Albie's Been Prepping for Gas!' Why, I'd thought it just a ruse; *until now.* Ach, for, the Jacker has it, he's cracked the code for some new sort of dread poison stuff.

I'm not surprised: he used to dream the stuff up all the time, then prattle on about it all night. As a rule, however, I was generally too drunk to listen; only now do I sense the import. Imagine, taking nitrogen from out of the air, then imprisoning it in some shell[48]; *like God dealing souls to Man.* Then, fire your ordnance, and—boom! Turn it back to gas once more.

Now it seems he won't even get to try. For, ever since my return, *peace it reigns at the front.* In fact, since Christmas they say there's been a halt, a truce. Why I even played football with some blokes from the *BEF*;[49] that is, until Winkelmann arrived to chase them off. It's hard to believe we should be expected to fire at each other again.

Oh, but ach—he raked me over the coals, he did; but it was worth it. For I found out a good deal concerning

---

48 [Thus for Jerry, being his 'stick grenade' was far superior to the Anglo-Frankish 'baseball.' At Loos however it was piped, via tubes, into the air; hence the calamity that soon transpired.—N.B.]

49 [*BEF*: British Expeditionary Force.—N.B.]

Jack. Yes, Tommy[50] says he's become a celebrity. Why what a stitch; I can't think of a more boring bloke.

The problem, as ever, is the girl; for theirs you see's just this side of a scandalous existence. I mean, the Jacker actually *lives* at Gabell House. I know where it is, too, for Jack and me used to throw stones at it. The fact they aren't married would be scandalous. That is, should it ever should become known; for the English are a savage race. Besides, a soul so sensitive as Jack's shouldn't be exposed to such tongue-wagging, which truly is the sport of the great unwashed; huh, save it for women and serfs.

Now it turns out this Philo's Jack's commanding officer. Seems he'd gone and gotten the poor boy a commission. And, being his lab houses the work, it's only natural where he should be quartered.

The poor sot. Whispers've begun to spread; for it's known the old boy's a niece. Still, truth be told, I'll bet the Jacker spends more time in the lab, than ever he does in Monique's boudoir...

Now, it's a curious thing this war. For, the English have no conscription: hers[51] is all-volunteer. Why the latest romp even has it the Kaiser, when asked what to do in event of a British invasion, is supposed to have said, "Well —call the police and have them arrested!"

Yet for the Jacker to avoid service would be seen as a sin in the eyes of the aristocracy; the which he so longs to aspire. In addition, Philo could use a hand with his experiments; which, the Jacker has it, are badly in need of funding. And not just any funding, rather, but that which only a government can provide.

---

50 [*Tommy*: An Englishman. In this case, those with whom he had just played football. In so doing, Hossbach proceeded to learn the latest regarding his mate.—N.B.]

51 ['hers': *i.e.*, army. Or, in this case, the *BEF.*—N.B.]

Further he writes: 'HMG'd[52] become alarmed to learn Philo'd once met Fritz Haber.[53] The First Lord was miffed; some young-buck by the name of Churchill. He grilled Philo for hours in front of the Lords.'[54]

Then so it is this dropout's become chief assistant to the head of chemical weapons; why, I fear he's over his head. Still, I must admit being a bit jealous; for, it seems, the Jacker no longer needs me to find trouble...

CO's HQ

Winckelmann's called me here to quarters, evidently for another of our one-sided little chats. Scarcely have I arrived, than he says he hears I'm quite the raconteur. Before I can utter a word of protest he hands me this notebook and pen, saying, "You can write your friend."

I'm surprised, seeing, ever since the English got here,[55] the censor's really been cracking down; letters to the enemy are strictly forbidden.

I end with a flush: 'May we never meet again!'

Back in the Trenches: Several Weeks Later

Innuendo abounds, and I am given to realize: my letter was never even sent. Great. Now my superiors'll know all about Betty the Shrew; well—why should the boys in Brixton be the only ones?

Curling up, my own little pile of mud, I immerse myself in the Jacker's missives. Schmidtie he proves more than a willing audience. Why the occasional shell isn't even

52 [*HMG*: His Majesty's Government.—N.B.]

53 Some Jew chemist, with whom P'pa's very much taken.[—W.H.]

54 [Churchill was merely being more pragmatic than the myopic men at the front. For, no sooner had the new year spread its good cheer, than fighting erupted once more. Any illusions of peace would not be entertained for another four years.—N.B.]

55 ['here': *i.e.*, to the Continent.—N.B.]

so much's a nuisance. Rather it directs one's attention from the stench of rotting horse and decomposed flesh; not to mention the rumbling going on deep in one's tummy...

He interrupts every now and then, explaining a term or providing historical context. That which follows's a compendium[56] of what we think the Jacker was trying to say:

The 'First Earl of Bottomsmack'[57]

Abiogenesis, the ancients had called it. Science however claimed to have put an end to such tomfoolery: *life it comes from life.* Inert matter can never beget living things. Oh, sure, they say, at some such point, in the most distant past, some such thing must have transpired; *but only once.* Then, after this 'Act of God', they set up a deistic dogma, stretching all the way from the Pulpit to the Academy. And ever since, 'abiogenesis' has been but fit for untrained minds.

Only, *Philo knew better.* Oh, how he must have gushed at the prospect that he, England's battiest Cockney, the 'First Earl of Bottomsmack', as the *Daily Telegraph*'d once dubbed him, should be the one to found a new age; *all in His Majesty's name.*

The irony must've given him cause him to reflect. For, the Jacker has it, a few years back, the Colonel'd been summoned by his fellows in the *Royal Society* to present his findings. Whereupon Philo, ears ablaze, set about castigating the very pillars of science for the past hundred years, culminating in his experiments with the 'life-energy'.[58]

---

56 [He means 'concatenation'—N.B.]

57 [Here, or so he imagines, we find Hossbach in 1915, giving us the skinny on his mates the year before.—N.B.]

58 ['life energy': A kind of subtle matter, according to Dr. Wilhelm Reich, a German Jew with a hand in everything from psychoanalysis, to something he calls 'biophysics.'—N.B.]

Silence. Next, whispers, echoing in an avalanche of reproach, employing much use of the terms 'buggery' and 'quack'. For, surely they said, the old boy must be mad; and it left him a bitter old coot.

Now, somewhere round this time Philo's brother—Monique's old man—had gone quite irrevocably mad. Seems the old b'd[59] more or less adopted the poor girl; before long his niece had taken over the day to day running of Gabell House.[60]

Thusly did the Colonel have much time to brood the Summer of 1914.

Then, *war came*. And, amidst the scare, HMG became desperate for the dread poison stuff. Rumors spread, alleging we 'Jerries' not only had it, but were prepared to make use of it. The old boy must've been energized by all this talk. So much in fact he'd gotten it in his head to approach the *Royal Society* once more. For, in addition to his experiments with the life energy'd lain his work in improving the nitrogen content of the soil. Which latter, called 'nitrogen fixation', Philo had pruned from no less a luminary than old Fritz Haber. Boasting the potential to feed billions, the process can be put to the development of deadly new weapons; then so at last, Philo had learned to speak the language of the Lords.

Yes, England would have her gas; and, with it, Philo his funding through war. Alas the very wankers who'd once had him on, would presently be lining up to fund his new age; *for the benefit of all Mankind...*

Further consideration still lay in the fact that Gabell House's been in hock since the 'Nineties.[61] The untimely onset of dementia in Monique's old man'd left a string of creditors in its wake; and for such things Philo had neither

59 ['the old b': *i.e.*, Philo.—N.B.]

60 [*Gabell House*: The London branch. Further properties obtain in Paris and New York.—N.B.]

61 [*i.e.*, just before 'The Girl' was born.—N.B.]

the ability nor inclination to handle. No, for the Colonel, the war could not have come at a better time. The Jacker under his wing, they set to employing the new fluorescence microscope; all at His Majesty's expense.

During the day, they made gas[62] in the study, following the work of Haber; while, in the basement, they pursued the life-energy at night. Yes, for Philo'd been able to convince the Jacker that, if one could just determine the conditions of the moment of conception, he could reproduce the process; thereby eliminating death.[63] Therefore no matter how many fell due to gas—for, surely the old b' must have reasoned—one day they'd be honored as saviors of the race.

Now what he did *not* say, I could nonetheless read between the lines: and, that is, *we are the enemy*; or, so the Jew-ridden press, what with their love of the lie would have it. You know, the kind of skullduggery a 'civilized people' like the English need in order to get man to kill man; for persecution you see's an adjuvant of faith.

Thus renewed by this young man, and his irresistible enchantress, Philo's work proceeded apace. Why he even had time to submit an article dealing with the 'life-force'. Perhaps, just perhaps the world would finally come together upon being offered the gift of life; and so at last lay down the weapons of war...

The Royal Society'd agreed to give Philo one last hearing, furnishing various experts to testify before the Lords. For surely Albie would be willing to enlist any such aid in so prosecuting the war. Indeed, this Churchill'd[64] sure done his homework; clearly he'd seen the obvious implications for the stuff.

---

62 ['gas': *i.e.*, chlorine based.—N.B.]

63 [The theory presupposes the fructification of a hard and fast delineation between inert and organic states; then, via abiogenesis, simply reversing the process.—N.B.]

64 [Churchill, Winston, *Sir*: First Lord of the Admiralty at the time.—N.B.]

The Colonel'd claimed their new microscope would demonstrate evidence of energies previously unseen in the very roots of matter. Thus, Jack ruler, Philo slide, they set to.[65] There followed certain mumbo-jumbo concerning 'sexual politics', followed by a schematization of something Schmidtie calls the 'Nitrogen Cycle'. Taking this gas, the most eminent on Earth, and preventing it from interacting with the atmosphere, had proved a stroke of genius. Politics aside, the men really did have reason to boast; eagerly they awaited the verdict.

Saith one prominent chemist: "It's just a trick of the over-magnification. He's distorting the absorption of light, via the affectation of artificial motility upon the medium."

The President summed up their findings: "Your lenses must be dirty old boy—and I don't mean your bifocals."

Yet it devolved upon Lord Lansdowne to say what was really on everybody's mind: "Why—it's all a bunch of bunk!"

There was one bright spot, though. For, the First Lord you see has all the greatest scientists at his own beck and call. And he was not above foaming at the mouth, regarding certain applications to which the Colonel had alluded. Yes, for Churchill, it was all a smashing success. Following his lead the Lords, and, later, Commons agreed to extend the twain's funding—for gas; they had no use for any other, more exotic stuff.

Thus was it a Pyrrhic victory; or, so it might seem at this time. Indeed, for, as my informant has it, these are not men to be taken lightly. Yes, if gas is the one means of securing them funding, then, dammit—*gas they will have...*

---

65 [The 'life force,' or so they imagined, is supposed to recapitulate via the undulation of divers organic and inorganic states, 'bathed as it were in the light of the sun;' indeed, from such things of which stars are made.—N.B.]

Chapter 6: The Second-Oldest Profession[66]

London: September 1, 1914[67]

Monique Gabell'd always adored the social scene. And, now, what since her engagement, she's an excuse to hold this endless procession of balls. Moreover, much to the Colonel's delight, he'd found his niece a masterful mistress. Indeed, for the first time in years, the books are finally in order.

Only, what Philo'd done was more brilliant still. Really, I've got to hand it to him. Oh, he doesn't give a damn for any ball; why I'll bet he doesn't own a suit beyond the Gladstone Era. Still, the Girl busy upstairs, her uncle was free to descend to the basement with Jack—giggling like two schoolgirls, I'm sure—to continue their illicit experiments.

Save all the festivities in the world couldn't keep a hussy like that from feeling all alone. No, what that slut needs's a man; *a real man.* Yea, she, a Frank; and I a Saxon through our fathers; and, wards of perfidious Albion via our respective mums.[68]

---

66 [Again, we find Hossbach 'in' 1915, digging for dirt during a lull, via interrogating a prisoner, with regard to the fate of his friends. He goes on to relate Monique Gabell's movements, much as he has with Jack, since the end of the Summer of 1914.—N.B.]

67 [The following was scribbled atop this sheaf.] I write during a lull in the fighting, circa 8 October. The swine attacked at Champagne. We had to retreat a few kilometers. But, Bettelmann assures us, we'll be launching an offensive soon, so's to get it back. And yet I know, as only a soldier can: *I will not survive*; thus this note for posterity. Windemeer Hossbach, Leutnant in the Bettelmann Regiment, 3rd Guards Infantry, 3rd Army.[—W.H.] [As a newly minted officer, Hossbach had been transferred to the *3rd Army*, probably due to the proximity of its *HQ* to Berlin. Jerry's counter attack came off later that noon.—N.B.]

68 [Actually, Hossbach has it reversed: Her *father*, as well as her uncle, represents that Norman branch of Nordic long since settled in London. Monique's *mother*, on the other hand, had been rumored, probably spurious, to be scion of Napoleon III.—N.B.]

Only, she made the wrong choice; and now the poor sot she's managed to snare's gone and run off with her uncle; huh, seems the bitch's reaped what she's sewn.

***

Pah, that English pigdog—this time, he's gone too far! Really, sticking his nose in everyone's business; all but to save this woebegone race.[69] I mean, it's bad enough they're even here. They'd gotten to the Continent before August[70] was out. I hadn't the slightest; until the bloodbath that was Mons.[71] Now, it's a curious thing this war. For, it seems some of our replacements fought thereabout; and they swear Albie used the dread poison stuff. Oh, I was sure they'd inhaled something; just not gas.

Now, it seems this 'Daughter of the Revolution"d[72] learned her beau was about to be sent. Why, something must've just snapped; for, you see, it left her a bloodsucker with no one to bite.

And yet, for a space, that fleeting waste in Monique's soul seems to've been made pure. Why who'd have imagined some silly bird, especially the likes of *that*, would ever put itself in harm's way; then again, I'd like to think *we* had something to do with it...

***

In between day-dreams of sleep, and digesting ersatz crème de la' dust, I make it my business to chat up the *POW*s; enough so's to present that which follows. Oh, I may be embellishing. Still, any news is good news; especially if, for even an instant, it takes one away from the front...

---

69 ['woebegone race': It's hard to tell if he means Belgian, divided as they are between Flemings, and Walloons; or French. More likely, he considered them all one and the same.—N.B.]

70 [August, that is, 1914; *i.e.*, a little over a year prior to the 'lull' before Champagne.—N.B.]

71 [August 22-23. The press had reported the arrival of the *BEF* as early as August 20.—N.B.]

72 ['Daughter of the Revolution': *i.e.*, French.—N.B.]

London

It was early September, just days from her beau's having been sent, that Paris itself'd stood in danger. Yes this was the one thing—or, so she'd convinced herself—the one thing she could not suffer. Thus, after ample attention to her toilette and buxom coiffure, Monique swore to do her part.

Now it turns out that old sawney[73] Beaverbrook knows her Uncle Philo. Pah, the diminutive sonofabitch you see owns these papers; that's how she got her start writing these broadsheets currently inflaming the nation. Yes, a tried and true method: rile up the women with *Kinder, Küche, und Kirche*[74]; the men'll dutifully follow, what the one outdoing the other for patriotic donations; you know, *blood-money.*

So it did not surprise me to learn that that sassy little slut's gained quite the following. Indeed, now more and more young men like Jack are being pressed into service, their women are just dying to get word from the front; consequently, half of London relies on 'the Mademoiselle' for all the latest dirt. Yes every opera—and, I'll be, ball—everyone who's anyone offers her 'advice'.

Everyone that is save Lady Beaverbrook, the hostess of a certain *fete*. Yes, our POW told me all about it. Seems he was 'confidante' to the Mademoiselle; one can only imagine. Oh, but ach—the picture that he paints! I reward him rather generous, filling his sleeves with foodstuffs, the which my mates would kill.

And he, in turn, weaves one hell of a tale...

Lady B's Fete: As Related to Hossbach by his POW

---

[73] [Derogatory term for 'Scotsman'.—N.B.]

[74] [The onus is rather less evident in English: 'Children, Kitchen, and Church.'—N.B.]

Pah, that venomous muff it seems can only function under the guise of some sense of victimhood. Indeed, for, just a few weeks back, her womanly feint of attending uni'd come to a precipitate end, her love of chemistry filed away; the which Lady Beaverbrook was bound to make sure the entire ballroom should know.

Chatting up Lady Wilson, a glance, or, perchance, scent, should've warned the Girl, from whence the next salvo might come. Oh, how she must've hated it, being these women, vicious as they are, would inevitably pour salt on the one wound Monique had been unable to stanch: *alas, the vast specter of infidelity.*

"You poor, poor girl," Gladys[75] had dug. "You mean, you haven't heard from Jack since Mons?"[76] Why, the very devil herself, what dripping poison in her ear.

Monique did not reply.

"I tell you my dear, that devil of a man's off plowing somebody else's field; oh, they all do it." And, with a smile born from the lethality of pity, the Lady adopted the hushed tones of a cold condescension. "But, then again, boys will be boys. What does it matter if Jack's new toy's a rifle, or, the village slut?"

Now, Monique had kept her composure long enough. "*Infernal wench,*" she'd gasped, withdrawing a blood-stained bicuspid; grinding her tongue what with her teeth, so's to gain restraint.[77] "Men like *your husband* make history: men like Jack. Or do you really think, you petrified slut, ten years from now anyone will actually remember you?"

Horrified, the Lady fled, not so expertly concealing a shocked indignation.

---

[75] [Gladys: *i.e.,* Lady Beaverbrook.—N.B.]

[76] [*Mons*: Rout of a well prepared British retreat, leading Jerry to the very gates of Paris. This set the stage for the *First Battle of the Marne*.—N.B.]

[77] [At least, that's the way his interlocutor fancies himself having envisioned it.—N.B.]

***

Monique left,[78] without so much's calling a cab; and, striding in those impossible heels, had braved the downpour to march to the City of London. Her hair a mass of disheveled insolence, she'd made for the ____ Hotel[79], which served as an embassy of sorts, then knocked upon the Ambassador's door.

Like a dying cat, it opened. The secretary shot her a glance, then returned to the rather arduous task of filing her nails.

A giant appeared in old-man's gear. Zeroing with his bifocals, he started: "*Prin-cess?*"

Gaily she jumped: "Oh Uncle Zach!"

"*Humph,*" he smarted, setting her down. "My dear, either you've grown; *or I've shrunk.*"

Now, I seem to recall the Jacker having mentioned something regarding some Frenchified uncle: studious, officious; why, here one fathomed less man than machine. Truly in such specimen Paris had found an able administrator.

Only, Monique didn't see it. Yes, they'd always had this chemistry, an understanding; and, alas, his niece saw the human within.

And, he, ever the diplomat, acted it.

"Pfft," she sneered. "Old Fuss and Feathers! I need this, um, *favor...*"

His gay demeanor quickly turned sour.

Monique came up from behind, gently taking his hand. And, meeting his half-soaked eyes, she ensorcelled him what with the one word Woman should not be allowed to say: for she said, *"Please."*

---

78 [Apparently, her 'companion' in tow: Hence the POW's tale.—N.B.]

79 [Paris had maintained no 'official' ambassador to England till 1941. The hotel in question is given in Hossbach's manuscript: It has been deleted by the Censor.—N.B.]

"Oh good God; how I've dreaded this day. Ptth, I know—a patriot much like your father!" Exhausted he exhaled, punctiliously refilling his pipe. "I can get you to the Continent. But, you have to understand... it will take weeks to set up your credentials. No," he added, as if trying to convince himself something. "It's a good thing, really; yes, the Red Cross truly's a wonderful organi—"

"No, you don't understand! But Monsieur... *it's Par'ee.*"[80] She pleaded, meeting his downcast eyes. Alas she stiffened: "Or perhaps you've forgotten the family crest."

"*Blast*," he uttered the Anglicism, much to his dismay; yes, for even the Anglo branch of Gabell House still holds fast to its Frankish roots.[81] "In this day and age—what is it with you ladies? You used to be so... so *tame*. Why would anyone wish to help—*like that*?"

Monique did not reply.

He struck a match, so's to have something to strike; then, re-lit his bowl, so's to have something to burn. Aghast he gazed. The Captain, who'd once led a cavalry charge, realized his niece was not about to budge. "But Princess, please, young thing like you... *the vilest things*—is that what you really want?"

It wasn't a very pleasant sight, really; at least, not the way my prisoner describes it: just this subtle twitch out three corners of her mouth. And, if ever that Jezebel were capable of tears, now was the time. But she said, *"Oui."*

---

80 [The manuscript reads 'Paris.' I have altered the spelling here, in order to conform with the pronunciation Hossbach presumably intended. In general, I have refrained from such tactics: Yet this as a reminder.—N.B.]

81 [For once, Hossbach has his genealogy correct. Yet still he persists in error: Philo Gabell was by no means beholden to any such 'Frankish roots.' Then again, these Cockneys always do seem to march to the beat of their own drum.—N.B.]

The blood ran thick to his skull, as though his cranium were too small to contain it, while he morphed into the various stages of officialdom.

And so it was as the Ambassador that next he greeted her, and said: "So—how's your *Deutsch*?"

***

As her Uncle Frenchy had admonished, it would take some time[82] to get her to the Continent. During the which, the Girl'd kept busy. Alas, the vanity upon which Lady Beaverbrook, and millions just like her feed, paved the way for Monique to polish her inborn skill at character assassination[83]; why it was Old Beaverbrook himself who'd given her the poison pen, with which to weave her invective.

One of the prisoners showed me this clipping, the which I dutifully recall:

<u>Why We Fight</u>—by Mrs. Jack Suffler[84]

"You know the type: The kind of empty-headed bag who thinks this war's about keeping her in the latest from Paris. I'm sure you'll agree, such debutantes have neither the mental, nor moral capacity to realize one simple truth: Man fights because *he's man. A force more powerful than any Cabinet, his is the one sacred quest: To find one's place in society.*

82 [Indeed: All of one week.—N.B.]

83 ['character assassination': He should talk. As the attorney for G.W. Pub. reminds me, the Lady was a paragon of eminence, elegance, and, well, downright upright virtue.—N.B.]

84 [I have been unable to locate the article in question. Hossbach's reconstruction here stems from recollections some thirty years past; with an anonymous prisoner at that. The tone however is in keeping with what she is known to have written at this time. Also, note the honorific: Engaged, but unwed, the device of adopting such pretense, may have been at the fiat of her editor.—N.B.]

Those who gossip about such types are even worse than the enemy. For they tear at the moral fabric of a nation. England owes a debt to such knights: I know I do."

***

Her article had begun as a reproof to Lady Beaverbrook, seeking to squelch the scandal currently threatening her reputation.[85] Yes, the beauty of it all in that sick tart's mind is, she'd used the Lady's own husband's press against her. Of course, Gladys herself was never even mentioned. And yet the caricature concerning the kind of dame who gets her jollies condemning the loose morals of the troops, could leave but little doubt as to whom she was referring.

The rumor-mill soon grew quiet; Monique's reputation was restored, almost overnight.[86]

The Valley of the Marne

The hacks in the Royal Navy'd conspired with the Cockroaches to send this flotilla of nurses French-side the Channel: twenty-seven in all; though, the way my prisoner has it, the rest were all on the up-and-up.

Not so the Mademoiselle, by which moniker she'd now become known. For, Zach, who like every French devil's sold his soul to the English, Zach himself had snuck her ashore. His niece had been given certain 'special assignments': watch us, befriend us; information would follow, the which she was to pass to the *Quai d'Orsay*.[87]

---

85 ['her reputation': *i.e.*, 'The Mademoiselle.'—N.B.]

86 [Apparently, her articles had proved so successful, she continued to write them, even after disembarking to the Continent.—N.B.]

87 They were desperate: why just one river'd stood between our trench, and leave in Paris. The swine eventually'd staved us off; by the skin of their snail-eating teeth. Oh, but that's alright: ah, gay Paris—I shall see thee again![—W.H.] [The reference is to the 'Miracle of the Marne,' September 5-12, whereby French heroics, and German stupidity, hand in glove altered the course of the war.—N.B.]

***

A makeshift hospital on the Marne's where that no-good piece of arse was supposed to have been sent; still, they shift her whenever a battle's been fought. And, through it all, her one thought must be, 'Don't let me miss the Battle for Paris,' finding herself, as do we all, intrinsic to her own side's success.

Meantime she moves among the wounded, what like some Black Death spreading camp to camp, inflicting defeatism on our men. Saying hideous, anarchical things; what with the inevitable pacifistic balderdash thrown in.

Occasionally there'll be an exchange of prisoners. In Monique's case, this seems to happen more than not: for, they're picked men; men fallen subject to her wooing. Then, then they're sent back like some bacilli; sometimes for no exchange at all. 'Humanitarian', they say; *my arse.*

The Mademoiselle's activities, my informer went on, upon having been smuggled the merest morsel of meat, are being funded through something called the 'Anglo Saxon League', a division inside the Quay d'Orsay; i.e., *French Intelligence*, composed mainly of right-wing anti-communists like her Uncle Zach.

Thus she lurks among the wounded, corrupting us through 'Wine, Women, and Song'; and we jealous, hard-drinking louts (for, what soldier is not?) fall for it. It is not without some pride that her own uncle refers to her as 'my own little Delilah.'

Now, Monique's handler (as if anyone could ever actually handle that cunt) is said to be this diminutive Spaniard, who goes by the name of *Count Ernesto Gonsalvo*: aristocrat-cum-mercenary tactician, whose specialty lay in the taking of beautiful women, and sneaking them behind enemy lines.

And Monique soon proved a quick learner.[88]

88 [No mention of 'Monique on the Marne', a spurious pamphlet, purportedly from the Interbellum: It does not exist.—N.B.]

Chapter 7: First Kill

Western Front: Indian Summer, 1915[89]

Perhaps my first mistake lay in wondering whether there were any life outside Twenty-nine Chancery Lane. The answer now it infiltrates my nostrils, the puke from my gut enmeshing my lips, even's I crawl; unwittingly become one with a pile of slush. Sulfuric acid it rains death from on-high, the delayed ring of artillery ringing out as aftermath of ornament.

What half-blinded and hunched, I can barely make out this pulsating billowing up and down my arm: *my arm, you see, my arm*; why, I seem to have smashed it. We're extricated from our funerary procession, losing half a company along the way to executing a forced march. Necessity's a sonofawhore; for, somehow, we run the six-minute mile.

Double-time it ceases to subsist, and the march proceeds in the ordinary fashion. Fewer and fewer drop out until, what forty-eight hours and no sign of sleep on, I can barely make out three Private Guttermanns plodding in front of me; *thank God Schmidtie's still here.*

Breaking ranks, he upends my arm; then, slinging it over his shoulder says, "*We march.*" But damned near carrying me, we reach our objective: the approach to the valley of Champagne.

The sun it comes climbing down. Squinting I marvel this nightingale settling into a tree; when two shots they ring out. *Sonofawhore*; why, they've taken the company commander. My soul is athirst, consumed by a thing I did not know. Shaking, I cannot remember to fire.

---

89 [Being Jerry's counterattack in Champagne appears to have not yet occurred, this chapter, as the previous note, *viz.,* 'October 8,' should probably be backdated a day or so. Cf. note 67.—N.B.]

Eyes half-closed, and brain half-numb, mine is not to think, rather; but *do*. And yet, somehow, somehow the awareness something is wrong comes creeping into my mind; and then, a voice, this new-found voice it says: *I am underwater...*

From the lake I leap, slitting the throat of two Frenchies I did not know I have been watching. I absorb their death; transmogrifying spirits now forever one with me. And, it absorbs me; or, *I it*; and the oddest of things enter my mind: *Grandpa; we're in the forest. He's teaching me the 'Rite of the Teutoberg'.*

Closing my eyes I cradle two corpses, chanting to the accompaniment of shells piercing all-about:

Odin, Odin
Long hast thou slept
Unbridled breath, possession divine
thou—Spirit of the Forest!

For, I am the Cre-a-tor
And I am the De-stroy-er
And I am the field
—and the blossom of the fruit!

Yea, I am Sky, so soft in its hue
Fafnir O Fafnir, slay amidst blue
For, all life shall shake, the world embrace
—our Teutonic steel!

Hail, Augusten
Father my seed
Hail, Germania, onward
—sieg![90]

---

[90] Thus sang I in the forest of Champagne.[—W.H.]

Chapter 8: The Rape of Europa

A Few Hours Hence

People are beginning to stare. The darkening sky, what the deadening din of battle now spent, awakens me. My uniform's caked in blood. Only, I'm not bleeding; at least, I don't think. It's just, there's this thing, a heart you see in my hand; and, muttering, I lay amongst the wounded and dead...

Morning hits.

Tucking my heart in my ruck, I join the line[91] for chow, then make as if nothing has happened; this seems to put them more at ease.

Several Days Later

To them, you see, *I am hard.* At least, that's what I tell myself; holed up between bottles of booze up in the middle of the night. The memories come rushing back, what this thundering haze which makes my college days seem as nothing. They come to me in these dreams; these dreams I've been having:

The plunder, and the mud, what the smell of unrequited love it lurks; even as the village it burns all-around...

Schmidtie says they aren't dreams at all, rather, but *memories*; the likes of which I cannot shake.

---

91 ['line for chow': Dark humor? Refinements such as chow lines had, by this point, become increasingly rare, being supply lines and baggage trains had long been thrown into an unholy mess. It's just as likely he meant 'having to forage' for his meal.—N.B.]

A Village in the Valley of Champagne[92]

Orders, they say; *orders*. Ach, for the *franc tireurs*, terrorists, have been taking shots at both officers and men. Alas are we given to do that for which so many have been clamoring: *fight fire with fire...*

We get drunk first; it's the only way. Yea, we set fire to their thatched-roofs, their wretched huts. And, like a scene from the Old Testament, the men we run through with the sword; then, we take their women one-by-one...

Fire it burns all around. This one hut appears to be untouched. I feel my way inside, what coughing smoke all the way: *a low-ceiling; a hovel; a sound.* I turn, only to see: this family baying in terror; *I ignore them.*

Oh, but ach—merry fucking Christmas to me! Yes, for I've stumbled on this delicate little number, what all dressed in white. And sardonically do I the atheist thank God the Very Most High. Moving towards her, I snicker; then, stumble—*huh?*

"Win-dy," she leaps, swaying with relief, wrapping her arms about.

"Yeah[93]—*Windy, bitch,*" I say with a cold, calculated sneer, strapping some rope 'bout my knuckles. *The stupid slut*; why, she thinks I'm here to *save* her. Curses; *ah, curses the cunt, she cries*; *cries as I thrust my manhood inside...*

And I cup, yea I cup those milky-white paps; administering a face-disfiguring grin.

"Win-dy... *no.*"

---

92 [Again, Hossbach believes himself to be reliving 'memories' from, what I can adjudge, events a few days past, *i.e.,* early October 1915. The passage, as much of the manuscript, is rendered as if in the present. Of course, over forty years have already transpired.—N.B.]

93 ['Yeah': English is the *lingua franca* for Hossbach, in his dealings with the 'non German speaking peoples.' For, to him, the Franks are decadent: Hence Sedan and the Maginot.—N.B.]

Yea, I pummel that gash, sampling her ample breasts; sticking my tongue 'tween her milky-white teeth. Her senses beyond repair, she just lay there; why, she just lay there and took it.

***

For an eternity it seems I've lain on top, protecting her what from the rest of the men; even as the village it burns all around. The peasants they must be either dead or dying. For slowly the wild, raucous cheers, ach the piercing of screams it seems to subside. Only, now, now our little love-nest you see it goes up in smoke; and I'm transported back to the world of the senses.

Gathering her unconscious body, I take it back to the barn; the which my comrades it seems must've missed. Any survivors I figure must be in here; *and, alas, a chance for revenge's revealed...*

Only, I can't do it, I can't *kill* her; for, you see, I *love* her. Oh, but ach—the bitch had it coming! Drape your dainties around me, do you? Teasing everyone like that, what the only stupid slut in a school just chock-full of men? *Whore*; why you stupid, filthy whore—I'll teach you look the other way!

Perhaps, perhaps in her eyes you see, I was just a child.

Only, now, she'll forever see me's a man...

Chapter 9: Jack's War[94]

Western Front: April to September, 1915

Alas the war'd finally come to Jack; or, rather, he to it.[95] Come Twenty-second April, the word came: we 'Jerries' had struck with the real thing[96]; with it, we routed the Frenchies.

Pah, the photos of the corpses of Ypres[97] must've wreaked havoc with the poor boy's stomach. Which would explain, in his last letter, the Jacker's mentioned something about having to quit. Only, as I've just gleaned from our prisoner—he did nothing of the sort.

It's no surprise, really. I mean, a young man desires promotion; besides, he must've been piqued we'd beaten him to it. Or perhaps his desire to stay on merely boils down to the fact that there are certain benefits which accrue, to being sequestered under the same roof as one's fiance...

Yes it seems this Philo's too old—or, valuable—to be sent himself into the fray; still, the swine needed someone to teach them to use it.[98]

---

94 [Here Hossbach 'finds himself' progressively learning, and thereby relating, Jack's recent movements, during a lull in the fighting. These had been related to Hossbach via an ever replenished supply of *POWs*, in addition to fellow *Boche* from decimated units, which, apparently, had been amalgamated by the *3rd Army*.—N.B.]

95 [His friend had been ordered to the Continent over a year before. So, how could war have 'finally come'? He must mean 'Jack's war,' *i.e.*, after the escalation of 22nd April: Cf. next sentence.—N.B.]

96 [*i.e.*, gas.—N.B.]

97 [*pr.* 'Eep-'ruh.'—N.B.]

98 [Being the Entente had been compelled to leap from experiment to mass production.—N.B.]

As a Second Lieutenant[99] did the Jacker find himself holed up with the cavalry,[100] detailed to instruct the infantry's to the use of poison gas. A task for which he'd seemed well-suited, providing as it were a certain kind of prestige; as well as that of a *rôle* of such import, so's to have kept him from the more menacing parts of the front.

Only, now, what do I hear, but that Tommy'd been hitting us for two days somewhere called *Loos*; inflicting us what with his own deadly barrage.[101] The real thing too; not this tear-gas one hears so much about from the still-wet-behind-the-ears. And, what's worse—if what my POW says is true—none other than the Jacker himself among them.

Imagine the Jacker's sense of pride when, binoculars in hand, he witnessed the Entente's first use of the stuff. And, one can just as well fathom the terror which managed to proceed, when he had to run for cover. For, the wind you see'd picked it up, flying in Tommy's face to the tune of some two-thousand casualties.

Thus went Jack's first foray at war.

Loos: September 28, 1915[102]

His squad had been sent to this field on the outskirts of town, seeing the battleground, straight as a blade, not only'd provided no means for cover, but the grass itself had long been blown to bits; and, war or no, an army can only survive, so long as the horses have fodder.

---

99 ['Lieutenant': Actually, *Leftenant*, as everyone save the Americans must know. On the advice of the publisher, I have catered my translation to the sensibilities of the American reader.—N.B.]

100 [In all likelihood, a detachment intended for the *125th French Infantry Division.*—N.B.]

101 [The Entente's 'first use of the stuff' had indeed proved counter productive. Nonetheless, gas continued to be employed for a couple of days: With, as surely Hossbach's prisoner must have informed him, occasionally devastating results.—N.B.]

102 Three days later, they'd become as've we, oh what holed up inside some bunker. And, in the chaos these last few days [*i.e.*, mid October 1915], I have been able to separate fact from fancy, interrogating both friend and foe, as to what has since occurred.[—W.H.]

Then so at last they'd come upon an opening in the clear. At which point the Jacker's horse had become unnerved by this artillery-laden chasm; his squad was forced to dismount.

Now, war is hell, mind you; and hell you see is the lack of any sleep. For, the judgment it becomes deranged; and, decisions once made, never can be taken back. Or how else to explain the command that they should just bed down, what scarcely a kilometer from their mates in their battlefield bunkers? Perhaps three in ten would have been assigned guard-detail, while the rest took their turn at the lost art of sleep.

Still, the former couldn't have been very vigilant. For, Bartholemew, the Jacker's horse, ran away in a conspiracy with some foals. The horses had probably heard it first: men appeared beyond the trees. In a moment, all was confusion; why, smoke it filled the very air. Yea, man grappled so close with man, both fist and the bayonet had become the weapon of choice.

The Captain he tackled Jack, dragging him into a shell-hole; then, amidst the smoke, and what all the panicky neighs, fumed: "You've got to get word to Haig! Tell him we're cut-off. *Here*," he dove, driving the Jacker ever-deep. Next he lay on top, even as boots they filed over his back, in search of ever-aimless kill. This being done, he lamented, "*Take Abigail*," a father giving away a son. *"Now,"* he sprung, spurring the Jacker on.

They made a mad dash before, dodging wild thrusts, coming on this lone baying mare; for, unlike the Looey, the Capatain had harnessed his horse throughout the night. Then, according to my prisoner, Sewell[103] he'd thrust him this map, yelling amidst the clamor that he might hear: "*Head west*; for—we've simply got to find that village!"

Now, this Sewell didn't know Jack from Adam. All he knew was, he was a Looey on loan, an instructor in

[103] [Sewell, first name unknown: Apparently, Jack's captain.—N.B.]

chemical weapons; he'd no idea he actually made the stuff. So far's the Captain was concerned, Suffler was an officer, just like any other. Map to the dirt, he instructed him where the village should be, before sending him on his way; then, bayonet in hand, had himself joined the fray, wending an opening through which Abigail, bearing Jack, might wade.

The Jacker would've driven her's fast he could. Until, about a kilometer on, the sound of shelling must've caused her to balk; for he'd dismounted, tying her to a tree. Gingerly he crept through wheat-bedecked fields, stalks chin high so's to provide for cover. Smoke could be seen issuing from the north, an eery mist obscuring the entire front. And, though he must've rued the prospect of losing yet one more horse, he'd continued on foot, so as to discover the source this river. Yes, for that's where the map said we 'Jerries'[104] were less likely to be. According to which, the waterline ran another three-quarters of a kilometer before turning into *Oesterdamm*.[105]

Which village was said to be 'Jerry Free', owing what to the natives' nasty habit of firing on our cavalry. Whence, a few weeks back, the General Staff'd decided: *Oesterdamm must pay*; why, we[106] burned it to a crisp.

This only seems to've encouraged them. For, the survivors they took to the hills; and have been wreaking havoc with our supply-line ever since.

Now, if he could just make it through, these bandits could get word to Haig.[107] Thus he low-crawled it through

[104] [The rationale being, it was more pressing to inform Haig with regard to what *might have been* merely the first trickle in a whole flood of reinforcements, rather than to risk bombardment in obtaining a transmitter, back at the coal field/front.—N.B.]

[105] [There was no 'Oesterdamm.' The village was probably a portion of woods, protected by a river, and thus accordingly bequeathed with the appellation. It had probably changed names several times, depending upon who had held it for any given stretch.—N.B.]

[106] ['we': *i.e.*, the army: Not Hosbach's particular unit.—N.B.]

[107] [Presumably, via transmitter.—N.B.]

this jungle of wheat, what every now and then holing-up in the prone-unsupported. Then he rambled uphill, as if headed downstream; where, stumbling on a deserted hill, the Jacker sought shelter beneath the trees.

That's when he must've heard the shelling; which, it seems, had been going on for quite some time. It's just, half-bold, half-scared, he hadn't quite realized until now.

What with relief did he come upon this sea of men in friendly gear, manning a slew of trenches. Such relief however was surely short-lived. Oh, how he must've cringed on hearing the sound—the sound of German thunder: hundreds, nay, thousands singing *The Watch on the Rhine*. Drums they delicately pattered—now rapid, now slow—like a procession of headhunters deep in the Congo: *tugga-tug-tug*; *tugga-tug-tug*; *tugga-tug*—boom! Then, our artillery having been spent, we[108] unleashed the cavalry.

He must've thought us mad, being his mates in the machine-gun nest had just laid waste to wave after wave of bloody helpless men; *yet still, we kept coming.* Bodies they piled so high, why no one could see what transpired. 'Oh good God,' he must've thought. 'I hope that's just a smoke bomb.'[109]

The thought it would've been arrested, ere he'd started to choke. Writhing in pain, sparks of terror unleashed in Jack's nervous system, forcing him to act. And, loosing a tocsin scream, he lunged with the bayonet; slash, then thrust, he gutted two onrushing men. Two, now three fell before him. He roared; horses they crashed—this one particularly beautiful mare among them—encysting Jack's head into an Earth not big enough to bury all the men who died that day on the farm...

---

[108] ['we': Again, his fellow Huns, being Hossbach did not take part in this battle.—N.B.]

[109] [*i.e.*, grenade, via which Jerry had been known to employ both smoke and gas indiscriminate.—N.B.]

Chapter 10: Isis on the Slag[110]

September 28, 1915

Monique had been ordered to Artois, seeing a major offensive was said to have just pittered out; and, before 'the Bosche' had any ideas, the Red Cross would have to do its job.[111] Why the sassy little slut you see didn't have the gumption to tell anyone about our little fling; that, or, her superiors just didn't care. Either way, the Mademoiselle went back to work.

Detailed for body-retrieval, she'd screamed on coming to a ditch: "*Ours.*" Then, the unthinkable: *the bodies*; why, they seemed to *move*. There was this man: he appeared to be unharmed; though it seemed he'd lost his voice. Presently she noticed this scar on the bloke above him what like some last-minute burial; and, whistling, had called for help in moving the corpse, so's to free the now-voiceless man.

While tending her mute, her eyes they followed the scar; then so at last fell upon Jack's earthly remains.

She wrapped herself about, coupling like an amoeba. His dying flesh penetrated her foul senseless being; his expiating warmth hallowing her ground-cleaving chest. Then, in that frantic state, she uttered the words whereby she should raise him from the dead. She prayed to God; Jesus next; then, alas she prayed no more. For, the life-force you see'd abandoned him; and even that cunt's malefic lips, couldn't put Jack together again.

---

110 ['Slag,' *i.e.*, coal field, a term Hossbach mistakenly applies to the whole of Loos. The battlefield alone, to which Jerry's reinforcements were then en route, fits this description. Again, it must be emphasized, these 'Stories of the Entente' stem from (Hossbach's recollection of the reports of) prisoners in German hands.—N.B.]

111 Or had she arrived simply to spy, knowing our counter-attack was soon to come?[—W.H.][No one but 'the Boche' could have had any such idea.—N.B.]

Straddling the now-lifeless corpse, she ripped her brassiere; then, grinding, screamed. Pounding the dead man's chest, she impaled herself up against that fumigant rot. Clutching pools of blood engorging her thighs, she grasped his hand beseeching: "Jack, dammit, get up. Get up I say—*rise*!"

A crowd began forming close-in from behind, consisting of the nurses and the soldiers assembled in silence. The Private, who'd helped free the now-voiceless man, tried to comfort her. According to my prisoner, he must've gotten too close. For, she'd hissed, then leaped on the poor sot; all in the frenzy of a decomposed soul.

Why, he must've been dense; or, beguiled, for, dammit, the Frenchified feline soon proved impossible to fend off. She cooed, caressing the startled young chap. What with relief she resumed: "And I shall love and I shall cherish..."; *over and over.* But it must have been their wedding somewhere in her diseased mind; then, shrieking, she collapsed.

Whereupon the Private decided upon a strategic retreat, followed by the whole lot of onlookers crowding behind; alas the nurses resumed tending the countless wounded and dead.

Rain came. And, with it, this pounding barrage[112], signaling our second, futile attack.

And Jack Suffler's corpse washed up on an unknown hill, somewhere between the slag and the farm.

---

112 [Probably overshots from the coal field, scarcely a kilometer off, dispersing both Red Cross and soldier alike.—N.B.]

Chapter 11: The Mission

November 13, 1918

Four years, and seven-million casualties too late,[113] the war's finally come to a close. Feelings of betrayal mix with Thanksgiving to the Lord Most High. Meantime we're forced to march back to the borders of the Reich. Forced not by any army, rather, than the political-police to whom our politicians have succumbed.

And I think of that queer chap I met while in hospital; the one who's wrought in me this crisis of conscience. I mean, how could anyone regret the end of the war? And yet, it's there; *the feeling is there.*

Through an inquiry I learn my friend's regiment fell victim to a gas attack back in October. And, now, what since the capitulation of November 11,[114] I'm granted leave to go visit.

***

The train-ride was traumatic; alas I'm free to just get out and walk. Oh, but ach, my head is all in a funk. Why I've scarcely any clue's to my surroundings. I mean, it's almost as if, something is happening; only, I can't tell quite just what it really is.

With relief I enter the hospital, whereupon I'm greeted by a certain Dr. Foerster. The balding chap, what with the thickest pair of bifocals anyone's ever seen, tells me I can see my friend, whose real name by the way is Hitler; *Corporal Hitler.*

---

[113] [The Germans suffered some seven million casualties, including two million dead.—N.B.]

[114] [The German here reads: '11 November.' I have reversed the order here, as elsewhere, being the English speaking reader is more accustomed to such civilian rendering.—N.B.]

Upon entering, I find my friend in somewhat of a fog. Poor sot, doesn't know I'm here... doctor says he's incommunicado. Nonetheless, I speak; I've no idea if he heard.

The nurse she pulls me aside: “For all intents and purposes, your friend Adolf here's in a coma.”

I insist this cannot possibly be the case. “Look,” I say. “Two arms, two legs, a nose—not a damned thing wrong! Get me his doctor.”

Dr. Foerster is produced; the balding bloke I met before. “Your friend,” he proceeds, stroking a mountainous chin. “Is suffering an acute case of *hypocondriasis*. Physically, there's nothing wrong. The problem's not with his eyes; but his *mind*.”

“Quatsch—the English are his problem!”

He smiles, condescending to a conciliatory gesture. “Indeed, that was the case when first they brought him. In fact, he'd only just begun to regain his sight, when...” Here his voice it trails.

Do I detect sarcasm; or, *sorrow*?

He takes a deep breath: “I'm afraid your Herr Hitler's taken a turn for the worse.”

Awaiting my response, and, finding the none, he proceeds to the attack; why all the charm of a leper. “Tell me—would you say this Hitler's the excitable sort?”

“Now what the hell's that supposed to mean?” I could just wring his neck; that is, if he had one.

He laughs. “I mean, is he a *fanatic*?”

“Fanatic for victory! Not some head-shrinker—especially one who's never seen the front—could ever understand; now could he, *Doc*?”[115]

---

[115] [Hossbach has *Ars*, which I have rendered 'Doc.' The German for 'doctor' is *Arzt*; *arse* the English for 'ass.' It appears a compound meaning is what our memoirist seems to have intended.—N.B.]

The swine; he seems amused by my attempt to outsmart him. “Your friend,” he returns, increasingly in paternalistic fashion.

It seems this Herr Hitler here's having a friend's helped humanize him a bit, in the eyes of this bureaucrat of the psyche; or perhaps he's simply amused by my mere existence.

“*Corporal Hitler*,” he resumes. “Is also suffering an acute case of *melancholia*, wrought by all the revolutionary chatter. And not just here—*all through the Fatherland, the people are taking to the streets.* The Kaiser himself has already fled. Just like Russia,[116] the riffraff've finally come out: '*Peace*', they prate. '*Peace at any price.*' Most of the ringleaders seem to be Jews, upstarts who—”

“Why—Wolf would have their heads!”

“I see,” he fidgets, unkempt digits fingering three-days' growth. One could carve a monument from the chin; indeed, I suspect he's well on his way. “It's just as I suspected.” Cold, calculating digits pluck plush porcelain skin when he says, “Say, Sergeant—”

“That's Leutnant: *Leutnant Hossbach.*”

He stares. “I'm glad that I've run into you. And who knows? You may've just saved your friend's life. What, what's that?” he adds, in response to my inquiry. “No, don’t bother coming here: he'll be on his feet in no time; you can visit him back at his regiment.”

[116] [Food riots had presaged the abdication of the Czar in March '17. His successors had nonetheless continued the war, with renewed, albeit maladroit vigor. In April, the *Great German General Staff* retaliated, packing a revolutionary called Lenin onto a train, then sealing it like the very plague. They dumped him off in Russia, where, as intended, he plunged the nation into civil war. The demagogue ceded Jerry a vast swathe of soil, in return for an end to hostilities. Berlin's gambit backfired at Versailles one year later. Following which, Bolshevik cells, backed by Lenin, conquered key cities in the very heart of the Reich. For the Anglo-Americans, the fighting was finally done. On the Continent, however, a greater war had only just begun.—N.B.]

He snarls, in response to the obvious, then fetches the nurse. She hands him this chart. Squinting, he reads, "*Six-teenth Bavarian Infantry Reserve.*"

My heart it swoons what with relief, and I thank him for all his care and kindness. On the way out however I realize: 'I've left my canteen with my friend.' It's a long way back to the regiment; besides, I doubt Herr Hitler will be needing it anytime soon...

I halt just outside his door, seeing there's this commotion coming from inside. Why, it's old man Foerster, lambasting someone called Kronen:

"Fine, if you don't believe—*observe.*" Like an actor he inveigles: "*A—dolf, A—dolf*—this is the voice of *Providence.* You—yes, *you*—you are the *chosen.* Rise, Adolf, rise—arise and make pledge your mission! But, first, first you must regain your sight; oh, oh yes yes yes, *regain your sight that the Reich may live.* Oh now cleanse us—cleanse us from the evil Jewish menace! Yes, you, Adolf, *you...*"

It goes on like this for quite some time. Only, every now and then, I swear I hear somebody snicker; yet stop dead in my tracks, upon noting this plaque on the wall: "Edmund Foerster: *Doctor of Hypnosis.*" An irrational, almost superstitious dread comes over me. Why, canteen be damned—*I flee.*

Searching my way out, I note this distinctly *un-German* scent: a hostile, downright almost alien air. Officers celebrating 'peace' what with the men; *all, all hailing the treasonous end to this war...*

Outside, it's even worse, like a mine fired-off inside the collective psyche. The people have taken to the streets; the inmates are running the asylum.

Germany's in revolution.

PART II
THE THIRTY YEARS WAR

Chapter 12: The Wolf of Weimar

Bremen: October 1923

Our money's worthless; still, that doesn't stop the government printing more. Worse, the Frogs have invaded the Ruhr, raping thousands of our women along the way. Their murderous blockade's starved millions. And yet, the people—the people, who had to eat dust during the war—the *people* are not to blame; still, just as sure, neither are *we* who served at the front.

For God's sakes, I mean, we were deep inside France; what a veritable empire carved in Russia: *all, all without surrendering an inch of German soil.*[117] I, I don't know what happened. Civilians they took over; and, now, now they've consented to a shameful peace at the barrel of a gun...

Never before has victor been so willfully turned to vanquished—ach, but for the bankers and fatcats! It's not true, mind you: it's not true the Jew only lusts for money; no, for that devil'd rather our blood than money. Gunboats they block the North Sea.[118] Finding work's impossible, seeing no one can afford to hire. Deprived of all food, save for turnips and war-bread what the consistency of mutton, I watch the old man simply starve. So, we sink; meantime, the Reich it turns to rot.

And so, caring not whether I live or die, I lose track of this earthly existence, finding myself wandering on the Marktplatz—when who do I run into but my good friend Adi Hitler.

---

117 [Save for a squabble over Alsace-Lorraine, which Hossbach conveniently omits.—N.B.]

118 [Actually, the blockade had been lifted, *over four years before*, in July of 'Nineteen. Whether Hossbach is confounding memories in trance, or repeating propaganda he believed at the time, one cannot say.—N.B.]

"Don't *say* that. I'm a politician: you may call me *Herr Hitler.*"

"So I've heard," I wink, grinning ear to ear. "By the way, Frau Zachreys sends her warmest regards. Why I've been meaning to thank—"

"Enough! You look like hell Hossbach. Well, I don't suppose you've been reading the news?" he glints, hands in this foppish coat what two sizes too large. "I've my own army now, the *SA*[119]: *and they listen only to me.* The men are housed and fed, though they aren't always paid; we do what we can. Say—why don't you come work for me? Put some meat on those bones!"

Herr Hitler is right: *why, I haven't eaten in days.* "I'd be honored, A—I mean, *Herr Hitler.* Yes, my father, and his *brood-mare*—"

Herr Hitler he slapped me!

"Um... *woman.*" It's good to have discipline; you know, *someone who cares.* "Really, I'd love to. It's just, I can't. For I mean someone's got to look after the old boy: after all, I'm all he's got."

"Now see here," he scoffs, scribbling on this piece of paper. "Get in touch with this man here, a Herr Maurice: he's head of the *SA*. I'll just have a few words with him. Then rest assured: he'll do what he can for you and your family. Well Hossbach, what do you say—I could sure use an old-hand like you!"

"But, *Herr Hitler,*" I flail, surprised at my own vehemence. "We simply *must* take back the Alsace—else how can we expect to feed our families?"

"Bah," he snickers. "Bigger, Hossbach—think bigger! For *I* see the rich lands of the Ukraine; then, after, the endless Russian steppe..."

"I have applied for the Army," I blurt; blunt like a schoolboy. "Only, the swine you see've turned me down.

---

119 [*SA*: 'Sturmabteilung,' lit. 'Storm Detachment.' The 'Stormtroopers,' or 'Brownshirts.'—N.B.]

Still I could be called. Well, what then? For surely I can't do both."

"Why not?" he smiles, ever the politician: always ready with an answer. "Then, once you have leave, come visit. But, until then, *join us*."

"Oh," I cavil. "How are we supposed to fight? Why even the government hasn't any arms;[120] nor tanks, nor planes; nor guns, nor gas."

Herr Hitler he grows stern, starting to shout: "And my army shall sweep across the plain, *painting the steppe red with the blood of my enemy...*"

It's a bit unnerving; and more than a tad unsavory. Still I sense the determination in his eye, what the sense of mission in his soul. And, for the second time, *I give myself to this man...*

I mean, what's the alternative? For, every day, every day the old man he simply turns to rot; what with Winifrid not far behind. Why, if I don't do something soon, surely we all must starve.

And so, weighing my options in the eternity of an instant, I come to a decision: "Of course, I must make certain arrangements for my old man and his um... *wife*." It sounds more a question; really, I'd meant to be firm.

"Oh of course, of course," he nods, fobbing my fear to the side. "Take a couple of weeks, and get your affairs in order. Then, should your duties with the Army not intervene—pay us a call! Do you own a weapon?"

"Yes but—"

"Bring it. Ammunition? Bring that, too. And oh yes —two pairs of boots; for, we're going to be doing a lot of marching." He smiles, completely transfixed. "Oh, just think—soon we shall be back in the fray once more!"

***

---

[120] [The Treaty of Versailles had limited the German army to 100,000 men, in addition to the prohibition of air power, tanks, and a whole slew of offensive weapons.—N.B.]

Heading home to break the news to P'pa, why I do what he would've done: get roaring drunk on the way.

Next day I start selling my things: a horn, some clothes, plus a batch of unfinished paintings. In return I receive enough Marks to get them through the next few months. Why I even sold my motorbike; for one cannot eat gears.

P'pa doesn’t so much look's I say goodbye. As for Winifrid why she just sits there, face in some book, what just waiting for me to leave.

“Go,” he says. “Go and get on with yourself.” Then, just to ruin the mood, adds: “Don't forget to send your old man some whiskey!”

Said it with a straight face too; clearly the old boy's given up.

“Well,” I say. “Good-bye.”

And, with a sinking feeling in the pit of my stomach, I walk back to the Army: *Hitler's Army.*

Chapter 13: Putsch

Munich[121]: Nov. 7, 1923

Despair it riddles the countryside, what the approach of winter ready to hand. And yet, they get by; they just barely get by. Ach, Berliners, sons of Brandenburg; *sons of the soil.* Yes, a family can count itself lucky if it hasn't suffered its children to starve. Worse, our elders, the heroes of 'Seventy,[122] now face utter ruin: just one loaf of bread now costs one billion marks. Why, suicide even seems sensible under such conditions. Rumors spread. In Berlin, the Communists and SA duke it out in the streets. A dim quietude prevails.

But I am in Munich.

Oh, I don't know how I got roped into it, but Herr Hitler here's intent on overthrowing the government;[123] and, somehow, I've agreed to join him. Dietrich Eckart, the playwright's our leader; Ludendorff our *cause celebrite*;[124] and Hitler their little drummer.[125] In fact, Wolf[126] has ordered me subordinate myself to Eckart entirely. Ach, the poet may be senile, but Hitler thinks his plan to be technically sound. Besides, it's inconceivable the police should actually fire on Ludendorff, the savior of the German people.

---

121 [*Munich*: An Americanization. The manuscript reads: '*München.*' I have, on occasion, replaced the latter with the former, in order to provide better intelligibility to the reader.—N.B.]

122 [*i.e.*, the Franco-Prussian War, 1870-71.—N.B.]

123 [the 'government': *i.e.*, that of the South German state of *Bavaria.*—N.B.]

124 [Evidently a play on *cause celebre,* being Ludendorff was, after all, a celebri-*ty.*—N.B.]

125 [Figuratively, of course.—N.B.].

126 [*i.e.*, Hitler.—N.B.]

The alternative's simply to do nothing. But that would mean the Bolshevisation of Germany; and, with it, the concomitant Communisation[127] of all Europe. The choice is quite clear; really it's no choice at all. I make my final dispositions with Schmidtie, with whom I've kept in touch since the end of the war.[128] In the event that it should prove necessary, he is to dispose of my earthly belongings; then, access my pension so's to pay for the funeral.

Off to the notary to make it official, we pass these malformed goblins: *Jews*. Just look at them what with their bellies; their wristwatch; their gall. Pah, the paucity of bread in the *Muenchener*'s stomach, couldn't possibly provide better contrast. Herr Hitler is right: *I learn to hate*.

***

"Tomorrow—*we march*," rasps Eckart, once we've gathered in Göring's surprisingly bourgeois home: the greatest heroes of the Reich assembled before me. Flush with fear—or, embarrassment—I cower in the corner. "*Ludendorff*," the old boy he says. "You are to lead the march. Now I trust I needn't tell anyone: the Feldmarschall is the pivot, upon which the entire operation must rest. He is to be protected: *at all costs.*"

"Ja," Adi seconds, this far-off look in his eyes.

"Good," beams the rosy-cheeked poet. "Once inside, fan out along the perimeter in staggered rows of ten, so's to constitute squads. That is, unless you're storming say a door: in which case then the march shall proceed via column. Herr Hitler," he coughs, ominously emplacing a revolver in the Corporal's hands: "Herr Hitler here will get their attention."[129]

---

[127] [Where the manuscript reads 'Bolshevik,' I have, as a general rule, hastened to translate it as 'Communist,' in keeping with more English speaking usage.—N.B.]

[128] [Following the armistice, Hossbach briefly let Hitler's old room, at Frau Zachreys', until finances dictated his return to Bremen.—N.B.]

[129] [While Hossbach has Eckart, the poet, reading the order of battle, Ludendorff was almost certainly the brains behind it. Yet, as the

It marvels me watching him study the mechanism. Yes, for Hitler, this is the greatest day in all his life. For, he's going back, back to the one place he truly belongs: *back to the front*; but then I realize—*so am I.*

"Create a diversion," the old boy resumes, sweating hard, making an effort just to stand. "But for Gods' sakes, don't open fire unless they do so first. Göring'll butter up von Kahr; plus that spider he keeps called Seissner. I'm asking a lot from you Hermann. But then again, *all Germany is.*[130] Meantime, Herr Hitler will keep them occupied with his revolver. It's unfortunate but, I'm afraid, quite necessary. Then so at last: *Hermann will come to the rescue.*" Turning towards the bright-eyed Swede[131] he says, "Get them alone, then make them a deal: Hitler, Chancellor; Seissner, President; and Ludendorff the head of the Army. If they argue however you must begin taking hostages..."

Glassy-eyed, the poet he gleams, the opium seeking its release in a tirade against the Jews. I catch the gist of it: "That pest has no business being in Germany. Oh, but one day, we'll fix them all—send them back to the desert!"

My, this is exhilarating; why, it's *history* in the making.

'spiritual fulcrum' underpinning the *Aktion*, Eckart indeed could have committed Ludendorff's orders to mind. Then, with the latter's approval, he appears to have issued them as his own. Provided the poet's infirmity, this was the limit of his involvement in any prospective 'putsch.'—N.B.]

130 [*all Germany is*: The German here reads: 'alles Germania ist.' I have taken the liberty of rendering 'Germania' *Germany*, as in the more common 'Deutschland.' The Censor concurs, being the dampening of any incipient German nationalism is, at present, in the interest of all concerned.—N.B.]

131 [re, 'Swede': Apparently, Göring, who lived there for a space. Hossbach's animus undoubtedly stems from the fact that that's where the future Reich Marshal had met his first, now deceased, wife.—N.B.]

We urge him to go on. Rather the poet wishes indulge us with some fatherly wisdom: “Either *we* shall wipe out the Reds; or the Reds[132] will exterminate us.”

His fever now spent, the poet returns to the matter at hand. “Once you've escorted Seissner and Kahr to the office in back, you must persuade them sign the Declaration of the New Republic. You must *charm them*, Hermann. Appeal to their pride as soldiers; as servants of the State. Then,” he snickers. “If need be, tell them Hitler's crazy, and's gotten hold of a gun.[133] And that, if they won't sign, there's no telling what he might do...”

Before I can question the wisdom as to his plan, the poet's back at work, charming us into a hypnotic frenzy; without the which an army is but a mass of men unwilling to die.

“It's high time that the *Nordic Man* should appear; *for he has conquered the ice*. Unleash, unleash oh my children the burning fire of the race—hail Germany![134] Hail Thule! Hail, *hail...*” His spent-face quickly turns white.

“Fear not,” Wolf he cries, helping the old-boy to sit. “It shall be our victory or—a glorious death!”

“No—you don't understand!” the Master he reels, berating the Corporal as if with his last. “You mustn't fail; *you simply must not*.” The poet he gasps, grabbing Herr Hitler by the throat. “Now I won’t hear another word.” He coughs, which isn't necessary; yet, through the arousal of such sympathy, stifles all objections. Besides, Eckart really is a sick man.

Dripping with sweat he continues: “With Ludendorff we have the Army; with Göring, the officials;

---

[132] [While entirely plausible that Eckart had become simply confused, in so seemingly switching the subject of his peroration, one should note that, for the Nazis, 'Red' might also mean 'Jew.'—N.B.]

[133] [Göring was, by this point, supposed to have already once wrangled a revolver from 'Herr Hitler,' a piece of mock bravado intended to impress von Kahr, 'and that spider he keeps called Seissner.'—N.B.]

[134] [Again, 'Germania' in the original.—N.B.]

and, with Hitler, the man in the street. Save that, for the Army to fire on Ludendorff would be the greatest betrayal in all human history! *Nevertheless*," he thunders, an old man, true; yet seemingly sick no more. "Don't think this allows a moment's hesitation: should they open fire, hit them with a murderous barrage, enfilading to a ten-foot perimeter, the closest man escorting the Feldmarschall to safety. I'm so sorry," he adds, what with a tear in his eye. "But anyone going down will have to be left; it's unfortunate, but quite necessary. For this is a *spiritual* operation: the Forces of Light arrayed against the dark, inferior races; organized as ever under the savage debauch of World Jewry. Of course," he snarls, re-lighting his pipe. "In case someone pulls a *schweinerei,*[135] First Squad will secure Ludendorff;[136] meantime, Göring shall be whisked off by Rosenberg and his men.[137] Herr Hitler, you might have to secure your own retreat. Still, I'll try and have Sepp Dietrich swing by and take you to the Hanfstaengls."[138]

"*Then what?*" says Hitler, glassy-eyed himself; not from any opium, rather, than the sheer strength of will.

The poet he empties his bowl; then coats his words with a sting: "You'll have to get out for a space; that is, in case of failure. I hear Switzerland's lovely this time of year; really you should see it. But I am an old man. And, if you should not succeed I, I..."

He clutches his heart then turns pale; Herr Hitler he bolts to the alert.

The old fox arrests him with his eyes, says, "It's nothing," asks for a towel, then bids us good luck.

---

135 [*schweinerei*: An especially odious act of betrayal.—N.B.]

136 [Or, I reckon, the 'closest man,' in the event of actual fire.—N.B.]

137 ['Rosenberg and his men': Ostensibly Second Squad.—N.B.]

138 [Actually, the home of Ernst 'Putzi' Hanfstaengl's mum. The former, Hitler's Press Secretary during the early years, had helped school that sociopath in the art of social mores.—N.B.]

Mid-morning, November 9

"Pre-sent——*march*!" sounds Göring, leading us down the avenue, headed for the square.

I'm bringing up the rear of Second Squad, SA patch on arm; and butterflies in my tummy. We halt at the Buergerbraukeller, then form a cordon that no one might enter.

Save the 'Big Three': Ludendorff, Göring, and Hitler; for, alas, they've come to negotiate with Bavaria's Ministers.

First and Third Squad filter in from behind, so's to sure up some muscle. Meantime we promenade about, much as we have since late last night, gathering support for the revolution we all know must come. We are filled with the utmost confidence. For we have Ludendorff: the George Washington of the German people—how can we fail?

Why, just last night, we feared, brother might fire upon brother—then, alas! The *people* they have joined us. The revolution, far from a struggle, in truth's a parade. Yes even the Big Three are marching lock-in-step. Why, things are going just swimming indeed!

The conifer-scented breeze wafts past, indwelling the nostrils, as I try to keep in step. Passing the massive stone columns on the Max Josephplatz, we come to the end of the Residenzstrasse, whereupon I'm entranced by the *Feldhernnhalle*: monument to the dead of the war.

Absorbed what by all the spectacle, I bump into the man in front of me; it's a pile-up. Ach, for the police you see won't let us onto the Odeonsplatz. Through the loudspeaker they insist that we should stop. Pah, they daren't touch us: *we march*. Oh, but ach, shrieks they break out in front; a burst of fire; and what the scent of ammo and fear's upon us. A car screams; someone goes 'oof'; and Ludendorff speeds off into the night...

Why, I think I've been hit; now I remember, *I remember the feeling*. My ribs; *my ribs they seem to have been crushed.* Barely managing to eke out a breath, I look up to see Göring lying in a pool of blood: the taut, twisted face; ominous what with one-eye open.

And, cursing under my breath, I scan the street; *but everyone's gone for cover.* Pain it pounds me what with its onslaught-beat, like some negro-jazz assaulting the very soul. I look for my friend; only, Herr Hitler's nowhere to be found. Smoke it assails me; and, praying for deliverance, I squint up only to see: the authorities menacing with spite.

The nation's betrayed; *the revolution has failed.*

Chapter 14: *Sitzkrieg* und *Blitzkrieg*

Hitler was sentenced to five years; for three of which I was to join him. Still, the suits in Weimar'd[139] decided to go easy. Really, Herr Hitler'd given them no choice. For, his oratory'd won millions; why even the judge was convinced. I gained my freedom first, on Third August. Then, alas, come Twenty December, the tides of justice could be held back no more: he'd served just thirteen months.[140] Now, he has emerged as leader, or *Führer*, among vast segments of the German people; the harbinger of change we all know must come.

I enjoy my work for the SA, beating up Communists in the street. Moreover, P'pa, while no friend of Hitler, is so pleased at my new interest in tactics, he's called in this favor; and, now, I'm a motherfucking *Major* in the German-fucking Army!

Life is truly grand. Why I've even discovered the joy of a good book, having taken up with Clausewitz, Moltke, de Saxe.[141] I've even expanded my interests beyond the purely military ken, delving into Goethe, Fichte, and Kant;[142] *all* thanks to the General Staff. Yes this institution's not only the greatest thing that's ever happened to me, rather, but for generations going on three centuries. And, well wouldn't you know? It turns out Hegel was wrong after all: the Prussian State is *not* the pinnacle of existence; no, for *that* sobriquet belongs to the German General Staff.

---

139 [While the putsch had taken place in Bavaria, the *federal* government had been housed out of Weimar.—N.B.]

140 [The trial had ended early April 'Twenty-four.—N.B.]

141 [*Clausewitz, Moltke, de Saxe*: German military theorists.—N.B.]

142 [*Goethe, Fichte, Kant*: Major German philosophers.—N.B.]

January '33[143]

Panic in Berlin. Yes, it's either the Communists; or *us*. As ever, the issue's decided in the streets. I earn my keep; plus a few scars to boot.

And yet, the final stage, just as immutably, is settled behind closed doors. What with their cabinets; their suits; their tails ensconced firmly between their legs—they can deny us no more! Come Thirtieth January, Herr Hitler is appointed Chancellor.

Ah, German people—rejoice!

1935

Time it begins to pass. Two years, in fact, as if in the blink of an eye; including a certain best-forgotten incident involving the SA.[144] Only, now, after two decades of unrelenting struggle, the German people have finally earned some peace and quiet.

I have been discharged from the SA, which had become a den of vipers as it were, becoming a *Führer Adjutant*: Hitler's liaison to the Army.

1936

Meantime, a *Volk*'s truly come into being; a National Socialist paradise the envy of the world. Dr. Ley's *Strength Through Joy* sends millions on these exotic cruises. Workers they fly like the very Gods amidst chariots thousands of meters high via the Hindenburg, and a whole

143 [As a general rule, headings and dates have been affixed by me. I take full responsibility for any errata obtaining therein.—N.B.]

144 [The *SA* was a homosexual gang of ragamuffins, led by one *Ernst Röhm*, hellbent on replacing the German army. Late June '34 found Hindenberg ordering Hitler to 'lance this troublesome abscess.' Scores of innocents died along the way to the settling of many a score.—N.B.]

fleet of blimps. The Führer's brilliant rearmament scheme's behind it, liquidating an endemic unemployment bequeathed us at Versailles.

And, now, in the Rhineland, our manhood is finally restored![145]

1938

Oesterreich's[146] incorporated back into the Reich; the Sudetenland freed; the Czech abscess finally lanced. At last the Reich is free from encirclement. Why life it couldn't be better: as proof, *Time*'s just named Hitler 'Man of the Year'.[147]

August '39[148]

Yes, the time has come to take what's *ours*. Ach, for the same swine you see who sought exterminate us at Westphalia,[149] are the very same Traitors of November.[150] For there are times in a nation's ledger, when only the most martial means will do; thank God Fate's sent *him.*

---

145 ['manhood restored via the Rhineland': An unprecedented bluff, allowing Hitler to reoccupy the demilitarized zone, in contravention of the Treaty of Versailles, in March '36.—N.B.]

146 [*Oesterreich*: Austria, *i.e.* the 'Eastern Reich.'—N.B.]

147 [Two omissions: The former concerns that of the *Reich's Kristallnacht*, an attack on Jewish businesses, resulting in some 100 deaths, in November '38. Hossbach, understandably perhaps, has failed to mention it. The latter, concerning the Olympiad in 'Thirty-six, was included in the original manuscript: It has been excised here at the request of the author.—N.B.]

148 ['Herr Hitler' had thought to render the Poles friendless, by forging a pact with Stalin, in late August '39. Many expected Warsaw to fall, bloodless, as had the Rhineland, Czechoslovakia, and Oesterreich before it, into the German sphere of influence. Yet the Poles, puffed by us posturing Brits, refused to take things in such a cowardly fashion. Jerry responded, via invasion, on September First.—N.B.]

149 [He refers to the *Peace of Westphalia*, 1648, which sought to eradicate any hopes for Teutonic unity, against a backdrop of insignificant, oft competing states.—N.B.]

150 ['Traitors of November,' *a.k.a.*, 'November Criminals': Left leaning politicians, who had signed an armistice, on the heels of the Kaiser's abdication, in November '17.—N.B.]

Oh, but ach, the English are being intransigent. Why they've egged on the Poles with a check they simply cannot back; *war's inevitable.*

17 September

The Polacks've fallen in a fortnight; save for some mop-up duty later. Speaking of which, the Ivans, as per agreement, now set in from the east.[151]

And—proost! *Poland is no more.*

The press they call us bloodthirsty. "Ridiculous," the Führer says. "Our new—or, should I say, *old*—territories[152] will take fifty years to digest."

"But, but what about a declaration of war?[153]" I say, lest *he* not forget.

"Are you joking?" he chides. "Like a *Dachshund*—I have that Chamberlain right where I want him!" He smiles, what this far-off gleam in the eye. "Well, one thing's for sure—never again shall we have to face the horror of a two-front war."

1940

Winter 'Thirty-nine soon gives way to spring Nineteen-forty; and so at last, *peace* it reigns in Europe. Oh, sure, London and Paris've declared war. Still, that was months ago. Save for some naval posturing, they haven't so much's lifted a finger; why even the neutral press calls it the 'Phony War'.[154]

Ach, but the Jew—i.e., *Moloch*—couldn't leave well enough alone. For, ever since the assumption of power

---

[151] [Missing from the transcripts of the trial is the fact that the Soviet Union invaded Poland on September 17, in accord with a secret protocol to the *Molotov-Ribbentrop Pact.*—N.B.]

[152] [Prior to war with Poland, Austria had been annexed, Czechoslovakia swallowed, in a series of 'bloodless coups,' between 1938 and 1939.—N.B.]

[153] [When the General first claimed to have said this, they nearly laughed him out of court.—N.B.]

[154] ['Phony War': *i.e.*, 'Sitzkrieg.'—N.B.]

they've continued harass us what with their boycotts; their atrocity-mongering press: it's *they* who've pushed us to war.

Proof is[155] to be found just in the nick of time. For, on April 9-10, we just barely beat the Brits to Norway—a so-called neutral—upon the heels of the greatest victory in maritime history. So much the Germans a 'land-locked people'!

One month later, the meteorologists, following a very different kind of front, declare the skies finally fit for gaining air supremacy. Armed with such information, the Führer decides to teach *Francois* an object-lesson.

Mid-May 1940: The Forest of the Ardennes

I trundle through the trees[156] in this tank, leading a battalion through the brush so fast, it takes the infantry days to follow. At length the rest of the division arrives ala pincer; then, via double-envelopment, takes Francois in the rear. And so at last, the French Army is no more.[157] Yea, for the first time in a quarter-century, German troops straddle the Channel.

Ah, England—I'm coming home!

The Summer of 1940: Wehrmacht Supply Depot, Paris

The English will just have to wait. For, as the Führer reminds me, it will not be the White Race who benefits, when their Empire is finally destroyed.

155 ['Proof,' since, in Hossbach's mind, only 'The Jew' could be so callous, as to engender war against kin: Especially as concerns the Angles and Saxons of Angleland, *i.e.*, England.—N.B.]

156 ['impenetrable forest': The Ardennes, thought by all, save Jerry, inaccessible for tanks.—N.B.]

157 [The French army was far from being 'no more.' Yet, as a cohesive, fighting force, their goose was essentially cooked.—N.B.]

I prefer not to think of it. To which end I could not have landed a better detail: posted to my old haunt as Quartermaster, in charge of a 'shed: *in Paris.* Dutifully I take my fill of the pleasure the city can bring. Well, as P'pa used to say—'Let there be drink!'

Jeffries, my superior, warns two Cockroaches might be coming to pick up some equipment. “Alas,” I say. “We're fairly out of skirts.”

Francois arrives, wearing that mien of insolence so peculiar to his race. I dig through the cabinet, fetching some gas-masks and a receipt. 'Tall bird,' I say to myself, eying his companion when—*oh good God...*

“*Monet,*” I fumble.

“That's Monique, you bastard.”

Oh, how I would but just to throttle her; to kiss her; to make her go away. “Now see here,” I sneer, unwittingly giving her a light: “You don't know me, I don't know you; and *that* is how it must be. I, I'm not the man you think... *I cannot be.* For, he died, *he died in the last war*; and the world's a better place for it. Now, nothing exists save the Führer. Madame,” I bow. “Good-day.”

Gentle I nudge her. Still, the sow, she persists twisting my arm; which, weakened with guilt, readily gives way.

“You always did hide behind something Hossbach, didn't you? I guess this Hitler's your new couch.”

“You—you Parisian slut, you!” is all I can muster. For, somehow, we seem to've become entangled; she winds up banging my fist against her face.

I made that hussy flee, what her cowardly compatriot behind her, without so much's taking their equipment; pah—just like the English at Dunkirk!

Well, I trust I won't be seeing any more of her.

Chapter 15: Fathers and Sons[158]

London: May 10, 1941

Pilot Officer Suffler[159] was just returning from his evening patrol over England's war weary skies. The Mosquito he manned[160] leapt with ease, as though it were not he at the controls, rather, but some mathematical force, endowing the machine with a mind its own; and, furnishing Jack with the gift of flight.

It's hard to think of a more unlikely ace for the Class of '41. His namesake'd been a hero in the last war, for which he'd paid the ultimate price; Jackie never knew him. And, being the boy's mother was always running around what with every Tom, Dick and Harry, Jack swore to follow in his father's steps. For, although they'd never met, through flight you see he fancied he'd come to know him. Oh, I don't know why. I mean, I knew the Jacker; and why I don't think he ever set foot in a bird[161] in all his life. Poor sot; perhaps it was just a cry for his mother's attention.

Speaking of which, Monique had recently dropped the surname, Suffler, the which she'd so dutifully, if somewhat fraudulently, borne since the end of the war.[162] It took her long enough. For, upon the Jacker's death, the anglicized hussy soon fell to taking a swarm of lovers. Poor Jack was always being fobbed off on some relative. Or, what's worse, the help; in the end, anyone ready to hand. He saw his mum less and less; and, so'd resolved to hate

---

158 [Chapters 15 through 18 are decidedly *not* 'trance based.' They are reconstructions, based on third hand information, obtained via discovery, in an effort to piece together *my* purported movements. Unlike the rest of his conscious, prison-house narration, I have *not* rendered such aberrations into italics, simply due to their length. As for their veracity, however, I must hold my piece.—N.B.]

159 [*i.e.*, the editor of the present work.—N.B.]

160 [*Mosquito*: A fighter-bomber—made of wood!—N.B.]

161 ['bird': In Britain, a dame; here, a plane.—N.B.]

162 For Jack, poor sot, died before he could make her an honest woman. [—W.H.]

her all the more. And yet, secretly even unto himself did this make him desire to please her come what may.[163]

Of course, society'd served its function in so ridiculing the 'immoral Frenchwoman'; albeit with bated breath. She was, after all, a war-widow; and filthy rich at that. For her fiance you see'd helped develop poison gas; which, as regards its effects, the world had become quite inured. His posthumous patents yielded millions. Gabell House was brought out of hock. In a sense, the Jacker's fared far better in death, than ever he had in life.

Still, thanks to the outbreak of peace, public opinion cast a wicked opprobrium against the dread poison stuff—so unbecoming this valid weapon of war. Now, children can be cruel; their teachers crueler still; Jackie bore the brunt of it. For, gas, previously seen's having won the war,[164] had become outlawed by all 'civilized' nations.

The boy found his solace in the art of fencing. At Cambridge, he became captain of the team. This seems to've done him some good, so far's confidence's concerned. Yes, for foolish blokes who'd get in his face, would oft live regret it. A tenacious devil-may-care, as all young men, with Jack you see it was more pronounced. Ever eager for a brawl, Jackie soon earned the respect of his mates.

Upon suspension from uni, he had been encouraged to try his hand at the military art. Now, I can't imagine how he kept himself out of the brig, but, somehow, he took a liking. Perhaps it was thc structure. Yes, it seems the one thing he lacked, was the one for which he truly had need. The Pilot Officer proved a natural ace, infuriating his elders with death-defying feats; the golden boy of the squadron.

So it was one memorable day—May 10, to be precise—that the Luftwaffe'd given Albie her greatest

---

[163] Wisdom bequeathed, over a bottle of schnapps.[—W.H.]
[Balderdash: I never touched the stuff.—N.B.]

[164] As for gas, its reputation was calumniated by that ridiculous plebe, the mass.[—W.H.]

thrashing. Jackie'd taken off with his squad, and so was lucky to've made it back with most of the team intact. After, he chanced to be completing that ever-odious paperwork known as the 'flight log', when he happened to receive the following baffling message: "Sfflr x Hq^{x2}—*Briggs*."[165]

Surely he must've wondered why the CO'd deemed speak to some lowly Pilot Officer. Still, Jackie'd endured enough unanswered questions during his childhood, and so had taken to becoming a man of action; you know, *the kind who gets things done.*

Employing much his own brand of bribery and bluster, Jack'd ascertained what rumors he could, then made a point not announcing himself at quarters. Helpless Miss Bramblewaithe'd looked on, as he stormed the CO's office.

"What the bleed?" she must've heard, no sooner had he entered. "You're sending me *where*?"

The Commander, an aged man, with unremarkable features, save one could say, 'here there used to be a drinker', had sat and simply said nothing. Only, this pained expression contorted his face, straining the interminable. Alas he shrieked, "An order I say—*order!*"

Now, if this Briggs had been the bloodthirsty sort, Jack could have wound up in the brig; *or worse.* Yet he was a carefree bloke, whenever possible leaving the disciplining to others. 'Smiling Jim', they called him. Not for his smile, rather, but because 'no one'd ever seen him frown'. As such was Jack at a loss to explain the apparition before him.

It turns out this Briggs'd lost a son, a fighter-pilot, about a year before, prior to the Blitz. Even still, the

---

165 [The censor has given me permission to correct a glaring omission, lest it give way to the most ridiculous nonsense. You will read how I was packed off, like some perquisite, to the States, when I was just a boy. Technically an 'American,' by '41 Mother had long since welcomed me back: Indeed, I had been in England for almost eight years. I won't say she didn't pull some strings; truly I've no clue. At any event, duly I *earned* my commission, in the RAF.—N.B.]

Commander hadn't lost his poise. Truly, a father to all the officers under him; *yea, in Briggs they could confide.*

This just goes to show how inferior they really are. For, in the Reich you see this Briggs would've been equally beholden to his men.[166] Only, in England, the hang-ups of class would've rendered such behavior downright scandalous.

Now, Jackie must've been scared, a feeling he probably hadn't felt in years; seeing he'd long been liable to settle any such score with his fists. For, Briggs was staring, staring at him what just like some common criminal. Eschewing the intercom, the CO'd yelled, “Miss Bramblewaithe!” Seconds later, two toughs, what with such deplorable posture[167], appeared. “Emerson, Lowry—escort our *Pilot Officer* on his, um... *way.*”

The way he'd said it, 'Pilot Officer', had seemed so menacing; as had the rather ominous pause before 'way'. On the trip north, moreover, Jack couldn't help but have noticed the Big Brass, sitting silent as the Sphinx beside him; heading for destination unknown.

They disembarked at a rundown jail in the midst of the Scottish hills, this picturesque panorama far from bomb-torn England. The brass they led him inside, as if he were some prized-prisoner. Uncomprehending he'd turned, only to find his chaperone letting themselves out; leaving Jack to face a lone prisoner in his cell.

Jackie—at least, for now—stared outside-in. The strange rake cocked his head, grinned a buck-toothed grin then said, “Ah, let me have a look... *splendid*! Absolutely splendid! You do remind me of your old man so.”

---

166 ['men': *i.e.*, the enlisted, 'rank and file.'—N.B.]

167 ['deplorable posture': The Censor has been so kind to allow me interject: I recall nothing of the sort. The British airman, as his counterpart in the army, is a paragon of the most upright virtue.—N.B.]

The swastika-armband, what plus the broken English, must've caused Jack's head to swim. For, almost against himself he'd said, "You... *you knew my father?*"

The prisoner he'd smiled, smiled as though he'd no idea how ridiculous it made him look; and cared even the less. "A great man—the Lion of Liechtenstein!"[168]

Jack was thrust to survivor-mode; you know, where everything runs in slow-motion. The smell of perspiration, what the primal stench of a fear once-known, seemed to've been propelling his hands behind the bars, so's to choke the life from the odd helpless man. It had come to him as a vision, a flash before the eyes. The only thing holding him back had been the gnashing of teeth. Jaw agape, he'd gasped, "*My father's dead, you kraut-eating sonofabitch...*"

The gay chap, what with the mammoth buckteeth, and swastika-lapel, appeared to have grown quite perplexed; no, this wasn't at all what he'd hoped for. "You don't understand: *your father's very much alive.* I should know, for I've seen him—seen him with my very own eyes! In fact, he's probably with the Führer right—"

And that was that. Even as the bucktoothed bloke had taken his hand, Jackie had him about the throat; *crash*, then *thud*; two MPs dragged Jack to the Rolls.

By the time his panting had subsided, he was well on the way to England. The Pilot Officer recovered his focus long enough, so as to have noticed this piece of paper in his hand: 'The prisoner,' he must have thought. 'He must've passed it to me while I was trying to throttle him.'

But then he realized: this was no piece of paper at all, rather, but a photo; *a photo of a man.* Or, two men, rather. In an instant did Jack recognize the 'buck-toothed Bosh', observing maneuvers with some other.

And, 'the other' was a dead ringer for—*himself?*

[168] ['Liechtenstein': Supposedly the 'name' of a village, which Hossbach is thought to have pacified. More likely, it refers to a brothel, concerning which our memoirist is said to have frequented.—N.B.]

Chapter 16: The Best Plot

Europe: May to November 1941

Britain breathed a sigh of relief, once our dread invasion failed materialize. In June, we turned east, so's to deal with the Red Menace. This bought Albie a new lease on life. All across the isle, a haughty optimism prevailed; indeed, more than a few romances were enkindled.

Jack resumed his correspondence with a certain Contessa. The exchange had ended rather abrupt, owing to events in the Spring of 'Thirty-nine. Ach, for the Führer you see'd pulled off a string of bloodless coups. Why Chamberlain himself'd even declared 'peace in our time'—then handed us Czechoslovakia! Then, that dagger, that dagger piercing Europe to the bone simply ceased to exist;[169] without so much's firing a shot.

This last was simply too much. Oh, they didn't mind our new acquisition; it's just, they never expected us to acquire it so rent-free. Yes, *they* were the one's with buyer's remorse. In Whitehall there was panic: *war appeared inevitable.* The letters they suddenly stopped; I mean, who has *time* for such things?

But, three months later—Barbarossa![170] Thus, the Reich having moved east, Albie rejoiced in the fact that she is to be spared. Regulations became lax[171]; alas, the dim art of courtship prevailed. Thusly did their dalliance resume.

Oh, just a little harmless flirtation through the mail. You know: older bird, younger bloke; why surely it must have flattered his vanity. Yes, the lanky young lad you see

169 [One need but consult a map to get the gist of it.—N.B.]

170 ['Barbarossa': Codename for the invasion of Russia, which commenced June 22, 1941.—N.B.]

171 [Here, he is purporting to explain the genesis behind my alleged 'amours'.—N.B.]

must've been convinced his exploits traveled fast. I mean, why else'd some rich bird be stalking him? Besides, it must've been exciting being courted by some mysterious countess.

That is until she let slip she knew someone in Berlin who could put him in touch with his pa; alarm bells precipitately went off. Save for *MI-6*, Jack hadn't told a soul what the prisoner had said in Scotland.

The Pilot Officer was just as shocked as anyone to learn that the buck-toothed bloke was none other than Rudolf Hess: 'Hitler's right hand man.'[172] Somehow, the Countess seems to've gotten wind of Hess's crazy scheme; and, for reasons her own, had gotten Jack involved.

Yes, it seems the boy was in danger of joining ol' Rudy in the Tower; *or worse.* Rather his savior appeared from a quarter which could not have been more unlikely. Ach, for, no sooner'd Jack returned to London, than the Führer himself already had spoken, alleging Hess to have gone quite mad. This appeared to have put an end to the matter once and for all. Jackie was brought back into the fold; his career as suspected Nazi-spy having come to a precipitate end.

Alarmed by the Contessa's latest intrigue,[173] Jack informed Major Oliver, his superior now that Briggs had been sent on assignment. A tall, grayish man in his fifties, Oliver'd won rank owing to a mission in Mexico City, concerning the which he never spoke; and, wouldn't rise beyond, due to an incident in Madrid some years hence. Still he possessed a keen mind for personnel, and the best ways of putting them to use. A man who garnered respect from both subordinate *and* superior. Duly he passed the

---

172 [After our supposed 'meeting,' Hess was taken to the Tower, where he was held for the duration of the war. At Nuremberg, he claimed amnesia, then recanted in the middle of the trial.—N.B.]

173 ['latest intrigue': *i.e.*, her reputed mention of my father.—N.B.]

Pilot Officer's information to MI-6;[174] where, par for the course, it rested for a space.

Alas, come 8 November, the boy was sent on 'leave', along with Captain Wally Best. Which leave had been concocted, thus that the Captain might accompany Jack for a meeting with the Contessa. Principally a fact-finding tour, there existed the possibility of kidnapping her for interrogation in London. That is, if things didn't go well; or, rather, if they went so well, further questioning was desired.

Of course, Jackie being green, he knew nothing of the whole kidnapping bit; after all, that's why they'd sent Best.

Yet even the Captain didn't have all the details as to this mission.

In Search of Dionysus

The Countess arrived at Cafe Dionysus, Dutch side the river Meuse. And, exiting the stately Bentley waltzed this broad-shouldered chap, deferentially nestling her nigh.

The Captain and Jack were sipping tea on the veranda. They rose, then bid their guests have seat. Arrayed in chauffeur's attire, the broad-shouldered chap he smiled, then waved as if greeting somebody. Then, almost in the same motion he pirouetted, pinning the Contessa to the table.

Jack rushed up to her aid. Yet the woman had already squirreled out of her assailant's grasp—only to meet the latter side by side, matching *Walthers*[175] in hand: pointed straight at the Britishers' heads.

---

[174] [Actually, 'SIS': *i.e.*, British Intelligence.—N.B.]

[175] [*Walther*: A pistol, favored, as we shall see, by no less than Hitler himself.—N.B.]

A snarling glance sent the diners a-scamper when, alas, the burly man he spoke: "Herr Best und Herr Suffler —you are under arrest!"

Best he laughed: *"We?"*

The Contessa she smiled. "Fools! Did you think you could outsmart the great *Schellenberg*?"

As if on cue, this pompous dandy stepped forth, cocking his head to the side. In broken English he spake: "Vell vell vell—if zees isn't zeh perfect gift for zeh Führer's birs'day[176]—the cream of MI-6's crop."

Jackie snarled: "Intelligence? We came for whores!"

The Countess she slapped him.

And, he smacked her right back; a good one, too, evincing a savage grin. Still he had but seconds to marvel those strange, asiatic eyes, which almost seemed to mock him; when two goons they stepped forth and beat him silly.

Jackie and Best were taken into custody.

[176] [The fact remains that Hitler's birthday was actually April 20. If the above even occurred, Schellenberg might have said it merely for dramatic effect.—N.B.]

Chapter 17: Interrogation

Berlin: November 1941[177]

They were taken to Berlin, then kept in gaol for special prisoners. So far, they'd been treated rather well. One of the guards however appeared to be harboring a murderous rage within. More ominous still, Jackie and Best had been separated from the population writ large, forced to inhabit a tiny cell all their own.

"What're they up to, Cap? And what could they possibly want with two jakes like us?"

Best begged him to be quiet. Something seemed to be bothering the old chap beyond their already dire predicament. For he'd this look of the schoolboy, who's been hauled before the principal for a variety of misdeeds, only some of which'd ever occurred.

Jack, though, wasn't taking it quite so well. Presently he began pounding on the bars: "I'm an officer, dammit—I know my rights!"

The which produced a chuckle from Best, crumpled though he were upon the floor, manipulating this magnifying glass he'd somehow managed to conceal. "Ain't no one wants to hear about you, or your stinking rights. Now, pipe down, and shut up: *that's an order.*"

Jack continued to scream, leading Best to cause the aforementioned magnifying glass to quickly disappear.

Just in time. For, the first guard you see approached, rapping Jack on the knuckles with a tiny, metallic object. His partner opened the cage, then grabbed the boy by the throat. "Tommie want trouble, eh? Well... *he gets it.*"

Best spoke up: "Leave him alone—can't you see he's only a boy?"

[177] ['My' purported escapades probably stem from the files of the Gestapo.—N.B.]

The first guard he entered, rendering a nightstick deep in the Captain's solar-plexus; then, absconding with the lanky young chap, slammed the bar behind.

"Hang tight," shot Best, still recovering from the shock of the blow. "When you get out you must get word; *must get word to the Consulate.* And, tell them—tell them to get me the hell out!"

It was an old trick, the planting of a seed: 'when you get out'. As if the boy were innocent and, therefore, had nothing to hide. Truth is, Best had no idea why Jack had been taken. Certainly not for a little rowdiness; no, for that, for that a good beating should've sufficed. Clearly these chaps wanted something more.

Extracting some cyanide from a false-lens in his glass, Best went about the undignified yet necessary means of concealing it; then, sprawling on the floor, made as if to sleep.

***

Jack was taken to interrogation where, much to his surprise, he was greeted by a bird: the girl from the sting. Slender, and clad in a black one-piece, this raven-haired beaut, what with the slant-eyes and rawhide whip, spoke in commanding tones: "*Leave him to me...*"

The guards dispensed post-haste. Divining thus this Asiatic's intent, Jack was quick to react. Lunging he wrapped his hands about her sinewy throat, only to find himself flying; then, come to a stop against the wall. Convulsing he looked up only to see: a cattle-prod in her hands.

Before he could move she was on top, pinning him with a force unbecoming a bird: then she said, "*Son.*"

'Oh good god,' he must've thought. 'How hadn't I realized it? You know, before: back at the sting.'

As if anticipating his question she said: "*It's what I do.*" The light it changed, and Monique became formidable once more. "I see there's a lot they haven't been teaching you: that's about to change. Oui, next time you see me, we shall be surrounded by the Sausage Eaters. Yet do not doubt for one minute that, what I do, *I do for my people*. Perhaps some day you'll come to know such meaning; the *hardness* it demands. For now I have but one question—do you still want to win the war?"

"Oh God yes!"

Why the simplicity of it all must've been a welcomed island of absolutism, a buoy midst a mounting sea of confusion.

"Then *listen*: henceforth, I am your commanding officer. Now, you will meet a man, a man of great import; only, he doesn't know it as yet. Now, this man, this man will tell you things: things you won't wish to hear. You *are* to hear them; then, when you do, 'we-port *back* to me."

She handed him a letter, the which he studied before, following this game she'd taught him as a child, he swallowed upon committing to memory.

"This man, whatever he might tell you, whatever he might say, this man is loyal to Hitler; and, in his eyes, *so am I*. And that is how it must be. Oh, and one more thing," she chided, the constant refrain of his youth. Only, now, with a twist: "You shan't mention this to anyone: that is, *on pain of death*."

They locked eyes. And, Jack, seeing she meant it, must have felt a new-found respect for the woman who bore him. Yea, impossible though it were, for the slightest of seconds it seems she lapsed into tears;[178] but then almost instant did she retreat to her cynical charm. "Get to know him," she hissed, noting the time was short. "Earn his trust; then, *turn him to the resistance*."

"Resistance?" he scoffed. "But, but there's no such thing."

---

[178] The way Jack has it; but I doubt that bitch ever cried.[—W.H.] [This is mere moxie: Hossbach belies such 'doubt,' on more than one occasion, throughout the course of the manuscript.—N.B.]

And her eyes, weighed by the gravity of a horror as yet to be born, sank with the swallowing of secrets about a future yet to be written. As if in trance she sighed: "*There will be.*"

Rearranging her wig, then fixing those fake slant eyes, she said: "Oh, and one more thing: tonight you will be shot trying to escape..."

"But, but what about the Captain?" he stammered, suddenly recalling the man in his cell.

"*Oui,*" she offered, deadpan's an audit. "For the time being, he will just have to make do. Oh, don't worry," she smiled, batting those lashes; false just like the rest of her. "I'll put in a good word—*with the Führer.*"

Chapter 18: Jackie Becomes German[179]

Berlin: November '41

Exhibit 57-A: Interrog. 117, Deposition by SUFFLER, JACK[180]

[“] The *Zum Nusbaum* was clad in darkness, wrapped in the stale, fetid odors of cheap cigar and war rationed cigarette. Sitting down had been my first mistake. But what was it to me? “I'm an American,” I figured. “They can't touch me.”

I should have gathered mummy's machinations had lent a false sense of security to all my movements. Relaxing at the pub, I recalled how she'd led me from interrogation, body convulsing, to simply just rot in the hall. Whence, I could hear her being read the riot act by

---

179 Poor Jack. Why he'd simply no *idea* what company his mother had been keeping; and now it was about to engulf him. As a boy, his tutors had impressed upon him his mother's wish that he should learn German. And, being the wily slut insisted that he should speak to her in French, or not at all, Jack learned three languages. Add a refresher from the blokes at MI-6, and this 'American' became a full-fledged British spy.[—W.H.] [No comment, other than to add that the chapter heading, as usual, though not invariably, is his. The date and locale, conversely, have been affixed by me. Additionally, I have taken the liberty of adding an opening, and closing, quotation mark in brackets, in order to indicate where Hossbach has purported to have 'copied' material written by somebody else. —N.B.]

180 Before they hung the swine [*i.e.,* Canaris], his files on Jack's interrogation had been kept under lock and key. My attorney has since succeeded in requisitioning them. While they've done nothing for my defense, they've at least given me some insight into the Flying Officer's state of mind. For such service do I hereby nominate Dr. Seidl for the *Iron Cross*, 2nd Class.[—W.H.] [Canaris was supposedly hung by the Boche, in April '45, though certain unsubstantiated rumors, regarding the lack of a corpse, abound. 'Interrogations,' including, allegedly, that of my own person, *could* have been passed to London, from whence Seidl *might* have obtained them. The crude aping of my literary style, on the other hand, argues for this chapter as a forgery.—N.B.]

some Corpulent Colonel Kraut. He was beside himself. The Boche proceeded to usher her into the commandant's.

I could see her, bobbing her head, a series of yeses and nos, before slamming the door behind.

Upon exiting, she led me back to my cell (I say mine because, by this time, Best had already disappeared.) Mummy whispered, "Change of plans," then proceeded to strike me square in the gut.

"*You*," she'd snarled, loud enough the whole block could hear. "If you cost me my job I will have you drawn and quartered then paraded through the streets, an enemy of the people." She was seething. *"Oui,"* she gestured, a loan word from her native tongue. An SS stud gave her a light. "The Ambassador has a soft spot. I might be just a girl: But he's the one acting a sissy. But *Monsieur*," she mocked. "'The *Americans*... one mustn't bother the Americans!' Ech, that's alright," she stared, indicating the door to Interrogation. "We've still Captain *Woerst* to attend. Now go, you oily swine: Live it up while you can! But, just one screw-up and..."

Here she made an unmistakable gesture, turning on the unfortunate Looey,[181] who happened to be standing nearby, then began barking unintelligibly.

Two NCOs ushered me out the door, apologizing profusely before setting me free. Not before arming me, much to my disbelief, with diplomatic immunity. The safest man, thanks to Mummy, in all Shitler's Reich.

The gents in the Wilhelmstrasse[182] feared an *incident* such that they set me up in a smashing apartment, overlooking the Tiergarten. The Embassy, that is, German, furnished me a stipend for my monthly expenses.

---

181 ['Looey': A Leutnant, *i.e.*, Lieutenant. I beg the reader please question the veracity of my having supposedly referred to an officer, even that of the enemy, with any such familiarity. If I had, I *might* have called him 'Lefty,' *i.e.*, short for *Leftenant*.—N.B.]

182 [*Wilhelmstrasse*: Street housing the Foreign Ministry.—N.B.]

As for Best, however, they weren't nearly so put out. Indeed, they were glad to have him, confident's they were that he could be broken. The accident of my American citizenship had meant for me the difference between life, and a fate far worse than death.

Nothing to do but wait for Mummy to issue my assignment, I took to frequenting this Gasthaus in the Fischerkietz.[183] So there I was, right, marking time with these broads from Heidelburg when he made me. I'd an uncomfortable feeling every time he looked over. I smiled, as if say: "I have nothing to hide." And it must have worked, too. Or so I thought, being he appeared to have turned his attention to the bit of crumpet gyrating onstage. Exhaling deep, I sank back to a well won anonymity.

Closing time. I was putting away my last *Pils*,[184] when the bartender stepped forth. "I beg your pardon: But that man," he said, pointing to a now empty chair, "is in back." He raised his brow to see if I comprehended.

I pretended that I did not.

"I said, is in back, waiting: *Waiting for you.*"

"Look pal, I don't know what you're into: But I got me a little woman," I lied, then made for the door.

With a snap, two uniformed toughs stepped up to bar my way. So, I got rowdy. "I'm an American: Get the bleed out of my way!"

But they just stood there, dumb as a stump, awaiting orders. At last the 'bartender' spoke: "Herr *Suffler.*"

The big galut—how'd he know my name? "Ptth," I reasoned. "Anyone could have gotten that, simply by checking with the Embassy."

"That's true," he concurred. "At least, so far as that kind of thing is concerned. You are correct: International Law protects you as a guest of the Reich. On the other hand, your mother..."

---

183 ['Fischerkietz': District in the drinking environs of the city.—N.B.]

184 [*Pilsner*: A delightful German beer.—N.B.]

"You leave her out!"

"Then this way, please, I assure you: He only wants a little chat."

"But *who*?"

"This way, please, *Herr Leutnant.*"

It was odd the way he phrased it, using the Luftwaffe term for Leftenant.[185]

"Alright," I said, "let's have at it."

My companions froze, thinking me fixing for a fight. The big galoot nearly walked into me. They marched me to an open door, upon which one of his cronies proceeded to knock.

"*Come*," rang a man with a deep voice, while feigning himself be busy. He bid me stand, while signing some seemingly important papers. The mahogany desk appeared well suited for a gray haired Kraut in his fifties, wrapped in a turtleneck and bearing a swarthy complexion. Surprisingly supple, he propped himself up on the desk. "So," he raised his eyes and looked through me, legs kicking. "Herr *Suffler*: We meet at last."

"Tell me," I balked: "Who is this 'we,' and what do 'we' want?"

"Ah," he smirked, "yes... yes! I'll come straight to it: We know the Gabell girl... that is, your mother... has been in the country now for quite some time: *Working for the enemy.* And no matter how much I'd like to get my hands on her, I'm prevented from so doing by Himmler."

"Your hands—"

"I am prepared," he resumed, "to offer a deal: Come, work for me! Then, when America comes into it... which, I assure you, will be any day... *I will protect you*: New name, rank, the whole bit. Should you refuse however then I shall have no choice but to deport you as an undocumented alien: For passports have a way of expiring. And you know what that would mean... to your mission."

---

[185] [Or 'Lieutenant,' as the Yanks would say.—N.B.]

"My *what*? Are you mad?"

"Ah, very good, very good: 'What mission' indeed, *Herr Leutnant*."

There it was again... that word: A code?

"Young man, see here: I've grandchildren myself. Really, I've no problem with a boy who just wants to meet his pa. Truly I—"

"My *huh*?"

"Your—you mean, you really didn't know?"

The air appeared to go out from him.

"In which case, then, my apologies: My apologies for your having to find out like this. You know, when all's said and done, I fancy myself a gentleman. Cooperate, and ask him yourself."

"Ask what? Ask who? And *who*, Herr Shadowy Figure, just who the hell are *you*?"

He laughed. "All in good time, my boy: All in good time. Oh, don't worry. You won't *really* be doing any Abwehr[186] work. I shan't be asking you to sacrifice any loyalties. No, there's just one thing, Herr Leutnant, *just one thing* that I want: Do that, and I will introduce you to this man people say's your pa: You will be free to come and go as you please."

I was disturbed, and perplexed, almost in equal measure. Plus more than a tad impatient. "Spit it out, old timer. Now, tell me just what the devil it is you really want?"

"I want you... *to introduce me to your mother.*"

I left the Gasthaus[187] baffled, and more than a tad sauced. Indeed, the same SA bloke[188] blocking the door a few minutes before, ended up driving me home.

---

186 [*Abwehr*: German Military Intelligence. Admiral Wilhelm Canaris was its head.—N.B.]

187 [*Gasthaus*: A tavern, or inn.—N.B.]

188 [*SA: Sturmabteilung*: A paramilitary force, which, after the Röhm Purge, continued to exist, albeit in truncated form.—N.B.]

***

Next morning, some ungodly hour, an endless reverberation shattered the tenuous grip on my hangover. Struggling to locate the phone, I cradled the receiver before me. "Hallo?"[189]

"Four o'clock."

Four o'clock: Mummy's code for danger. She'd taught it to me as a child, prior to packing me off to the States.

"*I hear the rain's lovely this time of year.*"

Another code, meaning, 'Meet me by the lake.' Only, which lake? Knowing her, it would be as far away as possible. Being she hadn't specified where, it had to have been Berlin. Then I recalled: The Havel crosses the westernmost part of the city. She had mentioned it once in passing, which I now hoped to have held some sort of significance.

Before I could verify my assumption, the line fell dead: Battle stations! I hopped in the Volkswagen, then headed for the Autobahn.

Forty minutes later I pulled up to a stretch of woods leading to the *Wannsee*[190] and parked. After a paranoid stroll through the woods, I fell upon a Scharführer eviscerating a deer.

The scene had been causing quite a stir. Shocked, outraged faces were deserting in droves. For they knew Göring had passed the toughest anti vivisection laws in the world. The miscreant was liable to be punished with death: And no one wanted to be around once the Gestapo arrived.

---

[189] ['Hallo': This is not a typo. I am neither confirming, nor denying Hossbach's claims with regard to my person. But it is common knowledge that, if one resides amongst foreigners, then one is apt to speak in a manner befitting the local inhabitants.—N.B.]

[190] ['Wannsee': The *Grosse*, i.e., *Greater*, Lake Wannsee, in West Berlin.—N.B.]

Keeping my disgust in check, I approached the sacrilegious figure who, on second thought, didn't much look like a *Scharführer* at all.

"Mother?"

"*Shsh.*"

And that's how it began. That's how we were united: Me, a horrified look on my face; and, she, she wearing this ridiculous mustache.

"*Jack*," she cooed, more slap than hug. "You are in danger. My people saw the *SA* leave your apartment: What did they want?"

"*Your* people? You mean, you just left me, left me there to—"

"Flying Officer! Now is no time. Now, tell me—*what did they want?*"

"They wanted to talk... yes mother, talk... talk to *you*." I said this with sarcasm borne of long suffering. "Something about this Kraut you want me to meet being my pa. Now, would *you* care to do some explaining?"

"There is no time," she said, repeating the mantra of my youth.

I was caught like a dear in the lights, able neither to speak, nor fix my attention, until she released me from her grasp.[191]

"*Names!*"

"I, I haven't a clue: They didn't say."

Mercifully Mummy exhaled. "Good: I think. *Oui*," she glared. "It means they wish to remain anonymous... for now. But, whatever they're up to—say, Jack: Do you remember the sight game?"

"Mother good god! That was ages ago."

"*Nevertheless*," she intoned, retrieving a piece of paper from her purse. "You've twenty seconds: *Go.*"

---

[191] ['her grasp': I can confirm this to be the case. It is not physical: More a sleight of mind. I fancy it has something to do with the modulation of her voice.—N.B.]

Frantically I began searching for something with which to write. Failing this, I started to draw a face in the sand. Panicking, I outlined it several times, attempting to relate my message.

She stomped it out before I was through. "*Good boy.* Now, Jack, tell those pigs next time you see them: *I* shall send for them when ready."

No sooner had I begun pondering the meaning of her statement, than a limo, all decked out in government plates, came to a screeching halt, ejecting a sandstorm of dirt and debris. Probably a smoke grenade, too, being I could scarcely make out a thing.

Until, like a homing pigeon, the sun bounced off my windshield: *I raced for the Volkswagen.* Unable to find me mum, I channeled my inner French and took to my heels.[192]

I must have broken the sound barrier on the way back to my apartment, where, like a mantra, I kept telling myself: *You are safe now, you are safe*. Sometimes, it's best to believe a lie, when the alternative's simply too much to bear. Moreover I was confident Mummy had set the whole thing up.

Behind my surmise lay an irrational fear that, somehow, I was being protected. Perhaps this explains why I slept with the door unlocked. That, or, I'd meant to say, 'Have at me if you will. Otherwise... let me sleep the bloody thing off!' ["]

---

192 [As repeatedly stated, I cannot possibly comment with regard to the veracity of my alleged doings. Yet, this time, Hossbach has gone too far: I am fully one quarter French. It is absurd to believe, interrogation or no, I could have written any such tripe.—N.B.]

Chapter 19: The Curse of Sisyphus

OKW HQ, appr. 16 meters under Zossen[193]: Dec. 8, 1941

Army Group Center's bogged down, just thirty kilometers outside the ancient city.[194] Reports reaching FHQ[195] speak of spearheads having sighted the spires of the Kremlin; but, alas, winter's come too soon. The tanks they will not start; the weapons they will not fire. Worse, the dunderheads in supply fucked up so bad, hundreds of thousands have been allowed simply to freeze. Amputees are rife.[196] Yet deadliest of all's the clarion call of retreat; and, with it, the panic which doomed the *Grand Armee*[197] some hundred twenty-nine winters ago.

Owing to such extraordinary scenes, two days ago the Führer[198] authorized Bock[199] to go over to the defensive:

193 [I have, in this instance, decided to use Hossbach's subtitle. Of course, it is hopelessly muddled: And, therefore, in need of some correction. The structure of the German High Command is more complicated than that of the nucleus: There is much we still do not know. OKW's HQ was, at this point, situated at the Wolf's Lair, in East Prussia: It did *not* move to Maybach II till January '45. It is possible, though not bloody likely, that OKW had set up a kind of 'proto-Maybach II,' connected to Maybach I (*i.e.*, OKH's HQ), via an underground tunnel, as early as spring '43. *Neither* would have been at Zossen: Maybach I, and, eventually, II, were in Wünsdorf, *near* Zossen, about thirty kilometers from Berlin.—N.B.] [Late note: Overriding the prisoner's most vociferous objections, it is my duty to inform the reader that the 'Home Command' of *OKW* was indeed housed in the middle of Berlin, in the very the same building as that of the Army General Office. No wonder the defendant has been less than forthcoming, with regard to pinning down *OKW*'s movements. For, 'The Bendlerstrasse,' as the place became known, has become inextricably linked to the major players behind 'Twenty July,' with whom our memoirist would rather die, than ever be so associated.—N.B.]

194 ['Thirty kilometers': Eighty more likely. The spearheads, however, had indeed gotten that far.—N.B.]

195 [*FHQ*: Führer Headquarters.—N.B.]

196 [Due to army supply's criminal lack of winter clothes.—N.B.]

197 [*Grand Armee*: Napoleon's army, disintegrated within months of its own Russian folly.—N.B.]

198 [*i.e.*, the day before the Nipponese attack at Pearl Harbor.—N.B.]

199 [*Field Marshal* Bock, Fedor, *von*: Commander, at the time, of *Army Group Center*.—N.B.]

to dig in, and surrender not so much as an inch, rather, but *fight*. Yes, *fight*. And, if need be, *die*; die that the Army might live.

Therefore, since Sixth December I've been sequestered here at the spartan, frenetic quarters of *OKW*,[200] implementing unglamorous, yet necessary dispositions.

Only, now,[201] the Ivans—who were supposed to be lacking strength for a major offensive—have simply ignored our calculations and counter-attacked along the entire front.[202] My brain is over, or, rather, *under* stimulated; being one cannot cope with so many troubles devoid of any sleep.

Ach, for the Führer you see kept us up till five, jabbering on and on about the theater; and pork; and God knows what. Why, he's so much nervous energy, and the concomitant need to expend it. Still I've dispositions to make; the secretaries memoranda to type; adjutants schedules to arrange, facts to check, and a million and one household items to attend.[203]

---

200 [*OKW*, 'Oh Ka Vay', *Oberkommando der Wehrmacht*: Armed Forces High Command, in theory super ancillary to that of the Army, Navy, and Luftwaffe. Each had its own staff. The internal stresses affecting the structure of the German High Command will be examined more closely as we proceed.—N.B.]

201 ['now': *i.e.*, December 8.— N.B.]

202 [The front circumscribing the Moscow Theater, under the aegis of *Army Group Center*.—N.B.]

203 [The Armed Forces High Command, *i.e.*, OKW (Oh Ka Vay) was, like most bureaucracies under *die dritte Reich*, subject to a multitude of competing, oft contradictory redundancies. Hossbach worked in Warlimont's section, with an eye to armor and supply, yet also as liaison between staffs. Moreover, while frequenting *FHQ*, he often was pressed into his old *rôle*, in what can only have been a most difficult act: The 'War on Two Fronts,' he called it. OKH (the *Army* High Command) had jurisdiction in the east (i.e., *not* OKW). Yet Hossbach, operating under Hitler, performed duties requisite to the entire eastern theater. The arrangement was supposed to have ensured cooperation between staffs. In reality, it merely exacerbated (for Hossbach, at least) an atmosphere already fraught with suspicion. The situation came to a head in January '45, a tangential factor in his subsequent release.—N.B.]

Juggling figures, what for the umpteenth time, trying to balance an impossible equation, out the corner my eye steps this beanpole of a man; some Leutnant I've never seen, yet somehow seems familiar.

He bears his presence before me like a lamp of interrogation, demanding he should be heard. Now, ordinarily you see such impudence would be met by a sound thrashing. And yet, on a whim, or perchance since I haven't the energy, I decide to humor him.

"*Colonel*," he begins, using the Anglicized term, what like some fucking piece of popcorn; rather than the German word, *Oberst*. Yes, I know some of our boys spent time in America; but, dammit, we're not *in* America. Heedless he plods. "I have come from the Abwehr. Henceforth the Can-ary wishes me brief you on a bi-weekly basis."

Brief you? Pah, spook-talk meaning 'thus that I might brief him as to *you*'.

"On?" I say, seemingly angry, yet simply assessing the situation. I gaze, gaining courage from a picture of the Führer, then bid him continue.

"Morale," he says. "Specifically as to the morale of your men."

Now I really do get angry. "Is there a problem, *Herr* Güntzler,[204] a problem with one of my men? Or perhaps it's just you've a problem with me?"

He backs off. "No, that's not it: that's not it at all."

You're damned right it's not...

"The problem involves the pedigree of some of your men."

"My *staff*? The best a man could ask!"

"Fully one-eighth," he resumes, lounging in my guest-chair. "Fully one-eighth appear to be of Jewish

204 ['*Herr* Güntzler': A slight, being it is customary to address an officer, especially one with whom one is not familiar, by rank, rather than such civilian honorific.—N.B.]

extraction. Moreover a disproportionate number hail from left-wing breeding grounds such as Ber—"

"*Who is your superior?*" I bark, what literally turning the table. Coffee it spills; papers they fly.

'The insolent kid,' I say to myself on seeing him sneer—or *smile*? And yet—pah, devil take it! Yes for I've this *feeling*. Why I used to hear Hess and his ninnies talk about it all the time; an *eerie* feeling, almost's if talking to myself: *deja vu*, I think they call it; my thoughts they begin to wander...

Composing myself, I reassess the situation. "*Herr Leutnant*," I smile, proffering a cigarette; the which he politely declines. "Haven't I seen you someplace—where was it you said you were from?"

"*München*,"[205] he lies. For, I know the Münchener accent: and that's not it. "I have been in the Abwehr now for three years."

As if that has anything to do with it. Still, that's about right, what given his age; though they don't usually take them so young. He hands me his orders. "These are from the Can-ary: I trust you'll find everything in order." Leaving me scarcely a minute to review he continues. "You are to deliver a report within twenty-four hours, regarding the morale of your men, including any suspicions as to their allegiance."

"I've one suspicion," I say, delivering a deadpan grin. "Only, not with regard to my men..."

Now, in the old days you see, the next step would have involved the issuance of a challenge. Oh, but ach, the Führer's strictly forbidden it, 'save for lawyers and priests!'

I hope he knows what he's doing. He's playing with fire, he is—for I've a line *straight* to the Chief.

Then—reverently?—he *bows*: "I understand."

You—*huh*?

"Herr Colonel."

---

[205] [München: *i.e.*, Munich.—N.B.]

There it is again!

"Really I do. Say, why don't we meet for cocktails? The *Officer's Lounge*, say Nineteen-hundred?"

Now, I may be feeble-minded, owing what to a lack of sleep but—*did he just give me an order?*

"I'm just in from Muenchen," he yawns. "Not a friend in sight. Really, it would so help put me at ease when making my report."

Pah—outmaneuvered by a lowly Leutnant!

I parry, "That will not be necessary. Besides, you've given me much needless work: especially at a time such's this." I rise, the which he readily concurs. The swine; at least he's *some* notion what's proper. Atop my toes I stare him down; or, rather, up.

The boy continues to baffle me. He makes this disappointed face, what that just tugs at my strings; *perhaps he really* does *have no one?*

He tries to make a joke of it, saying how awkward such meetings can be, then proceeds to let himself out. He must've said 'Heil Hitler'; though, for the life of me I can't recall.

The hour's getting on; and what the whiskey's run low. The map it resolves into a blur of disconnected entanglements. The thought occurs to rub my eyes. But then I realize: *I have been doing this for quite some time*. The last straw it comes upon the realization that the Smirnoff has been exhausted. I cannot quite recall gathering my keys; the lights it seems they shut themselves off.

Trudging the tumultuous trek to ground, I pop my head through the trap-door, eying Old Fritz, who proceeds to give me the all-clear. I am parked a good ways passed the barn. Still it takes a few minutes to recall: 'You're not waiting for anyone old boy.' And now am I forced not only to walk to my car, rather, but drive it myself; for Schmidtie you see's on loan to the *SD.*[206]

At this crucial hour, though we be sundered, he is in my thoughts more than ever. Merging onto the Autobahn, my mind begins to drift: 'Thank God for the war: the traffic would've killed me.' I strain to negotiate the sparsely populated lanes, struggling through nary a curve. Why, I feel like such a heel, what having taken his prowess behind the wheel for granted.

Eventually I get the hang of it, and so digress: *ah—Schmidtie! We went through thick and thin back in the war. Yes, you've stuck your neck out for me many a time; even going so far's to assist Winifrid when the Nuremberg Laws*[207] *were first proclaimed. And, what's more, you've been instrumental helping me lock up the bad apples, whenever the Führer had to go to—*

Oh—donnerwetter, nochmal! Since when do horses have right of way? Unwillingly do I receive the yeoman's ill-will, then repay him with an Italic gesture. Overhanging trees, and the freedom of dirt-roads ensue; alas, *home*.

Divested of my driving gloves and riding-breeches, I fall upon the cabin what just like a casualty; shell-shock, no doubt. No way I'm going to the Chancery like this, whether the Führer's in or no. Kicking off my boots, my poor feet demand be bathed. Next, my whistle insists upon being wet; *brandy always seems to do the trick.* Until, alas, a cigar and some sweets; then, then I get the old boy[208] on the horn.

---

[206] [*SD, Sicherheitsdienst*: Reich Security Service. Domestic intelligence wing of the *SS*. In the east, this entailed *Aktions*, indictable as crimes according to the charter of the *IMT.*—N.B.]

[207] [*Nuremberg Laws*: Series of anti Semitic decrees from 1935, painted by Hossbach during the trial as necessary to "[...] take back our *Kultur* from the grip of an alien race."—N.B.]

[208] ['old boy': Possibly Schmidtie. Yet he was supposedly on duty with the *SD*. Perhaps another shadowy figure, whose services Hossbach had more than ample opportunity to employ.—N.B.]

He digs for dirt on this 'Güntzler' and finds: *nothing.* Actually, an exemplary record; though he was denied the Captaincy owing to peace-time quotas. Only, now we're at war, this beanpole could end up my equal: *or worse.* Ach, they don't keep us old-timers glued to a desk for nothing.

Oh, but that's alright. Yes for, as the Führer said what just the other day, once the present crisis's overcome, he'll make a General of me yet. This imbues me with a bout of courage, confidence, and energy with which to proceed.

Now, I know my mind should be absorbed with saving Army Group Center, but I've rivals aplenty: I certainly don't need one more. Therefore do I make up my mind to mention this Güntzler to Canaris next time I see him. Yes, it's operationally imperative; you know, so's to help me concentrate on the matter at hand.

Speaking of which, I simply *must* find some lackey to steer this infernal contraption. Perhaps I can get Canaris to meet us at the Transportation Ministry; *let's just hope the Ivans aren't there to greet us...*[209]

---

209 [The meeting with Canaris did indeed take place. After repeated inquiries to Dr. Seidl, with regard to why the event is not registered in Hossbach's record as I have received it, I can do no better than quote the inveterate Nazi counsel: "The other day, I went to see the Lion [i.e., Hossbach], in order to convey certain documents, regarding which you have been apprised. To my horror I found him on his cot, laid out in the fetal position, afraid to move. It was if he were in another world. Following a little coaxing with some whiskey, he surrendered his position to reveal the tattered fragments of precious court appointed paper. From what scraps I could make out, the casualty was no less than the entire Canaris chapter. It appears that Hossbach, in a semi-sentient state, had feared being brought before the People's Court, owing to his congress with the Admiral. By the time I could disabuse him his illusion, the damage had already been done. He refuses to rewrite it, for, in his addled mind, the incident I have related never took place." Communication from Dr. Seidl.—N.B.]

Chapter 20: Jackie

Berlin: 9 Dec '41

DIARY OF A FLYING OFFICER: EXHIBIT 57-C[210]

[“] The Gestapo could be here[211] any day. Immunity? Pearl Harbor! For, the Nips have bombed Honolulu. Consequently, or, so the rumormongers have it, we'll be at war any day. At war with Hitler's Reich!

Well, what of your plans now, mother? Thanks to her, I've been given 'one last job.' That is, until Washington can convince London to send me back. I stare at the sky every day and wonder, wonder what it would be like to be up in the air once more. Instead I'm supposed to be passing documents to a cutout for Joe Kennedy tomorrow. I dunno, some rich oil sonofabitch, whose son Joe they say is gonna be president.

But yet I cannot sleep. The leaves keep stirring outside. Plus these shadows sure as shit ain't birds. And what's all this nonsense I keep hearing about my father? My father's dead you goosestepping pricks: 'Hero of the British Empire,' killed by you Huns the last bloody war. Then, back home, a pariah thereafter. And not just him. The whole bunch of Tommyrots refused me promotion. Simply due to my name.

---

[210] The following diary entries stem from discovery, concerning Jack's comings and goings during the course of the war. I suspect that they have been doctored, perhaps even re-written, by the good folks at *MI-6*; or, the *Abwehr*. Nonetheless, it's the best information I have with regard to his movements. Seidl'd introduced them in court, so's to show my alleged 'sympathy' for the resistance. Of course, that's only so much *quatsch*. Still, I humor him so's to hear it. I have appended a copy to this record. For, Jack's story you see touches not only me, rather—*but all mankind.* [—W.H.] [I am prevented from commenting on my alleged 'entries' by the *Official Secrets Act*. Suffice it to say, they are not even alleged to have originated from my journal, but a narrated concatenation of my supposed 'interrogation.' Take them as you will.—N.B.]

[211] [*Gestapo (Geheime Staats Polizei)*: Shitler's secret police.—N.B.]

Therefore, in order to win the dead man's respect, I've gotten it into my head to join Mummy, and all her crazy spying games. A flood of emotion's let loose upon me: Gestapo or not... no sleep for this bloke tonight.

Best, I forgot to ask mother about Best! Ptth, she would have just said: 'There is no time.' There's always no time.

As for the Gestapo, I could be worried over nothing. That is, until I make this drop: Then, then they'll have the goods to hang me. I hope she's thought of that. Then again, she always does think of something.

But then, I'm done. They can shoot me when I get back.[212] Save there's one more thing that I must do: Find Best, then race like a rocket rapier out of this godforsaken land. True, Washington and Berlin aren't at war: Yet. But any day, these politicians could get their panties all in a bunch. I'm running out of time: Best is running out of time.

23:00

I am lucky to be alive.

Startling me out from my slumber came this pounding echo off the door. Instinct said: "Pull the covers over your head and disguise yourself. Then, flee out the window down the escape." Ridiculous.

Unsheathing my blade, I tiptoed to the door. It came as a shock, for of a sudden I could remember this game Mummy and I used to play called 'Grandpa.' He was our fictitious neighbor: Used to lived under the floor. At night, one had to be careful not to 'wake Grandpa.' In which case, of course... he'd come eat us!

It helped me now moving by stealth, the *feel* of the grip against my hand. With relief I ascertained the unspeakable knocking to be coming from somewhere inside my whiskey diseased brain. Massaging my temples seemed to do the trick.

[212] ['back': Presumably, to London.—N.B.]

But yet it did not stop. Hefting my blade, I approached the door. Then, cringing, called: "*Hallo?*"

"Sir, it's Karl... the SA? We met the other night."

Ah: Someone really *was* knocking.

"May I come in?"

Well, why not? It would have been riskier still to refuse.

"Sure," I relented, feigning disinterest. I could reach the knife in the small of my back within seconds: Just like mom always said.

"Come," I offered. "Sorry for all the mess. I haven't had time to recover since our little *rendezvous* the other night."

"You're very brave, *Herr Leutnant*," said Karl, perhaps the only Jerry with whom I've any sympathy: Indeed, every officer should have such an NCO. Smiling he extended a hand: "The Admiral he... admires your work."

"Admiral?" I thought. "And just what is it with this 'Herr Leutnant'?"

"I'll be brief," I said, "*Scharführer,*"[213] purposely addressing him by his rank; since, as a pilot officer, technically I outranked him.[214] Holding my breath, I executed a duty I neither understood nor desired. "My... mother desires to meet this *Admiral*, about whom one hears so much."

I was bluffing, of course, being no one knows a thing about 'The Can-ary.' As a rule, it seems, the very blokes who call him this chance know him the least.

"Admiral Canaris, *Herr Leutnant*."

"Another thing," I quipped. "What is it with this 'Herr Leutnant'?" For it had been established he knew who I was.

---

[213] [*Scharführer*: 'Squad Leader,' SA rank, loosely equivalent to Corporal or Sergeant.—N.B.]

[214] [This supposed 'diary' is really very funny, since, as enemies, my rank would have meant nothing of the sort.—N.B.]

He smiled. "Your father... er, my *friend*—"

"My father's dead, you sausage-eating sonofabitch."

Nearly I struck him. For, I was mad, and drunk as an Irishman. Only the need to maintain my composure prevented my acting on impulse.

The Scharführer stood his ground. Besides, he's a likeable lout: Tall, blonde hair almost white. Plus a face that must have been etched by the forge of the gods. I said to myself: "Now here's a man who'll go far." But then I remembered: "*He* is the enemy."

Biting his tongue he spoke: "Would you like to see him?"

"See what? See who?"

"Truly," he gazed, a queer look in the eye. "He wants to meet you."

I fought the dread screaming from within. Nerves long assumed dead came springing back to life, punishing me with pain. Pain of questions unanswered. Pain of anger, pain of rage at me mum, for having abandoned me all these years.

Yet I too can wear a mask. "Sure," I said. "Let me get my coat."

An hour later we arrived at a one story villa on the outskirts of the city.[215] It should have taken all of ten minutes to get out of the downtown. But this SA stooge, obviously no slouch, kept doubling back, in case the Gestapo was following.

"Here," he piped, pulling up to a well mannered homestead replete with Pan nymphs frolicking amidst baths of alabaster blue, fed by a constant stream of pure water.

My companion entered the house unbidden. It was understood that I should follow.

---

215 My 'home away from home': an antidote to the onrush of the city. [—W.H.] [Hossbach's main residence was his apartment in the *New Reich's Chancellery.*—N.B.]

Darkness. No one appeared to be home. Then, a sizzle, a sizzle just like lightning. The scent of sulfur mixed with flame, flashing against the window as this tall barrel chested lout stepped forth.

He kept right on going, until nearly we stood face to face. Pressing cold, calloused hands to my head, he rubbed my cheeks, even as tears slid down his battle weary face. Then he said: "*Son.*"

I pulled back, releasing myself from his Titan grip, then rasped, "First off, pal, I'm an American. And my father? My father, you jackbooted prick, my father died during the war:[216] Killed by you filthy fucking Huns!"

Instinctive I turned to Karl for support. With an infinite pain, he hung his head and looked off.

The barrel chested Kraut stepped forth, only not so close this time and said: "You have a right to know: A right to know the truth. Should you wish to leave, I shan't try and stop you."

Mad as I was, I must admit being a bit curious. The picture that crackpot had given me in Scotland... it was him: This very same man. In order that this mischief might be buried once and for all I said: "Alright old man... start talking."

He bid me have seat. Stifling the urge to do the opposite of everything he said, I forced myself to occupy the Ottoman. The smell of polish ingrained on deep stained oak was relaxing, reviving memories of home. The finest Yorkshire wood. What this Kraut was doing with a flair for English furniture was beyond me. I reckoned he must be a hunter. This appeared to be self evident, though I fail now to see the connection.

"*Ordinarily,*" he began, "I would not countenance such blatant disregard of regulations. However, an officer must be able to adapt to mitigating conditions: And hell, these are as mitigating as any. Oh, don't give me that

---

[216] [*i.e.*, the Great War.—N.B.]

'America's neutral' stuff. I know that, somehow, some way, that godforsaken mother of yours put you—I said sit! I'm getting to it. That woman, everyone knows just *who*, and *what* she is. No, there's one reason, one reason alone I haven't had you shot: And, that is... *you're only here because of me.* There, I said it... oh, but what was I saying? Oh yes: It was my second tour..."

He strained, eyes closed, hands rapt as if in prayer, an awful pain contorting: "We were just outside Champagne, when orders were received to advance. Everything was going just swimming. We went from village to village, imposing curfew whilst collecting booty along the way. The people we met were simple but cooperative. Everything proceeded in an orderly fashion. Until, two shots rang out: one man lay dead, an officer wounded. Yet still the perpetrators were nowhere to be found. Chaos thus ensued. Why, it was just like chasing ghosts. We searched from hut to hut, until the CO appeared, rerouting us with orders from on high."

"'*Terror must be met with terror*'," he resumed, relating what the CO had told him. "'*Kaminsky, Hennemann, you: Get the flamethrower. The women? Ours for the taking! Animals to be slaughtered. The men? Well, they're animals too, right—to the sword!*'"

He seemed to be enveloped in some sort of fog, sinking into the couch recalling the scene. Kneading his eyes, he forced himself continue. "It's hard to remember what happened next. I imagine there must have been tears in my eyes. Or, at least, butterflies in my stomach. Anyhow, one of the women... you see, one of the women... oh, but ach... *one of the women was your mother.*"

It took me a moment to get the gist of what he was saying. "Of course," I figured, "it can't be true." Yet there was this look, this pathetic look on his face, as if he hoped I'd kill him, or forgive him: Only not walk away.

I opted for the latter. Only, not through the door. Really I didn't know what I was doing.

"Jack," he wept. "*You are my son.*"

I was over him in an instant, squeezing that great big neck with all my might. An utter waste. The big lug didn't even try fighting back. Then Karl, my enemy turned friend, pinned my arms from behind.

The old man gasped, "Let him go."

We locked eyes: Mine, blood thirsty; his, blood shot. Suddenly I found myself overcome by a murderous desire to stomp out the life of this lug, this Kraut who so dared speak of my pa. Then it all came rushing back: *the teasing, the taunting, the fights, the sonofabitch; the sonofabitch just went off and died...*

"*He*," the old Kraut wept, "he was my best friend. It's just, your mother, your mother and Jack were planning to be married. Pah, until she came along, the Jacker and me were's thick as thieves. Oh, but I have to admit: I didn't take their courtship quite so well. Yes you see I, why, I thought... *anyway*, England had nothing more for me. And so, I returned, returned to the Reich to be with P'pa. Meantime, Jack—"

"Don't you dare speak of my pa, you spineless Nazi —"

"*Jack*," he persisted, "was a brilliant chemist. And, like I said, my very best friend. Oh, but that filthy slut, she took him... why, she took him from me! *Ach,*" he relented, "I am so sorry: I meant no disrespect. It's just, it's just you see that's how I used to think of her. I was pathetic, drunk all the time, and trying to take the Jacker with me. I guess I was just bitter. And, if what the SD says is true, much as yourself, chasing both whiskey and tail. No," he concluded, "Jack Suffler wasn't your father: but he should have been."

He was fighting back the tears. Meantime, I, like ice only aching to thaw, coalesced, frozen.

Lifeless he spoke: "So, now you know," his words assailing, yet reviving me all the same, "the truth: The truth, that is, about me."

In my mind's eye, the knife I'd managed to conceal was already coursing through space, striking his jugular with the sweet splash of death. Blood engorged my imagination, bathing the carpet deep Kraut red.

Perhaps it was but happenstance. For, that very moment, the light bounced off a candle, reflecting his eyes and I beheld... *myself.*

Really, had it been in front of me all along? Simultaneous with my Bowie knife fantasy, I wrapped my hands about his neck; and hugged him a good, long time.[217] ["]

[217] Something's been bothering me to this day, the which no one'd deemed worthy to clear up in court (unless I was asleep—a distinct possibility): and, that is, how in the world did Hess know who Jackie was when, at the time, even *I* hadn't the slightest? It is my belief that the Mademoiselle—possibly via Beaverbrook—had briefed Hess on the whole bit. This treason seems to have been conducted via a series of missives, a scheme by *SIS* to convince Hess of the existence of a pro-German clique in Britain; through whose entreaties he might be able to broker a deal, pursuant to the impending invasion of the Soviet Union. Which latter offers the benefit of elucidating something exceedingly odd. Something Hess'd once said, shortly before his flight, almost as if in code; indeed, as if I had 'been in the know'. If true, it would mean that I—unknowingly—had a hand in robbing the Reich of one of its most gifted men. I say this but as preamble to my record, lest anyone should get the idea that *I* had anything to do with such things, on the one hand; and, to convey my utter shock and surprise, with regard to what happened next, on the other.[—W.H.] [So much the 'preamble': I have moved it here, in order that the reader might come to reflect on such things, in so far as that is possible, at the 'same time' as has our memoirist.—N.B.]

Chapter 21: Dinner with the Führer

December 10, 1941: Berchtesgaden, Bavarian Alps

A letter arrived at *OKW,*[218] which moved my colleagues to jealousy: an invitation to dine with the Chief.[219] Oh, I can understand their feeling jaded. Yes, I've been to so many of these 'tea parties'; just like the rest of the staff. And they've always taken place in some godforsaken bunker, or mosquito infested hell, such as Vinnitsa. Only, tonight, tonight I am to dine at the Führer's own private villa. Ah, *Berchtesgaden,*[220] a luxurious lair: truly fit for a head of state.

I'm being flown in by Bauer, the Führer's favorite pilot, this bright-eyed, lantern-jawed chap, what with a cherry-red countenance. One's first impression is, 'Here's a man grown old before his time'. What the ever-delicate fuzz atop his dome; why, one would think him almost bald. The heavy forehead, every line of which speaks of some sense of purpose: the countenance of a steelworker. And the eyes —penetrating, blue; why, they all but just *bore* into you. Charisma born of confidence. An able pilot; *totally loyal.*

Presently we land, whereupon we taxi via an unmarked cab up the panoramic hill ascending the mountainous beatitude which haunts the Austro-German border. The Boss's[221] villa's in the mountain: I mean literally *in* the mountain; an arena for statecraft, as well as a private retreat.

---

[218] [Again, this should be pronounced 'Oh Ka Vay.'—N.B.]

[219] ['The Chief': *i.e.*, Hitler.—N.B.]

[220] [*Berchtesgaden*: Location of Hitler's Munich *HQ*. Like his birthplace, the vicinity straddles the Austro-German border: The most beautiful spot in all Hitler's Reich. For what it's worth, my sources indicate that the meeting must have taken place at the Wolf's Lair, i.e., OKW *HQ* during the period in question.—N.B.]

[221] ['the Boss': Again, Hitler.—N.B.]

Flush with confoundment, I take in the magnitude of the Berghof's[222] construction: miraculous walls of plated-glass, arising midst the anchorings of earth; an elevator which essays one a mile up to this exquisite little tea-house[223], what with a view of the roof of the world.[224] The farthest thing from the cramped, spartan quarters, which constitute most *FHQ*s.

***

The dining hall's probably smashing; it's hard to say, being my head it simply won't stop spinning. Not from the flight, nor the cab, rather, than that air of tardiness which like a magnet attracts everybody's attention. We had to re-route, after coming into some turbulence before settling into the jet-stream. Or, at least, so says Baur, in proffering a reason for our being some thirty minutes late.

Dinner's already been served. I mix in some small talk, so the Führer doesn't have to. Ach, for, having been in charge of protocol for many such events, I know it would be a *faux pas* for him to discuss say the merits of the Eighty-eight millimeter shell. Therefore I do my best to divert the conversation into more frivolous channels; you know, like one does with a woman.

Unfortunately our tardiness's resulted in damage that cannot be undone. A discussion's raging between Goebbels and some loathsome Turk, hidden beneath a veil, as per their custom; and, gesticulating violent as per their wont; *talk of war.*

My ears they perk up; the Führer he frowns. For such talk you see is strictly forbidden: *and everyone knows it.* Abruptly we transition to the awkward strains of a tenuous silence.

---

222 ['Berghof': Pet name for Shitler's south German chalet.—N.B.]

223 ['tea house': the *Kehlstein*. Or, as we Brits liked to call it, 'The Eagle's Nest.' Hitler hardly ever used it.—N.B.]

224 [Actually, over Salzburg: Hence 'the Obersalzberg.'—N.B.]

Eva is here, too. Yes, somehow this dye-job it seems's succeeded in awakening certain amorous feelings.[225] Oh, doesn't she know there's a war going on? Besides, history's replete with the ruins of its greatest men, emasculated by the wiles of the most insignificant women.

And, now, this unsophisticate's succeeded in attracting the interest of Dr. von Braun, a brilliant savant, apparently a guest this evening; *but I don't trust him.* First, he's devilishly handsome; the which tends towards vanity in a man. *And the stories*; alright, maybe I envy him a little.

Still, too much a free-thinker for me. You know the type: the playboy, a spendthrift; why, he reminds me of myself when I was his age. But the irreverence! Why, you can see it in his chin, in the languid leisure with which he pets that granite mallet. Such men speak their minds; *such men are dangerous.*

Of course Himmler, who it seems brought him, is completely lacking in anything such; and, as the Jew Freud would no doubt say, is therefore overcompensating. Why one would think him almost the host, exhibiting von Braun like some exotic new toy.

"*Herr Doktor,*" Eva she squeals, what with such exaggerated coquetry. "Is it *true*?"

Pah, such blatant display of affection; only, the Boss doesn't seem to mind; the which merely incenses me all the more. He's such a good sort, he is. Really, putting up with the likes of *that*. Why, I daresay I feel more threatened than him.

"Do you really think this *rocket*," she proceeds, staring unladylike into his eyes, before breaching the ultimate taboo. "Can still win the war?"

Everyone is preoccupied with their own idle chatter, engrossed in fulfilling their basic social function. For once, however, the Führer is listening. And, while none of the hangers-on've hitherto paid her any mind, the Boss he

[225] [re, 'awakened certain amorous feelings': *i.e.*, in Hitler.—N.B.]

breaks off his conversation with Herta mid-way,[226] inspecting Eva's eyes.

Silence.

Braun he hefts his humungous head, thus that Eva's eyes might meet those of his own. "Well, *Fraulein*, if you wish to be technical," he says, enlightening her with facts the which this empty-headed kitchen-slut can scarcely understand.

Oh, but ach, I know what's on that hussy's mind: *this is the only way they can ever be together...*

"The A4[227] is just a prototype," he smiles, a thousand gleams in the eye; what manly pride belying a boyish grin. "In future, space-flight will be common. I should know: I've worked out the equations myself." His plump hand it smacks Olympian thighs when he says, "At present we shall colonize the Moon come Nineteen—"

"*A-hem*," the Führer he coughs.

I mean, he could stand the flirtation. After all, women simply adored the man: much as himself, albeit for different reasons; *God they're young...*

Still, escapism's no excuse; hell, in war, it's downright treasonous. Oh, why doesn't someone send this egghead back to the lab, that he might finish this rocket about the which everyone's been speaking?

As if in answer to my prayer, the Boss he speaks: "Braun my good man, in future please leave such *hobbies* for your leisure; of which I can't imagine a man such as you having very much."

Now, what the Führer *means* is, a man like this Braun's no right to be wasting his time on such far-reaching fancies; that is, until the Final Victory is actually achieved. Ach, but these scientists—unlike *us*—why, they've simply no need to stand up and fight. No, for they earn their keep

---

226 [Schneider, Herta: Best friend of Eva Braun's sister, Gretl.—N.B.]

227 [*A4* ('Ah Four'), *Aggregate-4*: Liquid fueled rocket, later called 'V2.'—N.B.]

pushing but pencil and pen: the 'Technocrat', the 'Man of the Future', who, having seduced nature her mysteries, has become all but indispensable to the modern world.

That's all well and good. But, first, first they must sublimate their genius to the good of the nation; especially in time of war. Ach, how my innards rebel against such 'men': men in whom matter dominates spirit. Yes, the problem of our century is, men have turned from Kant, embracing instead an empty materialism which measures its God in tonnage of steel: the 'New Man'—quatsch! The future is *now*: to dream is neither the right nor the privilege of the present generation. I mean, what good is space? You can't bomb England through space.[228]

The F.[229] for his part insists that the rocket should be mass-produced, then launched in one colossal assault; rather than piecemealed out as it becomes operational. Why he doesn't give a damn for any 'space-ship', nor any *quatsch*: “Wars are won by force of arms—not blueprints of the murky morrow!”

He's right. I mean, what is it to a man like this Braun[230] if the Russians were to occupy say Rumania? Half our oil—gone in an instant! To him, it's nothing: 'A man on the Moon,' he says—preposterous! Dammit, there's a war going on; and it's high time these dunderheads knew it: these days, only children can dream.

I've got to pee really bad, but've been waiting for a break in conversation so to slip off. Ribbentrop, our Foreign Minister, breaks into some long-winded harangue regarding today's date, corresponding with market fluctuations; or, something such, multiplied by the number of martinis he's managed consume.

---

[228] ['You can't bomb England through space.': The Censor has kindly allowed me to relate that, since October 3, 1942, such a sentiment espouses the apotheosis of ignorance.—N.B.]

[229] ['The F.': Yet another appellation for Hitler.—N.B.]

[230] [Later events suggest von Braun had taken umbrage at Hitler's remarks, and, on a pretense, had proceeded to make himself scarce.—N.B.]

Driving my molar into my tongue, so as not to scream, I listen for a damned near eternity before making my escape. And—ah! I let nature unfold when, who do I see out the corner my eye but Hans Frank, Governor-General of occupied Poland, at the stall beside me. I finish my business then freshen up.

Oh, but he just stands there, what this horrified look on his face. "Dr. Frank," I say. "Something wrong?"

He shoots me this look, the likes of which conveyeth something unsound. Alas, with practiced refinement, he transmogrifies back to being just a man in a three-piece suit. Actually, he's turned into something far, far worse: oh dear Lord my God—a *lawyer*.

And yet, the quavering of his lips, what the brandy on his breath belie the illusion. "*Oberst*[231]," he pleads. "Take my advice: if ever you should chance be in Silesia,[232] and are asked to visit a camp on the River Bug, please, don't do it—it's not my fault!"

Clearly, the alcohol's begun to take its effect.

"*Hob-sox*," he slurs, wetting himself whilst essaying the delicate maneuver of reaching the sink. "The *Ostjuden*[233] are simply impossible: two of every three're completely incapable of rendering any work. Plus, they spread disease, disease—oh, it's not my fault!"

"Governor," I venture, treading cautious. "Tell me, what's the *name* of this place?"

Darkly he plies the brimstone abyss of his mind then says: "Oswiecheim; or, as we call it, *Auschwitz*."

Pah, I've heard it all before. Can you believe, a man such's that, actually *listening* to the enemy? The Jews aren't the only ones who should have their radios taken. Ach, they said we used to use babies for target practice back in the last war; a shameless lie, the which today everyone knows

231 [*Oberst*: Colonel.—N.B.]

232 [Upper Silesia. Or, as it is now called, 'Poland.'—N.B.]

233 ['Ostjuden': *i.e.*, eastern Jews.—N.B.]

to be untrue. Still, I have to ask. "But, but what about the *children*?"

He stiffens: "Ask Himmler."

"Herr Frank, who is running the place, you, or Himmler?"

"Himmler."

"But, but what about the *Führer*? I mean, does *he* know such things go on?"

"The *Führer*?" he chides. "He's the one who ordered it."[234] He slurs my name one more time; then, securing his briefcase, makes as if to abscond.

"You're leaving?"

"It is best: the Führer's sacked me. Says I'm 'too weak'."[235]

"But, but the Führer just wants some honest work from these Jews. Why, I should know: I've heard him say so myself."

"Rest assured, *Hob-sox*: Sauckel, my successor, will show them no mercy. Work—ha! That hapless race has never known it yet. Oh ha—ha ha! Only, *they will once Sauckel's done.* You know," he haws, thrusting a hand on my shoulder, the which I instinctively repel; being it cannot be said to be exactly clean. "A funny thing, this typhus: for, it makes a terrible National Socialist. No, it doesn't give a

---

[234] Let the record reflect that only in court did I gain any inkling's to what this 'it' was supposed to have meant. Naturally, I totally disbelieved the atrocity-mongering in the Yid-controlled press. [—W.H.]

[235] The sniveling Governor—who, incidentally, is so unstable's to have attempted suicide *twice*—has converted to Romish Christianity while awaiting his verdict. An obvious case of progressive mental imbalance. For years he'd begged the Führer allow him resign. The upshot was, Frank was forced to fulfill his obligations—just like everyone else. The lout was either drunk—and, therefore, mistaken; or, less likely, the Führer indeed'd fired him, but then quite simply'd changed his mind. In any event, the words of such a 'man', especially whilst wetting himself in the latrine, can scarcely be given any credence.[—W.H.]

hoot if one's Gentile or Jew, prisoner or commandant. Of course, a dead prisoner requires no food. Meantime, a live one must be kept free of disease. Which, in turn, requires a modicum of caloric intake; nutrition; sleep. Start messing with formulae like that, and nature will make you pay—oh, she'll make us all pay!"

***

Unnerved and disconsolate, I return to table like a schoolboy: cowed, and unable to speak. I scarcely even notice Bormann waltzing past, plopping himself next to our be-veiled Turk. Digging into my salad, I mete out a hefty portion of beans, the which to fill my famished face.

"A-*hem*," the Führer announces, emitting a boyish glee. "Ladies and gentlemen: I want you to meet the most beautiful spy in the whole world."

Oh good god...

Mumblings erupt. Drowning them out with baritone and brandy, Bormann he rasps: "Spy for *us*, right, mein *Führer*?"

"Ja!" the F. declares, hair a mess, what fist banging the table. Deftly do Eva's hands brush the unruly mop. Undeterred he continues: "The Mademoiselle here's done remarkable things for our Reich."

"Really," she blushes. "You are being too kind: *I do what I do for my people.*" And, resting her hand dangerously close to his thigh she resumes: "Together we must fight: fight if Europe's to be free."

The Führer he froths: "Free from the Asiatic steppe!"

Unbidden a voice it chimes: "Listen here little lady."

Why, it's Schellenberg, chirping apoplectic: half-smile, half leer. "You Cockroaches really are so stupid as not to suspect you work for us? I find that fascinating. Really, I daresay: I'd never suspect it."

The Chief he shoots Schellenberg a look.

And, being one who knows when to make an exit, the General he dives into his plate, committing an atrocity upon etiquette: no one pays him any mind. It's out of our lips, and into his ears; and, out of his hands, and into his mouth. Oh, I'm sure it's just for show; then again, one never knows with the likes of that.

The evening it plods rather dreadful. Then, that woman, that godforsaken woman, stripped of her veil, leads us in song while awaiting dessert. Why yours truly's even coaxed into performing some Bavarian-risque upon the piano. The rest of the evening however's like breathing sulfur.

It doesn't help I've to sit next to Fatty. Göring and I keep trading barbs, as if it's expected. By what, or from whom, that I've no clue; perhaps it's just our own expectations.

You know, it's funny. For the piano you see's helped me put this damned woman's impossible presence here out of my mind. Until, with sobering angst, I recall the words of Frank: then chalk them up to the ramblings of an inveterate drunk. No, my mind is not on the Jewish Question tonight. Rather I'm praying for strength, strength so's not to sick the Gestapo on that impossible woman. I mean, everyone just sits there, sits there sampling her ample breasts what with their ogling eyes; even while shamelessly she flirts with the rest of the men.

The women exchange horrified looks; the 'Mademoiselle' ignores them.

Every now and then Himmler acknowledges me with this mischievous grin, ill-becoming his fat little face: the four-eyes; the double chin; *the swine.* He glares at me's if he knows all about my dealings with this Jezebel. Then again, Himmler wouldn't be Himmler if he didn't save such things for a rainy day: that's how people like that work. Yes, information for him's like an army its reserves.

Towards the end of our little meal Schulze, the new Führer Adjutant, comes strutting in to interrupt. He whispers in the Boss's ear.

The latter he leaps as if ejected; then, in a flash, he's gone. Frantic I begin searching all about, when I notice him heading for the study, closeted with Bormann and... *that impossible woman.*

The door it slams close behind.

***

Forty minutes later they emerge, the F. convivial as ever. Of course, dinner's long grown cold. Frau Exner[236] orders our plates removed for dessert. I know the act—I've seen it a hundred times: the Boss won't be receiving any guests tonight.

I set to, devouring Marlene's[237] wondrous dip, when the Führer resumes his explanation of market fluctuations almost mid-sentence, as though he hadn't missed a beat.[238]

Upon Schulze's return, a door it slams, and I note the Mademoiselle's gone. Her little *Kaffeeklatsch*[239] with Bormann and the Chief had been met by everyone, the women in particular by a conspiracy of silence. Truth is, I'm tongue-tied. I mean, that damned filly's presence here's reason enough to make one ill. And yet, the Führer, upon whom her treachery most devolves, chatters on and on as though anyone were listening...

---

[236] [An obvious mistake, no doubt engendered by over a year's captivity: Frau Exner, Hitler's 'vegetarian chef,' did not enter the scene until 1943.—N.B.]

[237] ['Marlene': The putative Frau von Exner, who, at the time, was busy serving Romanian dictator Ion Antonescu.—N.B.]

[238] "It has nothing to do with supply and demand; everything the machination of the Jew."[—W.H.] [Hossbach, quoting Hitler: Copied, with permission, from a passage in one of the General's letters.—N.B.]

[239] [*Kaffeeklatsch*: A spot of coffee, accompanied by an informal chat. Here, the term is strictly symbolic.—N.B.]

Why, it's almost worth it just to see Fatty claw his Reichsmarschall's baton: the plump, sweaty fingers, wrath increasing by the moment owing what to his having been left out; now's *my* time to gloat. Indeed, seeing the Fat One so worked up just about makes up for all the injustice in the world. I bask in this platitudinous whale's unseemly humiliation. He pretends to be listening to the Chief, what this mock intensity about his opium-stained eyes. And it almost worked, too; save the incessant fondling of his rings giving him away.

Thus into our gay little soiree does Frau Schirach reach for the line then cross it, like the Panzers did the Maginot. Feigning converse with Himmler, she sicks those devious she-eyes on the Chief: "Good *heavens*," she pleads. "The war's so *dreadful*—and I don't mean the bombing. Do you know, *mein Führer*," she adds, arresting him with those ever artful eyes. "Those Russian dogs are simply killing their POWs? I know for a fact: for I read it in a magazine when we were in Switzerland."

Snickers they proliferate.

"But that's not the worst of it."

The mare; why, she's been setting him up all this time...

"The same article went on to reveal how, in Amsterdam, we simply frogmarched a few-hundred Jews onto some trains. Oh, it must have been awful: children crying, mothers screaming. Ech, *mein Führer*—do *you* know such things go on? And, if so—*what do you intend to do about it?*"

The F. turns white as a sheet. Upon recovering his hue, he rises and takes leave, without so much's saying good-night.

Convulsive and indignant, I snap an accusatory finger at the offending Frau. It's implicit in everyone's silence that she should leave.

The sow she returns to quarters, where her husband's recuperating from a long drive in.

Morning hits. And, why Moscow be damned, she insists on causing a scene, demanding that she should see me. Thrusting my map askance, I don my adjutant's cap one more time; and, summoning Schulze, instruct him in no uncertain terms to keep the offending Frau at bay.

Still she's the audacity to show up for lunch; no one dare address her. Taking a hint, she flees, husband obediently in tow, causing the Führer to crack: "Tell me, Schirach: are you the Reich's man in Vienna—*or Vienna's man in the Reich?*"

Speechless he exits; or, rather, is dragged by that Valkyrie of a wife. And, amidst the bellicose jeers, I can hear Bormann say, "*Smashed!*"; indicating Schirach's career.[240]

Guest Quarters

Every now and then some ridiculous rumor makes its rounds regarding the Jews; ach, they're such a nuisance. I mean, here we are, in the midst of a first-class war. And yet thousands are still running around, what with the most dangerous notion that they've got nothing to lose; oh, it makes one's blood just boil!

Somehow, as the Jew Freud would say, my little run-in with Frank it seems has penetrated my subconscious. Yes for I had this dream, this nightmare why just last night: *there I was, right, walking down the Wilhelmstrasse, when who do I keep running into but these kaftan-wearers. Each time I'd see one, I'd gasp.*

Of course, I give no credence to the more insidious rumors; oh—why won't they just leave us alone?

---

240 [Schirach, Baldur Benedikt *von*: Former head of the *Hitler Youth*, this half American remained in Vienna, as *Gauleiter*, until the end of the war. He is currently on trial, along with Hossbach, Frank, and all the rest. As for his wife, Hossbach is once again conflating things: For, *that* incident took place on Good Friday, 1943.—N.B.]

Ach, this Jewish business keeps distracting me from the crisis out East. Sullen I excuse myself from the 'Bridge Club'[241] in the anteroom, then return to quarters.

Polishing off a bottle of whiskey, in lieu of any dinner, I set to. Really, mine isn't so much a bedroom rather than a map-wall. Oh, but ach, I have all the amenities one could need: telephone, teleprinter, and booze; alas, I work best alone.

Next thing I know, it's half-past midnight. So many red fucking x's; and so few black. And another thing. The bar, much's our reserves, is far from infinite; I'm afraid I've exhausted the one as well as the other. Fearing the Führer'll see it in my eyes on waking, I examine myself in the looking-glass—and don't like what I find: *fear.* For, with that, a commander is gone. Thus do I come to a decision: *this business can be put off no more.*

Of course, I can't very well go to the Boss without any proof. I mean, he's so many problems; he sure as hell doesn't need one more from the likes of me. Therefore do I make one last effort at sleep; yet still, the voice of conscience demands its due. Whereupon I decide to see Ribbentrop, who's staying just down the hall. He should still be up.

Begrudging he bids me have seat. He's in his bedclothes, he is, enjoying a good book. The old sot he gets me calm down, then fixes a drink; the which I politely decline. After the inevitable exchange of gentilities he sets his tome, a history of Friedrich the Great, aside, then begs me I should get to the point.

With a deep breath I relate the mendacious rumor.

"*General*," he admonishes, upon a spot of brandy.

I'm flattered. Yes, for all the whisperers you see insist the Führer intends promoting me on the morrow; that

---

[241] ['Bridge Club': Hossbach's characterization of his fellow staff officers during the aforementioned crisis.—N.B.]

that's the real reason he's invited me. Well that just cinches it: with just one word, Ribbentrop's won me over.

"Upon my word," he says and, with this curious witticism, reminds me he too spent time in England. "All the Führer really wants from these yids is a little hard work. Lamentably some incidents have occurred—you've been to the East, you know what it's like. But death camps, murder squads? Oh, don't you see—it's just the hacked-off hands!"[242]

Thank God. Ach, for Ribbentrop you see's convinced me the Jewish Problem's none of my concern. Indeed, it's just as I suspected: Frank was too soft; why, he blew it out of proportion. And, once more, *the Führer is right.* It may be the Jews will even *thank* us once all's said and done. Yes for, alas, they're finally learning the value of some good hard work; the which can only help them in the end. Truly, as someone once said, it really is the 'best of all possible worlds'.

Now, talking to Ribbentrop can be like watching paint peel. I make an excuse so's to extricate myself, then head downstairs for a snack.

The longer I've dwelt on my little run-in with Frank it seems to have sapped me of all desire for nourishment. Still, my encounter with Ribbentrop's served an aphrodisiac to my appetite. I tip-toe into the self-same kitchen I've snuck into countless times what in the middle of the night; yet never an once during the day: for Frau Exner you see's Führer of *her* kitchen.

At the icebox however I'm startled by this abomination in a nighty: what the stiletto heels; and that daftly moistrous cunt...

"*Windy* my dear: I thought I might run into you. For I just knew you wouldn't be able to catch a wink after some time to *really think* about that irksome little chat; ah, *mon*

[242] ['hacked off hands': Specious rumors regarding German atrocities during the Great War.—N.B.]

frer, Franky told me all about it. Simply capital! Really, I'm so glad I thought of it." She inhales through her cigarette-holder; *a prop, just like the rest of her.* "He obviously needed to get something off his chest. I chanced run into him just last night over a fag during supper.[243] Ah, don't look at me that way: you should be *proud*. Oui, for I told him how sensitive an ear you really are. How you'd never betray a confidence. 'Wait in the latrine,' I said. You know it's funny. For I haven't the slightest why he was so put-out: one can only imagine..."

"Why you vicious little slut you I'll—"

Tilting her neck, she feeds me this dry repulsive glance, wetting those obscene lips; my skin it swells what with a flush. And, tossing those luxurious locks, she pouts, "Really, *Herr General.*" Seduction on her mind, and cock on her breath, Monique massages my member...

Why I'm flabbergasted; offended; and what turned on all the same. Pulling out arm-hairs one-by-one, I calm down long enough to forestall the inevitable, then feed her one last warning: "You play a dangerous game! Now go, get out. Leave me my son—and stay well away from the Chief. Oh, I can only imagine what poisonous bile you've been dribbling in his ears. No, let there be no mistake—*I* shall enlighten him as to you and your ilk."

"*My* ilk?" she drawls, cigarette in hand, freeing John Thomas. "And does such 'ilk' include your son?"

"My, my... *huh*? No, of course not, I, he... I mean, after all, *he's an American*: they're still neutral. And besides —*we both know he's only here because of me.*"

"Then let me be the first to inform you," she heaves, paralyzing me what with her scent; *and God I want to fuck her.* But she says: "Haven't you just come from Ribbentrop? *Pfft*—but why would *he* know."

[243] [I doubt he was in England long enough to understand, but Mother's use of the word 'supper,' as opposed to 'dinner,' would have been a dig at either the company, the food, or, both.—N.B.]

"Know, know what?"

"Ah, *mon frer*: Germany's declared war—war on the *USA*."[244]

"What?" I flail, in English, communicating via our usual tongue.

"*Oui*," she stiffens. "Declared war." Face turned, why it's clear she's concealing something.

So, I grab her about by the throat.

"*Off*," she squeals, digging her claws into my side.

Why I'm *this* close to killing her; but I'm no hero. No, now I can see the Führer's dilemma: Monique may be a spy but, dammit, *we need her.* For, she can get word from the Foreign Ministry—before the Foreign Minister!

"*An hour ago*," she grunts, when I let go, folding her dress into place. A decoy for, with the other hand, she's back massaging my member; why I'd swear the slut has six pairs of hands...

"He is *my* responsibility," I flush, after an interminable, throwing her to the side, then pinning her wrists to the floor. "*I* shall take care of it. As for you, *Madame de la' Resistance*, I simply cannot have you parading around *FHQ* up in the middle of the night; or, sneaking off into top secret meetings with *him*." Then, just to hit home the thought, I put my fist through the wall.

Monique doesn't flinch. "That's very funny," she smiles—dangerous for a woman; especially the likes of *her.* "I said, that's very funny. Funny I should be conspiring in Adi's own kitchen... with his most *junior* General."

"Why, you worn-out—I shall give you one last chance: leave—schnell!"

But she flails, "What about my son?" Tears they begin to flow.

---

244 [I found it somewhat ironic when this exchange was presented during the trial: For 'USA' happened to be one of Shitler's many monikers.—N.B.]

Oh, but ach, I know she's simply pressing her toe into this blade she keeps in her shoe. Yes for that Cockroach you see has such contraptions built into all her finest footware; the *raison d'tre* being, in ordinary attire, one can always conceal something. Yet, dressing as she does—that is, like some two-bit whore—why there's simply no place to conceal it; huh, this tearing-up bit must be a new one.[245]

"He is *my* son," I say, calm's a man can muster; you know, like before you take care of a fellow. "And, thus, my responsibility. Oh, don't worry: I'll send him somewhere safe—say, Switzerland. Now, leave—leave, or I shall be forced to call the Gestapo."

At which she gets mad. "It may come to that! In the meantime, we'll just see what Adi has to say." She makes for the hall, presumably heading for his door.

Is she mad? Why, it must all be bluff. Still, I cannot afford—*the German people cannot afford*—cannot afford if it is not. For, without me, the Führer would fall prey to the most odious of beings. Fiends who for years only *I* have been able to keep at bay: toadies like Bormann; swine like Himmler; infidels such as the Mademoiselle...

Therefore do I come up from behind—and beg: "*Don't scream*," I say, cupping her mouth, what damned-near placing my life in her hands. "*Bormann's right there, passed-out in the hall.*" Gently I release her.

Straddling the Good Doctor's[246] desk, she leans against the bed, rubbing those obscene hands up and down the shaft of the lamp. *Sonofawhore*; why, it must be working, working what just like some magic incantation. Ach, for, I can hear myself say, "You've twenty-four hours:

[245] [Such horse twaddle is sheer speculation of the very worst kind: Not one iota of proof has ever been presented for any of it.—N.B.]

[246] [*i.e.*, Goebbels. Apparently, Hossbach had diverted her into the absent doctor's sporadic quarters.—N.B.]

twenty-four hours to get out![247] And remember—*this is for our Johnnie.*"

"That's Jackie, you rapist; and, though he's your seed, he'll never be your son."

Head down I blurt, with a force from I don't-know-where: "If you want that the boy should live, you will do best to keep well away from the Führer. It's not *my* fault we are at war. Still, one's vigilance can be pushed only so far. I mean, should a man relax his principles beyond a certain point, he ceases to be Man."

Deadpan she stares: "Is that what you told yourself when you raped me?"

My head it drops lower still. "Yes," I say. "I had it coming. If it helps, I was under orders at the time. Why if it wasn't for me, you would have had your little throat slit. Yes you see I, I protected, protected..."

"Blithering fool! You think it was *you* let *me* live?" With a chuckle she runs a hideous hand through those delectable locks. "I could have killed you any time had I so desired. *Pfft*, but I took pity—oui, you big lug—*pity.*"

I laugh.

She raves. "Test me sometime."

"It may come to that!"

"It may come to that!"

A silent exchange briefly ensues. Then, exhausted she exhales, "Alright, *you win.* Now I expect you to do your fatherly duty for once in your life. Of course, there's still a little matter of that reptile Himmler. Mark my words Hossbach: *he* will want to know all about your secret meeting. *You naughty boy.*"

"Secret what, secret who? Why, just what witcheries are you performing?"

She exhales: "You know."

Ach, I wonder if she's ever used that cigarette-holder as a weapon...

---

[247] ['get out': *i.e.*, of the Reich.—N.B.]

"That meeting with your boy: the one you so serendipitously chanced via a certain *Admiral*..."

I gawk, eyes askance. "You, you'd throw Canaris under the bus, just to take someone with—now who's the swine?"

She leans, swaying those amorous hips and says, "And *you*'d do the same to your son: really, how *interesting*..."

"Humph!" I say, then give her a shove. "Just what poison are you dribbling in his ear? Why, you were alone—alone with *him*,"[248] I cry, mad for all I'm worth; I mean, I just can't keep it all in.

But she says: "When it comes to fighting Russians, Hossbach, I..."

The curve of her breath sends me spinning; inward I collapse. Still I think she's trying to say something: "[...] which, is why... I am your *friend*"; intimating the one thing we both know that she is not. Pouting, what with those obscene eyes, she says, "Well mon frer—see you at breakfast! Ah, and, one more thing: *Jackie's not the only one, who's like a son to me...*"

With that she ascends the balustrade, cast betwixt pillars of ivory set in all their Grecian splendor.

'Oh good God,' I say to myself. 'Truly that's one slut that doesn't belong in the kitchen...'

December 11:
Just After Lunch

I am puzzled to what she might mean. At first, I thought she might've meant me; only, the Mademoiselle's the same age's I. Therefore I try broaching the subject of Monique—and, by extension, Jack—with the Chief.

---

[248] [Hossbach's still harping on that meeting during 'supper,' to which he was not invited. In which case, 'him' probably means Hitler.—N.B.]

Scarcely do I make it past her name, than he forbids me say anything against her.

Well, I suppose, one mustn't fight it. I mean, the last thing he needs right now's another headache: especially from one of his Generals. Yes, my silence is but one more sacrifice I must make for the good of my people.

Later That Evening

Beaming with pride, the Führer promotes me to General. Now, now I have power: *power to save Army Group Center.* Yes, to rally those nincompoops to make a real stand; and, to lop off the heads of those who do not.

Thus, for the good of the Reich—nay, the entire civilized world—this Monique business's quietly been put to rest. Nonetheless I suspect Himmler must know something; thank God he hasn't told the Chief. Only, *what does he know about Jack?* Well, whatever it is, he's keeping it close to his vest; you know, 'saving it for a rainy day'.

Of course, by then, the boy will long be gone: *I* shall personally arrange it; after all—I *am* his father...

Chapter 22: Suicide

Hossbach's apartment in the New Reich's Chancellery: August 19, 1943[249]

"Goebbels has ordered you to the Propaganda Ministry," grates this voice over the receiver. Why, it's Meissner, the 'Keys to the Gate of the Palace'.

"Um, can I come up and—"

"*Nein*: I have the Führer on the other line right now, and he is very busy—"

"Jajaja," I say. 'Leading us to the Final Victory." Pah, the *Wolfsschanze*.[250] "Which is exactly why I must see him." I mean, ach, I'm a fucking General: I shouldn't have to explain myself; besides, it wouldn't be proper even to hint at the secret weapons over the line.[251] "Please tell him the question of *artillery* is more and more on certain people's minds: that one must *concentrate*, so as to understand the possibilities inherent."

"My ears must be batty," he says. "I'm about to repeat myself: get yourself to the Propaganda Ministry!"

And, with that, I'm off.

***

It's so strange. From time to time you see Goebbels and I've bumped into each other in the halls of the New Chancellery. Only, this summons here reminds me where I truly stand; *pah, fucking civilian.* Ach, for the Führer's all but abandoned Berlin so's to prosecute the war; and now I've no one to absolve me from such bureaucratic fancy.

[249] [I have made repeated inquests regarding a supposed 'lost chapter,' covering the period December '41 to August '43, and have come to the following conclusion: There is no such thing. The time in question corresponds with the most ruthless fighting: Notably the twin debacles of *Stalingrad* and *Kursk*, events the author presumably wishes to forget.—N.B.]

[250] [*Wolfsschanze*: The 'Wolf's Lair,' *FHQ* for East Prussia.—N.B.]

[251] [Yet, as the very next sentence clearly shows, Hossbach proceeded to do just that.—N.B.]

Thus, chip on my shoulder I enter the *Propaganda Ministry*. Enveloped by legions of luminescence, what like some fucking actor's studio, I'm chaperoned into his office. Dispensing with my shadow, I fall into this chair, without so much's being asked to sit.

"So," he begins, this midget at a giant's desk, what the stink of nail polish filling the air: "*Where's the Führer?*"

"The Wolf's Lair," I smile. "Why, do you need to see him?"

"*Nein*," he fobs me off with but a flick of the wrist. "You will just have to do it for me. Well, but what are you waiting for? March on off to Baur straight off. Oh and, here, give him this from me."

Fumbling with his breast-pocket he retrieves this note, the which he hands to me. Something is off. Why, I can feel it, feel it in the lack of oiliness in his voice. With a deep breath he hoists a paltry paw to his ear and, scratching, says: "There's been an accident. It's Jeschonnek. Suicide, they say: *suicide.*"

Jeschonnek? Why I've known that grouse since our days at Lichterfeldte:[252] a storied tactician; indeed, he's taught me well. Still, it's no surprise. I mean, I saw him just a couple weeks back; man looked like hell. Oh—this is all Göring's fault! Yes for the Fat One you see'd made him the whipping boy for all the Luftwaffe's failures; *why, it's Udet*[253] *all over.* Well, I wonder what surprises this one's left? Yes, for that would firmly be in keeping with the Luftwaffe's tradition. Ach, for Udet had this hobby, and so'd left an uproarious drawing: Göring, the Slavedriver—*in tights.*

---

252 [*Lichterfeldte*: A Berlin base, used for officer training during the Great War.—N.B.]

253 Udet was the last swine who chose to bump himself off, rather than continue under the Reichsmarschall.[—W.H.] [Jeschonnek was the Luftwaffe Chief of Staff. Udet, a former ace, was head of equipment.—N.B.]

How appropriate. For Udet had become a caricature himself. Really, blaming the Fat One for one's own cowardly condition? Still, that ought to be Göring now up on the slab; not once, now, but *twice*.

"Now see here," the Doctor commands, sensing the thought.

My, such firmness of voice; what histrionic eyes; and that fulsome, unitary brow, the which seemingly exists so's to accentuate such sinister countenance. Why, I feel like a deer caught up in the lights.

Taking my chin in his oily, manicured digits, he squeezes ever so slight. Then, he looks me in the eye and says, "You are to go the Führer *post-haste*." The devil, why he chain-smokes so fast, I'm afraid he'll inhale a finger. "Someone has to explain what's happened, before Göring arrives and puts his spin on things."

Like a ton of debris ejected off a mountain, an avalanche of relief washes over me; ach, for, for once, the Good Doctor and I are on the same page. "So," I say. "You want me due to my difference with Göring?"

With patience and silence, he draws it out from me.

Cringing, I eke the very words out, knowing full well that, sooner or later, the Führer's going to ask, 'Well, who do you see as his successor?' "Alright," I say, relaxing, extending my feet ever so close to the germaphobe's desk. "I knew Jeschonnek; and why I've no doubt it'll be a tough nut for any would-be successor."

He stares, evincing a fiendish grin. "Galland may be just a pilot but, to the people, he is a hero. Oh," he rises, limping off his child-like chair, beginning to pace. "Just think, the propaganda value that shall en—"

"*Nein,*" I say, stunned at my own vehemence. Thrusting out my seat, I too begin to pace.

The swine; why, he's all but bumped into me. I mean, he must've offered me a cigarette, for, you see, one's dangling out my mouth; *God he can be charming.*

Still, recalling his station, I tremble; then speak truth: "He'll never go for *that.* But, say," I parley, squinting so's to stave off a migraine owing what to this vain-monkey's paucity of light. "How about Milch? Now there's an honest type: the kind who gets things done."

Oh, but ach, the truth can go to the devil: for Goebbels you see's already made up his mind. Ominous he chides: "Would you rather've Kammler?"

"Oh good God![254]"

"Ha," he smirks, rubbing his dainty little digits. "That's very funny: because that's Himmler's suggestion. Yes," he smiles, rolling those reptilian eyes. "We've just gotten of the phone, and *he* says—"

"I beg you," I blurt. "Really—I've no influence with the Chief!"

He stares, quizzical, seeking elaboration.

I give him the none, being he damned well knows this whole Stalingrad thing's torn me down a notch in his eyes.[255]

The Good Doctor he slithers, donning a seamless grin. "Ah, but you do—you most certainly do!"

Why, the transformation's simply amazing.

"You are the Reichsmarschall's enemy: the Führer will welcome your suggestion. What's more, Herr General, you are—or, rather, were—Jeschonnek's friend. This lends you a certain credence in his eyes."

And a dam, a dam nearly ten years making bursts. "*The swine,*" I say, meaning Göring. "But, but what does he have that I do not?" It wasn't a question so much's an

---

[254] I'd known nothing of this Kammler, beyond his most dire reputation.[—W.H.] [This was scribbled, unfortunately in crayon, atop the defendant's sheaf.—N.B.]

[255] [Hossbach had nominated von Paulus for field marshal, once 6th Army's end had appeared to be nigh. German field marshals had a history of fighting to the last. Paulus's surrender, along with some ninety thousand men, left Hossbach in Hitler's doghouse for quite some time.—N.B.]

accusation. I'm on shaky ground here; and know it. For, though we call him the 'Fat One' behind his back, the turn of phrase could be the death of me.

The Good Doctor replies, what with the most remarkable elan, as if nothing indeed had ever been said: "Speed, my good man, speed!" He nods, as if scoring a point.

I've no choice but to agree; though I haven't the slightest what he might mean. Nevertheless, aside from any trouble the midget might make should I refuse, God forbid Kammler should ever get within five feet of FHQ. No for, if that swine should ever get a whiff of any real power, it would be disastrous for all concerned.

Thus my duty—*I accept.*

The Wolf's Lair: Rastenburg,[256] East Prussia

The flight proceeds without incident. Ach, for the Eastern Front[257] you see's our last bastion of air supremacy; though even that's begun to dwindle of late. And yet, and yet I feel safe in Baur's hands. It's good being around an *Old Fighter.* You know, someone who'd gladly take a bullet for *him.*[258]

Yes, invited or no—*I'm coming home...*

---

256 ['Rastenburg': Technically, a woods in the vicinity.—N.B.]

257 [Actually, they flew to East Prussia. In 1943, this did not yet constitute the 'Eastern Front' as such. Yet this is but a minor flaw in Hossbach's reconstruction. As the reader will doubtless recall, the editor has on occasion taken issue with some of the General's statements. My apologia in presenting the work *as is* is, as a work of some historical import, the least adulterated, well, the better.—N.B.]

258 ['him': Obviously, the idiot corporal, *i.e.*, Hitler.—N.B.]

Presently we arrive at the Wolfsschanze. Linge[259] takes us to the study, whereupon we come across the Führer busy pacing. My initial appearance makes but little impression. After an exchange of gentilities, he demands me explain my presumption in so coming.

Therefore, like any good soldier, I march straight up and say, "*Mein Führer*: I have come from Reichsminister Goebbels, in his capacity as—"

"Please, Hossbach: spare me the nonsense."

Why, he looks sullen; he looks angry; he looks ill. Still, it's good to hear my name on his lips once more. Reaching in my pocket, from habit I fiddle for his spectacles. Rather the *new* Führer Adjutant, some swine named Schulze,[260] has already procured them. Sometimes, I forget: *I am a Führer Adjutant no more.* I mean, it hurts to just humbly look by. What's more, I realize how far I've fallen in his eyes; God, what am I *doing* here?

Squinting at the Good Doctor's pernicious writing, the F. he takes but one look and says, "You sound like a sniveling bureaucrat, Hossbach—is that what my Generals are teaching you? Well, now I suppose you're going to tell us the meaning behind our Little Doctor here's unintelligible script?"

Breathe, I tell myself. "Why, it's Jeschonnek. Ach, mein Führer, *ach*—the old boy's dead."

The poor soul's cut to the quick. Still, the Führer wouldn't be the Führer, were he not a cut above us all. For, just as quickly does he recover, gives a noncommittal nod then says, "Go on."

"*Suicide.*"

---

[259] [Linge, Heinz: Like Günsche, Linge is another candidate for the 'Last Führer Adjutant.' Being they have since disappeared, and, moreover, are last said to have been seen in Russia, one may safely award Hossbach the troublesome sobriquet.—N.B.]

[260] [Schulze, Richard: Führer Adjutant from '41 to '44. Currently in American captivity.—N.B.]

The F. he loses all color, then plops himself in a chair. The granite etching on his face, what the stoic visage it masks a pain which only the Immortals can bear. At last his color returns, the blood seeking its way back to his face when, aghast, his eyes they fall from the page. Fixing on me he rasps, "Well, Hossbach, what do you make of it? Quickly now, what do you say? Be honest."

"Well," I dissemble, then feed him Goebbels' suggestion.

At which he turns beat-red. "*Quatsch*—I said what do *you* think, *General*?" This last it rolls off his tongue as though it were a curse.

"Ach, mein *Führer*." Now, I'm not proud of it but, alas, *a chance to settle the score*. And yet, at the same time you see I'm convinced I'm doing it just to save my people; perhaps both are true. "It's like this," I say, guarded—then let loose: "In my opinion the problem begins, and ends, with Göring: *get rid of the Reichsmarschall, and the Luftwaffe shall redound to its greater glory.* Take Milch: now there's a specimen! Why he's worked miracles for Fighter Production."

"*Ja,*" he cheers, smacking a thigh. "Milch, eh? Very well." The Boss he brightens. "All that matters now Hossbach is *time*. Once we get the new fighter-bomber into production, I shall sweep the skies clean—put the fear of God into my enemies!" He stares into the fire; but, alas, the burning embers only serve to remind one of our crippling fuel situation.

"*About that.*"

It takes all the courage I can muster just to even broach the subject. The last thing I want's to hurt him; I mean, he's suffered so much already. And it's terrible. Really, I don't want to do it; nonetheless, somebody must.

Loosening my collar I say, "*That* is not entirely true: the ME-262 must be completely redesigned, else it will not fly. Not now, nor ever: *as a bomber.* As a fighter however it really is first-rate. Why—"

"Quatsch! I have seen it: *seen it in my dreams.* The ME-262 is the high-speed bomber I have prophesied. Yes," he repeats, "*I've seen it,*" staring far-off; as though this were an argument. "Mark my words Hossbach: the jet-bomber is the weapon that will turn the tide of the war!"

He's sweating, hair a mess: *just like the good old days.* It's good to see him back in his element. Ach, for the Führer you see's come to life for the first time since Stalingrad.[261]

"Otherwise," he says. "The Jew will stick his big nose out of the ghetto and exterminate us."

His ranting done, the F. he seems suddenly spent. Presently he recovers his composure. "Of course you're right: Göring's a fool, and corrupt to boot. Still, you mustn't *say* such things."

I reckon he's no longer talking about the Two-six-two...

"No," he says. "When it comes to a crisis, Göring is *ice-cold.* No, I don't like it: I don't like it one bit!" He stares, what this mischievous grin on his face, fingers a-tap. "Now I won't hear another word about it." Shifting gears he leads me by the arm, then makes as if to plead. "Ah, don't you see? Truth is I can't afford a reshuffle of the leadership at this time. Besides, Göring is my successor—what would people think?"

Now, years of service around the various FHQs have taught, there's only one way to break him out of such a loop: I repeat myself. "*Mein Führer*—how about Milch?"

His ears they perk up: "Go on."

I recite the Feldmarschall's admirable record; how he too's nerves of steel.

---

[261] [Hitler was actually pretty animated during the planning for the Battle of Kursk, regarding which Hossbach apparently had not been privy.—N.B.]

"I like Milch," the Führer concedes. "And shall consider him. Thank you; thank you for bringing this to my attention. Oh and, by the way, please tell the Good Doctor from me: I have the utmost confidence in this Galland, and should consider it a personal favor if he were to appear in the next film."

He stands, setting his glass aside: a sign our interview's done. Cold or, paternalistic perchance, his eyes they meet mine; but he says nothing. Dejected I return to quarters then begin to pack.

A few minutes later however Schulze arrives, bearing an invitation to dinner. I'm relieved: for, first, a decent meal; then, sleep—ah, sleep, in a proper bed no less. Yes sleep, in this beautiful guesthouse surrounded by countless acres of ancient ambient woods. And, what's more, everyone knows dinner with the Chief usually entails a sidebar once the women have been packed off. Don't let anyone ever tell you Generals don't play politics! Such wives' tales were probably concocted by Colonels who just couldn't cut it.

***

Silent we sit through our meal, as the Führer expatiates on the subtleties of theater. It's a direct dig at Goebbels, the which I'll have to leave out of my report. Still it skirts the F.'s own unwritten rule of no talk of politics at table.

Mineral water in hand, the Boss declares that, to be truly great, an actor must magnetize the latent sex-instinct of the mass: especially the women.

Why, such cynicism it comes as a biting shock; for, *this is not the Führer I've come to know and love*. Still, far be it from me to criticize. It's just, he's starting to sound more and more like Goebbels, less and less the prophetic dreamer who foresees the creative possibilities in all things...

"It's a good thing we succeeded in exterminating the bourgeois mentality," he says, evidently serving us monologue in lieu of dessert. "For this the world should thank us. Just look at the Russian: all he wants is his icon, his vodka and, every now and then—a good whipping!"

Why, someone's gone put these ideas in his head. I mean, even if such things are true—*why say them?* Especially at table; what with women present. No, almost it seems, in my absence, he's forgotten to be a gentleman. Now, I don't like to admit it but, more and more, I find myself tuning him out; oh thank God—*dessert*.

"Which, is why," heedless he continues. "I need Göring. Oh, he must be allowed his petty indulgence every once in a while; just like a woman. But, *Jesschonnek*," he flares, what with eyes of fire. "At the very least the swine should have come to me first—just look at the position he's put the Reichsmarschall! Now, you know me: I don't go sticking my nose in other people's business. Which is why I've decided to allow the Reichsmarschall to choose Jeschonnek's successor."

Nearly I fall out of my chair. Steeling myself to seem drunk, I slur my next words according. Or how else am I to explain this state of shock? I pick at the strudel heavy of heart, knowing that, henceforth, any criticism of the Reichsmarschall is strictly forbidden.

Pah, I'll bet that fat bastard cried his crocodile tears then threatened to resign; all from the safety of his phone. Yes he's probably off on one of his shopping sprees right now. The swine, he must've threatened to go the way of Jeschonnek; no doubt that's how he lured Emmy from me.[262] And, why just like her, the Führer he fell for it.

Once again, I've been outmaneuvered.

---

[262] [*Sonnemann, Emmy*: Göring's second wife; Hossbach's putative 'former flame.' The true story of their rivalry is somewhat less than Hossbach would have it. *His* version has been omitted, for propriety's sake.—N.B.]

***

Politics: I wasn't cut out for the stuff; unlike that cutthroat prick.[263] Yes for my *sole* violation of the Officer's Code's[264] served to place an inordinate share of blame upon my candidate.[265] You see I thought Milch would be sympathetic to these secret weapons I keep hearing about: some place called *Peenemünde*. So far, the Führer's told me of two: one, a pilotless missile, the other a liquid-fueled rocket; *both* are supposedly near production. Yes, the Führer has it—they shall *single-handedly* win the war. Why he looks with glee to the day we can unleash them on our cowardly enemies. Bomb cities full of women and children now, do you? Well—we'll raze London to the ground! Besides, the *Wunderwaffen*[266] seem to be the only means of extricating ourselves from our impossible predicament—*not* the Two-six-two; of course, one daren't tell the Führer the latter.

So it is that Peenemünde's been on my mind all night, saturating my dreams with a percolating thirst for vengeance: *I am up in the air: a plane, of sorts. Only, it's unlike any aircraft I have ever seen—no propeller! I laugh at this 'jet'. Until I realize:* I'm *the one piloting it. And, suddenly released from all cares, I circle with ease about the endless expanse guarding the picturesque approach to the Isle of Usedom, wherein lay the secret base of Peenemünde. The topography it comes into view, set amidst all the spacious splendor, borne upon the height of the blue*

---

263 ['cutthroat prick': *i.e.*, Göring.—N.B.]

264 ['Officer's Code': The Prussian officer, as a rule, eschewed politics much like the plague. Hossbach's electioneering for Milch flew in the face of this time honored tradition.—N.B.]

265 And yet the Jew-lawyers would have had us been more politically involved![—W.H.] [Here he refers to the prosecution's claim that the generals should have disobeyed Hitler on strictly ethical grounds.—N.B.]

266 [*Wunderwaffen*, 'wonder weapons': Alternately and indiscriminately referred to as the 'secret weapons.'—N.B.]

vault of space unfolding before me. Riveted to my seat, I take her in for a—

"Sir? Wake up. Sir—"

"*Huh?*" I snap, confronting this darksome figure approaching.

Why, it's Schulze: *the swine who replaced me.* "Schulze," I say, eyes pained on the first light of waking. "What are you doing—get out of my room!"

"My apologies: but there is no time. To the war conference—schnell!"

"What, what is the meaning of this?" I bark, stumbling into my trousers. Oh, but ach, I've forgotten to take off my boots; and so've stumbled back into bed. "Oh, alright alright—give me some room!" *I don't very much like being wakened.* "Five minutes I say. Now, please, do tell: what the hell's going on?"

He freezes. "Sir, it's Jeschonneck: he's taken his own life."

"I know," I say, what still fumbling with these accursed boots. "The point is, but *why*?"

"That, if I may be so bold to say, *that* is why the Führer wishes brief us."

'The bold swine,' I say to myself, thereby awarding him the moniker. Still I can't help but reckon: 'I think I like the sonofabitch.'

He plows on. "One thing is clear: this Jeschonneck sure did the right thing. Thanks to him, an entire base was hit."

"Where?" I smart, shimmying into my trousers.

"Funny name," he smirks, trying to pronounce it: "Pennay-*moon*-duh.[267]"

Oh—thunder and lightning! *The Führer is not going to be pleased...*

---

[267] [There is nothing funny, or 'moon like' about it: *Peenemünde,* the mouth (Mund) of the river Peene. The base is situated in the Baltic, on the Isle of Rügen.—N.B.]

Chapter 23: Hydra

The Wolf's Lair: August 20, 1943

It turns out the Führer knew about the bombing all along.

What, does he think me suddenly skittish? Or perhaps he doesn't trust me's a man? Why he should expect such hardness from me; *and I him.* And yet, what was that squeamish, dare I say almost cowardly look in his eyes? I mean, it's almost as if he wanted to tell me something but, rather from prudence, decided to hold back.

You'd think *I* was responsible when, after all, this is all Göring's fault. Yes, Jeschonnek was my friend: but that doesn't explain it. I mean it's not like him[268] to hold such a grudge. On the guilty, sure, but by association? Suspecting an intrigue, I convince myself to batten down, and not let anyone near where nerves have already once been frayed.

At the 'morning briefing',[269] the F.'s a complete nonentity. Why it's as if he's not even here. I can't see why: just a few hundred slaves were killed. The production works were barely hit. Oh, sure, a few scientists might've bought it. But so what? The raid, for which Albie seems to have committed his entire bomber force, resulted in nothing but a pin-prick. An ingenious exchange of witticisms ensues; the *RAF* bearing the brunt of it.

The Führer is not amused. He beholds such jabs with a deathly stare, what almost's if standing vigil.

Not talking to me at table now, hmm? I finish my meal then return to quarters. Why I've half a mind to request a transfer back to the front. I mean, if he no longer values my counsel, why should I not meet my end like any other soldier? Really, if he's so put out by my mere presence, he *has* to agree. Fritsch did it: paid with his life,

---

268 ["him": *i.e.*, Hitler.—N.B.]

269 ['morning briefing': Probably early afternoon, as per Shitler's notorious routine.—N.B.]

he did; and I'm not half the man. Yea, I should gladly follow his example. But like I said: *I'm not half the man.*

A bottle of whiskey taunting me gratis's all the excuse I need. Thus, like any good soldier—*I put it to use.*

Afternoon

Duty calls. Only, Baur says he won't fly with me in such straits, what since the whole Todt business.[270] The Boss he lends me this driver, Reynolds I believe's the name, so's to get me to the station.

The lad's particularly punctilious, determined I should reach the appropriate terminal in time to embark for Berlin.

Before I can board however a messenger arrives to intercept me: *Luftwaffe Boy*; probably Göring's adjutant. He's carrying a letter, he is: a truce, no doubt. The swine—it's about time!

Why, it's nothing of the sort—a message from the Chief: says I'm 'all out of sorts'. And that, for my 'own well-being', he's ordered me go for a cure.

Luftwaffe Boy leads me his Mercedes, boasting a toothy grin. “The Führer wishes me take you see Dr. Kersten[271]. Remarkable man—cured the Reichsführer using his bare hands!”

Oh dear Lord my God: I'm being led into the hands of a masseuse...

---

[270] ['the whole Todt business': Doctor Fritz Todt's plane exploded on February 8, 1942, killing everyone on board. The *Master Builder* had had a row with *der Führer* immediately preceding the crash. The official report cited a 'self destruct mechanism' in the cockpit of certain planes. The Gestapo hypothesized a tipsy Herr Todt, a pilot in his own right, might have stumbled on the tripwire, causing the plane to accidentally explode.—N.B.]

[271] [Kersten, Felix: Himmler's masseuse.—N.B.]

Hohenlychen

Escaping the hubbub of the city we head north, eventually arriving at Himmler's palatial estate. I use the term intentionally. Yes, it's only a sanatorium; at least, as seen from the outside. The interior however's all decked-out what like some medieval knight's idea of Camelot: flush with antiques and men-at-arms strutting all about; why I half-expect to be greeted by a moat.

Rather, upon entering the servant's quarters I see Himmler, crawling hand over foot in search of something. Weakly he croaks: "*Ker-sten.*"

The mas-seuse appears, what like some deus ex machina; gently he takes him by the hand. Gathering what seem to be vitamins, the which his boss is desperately trying retrieve, he turns my way, as if to say, "*You see nothing*." A real nervous breakdown, the likes of which, if I am to follow, hasn't happened for nearly a week.

The driver, obviously no slouch, disappeared ere we had entered. Thus, while trying not to seem too conspicuous, I set-to watching the diminutive Finn get to work. Gentle, yet firm, he helps the Reichsführer into a chair. He'd best be quick. For, or so I've been warned, the spasms currently wracking his boss's musculature could go on for hours. Donning a pair of gloves, he beckons Himmler recline then says, "Looks like someone's ready for mas-sage."

"But," Himmler pleads. "I haven't the time."

And, as if unloading on some two-bit whore, he slaps him; I mean he really, truly fucking slaps him. "Pull yourself together!"

In a daze, Himmler he rises what like some mummy, wraps his hands behind the back then slowly begins to pace. *Remarkable*; absolutely remarkable. Save the cigar, the whole thing smacks of the Chief. Why it's obvious: old Heine's copied his hero with all the fidelity of a pedant.

His panic having subsided, Himmler turns meek as a cat—or, kitten—then makes for this ungodly contraption. Lying supine, he melts into some sort of table, the which the mas-seuse proceeds to strap him.

Hands like knives, he slices the Reichsführer's back; then, taking that sweaty stink in his unwholesome hands, sets to.

Oh good God, if this is how he treats Himmler, why —*what's in store for me?*

"Ah," Himmler he preens, relieved and, for a space, seemingly forgetting all of his cares. Thus, having been kneaded and beaten like a loaf of fucking bread, he's battered in oil what like some lazy stinking Turk. Passing into Paradise—or, Seventh Heaven—the Reichsführer he unwinds like any old Jake at his pub, then proceeds to tell Kersten all that has occurred. "An entire base. Imagine," he adds before, alarmed, fixing on me.

"*General* Hossbach," the Finn intones, by way of introduction. "The Führer sent him." Glancing my way he smiles: "*The works.*"

Himmler he feigns offense before, just as quickly, seemingly forgetting my very presence. He sighs, "Oh Kersten, what am I to do? Where, I say where am I to find five-hundred skilled-laborers capable of replacing those we've just lost? Really, the Führer's been so *demanding*. I, I don't know if I can cope..."

The unsprightly devil, what with the pencil-thin mustache, he seems relieved when Kersten hefts his hand, strikes it with his fist then, completing the gesture, hands him the phone: "*Call.*"

Himmler he draws a series of breaths, then has the operator put him through. "Obergruppenführer," he grunts, what through the pain. "You must leave for Peenemünde—*schnell*!"

"I beg your pardon, *Herr* Reichsführer," I can hear come over the line. Why I've never: a calculated insult, the equivalent of a complete stranger slapping one's back.

Only, Himmler he lets it slide; truth is, I think he scarcely noticed.

"What did you say?" I'm shocked to, once more, hear come over the line. "You've a pfennig your mouth?" Why I swear the poor devil the other end's being's loud's he can; you know, jaking it up. "Must be a bad line."

I see why he's dissembling. Ach for, Himmler you see's breaking his own rule even mentioning it.[272] Yes it seems the Witch Doctor's taking effect. With halcyon calm Himmler explains, even as the former dissolves the 'knots' in the small of his back, "Kammler old boy, everything's changed: it's secret no more."

Scarface—is *that* why he sent me? Why I want no part. Still either this Kammler's said something I could not hear, or, the Witch Doctor's just hit a nerve. For of a sudden Himmler he loses his stones: "They've hit the whole thing," he shrieks, arms flailing. Why it's all poor Kersten can do to keep from him rolling off. "What? No, no real casualties; *thank God.* Just a few hundred slaves—and, oh yes, the chief of engine-design appears to be missing. What? No, I haven't told *him*. My stars, if we don't win this war—God have mercy on us all!"

"Pull up your knickers," I can hear come over the line; or, something such.

"Please," Kersten seconds, squeezing the bigshot's not-so big-toe: "*Calm...*"

Kammler continues, again loud enough that I can hear: "I know what to do: of course, the whole thing must be done *so oder so.*"[273]

Himmler he damned near genuflects. Poor Kersten secures his head, so's to prevent a repetition of what I'd

[272] ['it': *Peenemünde.*—N.B.]

[273] [*'zo o-dehr zo'*: 'Exactly as I say.'—N.B.]

encountered upon arrival. "Oh of course, of course," the patient he petitions.

"I shall require an army my own," the *Obergruppenführer* resumes, dictating an Architectural Order of Battle I cannot quite make out: "... hundred twenty-three units housed in… sectors: *so oder so.*"

Himmler he smarts, "You can't *do* that. Truly you mustn't—"

Kersten proceeds to crack his neck, producing upon the Reichsführer's fat little face the most congenial smile.

Upon the which Himmler he says, "I shall get authorization from the Chief. Select a site and get everything ready. It must be out of range or, at the least, at the very limit of enemy bombers."[274] The Witch Doctor he whispers his ear. "Yes," Himmler returns, confident; and, therefore, *dangerous*. "It must have access to rail. Now upon my word, make it—I didn't *say* start; you know how *he* can be. Who knows," he adds, suffering his back be kneaded. "He might even wish design it himself. Tear it down—yes yes, tear it down and... be ready to go on my command."

"*Jawohl*," Kammler concedes, just as loud; and yet, somehow, weaker in irreverence. Oh, how he must hate having to hear the Führer's name upon somebody's lips, being it must always presage the loss of some power.

Himmler hangs up then proceeds to the next call. The Witch Doctor he continues pounding the shit out of him; presumably for his own good. God, it looks so *painful*. "Dornberg—"

"*That's Dornberger.*"

Ach, I thought it was just Kammler; you know, typical blowhard. Only I can hear this Dornberger just as clear. I mean it's obvious: Himmler *wants* me to hear; ach,

---

[274] [This should probably read: 'At the very limit of enemy fighters.' Yet, being a bomber's useless without fighters for cover, it amounts to very much the same.—N.B.]

for gossip you see is power. Yes, for he knows I've a line *straight* to the Chief. Now, whether this Kersten can help me or no, protocol demands I should repay him. You know, one of those 'rainy days'...

"*Dornberger*—listen: get hold of Sawatzki straight-off. Then—"

"Oh, what's he done now?"

"Done?" Himmler balks; perhaps the 'treatment''s taken root too quick. "He hasn't done—I said, hasn't *done* anything. Just fetch him—yes yes, fetch him I say—on the double. And oh yes," he adds, almost as an afterthought. "Have him bring his drafting tools. Huh? Oh, oh yes yes yes: *Heil Hitler.*"

The Reichsführer, recoiling from terror, finished the call with glee. Yes he's been coveting the rocket now for quite some time.

Before I can process it all, the paunchy mas-seuse sets to work—*on me...*

A Few Months Hence[275]

Though all I remember's the pain, perhaps Kersten really did grant him a new lease on life. More likely it was the tragic—or, for Himmler, timely—turn of events. After Hydra,[276] he'd commissioned Kammler to build these rocket facilities inside this hellacious series of tunnels, deep in the bowels of the earth.[277]

---

275 [*i.e.*, late '43.—N.B.]

276 [*Operation Hydra*: A British raid, precipitating *SS* usurpation of the rocket industry.—N.B.]

277 Just outside Nordhausen.[—W.H.] [Actually, von Braun, like most of the engineers, remained at Peenemünde, even after the bombing. Occasionally, some were forced to visit the Mittelwerke, an underground complex near Nordhausen, where assembly and test firings occurred. As for Peenemünde, the raid had grafted the cosmetic effects of destruction, which, as seen from the air, constituted an ingenious device for keeping the Anglo-American air force at bay. Development resumed, even production, for several months before the bombers, inevitably, perhaps, returned.—N.B.]

And it makes sense—that is, from Himmler's point-of-view—that he should be the one to take charge. Ach, for the Army and Air Force you see've proven equally inept at preventing such catastrophes.[278] After all, the SS is the greatest industry in the Reich; unquestioningly loyal. At last, Himmler's his chance: no excuses, nothing left to block him...

Thusly have this Braun and his men come to live in fear. And yet character you see is a trait woven deep in the heart of a man; so much the more once it's been reenforced by the habit of class and all the authority which that used to bring. Now, they say it's the mixture of alcohol and oxygen which gives the rocket propulsion. It would be harder still to imagine two elements more combustible than Himmler and von Braun: the one, a pedant; the other, dreamer. This mind you for a weapon slated to go into production 'any day now' for almost a year. The clock it keeps on ticking; only, just like the last war, *time is not on our side.*

Therefore nothing remains but to crack the whip ever so hard, so's to get these war-winning weapons[279] into production. Otherwise, the remarkable contours of our engineers' skulls won't be worth a damn, once they've been made a head shorter.

---

[278] ['catastrophes': Such as the raid on Peenemünde during the night of August 17-18, 1943.—N.B.]

[279] ['war winning weapons': the *A-4,* a.k.a. 'V2,' and variants of same.—N.B.]

Chapter 24: Arrested Development

Berlin: March, 1944

The subtle flames of Bach rise up, burning all dross from my mind, even as the cognac it keeps this map from seeming all too real. With a thud I'm wakened from my work, i.e., stupor: why, the Mademoiselle; and the tattered remnants of the lock which once graced my door.

She bursts into tears; and, being a fool, I try to comfort her. But it's no use. I've even forgotten my rage at her having simply burst in, as if she's either too proud or just never learned how to knock. Unsure how to react, I fix her a drink; then, being there's much to attend, return to the study;[280] where, like the Plague, she follows.

"Ech," she whines. "Your Ribbentrop's a mouse of a man—he's ruined all my plans!" She hefts the brandy to her evil lips but, on second-thought, decides to smash it on my newly cleaned floor.

"*Calm*," I say, increasingly unnerved. Not her having broken into my home—that I'm used to. No, I'm just fed up seeing such strong men increasingly being put in such straits. It started at Stalingrad; and what now this raid's[281] really rattled us all. Yes for it serves to remind one

---

280 [Her visit appears to have taken place at Hossbach's 'getaway home,' on the outskirts of the city. As the bombing intensified, he spent less and less time in his beloved *Reichskanzlei* (Reich Chancellery), more and more here, his second home.—N.B.]

281 [On February 20, the Anglo-Americans launched 'Big Week,' an attempt to destroy the Reich's aircraft industry. Much of it had been moved, or was in the process of being moved, underground, by *Dr. Ing.* Hans Kammler. By the 25th it was clear: The Allies had failed to lure the *Luftwaffe* into a 'decisive battle.' Still, the Germans had lost some hundred pilots, whose expertise could never be replaced. This led to the idea that Berlin should be bombed *en masse*, in order to lure her fighter reserve. Thence the raid that occurred March 4, to which Hossbach already has alluded. The results, while mixed, proved A-dolt incapable of maintaining air superiority over his very own capital.—N.B.]

just how far the 'Final Victory' really is. I give her my coat so's to cover her. “Here,” I add. “Drink this,” then hand her some water; hoping for no repeat from the brandy before.

She looks up—and, I swear, this time, *those tears are real.* “Why won't he appoint a *real* Foreign Minister? Pfft,” she puffs, what her beret looking like that of the old *Red Cross*. Only now I see: *why, it's a Luftwaffe uni*; ach, the pants skin-tight must be some Frenchified adulteration.

She smiles, black nylons plus what the smell of warm cunt and booze caressing my couch and says, “You and Adi are about to have a little chat: Lammers has arranged it.”

“You, why you little—”

“I've tried,” she sneers. “It seems I don't have the requisite anatomy.”

Almost I say: *that's never stopped you before*; but, having amused myself with the thought, decide to let it be.

She snarls, suffering some water make its way to her face, seeming to have regretted her conduct with the booze before. “Adi needs a man, a friend to tell him to him the truth: the truth he must stop this two-front war!”

Two fronts, that is, because the Amis are in Italy, albeit bottled-up in the south; for now. Still, everyone knows the invasion[282] could come any day. Ach, Rommel has it, if such a force were ever to actually land, our goose will firmly be cooked.

I shoot her a look, recalling her little *Kaffeklatsch* with Bormann and the Chief. “Apparently, *Fraulein*[283]—that's why he has you.”

---

[282] [re, 'the invasion', *i.e.*, of France: Jerry could not be sure from whence the invasion would come. Thanks to code breaking, however, not to mention the influence of Hitler, Hossbach would have gathered either Normandy or the Straits of Dover.—N.B.]

[283] *Fraulein* simply means 'Little Woman'. An unconscious put-down, by way of recompense, for all the times she's called me 'Hun'. [—W.H.] [Hossbach liked to boast of having read Freud: A doubtful claim at best.—N.B.]

"But, De Gaulle—De Gaulle[284] won't come to his senses!"

I bury my head in my desk, so's to avert the Bosom of Ample Delight.

"It's so *hard* to find good men," she adds, swinging those dastardly hips. "Now we've bogged-down in Russia."

"We?"

Fucking Frenchie.

"Oui—*we*," she nods, glancing at her nails; what the sag on her face having taken it's toll through the tale of years. Truth is we're both riding the last crest of middle-age. Which, makes her all the more dangerous, seeing, what she once obtained with her twat, she now must procure with her mind; and why it's sharpened the damned filly up.

"Elite SS are fighting in the East, even as we speak: under the *French* flag; all because of *me*. So, oui: *we*. Himmler has English, even Russian units. We *all* wish to see Communism destroyed."[285]

But I am not to be trifled with. "You mean *did*—why, you, you and that English pigdog—you were in bed together! *Casablanca*—what was that?[286] No, your 'we' shan't rest, till the German people are destroyed. And our *Kultur*, our beautiful culture of a thousand years suddenly is no more. No, enough of your we—your 'we' can just go to the devil!"

She stumbles before the fire, despite the heat trembling all over. "Then, then this is it: *this is the end...*"

---

[284] [*General* de Gaulle, Charles: French officer in North Africa, who refused to obey the collaborationists in Vichy. His unsung recruits gave Jerry untold hell.—N.B.]

[285] [It is noteworthy that she did not mention the 'Blue Division,' being Franco had ordered it back in late '43: Only a few volunteers remained. A true 'European Coalition against Bolshevism,' the crux of Nazi propaganda, had, by this point, largely ceased to exist.—N.B.]

[286] [*Casablanca Conference*: January '43, (in)famous due to the Allied demand for 'Unconditional Surrender.'—N.B.]

I help her to stand. I mean, no matter how I'd like to see her get what's hers, now I have her in my power and I, why, *I just can't do it.* Pah, in her wretched state, a strong word's all it would take: you know, give her my pistol; why, *just leave her alone...*

And yet I cannot help but speak truth: a truth indeed I had not known until now. "Dammit... we *need* you. There, I said it: the Führer he needs men like us; *especially now.* No, not men, mind you—oh, you know what I mean! Only, if you say, 'all's lost, it's kaput'—why, think how *he* must feel. And so you see, we simply *cannot* let him down."

Massaging my scalp, she searches me out, what with those animalistic eyes. Caressing her, unconscious, I continue: "If the Führer were to abandon all hope, then, that's that—show's over! For surely you must see: *after him, the deluge*; Europe will never recover."

"Ah *Wind*," she soothes, caressing me what in turn; my knees they all but buckle. Why, that name, that name the which she only employs when she's up to no good. "Did you ever think," she stares, licking those lascivious lips—a dirty trick. "How *easy* it would be, just to end it all? You know: get him alone and—"

"Brutus!"

"Well!"

I snarl; then put my fist through the wall, seeing it's the first thing besides her face ready to hand. Oh, but why —*why does she have the power to make me feel so?* You know: to take away my equilibrium.

"Alright, you, you malicious slut you—*so what if I have?* And you know what? It's something I should never do. Yes you see I, I took an oath; and, even should all Germany should go asunder then, rest assured—*I shall go with.*"

She hides her evil countenance, saddling past the fire, pretending to look at my books; *as if the slut ever read.*

My head; why, my head it begins to swim. The procedure's a nightmare. Rummaging through my thoughts, I scramble: *do I call the Gestapo?* Scenarios they play out, footprints brushing the floor of my mind when, of a sudden it dawns: *that will not be necessary.* Ach for, this Jezebel—the most vile slut in twenty centuries—hasn't the *guts* to kill him. And then, it hits me, like a concussion it hits; and suddenly I know her deepest darkest thought. "It's him," I say. "The Führer: *that's* who's like your second son."

Once again she manages fob me off. Executing an about-face she turns: "There is no time: *we must talk.* This 'Unconditional Surrender'," she flails, scarf flying all-about; and almost I pray it gets stuck in the fire. "Churchill doesn't know it, but that motherless cripple[287] really means to see it all through. *Pffft*, up till now, Woolfie's pooh-pooed the whole thing. Says England's intent on keeping Stalin from Europe. And that, sooner or later, 'we'll have to come to some sort of understanding'. Ah, but Ribbentrop's a fool. Church-ill? The drunk thought it just a slogan: he's been outmaneuvered by Roosevelt and Stalin. I should know—I've seen the dispatches: the Casablanca Declaration is quite real. And you know what that means..."

"But," I shudder. "The Führer won't hear it!" Downright I scream, seeing the contradiction in our policy between East and West's playing on everybody's mind. Truth is, Casablanca scares the hell out of me. I mean—if this slut's being above-board for once in her life—Ribbentrop must've seen the dispatch, too—well, why hasn't he told the Chief?[288] Or surely I would have known.

---

[287] ['motherless cripple': FDR. Please note such language is more in keeping with my illustrious father, as opposed to me well mannered mum.—N.B.]

Shushing me to a subordinate silence, the Mademoiselle plumbs the depths of her Machiavellian soul; and, finding nothing, says the first thing on her malevolent mind: “It's like this: Hitler must be lured to a secure location then placed under arrest. Because, let's face it: *neither one of us has the guts to shoot him.* That, or, Germany must do something so spectacular, she can come to an understanding with either East or West. *Ptth*, I know, I know: 'the Führer'll never make peace with the Ivans.' Plus Churchill we know's already been corrupted.[289] But you are forgetting *my* people: we Franks still have some say in this war. De Gaulle! *De Gaulle's star is rising.* Oui, we'll just have a little chat—then who knows? He just might free himself from that troglodyte in Whitehall yet.[290] But,” she shrugs, pausing so's to brush those voluminous locks. “To pull it off, I'm going to need a savior in my back-pocket. A savior for all Europe; as once I'd so stupidly thought your Hitler would be. And, that savior is—”

---

288 It's come out only now, during the trial: Ribbentrop's the last true gentleman; to our great ruin. He was hosting the Ambassador in Turkey, when the latter's counterpart from among our enemies chanced leave his briefcase behind. What did Ribbentrop do? Did he take the documents and photograph them, like any good spy? Did he send them by courier, through the proper channels, pleading ignorance as to their loss? No the selfless sonofawhore you see simply summoned his enemy's attache, then handed him his briefcase in a sealed diplomatic pouch; not one word was ever spoken. The sonofabitch sure won the enemy's respect; the which won't help him a hill of beans now. Bump off the Jews—as I've only just learned—to *that* he might have been privy. But, betray a gentleman's agreement—never! Yes, that's Ribbentrop, the sorry sonofabitch; I can't wait to see him hang.[—W.H.] [This note was written with hurried, jagged lines, more than any other: That Ribbentrop must really rankle him.—N.B.]

289 [The Nazis had charged Churchill with having been 'in the pay of the Jews,' regarding certain gambling debts, as well as funding for his literary career.—N.B.]

290 [the 'troglodyte in Whitehall': *i.e.,* Churchill.—N.B.]

Please don't say Göring; oh please *don't say Göring...*

"—our son."

"Our *huh*—are you out of your goddamned mind? Why, what's Jack got to do with it?"

He's riding out the war in Switzerland; at least, that's what the Admiral told me. Why he said Jack barely escaped her demonic grasp; even told me where I should write. Oh, what's he done? I should have known: *Canaris*, the religious man; *Canaris*, who used to live next door to Heydrich; well and now one of them's dead...

And now, as the Führer once said, with regard to a slightly different concern: scales they fall from my eyes. Now, I've never been one to strike the weaker sex; at least, not with a closed-fist. It's just, it's just, I'm carried away.

"*Unhand me*," she squeals, terrified lest I've broken her precious little nose; for, without her already degraded looks, why what asset could she possibly have?

Only now do I realize what I have done; and, worse yet—*so has she.* "Stop!" she screams, battling my guilt-weary grip: "I know where he is."

Mistrustful, I take a step back.

"Tell anyone, alright, and he's dead: let *that* be on your conscience. The scoundrel—he rapes, he crawls—yesterday through the mud, today on his belly before his Führer; then, to top it all off, he strikes the object of his violation. *Pfft*, if you had an ounce of self-respect, you'd run yourself through with the sword." Then she brightens. "But not now: for I have need of you yet. Now, for once in your miserable life—*listen*."

Why I can hear her loud and clear; and yet, in my mind's eye you see the only possible recourse is but to just reach into my pocket, and feel the cold impress of steel; then, pump two holes—one, her head, the other, mine. I know I simply must get the order correct. I mean, otherwise, *she wins*. And we can't have that; *mustn't have that...*

What I really mean, is, stunned—I listen: "Some time back," she enjoins, tempting my smoke detector whilst ashing on my newly cleaned floor. "Our Jack chanced fall under the spell of a seductive little slut, who put him in touch with Dr. von Braun. The devilishly handsome young man is, as you know, one of your top scientists. The minute I learned of Jack's involvement with the disreputable debutante, my people kept me abreast of his movements."

"*Your* people?"

"Never mind. As I was saying: I was pleased at this new development.[291] For, in it, I saw certain advantages."

Mechanically, what almost against myself, I respond to her wordless entreaty, thereby rekindling her flame.[292] *Why I wonder if she's ever used that cigarette-holder to pluck out somebody's eye?* Uneasy I take a step back.

"When it comes to rockets," head-back she exhales. "The sky's no longer the limit. Ah, how I have been waiting for this moment! *Oui*, England will have to suffer; but only for a minute. It's like I've always said: you can't fight a war, or raise a son, with an eye on only the moment. Save this Braun's been very naughty indeed. Here we are, braving the air-alerts and all the sleepless nights that go with them; believe me, darling, at my age it doesn't matter a lick if they're ruses or not. Meantime he's secreted himself on some desolate isle in the midst of the Baltic, to which the war has yet to come. Jack's one saving-grace? He's engaged in revolutionary work—it's all very hush-hush: a *liquid-fueled* rocket. Imagine, a projectile, hurling through space, several times the speed of sound..."

---

291 [re, 'new development': *i.e.*, my *alleged* departure from the aforementioned woman, and subsequent affiliation with Doctor von Braun.—N.B.]

292 [By this point, black market cigarettes had become even harder to come by. 'Rolling one's own' left much to be desired.—N.B.]

"But," I stutter. "But *Dr. von Braun*," what wincing so hard nearly I hæmorrhage. Ach, this woman, this godforsaken woman—you mean, she doesn't *know*? Why I heard it from Himmler only this morning. No wonder the glint that glib sonofabitch's eye.

"But," I repeat. "*Dr. von Braun*," thoughtlessly caressing those lithesome locks. "Is, I mean, he is... *he is under arrest.*"

"He *what?*"

"Arrest, under arrest," I say, as if repetition somehow sets everything to right. "For, defeatism; *defeatism.*"

Actually, sabotage, too; only, I daren't mention it, lest she might take it out on me. I mean I know Himmler and that squirrely ilk've been trying to wrest the rocket from the Army now for years. Oh, but this sort of thing happens all the time; why I'd scarcely even noticed. Ach, I might take issue with Braun's a man. Still I'm not so stupid so's to completely fail to recognize his worth.

"The staff?" she stabs, reviving me what from these internal deliberations.[293] The tension's like a rattlesnake: it could strike any moment.

I reckon she must be diddling one of the men; *whore.* Must be too much an antique to've landed von Braun; I mean, why else inquire about the staff?

"As soon as the paperwork's in order," I return, fixing a brandy, seeing I'm going to be needing it. "They too will be placed under arrest, then put on the next train for Dachau."

Then that's that; like a howitzer she's all over, what these sinewy little claws grasping my throat. Weary I thrust her askance; we collapse in front of the fire. My head, her

---

[293] [Here Hossbach indicates internal dialogue, *viz.*, in the preceding paragraph, without having gone back and attaching single quotes. To my mind, it is too long to render into italics.—N.B.]

lap, she screams, "*Kammler*; I never should have trusted that reptilian-eyed fool."

"Who?"[294]

"*Pfft*, just some Boshe who wants to take over the Luftwaffe—that's who; and, like all you Nazi swine, is willing to back-stab his own in order to do it." Then she gets ugly. "So help me, Hossbach, if you look at me one more time with that stupid smirk on your face, I swear, you'll never make it to tomorrow."

Not very ladylike; then again the Mademoiselle, while certainly all-girl, just as sure was never much a lady. Still she hasn't the strength she used to. So, she pretends: sweetens me up, then threatens me just for good measure; you know, the kind of thing that passes for reasonableness in a dame. This being done she moves on to specifics. "Alright, what about Speer—does he know?"

"Not yet."

Truth is, I've no idea. 'A misunderstanding', I'd told Himmler why just this morning, banking on accruing capital once I'd been proven correct. Yes I'd left our little meeting convinced he must feel the same; otherwise I'd never have said it. Ach, for the Reichsführer may be many things—but daft is not one of them. If the Führer says we need this Braun, well, then Himmler's hands must surely be tied; besides, a little spell in Dachau never hurt anyone. It did not concern me.

[294] Let the record reflect that, until now, all I knew of the man was his reputation, as evidenced by Himmler's call. Otherwise I didn't know him from Tom, Dick, or Harry. As an adjutant, or General for that matter, one rarely comes up against such types. Much of the prosecution's case imagines us higher-ups to have consorted with such brigands. In fact, we had precious little to do with such fiends. [—W.H.] [Hossbach's attorney, Dr. Seidl, said as much during his closing remarks. Unfortunately, this is a case of the story getting in the way of the facts: For Kammler clearly outranked him.—N.B.]

Until now. I mean, if Jack's tied up in all this, it's liable to lead back to me; oh, didn't the boy's mother ever teach him to be careful when choosing his mates?

Now, Speer you see may be a little artist sissy-boy but, these days, he's practically buddy-buddy with the Chief; hence the real reason his career's surpassed mine.[295] Plus, what with the untimely death of Dr. Todt he, a lowly architect with no military background whatsoever, has been given the Ministry of Armaments. Oh, it riles me no end that sonofabitch's responsible for the greatest revolution[296] since the Model-T. At least he—unlike Göring—earned it. Yes, just like the F., he too's an oddball intellectual who, throughout his life, has simply refused to go along with the pack. Ach, how I yearn to loathe him; yet, truly, I've no choice but to respect the man and his work.

This maverick streak—so incongruous, even seditious until now—found in Speer the rocket's lone defender. Yes, when it comes to the *Wunderwaffen* it was he —not Monique, nor von Braun, less still Himmler—*he* who got the Führer to finally come round.[297] And no matter how ephemeral such contraptions might seem to us Army-types —men used to dealing with *facts*—such pie-in-the-sky dreams just might turn out to be our last hope.

"*Get Speer,*" she says, snapping those dirty, ancient fingers. Why, I could just wring her neck; the gumption, the gall. Really, ordering *me*. "Oui," she sighs. "He is the one

[295] [As Hossbach would soon learn, Speer's world had been turned completely upside down.—N.B.]

[296] [re, 'revolution': *i.e.*, with regard to production.—N.B.]

[297] [This is absolute crap. Speer had indeed been key in getting the Idiot Corporal to 'come round' with regard to the rocket. Yet his role was only a necessary, far from *sufficient*, condition to the weapon's advent. The *real* 'getting the Führer to come round' occurred on July 7, 1943. We had given Shitler, theater maven that he was, a taste of his very own medicine: a cinematic salvo, starring the *A4*, explicated with pointer and pizzazz by a charismatic Doctor von Braun. Hitler, himself a captive audience for once, was like putty in the great man's hands.—N.B.]

man who knows what it would mean, what it would mean if anything were to happen to Dr. von Braun. For, the Jews—thanks to your Hitler—the Jews have already gone. It's the Professor, and Jack: they are our last hope."

"Jack? Why, what's he got to do with it?"

I mean, guilt by association's one thing: *I'll have Schmidtie take care of it.* Only, if their relation goes beyond that of mere acquaintance, saving Jack just might prove a whole world of trouble. True, one cannot hang a man such as Dr. von Braun: for engineers you see are hard to come by; but, their *friend*s...

"Ah," she winces, fleecing my cooler some *Cabernet Sauvignon*. "Haven't you been listening?"

I throw up my hands, then poor myself a double.

"It's like I said," she resumes, kicking-off her heels, what damned-near spread-eagled on the couch. "They are engaged in revolutionary—"

"*They?*"

"Oui—*they.*"

"But but, but *you*," I stammer; and what damned near sever an artery. "Why, you impudent little slut you, I..."

Oh, but ach, my mind's moving much too fast. Thus I revert to battlefield conditions: *one*, get Schmidtie; should he fail then *two*: go to Canossa[298] with Speer; and should *that* fail then—then Jack will be no more; *and then, alas, alas they shall come for me.* At which point, why, why what will be left—why what will be left of our beautiful Reich? The worst-case it plays out in my mind, even as I hanker for a final solution: "What about Heisenberg, and all that ilk?"

"'That ilk'? Please, spare me the invective: even your kooky Führer doesn't take *that* serious. Ah, *Wind*: there's no use probing the secrets of the atom. Now leave:

[298] ['Go to Canossa': Essentially, beg.—N.B.]

leave and tell Speer what has transpired. Only, not over the phone."

"But, but you just said—"

"You'll just have to go to him: I hear he's really quite ill. *Oui*," she preens, eyes perilously close to the map on my desk. "They say he's laid up in hospital. It's up to you—you, you big lug: *you* must convince him, convince him to get a *Führerbefehl*[299] freeing von Braun. And, of course, Jack. Got it? Good."

Pah, I resent some mesozoic twat's prancing all around, what with all her self-righteousness, giving *me* orders; especially some Cockroach of dubious allegiance. Yet the ability to command you see's its own justification; and, right now, Monique's positively exuding it: *I obey.*

"Hey," I yell, once she's half-way out the door. "Where are you going?"

And, with an arse, an arse that's lost none of its charms, she prances into the staff-car awaiting, swastikas-ablaze, and, looking me in the eyes, says, "*Zum Teufel.*"[300]

---

[299] [*Führerbefehl:* Führer Order.—N.B.]

[300] [*Zum Teufel*: 'To the devil.' Rarely do I recall her having had recourse to 'that barbaric tongue.'—N.B.]

Chapter 25: Jackie's War[301]

Cell Nine: Summer or Fall 1946[302]

March '44 found me wasting precious time trying to track down Jack. When really I should have been preparing for the invasion. Ach, for the Anglo-Amis already stood on the Continent, like locusts creeping up Italy's heel. Moreover the invasion[303] threatened commence any day; or, not at all. To top it all off I'd been up to my elbows trying to stem the bleed in the East. Alas the Reich'd become but one cordon of river, mountain, and all-important Channel. These alone had kept us from ignominious defeat.

Goebbels, the sly dog, had invited me up to his suite. A gay night of wine, then Delectable Leni showed me the stills to her film. Visions of her breasts they danced in my mind, apropos my proposal that they should grace the cover of Signal. *I knew only too well my presence there was but to partake of the latter. The Good Doctor lent me a photographer, equipped with a phonograph. Much brandy was imbibed. Together we dictated the 'River and Mountain' issue.*

The Little Doctor adjured that I should do my duty, assuring me the Führer had placed great hopes in it; that the "propaganda would be of inestimable puissance." Staring at Leni's chest, I plunged into that river wherein she is naked; and, in it, the Russians gat no hold...

Of a sudden did such thoughts take but backseat to springing Jack. Why I'd no choice but to enlist the aid of Schmidtie, dispatching him to Speer. Which latter was in hospital, recuperating—or, so I'd been told—from a rather

[301] [The title, in this case, my illustrious father has assigned. As for war, however, one must keep in mind that the General, as the rest of the 'elites,' rightly regarded us scientists as completely uninterested in perpetuating any such insanity. In the final analysis, theirs was the only lab in town: And, by town, I mean 'planet.'—N.B.]

[302] [The date was actually September 5.—N.B.]

[303] ['invasion': *i.e.,* of 'Fortress Europe,' through, it turned out, the north coast of France.—N.B.]

serious condition. And then, the word came: Speer'd take care of it. *For you see he had a personal stake seeing the rocket succeed: the Führer would never know. There the matter rested for a space.*

Now it may be instructive for the reader to afford a luxury I could not, and see what Jack was up to—under my nose the whole time—in the uttermost recesses of the Reich. That which follows is based on a questionnaire given to my son by his new masters, copies of which my attorney has surreptitiously obtained. Dr. Seidl believes it has been re-written by his interrogators in the third-person, presumably to impress upon their *superiors the authenticity of the facts alleged therein. He's allowed me copy this note, the which once'd graced the original. It seems to have been blacked out in mine:*

["] *To Whom It May Concern: FLYING OFFICER SUFFLER, JACK, appears to have gone native for a while while operating under the non-de-plume of LEUTNANT Güntzler, GERD VON. Subject forbidden to testify before the Tribunal, owing to reasons of National Security. [Signed] Dwight D. Eisenhower, Commander in Chief, USFET. 11 OCT '45.* ["] [No comment.—N.B.]

<u>Suffler at Peenemuende—by Staver & Lee</u> (Interrogators)[304]

["]HANNA REITSCH was returning to her apartment, sometime towards December '41, when she heard a noise coming from the bush. Fingering her pistol, she fired left, ferreting out a tall man in a gaudy hat.

Her wiry prowler raised his hands: "Don't shoot!"

[304] [Source: The 'Apologia,' an (unpublished) annex accompanying Hossbach's manuscript. The veracity of the statements alleged therein must be particularly open to doubt. Anything more I cannot say.—N.B.]

Closing in, she locked onto his chest. Nervous, her aim yet held true. Then, as if remembering something, she said, “Give me your wallet, Slim. Quickly: I've half a mind to shoot you already. *Don't test me.*”

“Jeez,” he swore, sounding like a Bavarian. Yet the Fraulein thought she might have detected something more: Something hostile, alien, lacking in all culture. Perhaps it was just the malapropism, like one of our Holy Joes. Or, worse, an American.

Reaching in his pocket, her Mauser held his attention: *Click.* This lady sure meant business.

“There,” he smiled, doing the one thing surely he had been taught never to do: For, he threw away his weapon.

“*Güntzler,*” she squinted, scrutinizing his ID, which she then proceeded to pocket. Her eyes flashed: “I know who you are!”

Impudent he met her penetrating gaze. After a space, the Fraulein resumed: “You've two choices, Scarecrow: One, you tell me who sent you, and why. Two, you do not, in which case I will just—I said, don't move! I don't carry this thing for my looks. Now, as to the first option, I'm afraid you're out of luck: You’re one of Canaris’s, aren't you? I can tell by your ID; that, and, your sneaking around in my bush. Now, as to *why...*”

“Would you mind putting that down, so we can talk? Perhaps a drink? I don't know about you—but I’m starved.”

She shifted her aim from his chest to his face, prompting the 'Leutnant' to turn serious, which, try as he might, he could not do without evincing a certain *machismo*.

Piercing her with his sun kissed eyes, he added, “But to meet you, Fraulein: I came to meet you. By the way, you were right about the *Abwehr*: Though it's not what you might think. Oh, I can't take it... I just want to pursue my one true love: I want to work with Wernher von—”

"*Shsh,*" she hissed in downright funerary tones. "That's 'The Professor' around here."[305]

"Alright, him. Truly, Fraulein, I hate this spying game, really I do: What I want's to go to the Moon!"

"You know," she said, in her mousey little way. "The next call I make will be to the Admiral. If he can't corroborate your story, it's straight to the Gestapo. Come," she demanded, directing him to a tasteful flat, weapon entrenched in the small of his back. Once inside, she proceeded to tie him up.

'Saucy little thing,' he said to himself. 'Bet she's done this before.' With practiced spontaneity he seduced her with the bit: "You 'gonna gag me too? I'm into that rough stuff."

She gazed at her prisoner, flashing darting doe eyes. "Perhaps another time, Slim. For now, I trust you'll find drawing attention to yourself to be to my advantage." She picked up the receiver, identifying herself, then asked the operator to put in a call to 'Tom.'

"No funny business," she warned, handing her intruder the phone, "lest I be forced to explain," returning a deadpan grin, weapon flush to his back, "why I had to shoot you before they could arrive: Being a woman has its advantages." She smiled, the intonation giving him to understand this was not mere threat.

Swallowing hard, he tried to keep serious, then asked the operator to connect him to a longish series of letters and numbers. Long because, in addition to the ordinary jumble came a few for a private extension. Minutes elapsed, during which neither spoke. Eventually a voice came over the line.

"*Hallo?*"

"Melanie."

---

[305] [Braunie did not receive this prestigious title till July '43. Let the reader take this into account while weighing the evidentiary value of incidents alleged to have involved my person.—N.B.]

"Mindy: Your access code, please."

"Er, five nine two, zero three eight."

"Ah, Herr *Güntzler.*"

"The one and only," he grinned, his stupid smirk enjoying a life of its own.

The Fraulein gasped, being it seemed to fuel his whole organism. Without it, she mused, her captive would be but skin and bones. She placed an ear to the receiver, weapon firm in hand.

"Very well," the secretary proceeded. "How may I be of assistance?"

"The Canary... *schnell.*"

"Sir?"

It was obvious this Mindy was one of these 'modern types.' A certain species of women who 'don't like to be bossed about.'

"I'm so sorry," she said: "Must be a bad connection."

"Listen here you troublesome shrew. Connect me this instant, or it's on *your* head that he's a dead agent on his hands."

"*Hallo?*" the hostess gasped, grabbing the receiver. "This is Fraulein Reitsch: Yes, that's me. I caught him snooping the bush... says he's one of yours. Oh, just wait til I tell the Führer. You know, he and I—"

"Calm down, Fraulein, I beg you—everybody just calm down!" Surely the secretary was just as weary as her boss of dragging Herr Hitler into the Abwehr's duplicitous nest. "There's no need for anything like that."

"Alright," declared Miss Reitsch. "Then listen once, and listen good: I am going to count to three. And, if by that time I am not speaking to the Admiral, he can kiss Herr Güntzler here good—"

"Ah, *Fraulein,*" an ingratiating voice came over the line. "It's not every day the Führer's favorite pilot decides to pay such tribute: To what do I owe the pleasure? (You can hang up now, Minn'd.) Now, *Fraulein*, would you be so kind as to point your weapon other than at my agent's person, thus that we might get to the bottom?"

"Gladly, Admiral. Yes I'm sure the Führer will clear the whole thing—"

"Fraulein! It's state business you've stumbled onto. You know I could have you—he *what*? You don't say. Really? Yes, that's true. Quite. No, no I do *not* know what he was doing outside your apartment... Nonetheless Fraulein I'd prefer you'd take such matters up with me, rather than drag in the Führer. You know how busy he is. Why don't you stop by my office, say, an hour: Then we can sort everything out. But, until then, let the poor chap go. That is, unless you plan on entertaining the Gestapo..."

The martial filly re holstered her pistol, emplacing the receiver in her intruder's hands. Then, collapsing from the stress, she retreated back to bed.

"Herr Admiral I, really I... *nein.* But, Herr Admiral, I swear: I never touched her. Really I wanted to..."

An outpouring of wrath filtered out the other line, inducing her prowler to extend the receiver at arm's length, accompanied by a certain gesture.

Through the open door she laughed.

"I'm sorry," he said, "I got scared. That's why I hid. Yes I know, I know: I know you could have me shot... *and I'll never do it again.*"

The line fell dead.

"How'd it go?" she quipped, fluffing her pillow.

He smiled, "could be worse," helping himself to a seat at her side. "Save that, one more strike, and it's the Russian front for me."

"Oh?" she said. "That would be great: We need more men like you."

"Naw," he drawled. Like a tiger he pounced, pinning her arms: "A man like me's hard to come by." He thrust his tongue against her lips, with permission delving inside. Clothing shed, they met with convulsive embrace. They made love with utter abandon, such as happens only in time of war. 'Something else,' he mused, 'clearly this broad's done before.'

Next morning Agent Suffler woke next to Hanna Reitsch, famed aviatrix: And personal friend of Wernher von Braun. [”]

<u>Interrogation II: Suffler's Road to Peenemuende</u> —by Staver & Lee

[“]Being a test pilot has its advantages. And Fraulein Reitsch, the Hitlerite's lone female flier, knew it. Thus did she deliver our agent to a secret base on the Isle of Usedom, wherein God's green earth still teems midst the primeval forest filtering in from the Baltic.

She manned a Fieseler Storch, unlike any he had been briefed on in London: A two seater. Training purposes only. One might think our Flying Officer suffered the indignity of being chauffeured about by a woman. Save that Fraulein Reitsch was no ordinary pilot. The fact of being a woman was, in this instance, completely beside it. Indeed, if the Luftwaffe had it, chances are she'd not only flown it, but had even helped smooth out some of the kinks.

Thus was it easy for her to get hold of a trainer, thence to obtain clearance to land on the desolate isle. There she was met by a dashing Wernher von Braun, to whom she then introduced our agent as “Leutnant Güntzler, an engineer just graduated from uni.”

The three hit it off. Secluded with these playboys, far from the *schadenfreude* enveloping overworked and underslept Berlin, one can't help but wonder what decadence might have ensued.

Over drinks did the Fraulein let slip that 'Leutnant Güntzler' had been mulling an offer from the faculty of the Berlin Polytech. To which von Braun could only sneer. The gesture confirmed the Fraulein as to the wisdom of having smuggled 'Güntzler' into one of the most secure bases in Hitler's twisted Reich.

Somewhere along the way our Pilot Officer appears to have acquired a taste for the new trend in rockets. The genesis of this development are not that hard to decipher. And while in uni he appears to have majored in brawling, the RAF soon brought out a latent desire to learn. He even started supplementing his fighter training via a self appointed study of mechanics. Through it all the common thread seems to have been the conviction, possibly need for ever greater access to speed.

Our Agent's enthusiasm was matched by that of Doctor von Braun. They saw it all as a puzzle. The Doc, heedless of security, was willing to set the gaunt one's accent, which he hadn't quite placed, to the side. Rather he picked 'Herr Güntzler' 's brain through the sheer technic[306] of number. The Flying Officer passed: With flying colors.

Fraulein Reitsch was to leave later that night: Alone. It had to have hurt, having to surrender these two Titans with Siegfried's charm. Perhaps she consoled herself that hers was an act destined to redound to the greater glory of the Reich. For these were men after her very own heart, devoting themselves, or so it had seemed, to the greatest of cause: service to Führer and Reich.

Our Agent had arrived at Peenemuende full of the most childish notions, such as a puerile longing to 'travel to the stars.' Surely this acted as grist to von Braun's mill. Thus enthused, they stayed up all night, brushing up on engineering problems: The better to help von Braun pull off the swindle.

---

[306] [*technic*: 'Technique', as considered from the point of view of emergent *technology*, inseparable from the accompanying world view of the 'brain men' intended to employ it; *cf.* the work of Oswald Spengler, especially *Man and Technic*.—N.B.]

Their pursuit was aided by the fact that Herr Hitler was intent on seeing the rocket come to fruition, insofar as it was thought to be capable of surpassing the speed of sound. If it worked, the Hitlerites could drive our invasion fleet into the Channel. Just thank god those dreamers were more interested in going to the moon, rather than the more immediate task of sinking our ships.

As for the rocket, one spectacular failure followed another. In front of big brass, too: In front of Himmler. The Rocketeers were so consumed with the nebulous notion of 'space,' the Boche couldn't pull off a launch without having it explode in their face. How on god's green earth could they expect it to ever reach England? Let alone go to the moon![307] By the time they'd gotten it to production, the war was all but lost: That's where their 'big dreams' got them.

No one will deny the achievement, from a purely technical point of view, that these men have engendered. However when one notes that more men perished on the launching, as opposed to receiving end of such weapons, the whole thing must be considered the most ridiculous lark. Of course, no one wanted to tell von Braun the rocket was doomed, whether with regard to winning the war or taking the weekend with The Man in the Moon.

Therefore it devolved upon Agent Suffler to relate the whispers then making the rounds. The experts concurred that, even if a launch should happen to succeed, it would be torn apart by the forces subsisting beyond the sound barrier. Or, another scenario had it: It would sail on forever amidst the endless vacuum of space. Either way, the *A4*,[308] or, so they reckoned, was doomed. The project

[307] [The tone of this 'interrogation' should suffice to show even the most gullible that it could not have been written by me, rather, but skeptics despairing of man. Their astuteness however may be gleaned from the observation that our real desire lay in penetrating outer, not England's air, space.—N.B.]

[308] [*A4*, 'Aggregate 4': Technical name for the first (operational) series of liquid fueled rockets.—N.B.]

should be abandoned, and Peenemuende's resources diverted to the fighting men at the front.[309] Men like our Agent, who, we hoped, would soon be firing rifles rather than missiles.[310]

Yet 'Braunie,' as the Professor is sometimes called,[311] is by nature a charismatic force. Thus did our Flying Officer choose to stay on at Peenemuende, indulging his scientific fancy: In blatant dereliction of duty, to say nothing of treason to England. Let alone the States, his adopted homeland. The fact that, if the weapon were to succeed, as indeed eventually it would, it was to land on his very own England, was implicit in his work.

Whether this bothered Agent Suffler, one cannot say. To hear him tell it, the slaughter of his fellows was but one more casualty of war. For, "Deeper still," he'd written, in an *apologia* sans *apology*, "lay the age old dream, a longing rooted in the very heart of man: That dream which says, *'O thou man—build me a path to the stars!'* "[312]

Thus they made their Faustian pact: For Hitler, a weapon to win the war; and, for man, this harebrained quest to 'travel to the stars.'

Signed: STAVER, R., COLONEL; LEE, R., MAJOR. 18 JUN '45. ["]

309 The English, as usual, hadn't a clue: our deliberations had considered pulling the plug on the rocket, so's to provide a fighter-umbrella for the *home* front. [—W.H.] [In which case, thousands of technicians would have found themselves slinging rifles, on any number of ever growing fronts.—N.B.]

310 ['missiles': Actually, rockets. Simple minded amateurs persist in perpetuating the myth. For instance the *Fi-103* required a catapult, plane, or even submarine in order to launch. All *we* really needed was a launchpad, a little alcohol and hydrogen peroxide, plus the ingenuity to keep the tanks housing such components separate and intact.—N.B.]

311 Bloody English, don't know their German: that's 'brownie', as in the confection; not 'brawny', i.e., thick and muscular, which is how 'braunie' sounds when rendered into English. It's not Jack's fault for speaking such a barbarous tongue. [—W.H.] [The reader may pronounce what he will: Either way, the spelling remains the same.—N.B.]

312 [There exists not one iota of proof for my ever having written any such tripe. Actually, as the Censor reminds me, this applies to these 'interrogations' as a whole. They are included, apropos the former's indulgence, for the sheer sake of fidelity to the work.—N.B.]

Nuremberg Prison: September 6, 1946

Seidl; why, he woke me from this trance, ere I'd even begun to write. For, I'd stumbled on seeing the guard. 'Whew,' I thought. 'Not an Ivan.' He moved on. Not before depositing my attorney, leaving time to pick his brain.

The old boy proceeded to let the air straight out from under, saying he'd no letters from Jack. Apparently they've begun to monitor him more and more of late.

Yet my elation returned, for the sly sonofabitch you see'd smuggled me Jack's response to this survey his captors-cum-employers've fed him; pah, that's how these eggheads fancy one's supposed to conduct interrogation...

It makes a damned good read. This despite the fact they're mainly interested in his work with Dr. von Braun; which, at least, helps me fill in some of the gaps.

My immersion in this boon's convinced Seidl to take his leave. Thus, with this clever device he's lent—a pen, with a little light that comes on when pressed—I shall append his responses, in essay form,[313] into this record:

3 DEC '45: Interrogation 013A: Flying Officer SUFFLER, JACK
JAN '44: Peenemuende East: Wehrmacht base, Isle of Usedom

[“]The bombing of Peenemünde, in accordance with Merton's notion of unintended consequences,[314] actuated a feedback effect, double blind in nature. For months we raced between Peenemünde and the subterranean base in the Harz.

---

313 [Again I am forbidden from either confirming or denying Hossbach's allegations with regard to my person: A precondition for the publishing of this work. Yet, as concerns my editorial position, I beg the reader please note the ambiguity as to whether my alleged response was via essay, or, if that which follows is his concatenation of such.—N.B.]

314 [In a closed system.—N.B.]

Sometime in the early New Year,[315] shifting priorities, much to our relief, had become readily apparent. The war was going bad, both in the air and the east.[316] Moreover, rumor had it, the invasion could come any day. Into this milieu did Berlin at last attach highest priority to our efforts. At last had Shitler foreseen our revolutionary yet embryonic technology as a means for rapidly ending a war he had so wantonly begun. Who were we to disabuse him his illusion?

The other end of the feedback had found us far removed from the privations of war, desperately engaged in our own private struggle. Speculation was rife, space chief among them. Therefore I was not surprised when, once Peenemünde was up and running, Braunie approached me with yet one more koan. Or, so it had seemed at the time: “Ever hear of a man named Newton?”

We'd been debating whether our rocket, upon which Berlin had been pinning all its hopes, would ever come to fruition. “Gravity, my boy. And you know what he did with it? He conquered the Earth, he did: *For Newton too prayed to the God of Science.* Now, tell me,” he whispered, as ever when launching into theory: Especially in barracks. At least, since the whole Himmler Incursion.[317] “What would happen if one were to fire a projectile, say, an *A4*, out into space?”

“Well, the gravitational force, for one,” I'd said, as everybody knows, “would prevent it from ever leaving the atmosphere.”

---

315 ['New Year': Apparently 'forty-four.—N.B.]

316 [The Allies had indeed invaded Italy. It's just, thanks to the Apennines, no one had taken it very seriously.—N.B.]

317 [re, the 'Himmler Incursion': At this point, that is, early '44, this might have entailed the increasing presence of the Gestapo and SS at Peenemünde. After the raid the previous August, the SS had absorbed the rocket from the army. As the diligent reader will no doubt soon learn, their ubiquitous presence was no mere threat.—N.B.]

"And that it should: And that's because speed[318] is energy[319] sans gravity, as influenced by that of the earth. Or so they say. Yet they have neglected to take into account one simple thing: A very basic property," he smiled, reaching into his lunch pail, retrieving a plumb. "Say I take this ball, right, and fire it at your face. What would it do?"

"Leave a nasty bruise for one."

"And it would at that. But stay with me now, Güntz, stay with me: For it *bounces*."

Well, I just about shit myself. Indeed, for, had he asked about some merely inanimate object, no *way* I'd ever get it wrong: For physics is phenomena. Save, I was so fixed on my position as observer, I'd forgotten to take into account the rest of the universe.[320] I swear to being thus enlightened; though it hadn't hit me as yet. Rather I said, "That's 'cause I'm hard," grinning a saucy-faced grin.

Me and Braunie can relate. Though he's my elder, he's still sprightly: We had our little laugh. Indeed, it was an honor to room with him.[321] The difference is, he knows when enough's enough: Looks like I didn't get that gene.

"Be-*cause*," he corrected, "your bones are hollow," ignoring my stupid smirk. "Take this ball, right, and fire it into a stream. Say, our sink." He demonstrated.

"It goes through."

"And it does at that. Now, do I use our last roll of toilet paper, to see if we should get the same result?"

"One would hope not," I said, blocking the entrance to the latrine.

---

318 [The schoolbooks say: (**S**peed)=(**D**istance) divided by (**T**ime). Yet this is a completely teleological assumption, biased from the point of the observer. As such it fails to take into account the existence of said object, measuring merely motion. The alternative is more scientific, being it involves a framework within which to manipulate, rather than merely measure, the motion of any given object.—N.B.]

319 [Actually, *kinetic* energy.—N.B.]

320 [A nod is as good as a wink, to the intrepid quantum theorist.—N.B.]

321 [It still is.—N.B.]

But then, it stirred, something I seemed recall: Slowly the veil of space unfolded before me, and I could see one equation: that nameless, formless possibility enfolding itself through streams of infinite quanta, each some point event of one discrete moment come together with some other, midst the realm where matter time begat. "Beyond the outer," I grit, entranced, while the new idea gat hold, "gravitational field,[322] there should be no encumbrance whatsoever. *For space is a vacuum.* No atmosphere, therefore, no medium in which to accelerate. There," I returned, re-cognizing my surroundings. "I have covered all the bases: no medium, therefore, no means of racing around the massive force field which surrounds the earth. Alert the Academy: Newton and his immutable laws hold. The mathematics makes it quite clear. I'm so sorry. I'm sure you'll understand."

"You're a fool, Gerd, a goddamned fool! Still, you're the best I've got: There may be hope for you yet. Now *listen*," he commanded, of a sudden become serious.

I'd never seen him like this. Save the lab. There, there those deep blues can breathe fire on the nincompoop who so dares threaten an experiment. But this happens so rare, being Braunie, unlike Shitler, is a good judge of character. Mother was right: Breeding *does* have its place.

The Prof surprised me by tearing a sheet from his easel, revealing a crude sketch of a rocket emblazoned above three equations in red.

I winced, "These have force going *up*. How do you manage that in the face of all of those gees? Plus look at your arrows: You've drawn them all wrong. They're only going in one dir—*oh my god*: You're *bouncing* it."

"Off your face," he clucked, taking a bite from his plumb. "Dammit, it's a slingshot."

I stood uncomprehending. "How on earth can you tell where it's going to land? I'm sorry, Professor, but we'll

---

322 ['gravitational field': *i.e.*, that produced by the earth.—N.B.]

just have the same problem the Luftwaffe does now trying to find London."[323]

"Ah," he exclaimed, seizing the moment with his own brand of showmanship. With the smile of a rake, he pointed to the pantomorphous equation on the board: "That my boy's where our friend Newton comes in."

It was odd how he persisted in calling me that. I'd never known the man whom, for so many years, I had considered my pa. Me mates used to call me 'Bastard Jack.' I didn't understand, being, just a few years before, they had called me the 'son of a hero,' and had treated me according. Only later was I to learn that my putative father had been instrumental in the manufacture of gas.[324] Then, before Mummy'd gone and packed me off to the States, I'd found some notes with regard to his private experiments.

It appears he had been seeking a means of eliminating death, through the study of the fructification of life. Then, from that moment, I knew what I was going to do: *I would become a scientist.* Hell, even getting kicked out of uni couldn't stop me from marking the shit out of the books in the library.

"Then so you see," Braunie concluded, appending what might have been the greatest lecture in history, if only I had been listening. Indeed, nostalgia comes at a price. "Last," he appended, "gravity's become our ally. Or, I should say, the lack thereof. We shall use the slingshot effect: And, with it, propel our spaceship to the farthest regions of the galaxy."

"Galaxy?" I gasped, unable to follow.

"Galaxy indeed. The absence of gravity will allow our ship to propel itself long past its fuel having been spent. Almost indefinitely in fact in any direction soever. Whence, it shall continue. For all eternity, endlessly lilting through the vacuum of space. A pity, really."

---

[323] [This is pure bunk: The Luftwaffe's problem was radar; ours, guidance.—N.B.]

[324] [re, gas: Specifically, chlorine-based.—N.B.]

Somehow, something just didn't sit right. "Unless," I challenged, thinking myself once more a sounding board for Braunie's ideas. "Unless our ship is made to stumble on some gravitational force, a body many times more massive than its own. Say, the moon."

The handsome chap swallowed a sardonic grin. And, in that moment, he watched me deduce the greatest discovery in history. I gasped, not knowing why. "It's impossible. What if Himmler finds out? It would be straight to the Gestapo. You heard him: 'It's your business to build rockets. Not spaceships fueled by adolescent fancy.' And besides, if our goose is really cooked, who'll be around to build the new age?"

"Leutnant," he commanded: "*Observe.*"

I scarcely remember his having ever used such a tone. I stood very, very still, and listened.

Prof passed me a news sheet, probably smuggled through Switzerland, depicting the destruction of the Reich's ancient cities.[325] "Just look, look at all the destruction. Not a goddamned thing's going to survive this war... not a goddamned thing! And yet, you expect to just sit around and wait? Germany's done for, I tell you: *And everybody knows it.* Everyone that is except that twisted fruit with a piece of shit under his nose."

He demonstrated, peering out the window, before thrusting a surreptitious finger above his lip.

I laughed.

"What," he persisted, "what if the enemy were to get hold of our 'ordnance,' as Ol' Adolf likes to call it,[326] and conceives the rather evolved idea of building a ship? It goes

[325] [This must have meant Hamburg, which had been laid waste in July '43, preceding by a few weeks the raid on Peenemünde. Also, Berlin had begun to suffer the effects of the heaviest raids, beginning that November.—N.B.]

[326] [The *A4* had grown out of the Artillery Department of Army Ordnance. That's how Dornberger and the army writ large had come on the scene. Yet, to all except Shitler, there existed a world of difference between a rocket and 'ordnance.' True, the 'Arsehole in the Berghof" eventually came round. But, inevitably as with such triflers, it was already far too late.—N.B.]

without saying it would have to be rocket powered, just to get out of the atmosphere. Well, who do you think they'll need to keep around in order to build it? Surely the Amis will sense the import, even if the English do not. Just give me five minutes, I say, five minutes. Then West will do anything to keep us from the Russians!"

"But," I shivered, "the SS," wondering how *they* had intended on 'keeping us from the Russians.'

"Herr Leutnant," he laughed, the spite of good birth, extinguishing a contraband cigar. "We're prisoners anyway. Take a look around: Do you think Old Four Eyes[327] would let you leave, say, to visit a bird? Why do you think I have to sneak them in here? Ech, what is it you Englishmen say, 'bother'? Yes, that's it, *bother* the SS..."

"My god, I—"

"That's alright. I know you're a Limey: Knew it day one. I *also* know you happen to be a man in love with mechanics. Do you think I give two hoots your opinions on the SS? They know nothing, I say, nothing! Let's just leave it at that. Besides, you're the only one who knows the real reason behind the redesign."

The redesign: The 'A4,' despite its maddening inability to fly without being blown to bits, had been redesigned as something much snazzier: the *A9/10*.[328] Braunie was able to sell it to the bigwigs in Berlin as a means of someday 'taking it to the Amis.'

In reality, The Great Man[329] had far bigger things in mind. His eyes traversed the microscopic movements of my face, like some wildlife assessor observing some new

---

327 ['Old Four Eyes': *i.e.*, Himmler.—N.B.]

328 [A9/A10: I know nothing of any such designation. There *did* exist an extended range variant, the *A4b*. But we're talking hundreds, not thousands of kilometers. By no means was I, nor anyone, working on anything so exotic as bombing America.—N.B.]

329 [Being Hossbach insists putting words in my mouth, I have been given permission to state that, if indeed I ever uttered such a thing, it could only have been in reference to Doctor von Braun.—N.B.]

species. Then, I beheld the face, a face I thought I never would see: A father, a father proud of his son. That instant, I realized: *I'm home*. No, not that free range prison on the Baltic, but in the company of a man like Doctor von Braun.

Meantime, the nations were engaged trying to knock out each other's teeth: Only *we* offered something truly new. *We*, the guardians of the future; *we*, the progenitors of space. Pressure out the back my skull meshed with my cranium, unfurling the physics parts of my brain. Wading through memories one by one, I traversed the albatross of obsolete discretion, bypassing roots of personality worked out long since. And, in the orgy of an instant, a veritable omniform of ideas proliferated. Permeating protuberant lesions enkindled, ripping and tearing synaptic gates, constructing curvilinear passageways leading to visions ever anon. Problems I'd shelved from fear of Himmler came into focus once more. Solutions started flying out left and right. "I'll do it," I cheered, triumphant, plugging new variables into equations of space time coursing the boulevards of thought. Laughter it leaped. And I shivered, shivered as so often's the case with the onset of some new idea. Eyes closed, I took cognizance of the new streams of data, which otherwise would have just floated by. Then, I inhaled, like a great transceiver swallowing the sun and said, "The problem of reentry is the *Alpha and Omega...*" ["]

Nuremberg Prison:
September 7, 1946

Thus the interrogation of my son. And, while I should be wroth with some of the things he had to say, in truth Jack's words have been my sole companion; yea, a constant source of solace on many a darksome night.

Oddly I've Speer to thank for helping me piece together Jack's run-in with the Gestapo. Nominally, the former was in charge of the rocket; that is, until Himmler took over. Now, Speer's harebrained scheme of trying to depict himself as part of some non-existent 'resistance' has led his attorney to requisition some rather curious files: interrogations of my son, obtained via discovery.[330]

Seidl, the Bulldog, somehow'd gotten wind. And, better yet, copies. True, too late for me[331]*, save my own edification; which truly must be infinite. For, why that's all I've got.*

***

I have had time—pah, time!—time you see to digest them. And, what had begun with a few unguarded remarks, led to the near-unraveling of everything for which I have ever worked...

330 [The testimony to which Hossbach alludes, pertains to my *alleged* interrogation by the Americans. After adjusting a few things at the behest of the Censor, the account as hereby presented remains otherwise unaltered.—N.B.]

331 ['Too late,' that is, being the trial has long since run its course.—N.B.]

Chapter 26: Scientists: Can't Win With (Or Without) Them[332]

Peenemünde East[333]: March '44

[“] We threw a party in March,[334] to commemorate a series of brainstorming sessions culminating in the radical redesign of the *A-4*: the *A-9/A-10*.[335] The Prof had begun by regaling the ladies with a dash of racy speech, administered with a pinch of dashing smile. This one particularly well endowed Spanish beaut appeared to have taken an interest in his dissertation cum debauch.

Unfortunately Braunie couldn't refrain lighting up every other minute, which seems to have disturbed our nubile Spaniard. Moreover, by that point, he had become increasingly intoxicated. And more than a little crude.

The Spanish bird had had enough, and was preparing to take her leave. The woman, whose identity we were never able to ascertain (being no one could ever remember having smuggled her in) was on the way out, when one of the engineers began expatiating on all the mysteries: Gravity, fission, light: Courtship to a man of science. I watched in astonishment as this, not my more 'hands on approach,' chanced pique her interest: She decided to stay.

---

332 [This chapter consists of Hossbach's 'reproduction' of my *supposed* interrogation.—N.B.]

333 [The Luftwaffe had their own base, on the western part of the island, home to the rocket's chief competitor: A crude, pilotless missile, the *Fi-103,* popularly known as *V-1*.—N.B.]

334 [1944.—N.B.]

335 [Part of my 'interrogation,' as 'recreated' by the defendant, has been stricken at the behest of the Censor. In this connection it is my duty to inform the reader that the term 'interrogation,' as used in the manuscript, is entirely misleading. Anything I *may* have said to the Americans, was done of my own free will.—N.B.]

***

Several *Pils* later, another engineer began remonstrating for 'greater artistic freedom.' Probably one of the blokes from the wind tunnel. I remember some such ridiculous statement, supposing a 'climate of regimentation' to have stifled his alleged creativity.

The Prof, even in that sorry state, let it be known he takes such things quite serious. Rearing his humongous head, framed with bloodshot eyes, atop his lungs he roared, "Gentlemen, goddamn, goddamn this stupid war! Oh, why don't they just leave us all alone?"

The room fell silent, as eyes, if not yet heads, began to roll.

"Give me six months, six months I say without Berlin breathing down my throat. Ach, *mein Gott*: We'll take man to the stars."

"But, but what about the war?" sniped the supple little Spaniard, aghast amidst men trying to hide.

Braunie slurred, "*Fuck* the war: *I* want to go to the moon!"

We had to apologize for our host, who, we lied, 'isn't used to touching the stuff;' *i.e.*, drink. Ah, but then Braunie had to go spouting such nonsense once more. Luckily, no one understood a single thing he said. Then, mercifully, he passed out. Huzel and I carried him to quarters.

The boss away, our gala became a smashing success. Needless to say, most of our guests were a certain species of athletically gifted women, disguised as nurses (Braunie's touch.)

In addition, several physicists were ready to hand. Braunie had had them fetched from off base, in order to break up the monotony. Such breaches could have cost him his head. Then again, he gets by with his smile, as Hitler with his will.

We forgot all about the offended woman. I was quite pleased with myself, presuming my intervention to have somehow succeeded in alleviating the situation.

Unfortunately, this doesn't appear to tally with facts that have since become known. True, some were disappointed. Yet we all knew our fate was inextricably intertwined with that of this man: No one would squeal.

So we thought. For, like Hitler, our luck had already run out.

We just didn't know it as yet. [”]

Chapter 27: The Trojan Whore

Nuremberg Prison: September 9, 1946

A reporter once asked me my most embarrassing memory of the trial. Pah, he was just trying to humiliate me over that whole East Prussia thing; the which surely I'll get to in time. Oh, but I showed him. "To me," I said. "The most embarrassing thing was Fulton. You know, Churchill's speech. For Göring was convinced it must mean war. Oh, but the Russian, the swine, for once, he didn't make a stink." He snapped my picture, then absconded to the anonymity of a mealy-mouthed silence.

Ah, Fulton. Yes we were all on our high-horses then. Why, we thought, 'We'll be released any day—we'll take Moscow yet!'

Somewhere round this time, my attorney played a very dirty trick. Behind my back he'd requisitioned some of the Mademoiselle's diaries, illicit copies of which had been found among Canaris' papers, pursuant to his arrest.[336] *Thusly did Seidl intend to prove I'd not only made contact, but had been 'keeping up with' the resistance all along.*

I could have strangled the swine. Oh, but what does it matter? And besides—it just might save my neck; which, you'll understand, I've grown rather attached to of late.

As for Braun's ill-fated fete, the Mademoiselle's diary makes quite clear: the SD had taken an interest in certain seditious utterances. And, while such drunken babbling wasn't yet enough to hang a man such as von Braun, it was *sufficient to attract the attention of the Gestapo.*

Which explains why, that March,[337] *Jack, Braun, and some other engineers had been placed under arrest.*

I'd put Schmidtie[338] *on it straight off, and was just waiting to hear back, before dragging in Speer.*

---

336 [*i.e.*, his second, and last, in the aftermath of 20 July.—N.B.]

337 ['that March': *i.e.*, early '44.—N.B.]

338 ['Schmidtie': Perhaps he was on leave from the *SD*. Or, it may be, Hossbach is merely protecting the identity of his helpmeet's replacement.—N.B.]

As usual, only now do I see: the Mademoiselle'd been one step ahead of me. Rather than leave it to me, she had decided to take things into her own malevolent hands...

THE DIARY OF MONIQUE GABELL

March 27, 1944[339]

[“] We snuck through Himmler's gate, like Greeks bereft of gifts. Canaris pulled rank with the sentry, while I produced the name of 'the Führer' on my newly painted lips. He called off his goons, then let us through. I'd like to think my cleavage had something to do with it. More likely it was the Admiral's Mercedes, all decked out in swastika flags and government plates just like the bigshot he is. Every day, each accretion of age brings some new defeat. A woman past forty's no use to anyone. Or so *they* say. And, after all, who am *I* to argue?

We found the Reichsführer hard at work in his garden, all dolled up in these ridiculous shorts commandeered far too high for a man his age. Such decadent disregard for fashion only goes to show these Jerries really are a barbarous race. His faux-pas was trumped by an unseemly shirt. Really, how unbecoming a man such stature, that he should be seen to sweat.

Old Heine was surprised to see me. Or, I should say, us: For I keep forgetting Canaris was there. Setting aside his drink, thus that he might not precipitate on his precious lawn, the four eyed fool bore quizzically upon me. “Guests,

[339] I have reproduced the Mademoiselle's record here, exactly as it appears in Dr. Seidl's papers; I have sought neither to omit, nor embellish it one bit.[—W.H.] [I have been unable to verify the veracity of this statement. Either Seidl, or one of his staff, has rendered the following translation, based on Hossbach's copy of the 'original' French.—N.B.]

unannounced? No, this won't do. This won't do at all. You know I could have you shot? You too, Admiral."

This was no mere threat. Very few people know this, but 'The Canary' was only recently placed under house arrest. For some reason, the Underground insisted I 'spring' him, then, flauntingly, bring him with.

I suppose I should have felt bad for Himmler's ill informed sentry. Rather I laughed, "Surely the Reichsführer wishes to know *why* we've gone to such lengths in order to see him. You know... *before* he has us all shot."

He smiled. "Yes my dear, he would," cupping that weaksome chin, suddenly social once more. "Have a seat, will you. Tea? Very well—out with it."

"*Reichsführer,*" the Admiral rejoindered. How oily yet... familiar. So obsequious, yet firing salvo after salvo. My estimation of 'The Canary' rapidly went up. Am I deluding myself thinking I've seen him someplace before?

The swarthy old fox protested: "Why didn't you *tell* me?" He knows damned well why he didn't tell him.

A tad more sincere, The Canary resumed: "This Braun... you know the Führer does esteem him so. Now, let me tell you, one friend to another: Without him, our goose will most certainly be cooked. No, I shan't pussyfoot about: The secret weapons are our last hope."

I'd feared he'd spoken too blunt. Making an example, I eased myself into one of these ridiculous seats. I laughed, being I could not help but think, 'Lawn Chair Deco.' Taking my cue, the Admiral followed.

I'd hoped to have put Heine at ease: But men are weak. He paused, squeezing those girlish fingers, as if sharpening a pencil. "Braun? Man's a defeatist. Foreign contacts, too. Speaking of which, *Admiral...*"

"Herr Reichsführer," I intervened, interrupting the most dreaded man in the Reich. Better yet, doing so with the formal 'Herr,' which only Dietrich dare use.[340] "I swear

[340] [The reader will in due course encounter a third exponent of such cheek.—N.B.]

on my husband's grave: If you kill this Braun, you'll forfeit the cooperation of every scientist: Those left, at any rate."

Himmler seized with a start. With fear he sought Canaris for confirmation. "Is this true?" the four eyed fool plead, suddenly meek and mild, depositing trust in the intelligence chief long known to be in league with the enemy. How touching: Really, I'm so glad I brought him.

And the Admiral said: "Not a one."

Himmler raked those dainty, manicured digits atop his ever balding chrome. Sizing the pros and cons, he said, "I shall consult with my advisers. Thank you. Thank you for bringing this to my attention." Then, incredibly, he *bowed*. "Madame: Please excuse me."

The cordiality was frightening, a tundra weighing down all enthusiasm save for regulation, work, routine: *Himmler*. But appearances can be deceiving, secret police so by their very nature. These days, he gives the impression of one just going through the motions, for something of which he no longer wants any part. I must share this with my friends in Monte Cristo:[341] It could come in handy later.

I heaved a sigh of relief. The man's stalked Braun for years, since, being a man, he fears that which he can't understand. Soothsayers and herbalists are one thing: Those he gets. It's the visionaries of science whom for Himmler hold a mortal dread.

But he's not dumb. At least, insofar as that statement may be said to apply to any man. He hasn't usurped the secret weapons for nothing. Plus he knows damned well that, in Canaris, he's an ace up his sleeve: A way out for when the time draws near.

Ah, Heine: We're about to become the closest of friends. ["]

---

341 [*Monte Cristo*: A codeword, since cracked, meaning 'Switzerland.'—N.B.]

Chapter 28: At the Führer's Mercy

Berlin: March 27, 1944

While the war cannot be said to be going exactly well, I manage to keep busy. In the day I ensure that the Führer's orders are being carried out at OKW. Such personal time's I have's spent entertaining guests at my villa on the outskirts of the city. One may even say life has been normal; hauntingly, abnormally so.

Schmidtie just called, on the way to Speer. Seems he spoke with his assistant, which latter insisted that the Minister could not be more with us. He will sign the petition for clemency: the teleprinter will take care of the rest. Jack and the gang'll be free in a matter of hours.

***

As such do I abandon the ennui of my suburban retreat, and return to my apartment here in the Reichs Chancellery. On a whim I hasten invite P'pa, and his broodmare, to dine. Perhaps it's just the irony: imagine, ex anti-Nazi and his half-Jewess, cavorting what with me: *under the Führer's own roof.* Yes for, thanks to the Boss, Winifrid's now an 'Honorary Aryan'. What, and Vati? Why, I cannot say what he loves more: the Führer, or—my new apartment!

Speaking of which, the 'Baron von Hossbach', as he styles himself these days, wears his sixty-seven years rather well. That is, for an inveterate drunk, who's more than his share of run-ins with the law; or, as he used to call us, 'those degenerate Nazi skum'.

Yes, those were iron days. The attitude of P'pa didn't exactly bode well for my career. In fact, once the Führer came to power, I had to resign my commission in the *SA*. The intrigue, while draining, probably saved my life. Yes for, there comes a time you see when every man must put his stamp on events. For me this meant executing a most difficult task. My performance so impressed the Chief, he made me his adjutant and liaison with the Army:[342] thus my apartment here.

Ach, for the first time, mine is not a pig-stye. Oh, for the first few months, I was afraid to touch anything, lest I should soil it. Whereupon I became drilled in manners, immersing myself in the cultural life of the city.

A more fascinating transformation still lay in P'pa's having become endeared to the regime; eventually. But, first, I had to extricate him from a rather precarious predicament. Pah, for my stepmother you see'd attracted the attention of the Gestapo; something concerning her pedigree.

Oh, people were always taking the Boss's words, and twisting them to their own harebrained schemes. Why science itself soon fell prostrate before the altar of such fanatics. Experiment had become a heretical act. Until, thank God, the war, separating as ever the wheat from the chafe.

Now, in my own sphere, I was constantly having to restrict the F. to operating within the bounds of reason; i.e., to the 'art of the possible'.[343] The process entailed coaxing the artist-within to entertain conflicting counsel before, as Head of State, drawing the necessary conclusions. In effect, I was Chief of Staff for turning his ideas into concrete, practical demands.

And, though he could be incorrigible, the overcoming of crises only served to bring us closer. For instance, when the Nuremberg Laws were first proclaimed,[344] he'd gone to the Gestapo Chief himself, some brutal young buck by the name of Heydrich, insisting he drop my 'little family matter'.

---

[342] [The 'most difficult task' probably pertains to his still obscure role regarding the liquidation of the SA, to which he had so recently belonged. Hitler, under pressure from Hindenburg and the army, had ordered the massacre, to the delight of the press, in late June '34.—N.B.]

[343] ["Politics is the art of the possible."—Saying attributed to Bismarck.—N.B.]

[344] ['Nuremberg Laws': Anti-Semitic decrees, issued in 1935.—N.B.]

Next thing you know, Winifrid had papers 'proving' Aryan descent. The fact she's well-beyond childbearing was the crux of it; a position the Führer readily endorsed. And ever since, she and P'pa've been frequent visitors to my luxurious apartment; *here, in the Reichs Chancellery.*

Yea, here I sit, amidst appetizers, recalling all that they have been through; and so appreciate their being here all the more. No sooner do I consider this, than P'pa forces me eat my own stew. Ach, he's as incorrigible's ever; I daresay he's going to drink me out of house and home. Almost I say something, when Winifrid, with but a flick of the wrist, appears to achieve the impossible; for, the old boy's thirst you see's been brought to a grinding halt.

Amazed by her bit of witchery, I make up my mind to thank her, when I'm forced to excuse myself, seeing Schmidtie's waiting in the hall. To the smoking lounge we retire. I beg him say whatever's on his mind.

Without ceremony he proceeds. “Sir, it's Jack.”

“What, he's here too? Hey—P'pa! I want you meet your—”

“Shsh. He is with the Gestapo right now, undergoing interro—”

“What? But, but *Speer*; why, I thought *Speer*[345]—”

“They wouldn't let me see him; I'm afraid he's deathly ill.”

“What—but, but oh good God!”

“*Ha-bay,*” he says. “You must leave—s*o oder so.*”

***

The unmistakable baritone of the 'Baron Von' rifles the air. And it breaks my heart; *pah, the old boy must've seen me.*

---

345 At the time, I was concerned lest any fallout from the raid should lead to trouble for me and Jack. It's only here, in prison, I've learned Braun and his big mouth were to blame.[—W.H.] [He's referring to our arrest, and subsequent imprisonment by the Gestapo. The Censor has allowed me to corroborate this. Yet I must demur the assignation as to any blame. Our arrest was bound to occur, being all Peenemünde was, at the least, hostile to Hitler.—N.B.]

"Winifrid," he shouts, so loud why the whole Chancery must hear. "Kommen sie—*schnell schnell!*"

"Aug-gie," she screeches, piercing the air, whilst stomping those high-heels cum-boots. "*Look,*" she gasps, pointing at me: out on the ledge two stories high.

"*Shsh,*" I motion, nodding towards two jack-booted men, setting up some equipment in a truck.

Like a criminal I'm forced to scale the gutter of the Reichs Chancellery, my home of nearly ten years, almost every inch of which to me is known; but not the facade. *The trap door will buy me time*, I gather, eying the roof; then almost as quickly amend: *not if they have dogs.*

Shuffling my feet I crawl, hands over elbows two-stories high then inhale. The smell of incense it comes wafting from within, lilting me to a place long-embedded in my mind. Pictures of M'ma—Muti, not this usurper: *why, she's scolding me. Same thing every time: playing in the sewer. Yes, I can see her now, fragile blonde; if only we knew how fragile. Oh, but ach, Vati needed whiskey, more than he needed a wife. And then, she got sick; wasted before our very eyes...*

Shimmying up the bird-befouled buttress I recall the warmth of her ancient rhythm, the dignity of her speech. A Victoria in reverse, she forsook her native England to raise her son *als Deutsch*. And yet, of all the names she could have chosen, she had to go and pick the most English;[346] worse, she had to go misspell it. Of course, it seems just right coming from her. What I mean is, I'm shocked to see her: you know, *up here.*

Muti she dissolves, and I'm struck by the realization: *I am headed down*; down, albeit still some two stories high. My feet are fully aware, yet still, the rest of me feels—or, perceives—still perceives her presence. The darting blue eyes; oh, how they shone like flame, whenever I'd done something wrong.

346 ['Windemeer,' as in *Lake Windermere.*—N.B.]

To the basement, the thought it comes to mind. Only now do I become conscious as to my plan, self-preservation lilting me out of the past and back, back to the turbulent now. Down the gutter I slide, palms-up burning all the way elbow a-glide. With my left-hand I bash in the window; while, with the right, cling desperate to the rail. Mine's all reaction now, not to think, rather, but *do*.[347] Scrambling for the water-closet[348] I fall to my knees, uprooting tiles in search of this tunnel Fatty's supposedly sequestered.

The rumor it soon proves true;[349] *and, once again, Schmidtie has saved my life.* Venturing under the floorboard I squeeze into this dark, ever-narrow passage—devil knows Fatty ever fit—issuing out the other side of the Chancery; then, up the escape, ascending the other side, ditching security as I climb. Pinioned hands grip the uppermost step, leaping several at a glance: right hand, left, right hand, left; repeating as I go. And so finally come to the fourth floor where, somber of mien, I approach the Führer's door.

I make it as far as the anteroom, whereupon I'm accosted by Bormann.[350] "*Reichsleiter,*" I flail. "Out of the way. I must see him, I say; oh, oh yes yes yes, see him I must. For, I am in danger; *great danger.*"

The smug, satisfied tough, what with no neck, looks all the more ridiculous in a three-piece suit. Why even his hair, all six of them, are nice and neatly apportioned. The swine, I bet he's been primping ever since the Führer left East Prussia; which, as luck would have it, was just last night, for a meeting in Berlin today.

His eyes they flash like blackest pits of empty night: bleak, obscure; why, the Devil himself could not see

---

347 [I had to laugh, being these soldiers are always sniping at us 'eggheads.' For, by now, all he had to do was simply jump.—N.B.]

348 ['water closet': *i.e.*, loo.—N.B.]

349 [Göring was said to have used a secret tunnel, after having set the Reichstag on fire, in Feb. '33.—N.B.]

350 [Bormann, Martin: Hitler's private secretary. The *de facto* head of the Nazi Party.—N.B.]

through. Likewise his soul; that is, if such a foul thing even has one.

He does not speak.

"*Bormann*," I rail, in a tone leaving little doubt's to my desperation.

"You," he harrumphs. "*Wait here*," then extricates himself. An eternity later he appears. "The Führer will see you *Herr* Hossbach."[351] He grins, snoot in the air, then leads me through.

The Führer's busy pacing. Upon seeing me he comes to a decided halt: "Sit!"

I obey.

A web of shadows it comes creeping over his desk, near the window to the study. 'Branches they flutter, a pageant of fully-formed life.' My head it jerks at such out of place thoughts.

Bormann begins to take leave, when the Boss he interdicts him. "Bormann: I want you to hear this."

Beholding me with a frown, the F. he sucks in his face. "I understand, *Herr* Hossbach," indicating a dossier in the Reichsleiter's[352] hands. "I understand you've become quite chummy with this *boy* I happen to know's been working on our most secret weapon: a certain *Herr*, or should I say, *Mister* Güntzler..."

It is not a question, rather, so much as a noose around my neck. "*Hossbach*," he barks in dark, staccato tones. "The Gestapo's outside this door right now, just waiting for my word to place you under arrest. Now please, pray-tell, give me one reason why I should prevent them doing their job."

---

351 [The omission of rank, in exchange for such civilian appellation the equivalent of 'Mister,' is a decided insult, the likes of which Hossbach could scarcely have missed.—N.B.]

352 [*Reichsleiter*: 'Reich Leader,' *i.e.*, Bormann.—N.B.]

"But, *mein Führer,*" I beseech, falling to my knees, like a child rapt in prayer. "I'm no rebel, really. This man, this *Güntzler,* isn't my friend—*he is my son.*"

His eyes turn black with bile, fixing on their prey...

Nonetheless I proceed: "When we first met—I mean, we hadn't met *before*. It's just that—"

"Guards!"

Now, mamby-pambyness you see's the one thing the Führer won't suffer; thus I pull myself together. "It was just before Pearl Harbor. This boy, this 'Güntzler' after all's an American; and we weren't at war as yet. Somehow, somehow he chanced track me down. So, I tried to convert, convert him to... *the cause*." It's all I can do but to go on. "For you see my son was begotten… *in an unnatural way*: we were in Champagne, back in the early days of the war. Oh, I was all of nineteen—an imbecile really; why, not long after I'd first met you. 'Orders', they said: *orders*. Ach, for we'd stumbled on this village. Captain said the Kaiser was behind it: 'tit-for-tat', he said. The policy demanded we should punish these *francs-tireurs*[353] who, at the time, were busy sneaking around, shooting our men in the back; well, so we did. We set their pathetic village to the torch. The women, pah, the women were sanctioned as spoils of war; the men, the men we put to the sword. Oh, but ach, *mein Führer,* I was a different man then; we all were. So you can imagine the look on my face when I set eyes on this saucy little number, what with her Red Cross uni when, of a sudden, I realized: *that's no lady, rather, but the very Devil herself!* We'd known each other before, in England. Oh, but ach, the stupid slut you see'd gone and run off with my very best friend: the only friend I'd ever had. Pah, she picked him—*him* instead of me! And, what's more, she took him; *why, she took him from me*. The whole thing was like a dream; *a dream verily come true*. I, why, I..."

---

[353] [*Francs tireurs*: Terrorists, from the German point of view, mainly French and Belgian, during the Great War.—N.B.]

The Führer he stares disconsolate, what this horrified look on his face: of shock, of shame, betrayal; and, what's worse, of *disrespect.*

I plead, peeling my fingers, denuding a swath of callused ancient skin: "When I was done I lay on top; on top that the rest might pass by. I mean, it was awful, fires all around. And yet, it was I—*I* who saved her! But, but the war... *I never saw her again.* Years they passed, and I built a new life. Why it was only due to *Yellow*[354] that I chanced run into her, whilst manning the cage in Paris. Pah, she must've told Jack all about me. Naturally the boy must've wanted to meet his pa. It was right before Pearl Harbor when I realized who this 'Güntzler' really is. And I—-I mean, after all, *he is my son.* Ach, mein Führer, *ach*: I am so—"

"And *I,*" he erupts. "*I* have no choice but to mete out summary justice: you can come out now." And, from the curtains comes—*oh my God...*

"Bonjour," she drawls, cigarette-holder as ever attached to her hand; though, in the Führer's presence of course it's just for show; *pah, just like the rest of her.* Still, it suits her: what the black fedora, and the ob-scene one-piece.

"I," I stumble. "I don't understand."

"*Silence.*" Almost instantly he moderates his venom, much like turning a steak. "That's alright; or, rather, it will be, once you've made amends. Now, let me tell *you* some history—secret, *Party* history: I was in Landsberg, not long after your release. Dietrich Eckart, you may recall, recently had died. The Party was badly in need of funds. And yet Providence, Nature, whatever one wishes call her, abhors a vacuum just the same. Then, along came a certain war-widow known to a mutual acquaintance.[355] And she, rather than mope herself into an early grave, decided to

[354] [German invasion of France, and the Low Countries, in May 1940.—N.B.]

[355] [re, 'mutual acquaintance': Possibly one of the Mitfords in England.—N.B.]

exploit her status; and in so doing'd accumulated a small fortune. More important, so far's the Party's concerned, she helped smooth the way with these bankers close to the Duce.[356] Almost alone did she and I convinced the Duce of the need for a united front. We pooled our resources, our sole aim being that of squashing the Reds. Unfortunately Paris was too Jew-ridden to go along. Only, now, that's all changed: *thank God*. Yes Hossbach, the Mademoiselle is—and was—the best friend we have ever had. Really, I'm so glad she came to me about this in the first place..."

I rave, what murder in my eyes: "*Whore*; why you stupid, filthy—"

The Führer he slapped me!

"Ach, mein *Führer*, I am so—oh, what do you want me to say? I—"

"*Silence*," he roars, beginning to pace: and everything hangs on the very next word. "As I was saying," he grunts, unconsciously hitching his pants.

I'd had them altered, you see—secretly, of course, seeing he's begun to put on the middle-age spread; and, well, had so wanted to save him the trouble.

"Bormann, tell the General here what the SD has to say about his son."

Parroting his Chief, he pounces: "Treasonous remarks about the Führer!" jutting that thick, unshaven chin; so much the better to bask in my misfortune.

"*Ja*," the F. resumes, gaining control of our impromptu little gathering. "You will make amends, Hossbach: from now on you, you and you alone shall keep the reins on that rot of a son. Oh, I have to admit: rocket-men aren't a dime a dozen. Still, it was wrong of you to have concealed him. Yes I know, I know: I said I wouldn't hear a word against the Mademoiselle—that much's true. On the other hand, you never *once* tried twisting my arm.

[356] ['Duce': *i.e.*, Mussolini.—N.B.]

Then again how could you—knowing what you know! And, for that, for that I should have you shot..."

"Why, I'd do anything, I—"

"*You'd better.* Hopefully, it won't come to that. But mark my words, Hossbach: this business's liable to gain the attention of Himmler; in which case then it's beyond my control. Now see here: I don't give two hoots whether your boy's a model National Socialist or a raging Tory. I *do* care if he happens to be harboring opinions about which he can know nothing. For, in Germany, only one man's qualified to play politics." He seems to upbraid himself, as if begrudgingly being forced to make some concession. "The Wunderwaffen are... of incalculable import: *that* is why I'm having them released. Hossbach, I'm intervening with Himmler—which, as you know, goes against my most basic tenet. Next time, however, I shall make no such allowance: *Wunderwaffen or no.* The boy has a job: he is to build *rockets*. Rockets, Hossbach, rockets; *and, with them, I will crush the blood of my enemies.* Of course I needn't remind you: any slip-ups will be dealt with in the most dire fashion. Now, I want a report, and I want it in one week."

"Jawohl," I say, clicking my heels, then exit the Chancellery; this time, however, taking the stairs.

Why I've risked my life protecting him now for twenty-odd years—and I'd do it again. And yet, and yet I cannot betray my son. Therefore, should Jack prove too much to handle, but one solution remains: *and the Führer and I know it.*

Heading for the gate, the guard returns me my weapon. And, in it, I feel the impress of steel; and yet, the warmth, the warmth of a long-lost friend.

A friend who just might be the last means of protecting my honor...

Chapter 29: Under the Mountain

Hossbach's Cell: September 13, 1946

When all's said and done, I am a simple man: my job is but to command. Say there's a bridge that needs to be blown: I am your man. Send in the sappers; alert the NCOs;[357] *and, goddammit, get me the Chief of Staff!*[358]

Still—and, God's going to punish me for saying this —but that woman, that godforsaken woman is... someone on whom I've learned to rely. 'Oh Monique, you guileful slut you, here're your orders—now get to it!' Yes, that's what I used to tell myself I'd say; in reality however I did nothing of the sort.

I say this but as preamble to the fact that it was she *who secured Jack's release: under* my *supervision. Yes for, thanks to my new clearance, I was able to obtain access to the most impregnable bastions in the Reich. Each Wednesday my batman would drive me to Peenemünde,*[359] *thus that I might light a fire under the rocketmens' rears. For, up to that point, you see, I hadn't occasion to visit the Mittelwerke. Regarding which, skimming Seidl's voluminous files, only now do I see: once again, the Mademoiselle'd beaten me to it...*

---

357 [*NCO*: non-commissioned officer; a Corporal, or, more likely, Sergeant.—N.B.]

358 Thus when I used to lead from the front. Still, the Führer thinks [sic!] I was too valuable; i.e., *that I knew too much.* Therefore did the telephone and telegraph become the most potent tools in my arsenal.[—W.H.] [Hossbach had said as much during the trial, leading some wag in the press to dub him 'The Desk General,' much to the former's distaste.—N.B.]

359 ['drive to Peenemünde': Of course, that would have taken him only as far as Kröslin. From there, he would have had to have taken the ferry.—N.B.]

Monique's Diary[360]

March 29, 1944

["]I saw Himmler today, on the heels of a most edifying conversation with Wolf. The latter'd no objection to Jack's release: However, he warned, some 'loose cannon' might always go off half cocked. A middle ground was reached: Jack, Von Braun, and the rest are to be released, under the following conditions: First, the SS is henceforth authorized to submit them to strictest surveillance. Second, those monsters in the Gestapo now have the right to inspect both Peenemünde *and* the Mittelwerke. A thing previously unheard. For, they hadn't the clearance.

Himmler proceeded to receive me at his palatial rest and resort at Hohenlychen. A pass from Mann[361] had won me admittance, warding off all but the most lurid of looks. Heine wasted no time depicting how devastating it would be if the Russians were ever to get hold of such weapons. In this vein he spoke quite candid of Braun's liquidation, 'if the Russians should ever get near.'

"The rest?" I said, vulnerability in my throat. Now I had his attention, I proceeded to answer my own question. "Chances are, they too will have to be liquidated."

I watched his fat little face slowly contort. Involuntarily I attempted to decipher those squeamish black dots he calls eyes, hidden beneath that stupid pince nez.[362] He swallowed, fixing a glance which said, 'Woman—*what*

---

360 [Again, Hossbach appears to have copied her purported entries. A third party has since subjected them to translation.—N.B.]

361 [A blind, since cracked, for Müller: Head of the Gestapo.—N.B.]

362 [*pince-nez*: Himmler's infamous eyepiece.—N.B.]

hast thou to do with me?'[363] Or, as I call it, 'Hossbach's Perpetual Look.'[364]

Knowing my suggestion would, if adopted, result in the probable death of my son, Heine lost all faculty of speech. He recovered just enough to polish his already spotless lens. Then, like all men, unconsciously fixing on my breasts, he relented.

They're quite firm, even after all these years: Or so he thinks. I'd made sure to pad them before our meeting. Men are such suckers: Especially puritans like Himmler.

He bowed: "I see we understand each other." There followed an awkward attempt kissing my hand. While he was bending, the seem of his trousers began to give way. How I wanted to smile. But inward I said, "You have no right." Indeed, for youth is equally behind me. Ever since my... condition,[365] I knew the sands of time would be merciless. Well, now his tailor will know, too.

I affected not to take note of the severed hem guarding his tiny bulge. I trust my discretion was duly noted: For which he'll be forever grateful. Men!

If the Russians ever do get near, and, they're getting closer all the time, it's going to fall on me to get Jack and the Prof out of this pestilential land. Hossbach? That Hun's his Führer so far up his derriere, he has to pee sitting down. At least I have an excuse: And I'll be damned if I'm not going to make it work for me.

[***]

I'd set off for the Mittelwerke, papers forged courtesy of _____.[366] As representative of something called the 'Gestapo Chief Inspectorate,' a name I simply made up, I headed for the subterranean lair.

---

363 [John 2:4.—N.B.]

364 The Mademoiselle has told the truth here for the first time in her miserable existence.[—W.H.]

365 ['condition': Apparently, pregnancy.—N.B.]

366 [Deleted by the Censor.—N.B.]

Ordinarily, Jack's at Peenemünde. On occasion, however, he and the Prof have to inspect these underground facilities far to the south, near Nordhausen. Which, being farther from Berlin, I figure's less likely to suffer any Russian incursion. Almost as soon had I secured their release, than my people sent word that now would be a good time to go see them. For, any day, they'll have to return to the Baltic.[367]

Thus, the Mittelwerke. Lots of stories have been put out regarding the place. Unfortunately, some of the laborers were under suspicion of sabotage. At least, that's what my 'orders' said. Plus, the 'signature' of Kammler himself affixed them: And he's an Obergrüppenführer. Now, not only does one not question such a man but, as a rule, one does not even acknowledge their existence. At least, so runs the rumor that 'ridiculous woman'[368] has been allowed to put out.

I was taken to the Harz,[369] under armed escort: For my *own* protection. Of course, I didn't need it. Still, everything had to look just right. Plus it didn't hurt Private Hennemann has a cute butt. Handpicked, you might say.

Dr. Theiles, liaison with camp security, led me down a ladder into the subterranean dark. I tried to put the more ugly rumors out of my head with regard to the slaves, property of a local KZ.[370] An artificial sun much akin to twilight reared to greet me. Coughing from the impact of the soot, I navigated the twists and turns while he led me to the Development Works.

---

367 [Her logic being, the more distant *Mittelwerke* would have a longer lease than Peenemünde, before being paid courtship by the Russians. As such was the former supposedly chosen to erect a tunnel, in order to affect our alleged escape.—N.B.]

368 ['ridiculous woman': *i.e.*, herself.—N.B.]

369 ['Harz': Mountain range, whose southerly region incorporates the environs of Nordhausen.—N.B.]

370 ['KZ', *Konzentrationslager*: Concentration camp.—N.B.]

There I was greeted by a tall, breathtaking man, with cheekbones for which to die: This I was told is Doctor von Braun, i.e. 'The Prof' one hears so much about. There he loomed, surrounded by colleagues about to witness a test fire.[371] If successful, it would solve the air burst problem which, the Doctor ('Call me Professor, please') explained, a bit too familiar, perhaps, has been intermittently dogging production. Ah... but under any other circumstance!

I was catapulted out from my swoon, and damned near almost swept off my feet, by the stench floating in from nowhere; and yet, everywhere all the same. Concealing my distaste, I twisted some locks over my eyes, blocking sight of two skeletons, which just days before had been men.

Miraculous they sprung to life, enough to haul what appeared to be a backbreaking tank into place. An onrush of pity enjoined me. Quickly I recovered, then said to myself, 'Now is no time.'

The episode had thrown me for such a loop, the fish I was trying to catch had already begun issuing orders to his men.

"You," I summoned the thinner abomination, this lopsided parody of a man with a beard on his face and terror in the eyes. "Tell the Professor his demonstration is done: He can finish later. The Gestapo is here: *and it's time for inspection.* He is to bring three... no, four... *four* of his best engineers. Well, are you deaf? I said go!"

A minute later the agitated, gesticulating figure of the man with the golden locks and rock chiseled features approached: Only to let into me with fulminating force. "How *dare* you interrupt one of my experiments?" He gave me the once over. "The Gestapo's using women now, hmm? Klein, run a check on her credentials." He stared, ominous. Never have I so wanted a man.

---

[371] [re, 'test fire': Possibly one of the engines.—N.B.]

A few minutes later the verdict was in: “Her papers check, Brow... I mean, *sir*: Major Oster here's investigating a tip on behalf of the *Abwehr.* She's been granted special powers by the Gestapo, owing to an arrangement between General Müller and Admiral Canaris: Everything appears to be in order.”

The Prof tore the dossier from his sergeant's hands, then pretended to flip through it. Grunting every now and then, to give the impression that he was actually reading it, he shook his humongous head and said, “Well well well, what will they think of next?” Hands in the air he sighed, “Alright, let's go Frau—err, *Fraulein*... ?”

“That's Major, Doctor: Major to you.”

He couldn't get over the shock, and just stood there, stood there shaking his cyclopean head. Eventually his senses returned. “The patronymic... you wouldn't happen to be related to a certain *Colonel* in the Abwehr, now, would you?”

Eyes seething I raged, “I will ask the questions!”

By now, the big lug had become deathly afraid. Ostensibly I didn't have 'rank' to punish him, being the Prof's an officer of the *SS.* Of course, everyone knows the Gestapo doesn't give a hoot for such distinctions: Well, why should I?

Save, for some, fear is readily supplanted. “If you've something to share with my men, Major, perhaps you'd better just say it to my face.”

As ever, bravado only goes so far. He thought he could scare me: Anything but. Indeed, the Prof has won a place in my heart. After all, the man's etched like a God: And knows it.

“That will not be necessary,” I returned, indicating one particularly panic stricken Leutnant I'd noticed trying to hide. Executing an about-face, I unloaded on Von Braun: “The man's name!”

"What, him? Ech, that's just Leutnant Güntzler," he soothed, flashing the most congenial smile.

And, ah, how I would to have been but putty in his hands. But, as the Boche like to say, 'duty calls.' I waited for him to continue.

Defensive he snarled, "One of the best engineers on the island. Which is to say, in all the Reich: Else I would not have him."

"Silence. It's obvious he thinks there's something funny about my being here, don't you, Herr Leutnant?"

"Um, sir? I mean, no ma'am! Nothing funny at all. No sir sure as sh—"

"Klein!"

"Major?"

"Take this man to interrogation. Place two guards outside, then come back and escort me."

Thinking on my feet, I didn't know what I was saying. Smiling I circled smoke-rings in his face. I guess I was just winging it: It's served me well before. "Bring me everything you have on this man—schnell!" Then off he went.

"Indeed," I said, addressing the Prof, then prattled. I could have recited every capital in Europe, yet his terror wouldn't have abated one bit. "One must make an example, that's what I always say. Braun my good man, something here is rotten: And I intend to get to the bottom of it."

"Jawohl, Herr, er, *Major,*" came a cowed response, less cocksure than ever until, as if doing something beneath his station, he summoned a strength I did not know he had. Thus he loomed ten feet tall: "Dammit, ma'am, don't be too hard on the boy. Güntzler's a model assistant. And his work... yes, Major, his work is something I cannot do without."

"Then I shall keep that in mind," I curtsied, savoring him with my mind's eye, before disappearing behind the concrete wall to interrogation.

Just me, and 'Güntzler.'

"*Jack,*" I hissed, as soon as we were alone. "What are you trying to prove? Do you've any idea the lengths I've gone in order to find you?"

"That's my business: As if you ever cared. No, Mother, whatever you're up to, I want no part. Please, don't go explaining yourself, I'm sick of it: Sick of your lies, your explanations, your Hitler loving games. I understand it all now, really I do: Daddy's a Nazi swine, and mummy... well, mummy she sleeps with the football—"

The blood ran curdling off of his lip and onto his Leutnant's uni.

"Mother, good god, what would you have, save me? Better save yourself! Now leave, leave and take this stupid war with you. That is whoever you happen to be fighting for this week. Who is it now, mummy, hmm, Hitler? Or perhaps the French? Only, which French? For there's the Resistance, then there's Vichy. I hear there's even a Charlemagne Division attached to the SS."[372]

"You shouldn't believe everything you hear: Even if it is true. Ah, don't you see? This is no mother son reunion: I see it's too late for that already. Yet never would I have imagined my own flesh and blood to be firing missiles—"

"Rockets, mother: They're called—"

"Rockets at his very own England. I must admit, the whole thing's beyond me. Or perhaps it's just you give a damn about no one but yourself. Really, how dare such a 'man' presume lecture me. Now enough. Enough of this foolishness! I have come, Jack, I've come with a warning: Himmler's wrested the rocket from the army. You're all in terrible danger. Or I should say you will be once the Russians get here. For Old Heine's given the order for Braun and his team... and that means you... to be liquidated

372 [French volunteers, under German suzerainty, fighting on the Russian front. The comment, if ever I made it, would have hit home, being Mother had played a key role in its formation.—N.B.]

if the Russians should ever get near. But, these skeletons, your 'labor force.' The Mittelwerke—some marvel! More a chamber of horrors. And yet you, you would preach morality to me? You'd better shrug, boy. Because, once Ivan gets here, the whole thing will have to be liquidated. A sensible decision, too."

Beneath the pain, I smiled: It's been a long time since I've seen myself in him. Then, he said, "The kind of decision you might well make yourself, mother, hmm?"

"I'd liquidate the lot of you," I said, "rather than let doomsday weapons fall into the hands of the Russians.[373] But come, Jack, listen: It doesn't have to end like this. For I have this—"

A knock at the door caused me to cringe. Panicking, I changed gears, "*I'm so sorry*," whispered, then, closing my eyes, put a baton in his ribs.

A knock.

"Come!"

Klein, sickened at the sight of his Leutnant, went white as a sheet, then handed me a stack of papers.

"Leave," I said. "We aren't finished. Ah, don't fret: Your Leutnant just needs a little... encouragement. Encouragement, help him recall."

Klein couldn't leave quick enough, resembling a rocket himself with his speed of departure.

"Now," I said, facing Jack, "where were we?"

He writhed, crumpled on the concrete, when I caught the look in his eye. Then I realized: *Tread cautious.*

Gently, yet firm, I whispered, "I'm having a tunnel dug beneath Nordhausen, so you and the Prof can get out if there's still time. Until then, just keep doing whatever it is you've been doing. My sources say, (I was bluffing, of course... but was I? I'd meant to say, 'My intuition tells me')

---

[373] [She must have been referring to the delivery system, which we did have, not 'doomsday,' or, atomics, which we did not. The Censor insisted my making this clear.—N.B.]

your work is of the utmost import. That, 'Upon it the world of the future must stand.' Unless the Russians get hold of it: In which case there might not *be* any."[374]

He kept trying to bolt, so, simultaneous with a tender caress, I let my nightstick into his ribs. Several blows later, I needn't repeat. I cannot tell whether it happened at once or as a battle on and off. Point is I managed to convey what had to be said. "As for your file," I went on, whispering as before, "Your file will disappear: I have a friend in the Gestapo. Now Jack, all I ask is ten weeks. I'm sure the front will hold out a few months more, provided of course Herr Hitler doesn't go and do and something stupid. Okay, six. That's still enough time to build a tunnel. Tell no one: Especially von Braun. He has loose lips, as all you scientists. As soon as the Russians are within one hundred kilometers, you are to act. Then, and only then, you will tell the... er, Von Braun, about 'your' plan. And, if necessary, abduct him by force."

Violent he lunged. I had to knee him just to continue. "Assemble all documents," I said, lips to his ear, whispering more at rather than to, suppressing any tears which might have clouded my mind. "Documents which might be of any use. Sequester as many scientists as you can find. If the Russians get within fifty kilometers of either base,[375] Himmler has been authorized to liquidate every last one of you. Moreover, thanks to the speed of armor nowadays, anything's possible. Here," I deadpanned, nonchalant, handing him a silver ampoule, "I am so sorry: It's not what I had intended. Then again, you might have need of it yet."

"Poison, you're giving me *poison*?"

Locking eyes, I gazed, hoping he'd *feel* the turmoil inside. Plus, does he know that, now, I've no poison my

---

374 [*i.e.*, 'any future.'—N.B.]

375 [re, 'bases': Peenemünde, in the north, and the Mittelwerke to the south.—N.B.]

own? He mustn't guess, else he'll never accede. Fear? Damned straight. Only, I can't show it: It's just not in my nature. Words were neither necessary nor desired. Point is, he should feel the warmth, the maternal bond... then pocket the damned pill.

Mechanically, he did. A smile then broke out. “Mother,” he started, after I'd helped him to sit. “I’ve been really busy,” grunting and groaning, recovering from the shock of the blow.

I moved in, emplanting a kiss on his face, then rendered him one piece of advice: “You must bite down *hard*,” indicating the ampoule, “in order to break the seal. Here, keep it here in this locket.” Ominous, I passed him the necklace. Some keepsake, with a perfectly hideous Prussian woman to grace it.

“*There is a secret compartment*,” I hissed, secreting the ampoule inside, then clasped it about his neck. “Try and make it to American lines, even the English. Just promise me one thing: You won’t fall into the hands of the Russians!” [”]

Chapter 30: The Middle of the Earth

Nuremberg Prison: September 15, 1946

From the Spring of 'Forty-four, we expected the invasion[376] *any day. Everybody was on tenterhooks, hoping they'd 'just get it over with'. Either we should kick them in the teeth, and drive them into the sea; or, we should not, in which case then the war would irrevocably be lost.*

And yet I was only obliquely concerned with the endless expanse of coast; how much less the inexorably retreating Russian Front. Ach, for the Führer you see'd insisted the Wunderwaffen were our last hope. All the generalship in the world wouldn't amount to a hill of beans if I couldn't convince Jack to snap at it, and get production rolling before the Anglo-Amis attempted to land.

I felt like Metternich, knowing my task would, for better or ill, reshape the map of the world: it's just, like Christ, I had to descend to Hell in order to do it...

The Harz, near Nordhausen: May 3, 1944

The Führer's ordered me to the Harz where, buried in the bowels of the earth, lay Jack's new abode. But nothing's permanent. His detail'd begun as an inspection but, for some reason, they've decided to keep him over a month. Dornberger,[377] indignant, demanded Jack be returned to Peenemünde: *I wouldn't hold my breath.* Yes, it looks like my Wednesday sojourns on the Baltic will just have to wait.

---

376 ['invasion': *i.e.*, of the West.—N.B.]

377 [*General* Dornberger, Walter: Head of army ordnance, in charge of *Peenemünde* until the SS took over. I am allowed to state that he remained *de facto* chief, albeit largely stripped of any real power, from the Fall of '43 on. This renders him innocent of any crimes which might have been committed at the Mittelwerke: Those were all the doing of Himmler.—N.B.]

But that's no excuse: *there's a job to be done*. It took some strings, but finally I got Schmidtie on loan from the SD to drive. Oh—it's going to be just like old times!

***

We've come for business, not pleasure. "Everyone's hurdles, right?" I rasp, imbibing the remnants of three-year old whiskey. The Führer wants that I should stay sober, in case of the invasion. Oh, he's yet to drive with Schmidtie. Not that I mind. It's just, so few people know how to really *drive*. It's a task, this shifting in and out, tackling mountain alternate with molehill.

Motor revving, and sunglasses on, his answer it comes as we swerve, swerve almost off the side of the pass, overtaking a bus of children—or, is that troops? "The past is past," I say, taking the liberty of speaking for him. "Oh, Schmidtie, of course you're right: *there is work to be done*."

Eyes to the road, lest we should take a header off the cliff, he hands me his kerchief. Sonofabitch, why, he knows me better than myself. Ach, I'm bleeding. It's all this height you see; for mountains have a way of worming inside. I'm convinced Old Rudolf must have gotten his name while compassing one of these.

A goodly hour recedes before the whiskey, and what my equanimity along with it is exhausted. I've given up trying to recite this speech, intended to talk some sense into these boys, seeing Schmidtie either can't hear, owing to the wind; or, more likely, is simply sick of having to listen. The gist of it runs: 'The rocket-men whine they've been out of jail just over a month—and yet, the A4, the fucking A4's maiden flight is over a year and a half in the past; still next to nothing's rolled off the assembly-line as yet. The Führer intends that I should change all that: *in no uncertain terms*.'

***

Schmidtie and I process through the niceties at checkpoint, then some SS tough lets us through. They call this the 'Mittelwerke'. "Hah," I chide, upon being led to the depths of this dungeon. “More like 'Middle Earth',” referencing P'pa's reading of Wells.[378] The guards, cut from the same cloth as their chief,[379] have no sense of humor; then again, if I had to live here...

Actually, it's not half-bad. Oh, sure, I've heard rumors. You see, back when the barracks were being built, a lot of men died, owing what to this chill running through the tunnels. The workers it seems had to sleep there for a space. Still, no sacrifice's too big for this war. Besides, the men—criminals, for the most—have thereby atoned for any sins they may have committed in this life; surely they shall receive the blessings of Valhalla.

Now, the barracks are fine. The tunnels, a marvel of engineering. Pah, it serves me right having listened to such rumors. In future I shall make a point to, as the Führer says, close my ears to such *quatsch*.

Still, some liken this place to 'a great heat', bearing its blight upon the soul. Yes an 'endless torrent of sunless day, indistinguishable from empty night'. To them I say—you should try living with the Führer! Like that hellhole he keeps at Rastenburg. Why I swear, there, it is not he who rules, rather, but the mosquitoes. Well, I suppose each man has his hell; this one's no worse than any other.

It was goodly of Sawatzki, therefore,[380] who's run of the place, to lend me his office for the duration of my visit. Knowing one comes from the Chief sure puts things in perspective.

I have Jackie fetched then brought to the office, which's really more a study. Like the Berghof,[381] it too is carved into the living rock. I lean back in my chair, hands towards the vastness of space which, incidentally, one

---

378 ['stories of Wells': Probably *Journey to the Center of the Earth*, by H.G. Wells, as read to a young Hossbach by his pa.—N.B.]

379 ['*their* chief': *i.e.*, Himmler.—N.B.]

380 [Sawatzki, Albin: Technical Director of the Mittelwerke.—N.B.]

381 [*i.e.*, 'The Eagle's Nest.'—N.B.]

cannot see from down here, and say, "Jack my boy, what is it you *see* up there? The things I hear: spaceships, Moon-landings, visits to Mars; and other *quatsch*. I mean, why go through all this trouble, just for some godforsaken dream? There's a war going on—and it's high time you knew it. Yes, the Führer wants that you should build rockets; *rockets*, not whittle your time chasing some childish dream. Big things are happening, Jack, big things; things of which you know nothing. Yes, the Boss you see has this plan. Oh —if only you knew him as I! Maybe then, maybe then you'd see things different. The war is not lost; not yet, at any rate. For, *the Führer*," I lean in, taking him into the confidence stemming from my privileged position. "Has seen it all in a vision; and has prophesied. And yet you, and yet you would make him the fool? Why he's told everyone that this rocket shall soon take to the air—well, where is it? You must work harder, son, *harder*; all is not lost. Yes, the Führer thinks this rocket—your rocket—will render any invasion simply impossible. Oh, don't you see? They will be torn to pieces before they ever make it off the beach; pah —just like a beached whale!"

Now I turn grave, hamming it up; for, perhaps I don't quite believe it myself. Still, I *do* believe in the Chief. And besides—*I am just a messenger*: "And that's not all: soon, soon we shall unleash the latest Wonder Weapon[382], the *ME-262*—the high-speed bomber the Führer's always prophesied; and, with that, with that we shall force the English to their knees."

Why, I'm carried away by my own vehemence, by the possibilities latent in the moment. But then I realize, rather too late: *the poor boy's spent half his life among the English...*

"Ha-bay," he riposts, using the German way of shortening my name.

An affectation—a good thing.

382 ['Wonder Weapon': *Wunderwaffe* in the original.—N.B.]

"The Two-six-two is far too heavy: as a bomber, she will not fly. Any five-year old—which *der Führer* obviously is—could tell you—hey!" he thrills, eyes heavenly. Distant flecks of corona sparkle, seemingly inducing decadent visions ever anon when, without warning, he shrieks: "The Fibonacci Set![383] One, one, two, three, *etcetera*, concerning the proportion of mass to thrust —taking for our model of course the Earth's gravitational force." He smacks himself. "It's obvious: *one-to-one*," he adds with a start, returning to Earth himself; though I'm not so sure I follow.

Luckily he remembers yours truly's still here. Pah, flights of fancy; another blessing-cum-curse of a Hossbach.

Yet still he persists. "Our first Fibonacci pair, that of one-to-one, conforms to the world of Newton: the corresponding law of physics is adumbrated by the *Second Law of Thermodynamics*. Our next ratio concerns the proportion one-to-two, which—hey!" he rails. Fingers they snap, lest I should cease to be silent: "I'm working!"

Why I could slug the poor sap; imagine, saying such things about the Führer. But then I realize: *something is happening*; something the which I daren't interfere. He paces; I brood.

"Our next ratio," he returns, lecturing me like I'm back in Leicester; *God I hated school.* "Concerns the proportion one-to-two. Here we see the zygote in nature; our monad split in twain: one female, one male. And so, Ha-Bay, we come at last to our miraculous two-to-three, being some third thing—or, number—necessitated by the union of any two others: that is, the aforementioned one and two. *Two* things, two things unlike each other and their offspring alike: our blessed number three! And yet, intimately related thereunto. Got it?"

---

[383] [Fibonacci Series: Set of numbers {1,1,2,3,5,8...n} wherein the median proportion of any two contiguous numbers yields approximately 1:1.618, *i.e.*, 'The Golden Mean.'—N.B.]

I most certainly do not.

"The magisterial wonder of the infinitely repeating set! Hence—and, here, I hesitate to offer—"

Hesitate indeed; *why, it's all a bunch of gobbledygook.* The poor boy's in ecstasy, or hysterics; I can't tell the which. Still, I don't understand; ach, this is arithmetic all over...

I *do* however chance hear one word which awakens my fancy: "Therefore, our infinitely repeating set just might serve a solution to the problem of encumbrance—say, the jet-engine?"

He looks at me's if asking a question. The poor sot: better ask the wall. And yet, somehow, somehow I manage to push my sarcasm—that other blessing-cum-curse of a Hossbach—aside. For, at the word 'jet', I know that I must listen.

Luckily he returns to his solipsism, lest we should be here an eternity awaiting my response. He jerks, what damned near leveling poor Sawatzki's jar of perfectly sharpened pencils: "That's it!" Alas, acknowledging my presence, he continues. "Say you've an object, right, the mass of which—say, a rocket—the mass of which may be thought as being in proportion to that of the Earth. Well, substitute the speed of the latter for that of the former, requisite to generating optimum thrust, and one ought to be able—I daresay—one ought to be able to find some means for overcoming the Earth's gravitational field. And, further —oh, Braunie's gonna love this—if our friend the *Fibonacci Series* contains a solution, via undulating proportionality, well, then there's nothing to say one can't do the same with, say, a spaceship, theoretically infinite in size. Moreover—"

"Stop! My head's beginning to swim. Oh, you're as bad as Rosenberg," I say, meaning the Party philosopher. I lean back in Sawatzki's swivel, sweat burning the back my neck like some great weight constraining, what the very life-blood seeping out my ears... and beg: "*Jack.*"

He bolts to the alert; with sadness his wide-eyes turn rigid.

With a gasp I say, *"Don't do it!* Man was not meant to play God. No, there can be but *one will*—that of the Führer: and *he* says—"

"I don't give a damn for your fruity Führer!"

I cover my ears, and pray to God no one's listening.

Still, like a death-sentence he drones: "Ten years from now, a man will walk on the face of the Moon. Space-flight will be common. Do you really think your medieval weapons, and obsolete forms of government, can do anything to stop it? It's space, father, *space*; and it is our destiny."

The lines being drawn, an uneasy fidgeting prevails. Slowly do I slumber under the dawning light of defeat. Prying sunken eyes, I stun the poor sap with a delicate pat. "Well," I say, "*I tried*," then, breathing out loud, head for the exit.

"Fancy that," he taunts, following me into the hall, our confrontation apparently not at an end. "Just walk away do you? *Of course.* It was so easy the first time: you know, after you raped me mum.[384] Well—why should it be any different now?"

The swine, why, I would but just run him through with the sword:[385] I stand very, very very still...

---

384 [If indeed I ever set foot at the Mittelwerke, or, for that matter, any secret base, it would have precluded speaking anything but German: It would have been suicidal to have done anything else. As such do I call into question the use of the words 'me mum,' a phrase I ceased to employ when I was but a child. Hossbach has mistakenly recalled our 'conversation' in working class English. While I was born in England, I'm as American as they come.—N.B.]

385 [re, 'sword': Ceremonial officer's sword. It would have been highly irregular to have negotiated any such object betwixt the aforementioned spaces.—N.B.]

"I *see*," he says, feigning embarrassment. "But *der Führer.* Well, let me tell you a thing or two about *der Chef*, he and his wet-dream, the ME-262: *both* shall reign from on high—in cloud-cukoo-land!"

"Dammit," I explode, in my fury seeming to have smashed poor Sawatzki's vase. "I know, I know—yes, I've known it a long time; the plane, you fool—*not the Führer.* Yes you see, I'd told him. Why I'd said, 'But, but this *thing*,' meaning the Two-six-two. 'This *thing* simply will not fly. One can't take a fighter and make it a bomber just because they're Führer.' Oh, of course, I didn't *say* it just like that—which, by the way, is the problem with you young people; why, you've simply no respect for your elders."

Gaily swiveling poor Sawatzki's chair, Jackie wreaks havoc on the carpet, eying me with disdain; or, what's worse, *disrespect*. Only now do I realize what I have done: 'in my day', the same thing for which I'd chastised P'pa so long ago. "*Windy*," the old goat he'd grouse. "Let it be: trust me, no good can come of this Hitler. Has the world gone mad? Give me my monarchy any day." And blah blah blah; *ad nauseam*. Thus it was with pride when, on coming to power, I made him eat stew. Yes, he was my guest at the Reichs Chancellery. Why I even introduced him to the Boss himself. Oh, but ach—devil take it! By then the old boy'd convinced himself he'd been a good National Socialist all-along.

The earth it shifts; I mean, literally, the cavern threatens collapse.

He laughs. "Just a little test-fire: probably the engine-works."

The which brings me out of my reverie. For, for a split-second, it seems, I'm actually relating. I try, you know, try to 'just reach out'. "Your father's not so old-fashioned's you might think. Yes, Göring explained this whole technology thing long ago; and *he* thinks—"

"Göring?" he stumbles, shocked, and more than a little embarrassed for his pa. "Since when do you give two hoots what Fatty has to say?"

I cry. Outward, no; but, inside, *I die a little*, desperate for something, anything, no matter how vile, if only but to save the poor sot. I cringe; *pathetic*.

Then I remember: I *used* to be a soldier. Oh, we may be in somebody's basement, what this colossal coal-mine where Pharoah's slaves hath built the Seventh Wonder but, to me, *this is Smolensk*[386] *all over*; only, now, now I shall make a real stand...

Yet it's only a mask, and shall disintegrate upon the first repulse. To myself I chide: 'Next thing you know, you'll be quoting the Mademoiselle.'

He gawks, what this puzzled look on his face, as if the storm's finally passed, short-circuiting Valkyrie flights in his brain. Much to my chagrin—and great hope alike—he too realizes the score.

Now, some people sacrifice their lives, their beliefs. But, for me, Jack's about to sacrifice something more—I can tell by the look on his face: *his defiance*. Yes for it's the same look I must've had when they broke me back in the war; *and made me a man*.

"What I *mean*," he says, redeploying his face, not daring look me in the eye. "Is, if *the Führer* insists..."

"Oh, but he does. He most certainly does!" I cry, mad for all I'm worth, then give him a hug; a great big hug. An eternity, or, perchance, a few seconds later, what the weakness having passed, I swear one more time: *this is the last time I shall cry in this war*. And then, not me, rather, but that which is *best* in me takes over. "If not,"[387] I add, with a gesture, indicating the consequence of such failure. "For you; for you and that idiot professor."

---

[386] ['Smolensk all over': Evidently an engagement in which Hossbach had failed to stand fast, resulting in his 'desk job' at OKW.—N.B.]

[387] ['if not': *i.e.*, if 'I' had refused to go along.—N.B.]

"That 'idiot professor'," he glares. "As you so wantonly call him, happens to be the greatest man in Europe." Inarticulate with rage and, like his old man, frothing superlatives impossible for any man to fulfill, he terrifies, yet strikes me with pride all the same.

Like lightning I roar, then grab him about the scruff. He might be tall: *but I'm stronger.* My hand it closes flush against his trap. "Don't *say* that; you mustn't *say* that." And then, my hand, but only my hand, lets up. "Oh Jack—I didn't want to do this..."

What hurts most's having to choose my words with the utmost calm—just as I would with any other officer. "I will be back in three days. By which time the rocket must be ready for mass-production. Now I don't care how many must explode along the way. Just make it happen: *so oder so.* Consider it a Führerorder. Oh, and oh yes: *Heil Hitler.*"

He returns my salute, more from astonishment rather than any in-born feel. Still he recovers his verve—another curse of us Hossbachs—enough's to say: "The Two-six-two will not fly: not now, nor ever; *as a bomber.* As a fighter though it really is first-rate. I swear, with such a machine, even you Jerry's could kick us Tommies out of the sky." His back-handed compliment having been issued, he exits.

Half-way out, I bid him wait, while doing what I can to repair Sawatzki's sentimental clutter; yes for, it seems, that stupid family picture took a spill upon my having lunged at the poor boy.

This being done, I make as if to lead him out, but then realize: why, he knows the place far better than me.[388]

He laughs. "Follow me."

---

[388] [While not violating the stipulation of the Censor, I must state that any traffic I might have had with such a place would have been tertiary. Otherwise the Americans would not have employed me, and I would be in the dock with our defendant: Or worse.—N.B.]

We spiral through a dim, tortuous mine, ascending the stairwell seemingly built into the living-rock. Emerging out the trap-door into this sham commissary, I bite my tongue as he recites a series of meaningless notions, bearing no relation whatsoever to the current war.

Alas we reach the garage, where diligently Schmidtie's been waiting; and, thank God, the gate beyond which Jack can go no more. Escaping to the safety my Mercedes, what I damned near trip while essaying the mat. Then, addressing the boy in a tone I'm ashamed poor Schmidtie has to hear me use, I say, "*You* are not the Führer. Now stop playing games with these Fibinazi numbers, or whatever they are and—*and get back to work.*"

I slam the door with but one thought: *thank God Schmidtie's still here; he'll know what to do.*

Reaching over, he rolls up my window, then hands me his kerchief, the which surely I'm going to need for the ride; then gets me the hell out...

Hossbach's Cell: Roughly September 21, 1946

Now, what I did not *understand, that is, prior to receiving his letters through my attorney, is the fact that Jack's discomfort lasted but seconds. Our interaction, a battle of wills, had simply served to stimulate him. Like a blow to the head, his focus had settled on the immediacy of the moment. Everything else it dropped to the side: the one thought remained...*

The Mittelwerke, Part II: May 3, 1944[389]

[389] Through Jack's letters, surreptitiously obtained via counsel, I have managed to piece together that which transpired, upon my having left the Mittelwerke. I have reconstructed the gist of it here via narrative, seeing prison leaves one but little ambition for becoming anything but a writer; or, loon.[—W.H.] [Let the reader, or, for that matter, any gung ho would be prosecutor, take this into account, when weighing Hossbach's allegations with regard to my person.—N.B.]

“That’s it!” Jack cried, in the fury of a mathematical frenzy. “*The Fibonacci series.* The distribution of armor along the fuselage—what if it were related to bomb-mass in proportion to, say, *Phi*?”[390]

He raced back to quarters. Rummaging frantic for a few bits of scrap, he set forth page after page of calculations before, alas, smiling in triumph. And then, Jack Suffler, just as the man who'd borne the name before him, knew how it felt to be one with a higher force: a power competent to alter the destiny of nations.

Still, unlike the bloke who for some twenty-odd years he'd mistakenly called 'pa', *my* boy's sure to make good: on the promise, *that Faustian promise*; the which no Gestapo, no MI-5—or whatever the hell Monique is—can ever make any use...

[390] ['Phi': Again, approximately 1.618.—N.B.]

Chapter 31: The Summer of '44

To hear the neutrals tell it, the sky is beginning to fall.

Claustrophobia however has yet to set in in the Reich; much to our enemies' dismay. Nonetheless a sense of doom has begun to infiltrate our once invincible morale. Ach, for 'Unconditional Surrender' you see has scotched any chance of a negotiated settlement. Thus we've no choice but to fight, rather, fight for our very existence. We, descendants of the self-same knights who more than once had to repel the beast-men from the steppe; who, under Odoacer, put to the sword the 'grandeur that was Rome'. Why the very notion of our defeat's an historical impossibility.[391]

All talk of victory however's simply ceased. Thus do we proceed: no hope for victory; and yet, no chance of defeat. Sooner or later, someone's got to grow tired of it all; and, if 1918's taught us anything, *that someone's not going to be us...*

With every fresh defeat, the Führer's become more and more enamored with these 'secret weapons'. Pah, if only Jack and that idiot professor would but do what they are told. Why I've told them time and again: the A4 must be ready *before* the invasion, seeing the Luftwaffe, like its boss, isn't worth shit.

Only, now, not only have they landed,[392] real beachheads have actually been formed; and yet, where are

---

[391] [The defendant could use a lesson in history: The 'Teutonic Knights' lay at the center of Nazi, particularly *SS*, notions of culture and chivalry. The latter, *i.e.*, those who fought 'under Odoacer', appeared some eight hundred years earlier, illiterate savages with neither culture nor any semblance of a viable state.—N.B.]

[392] [They did so in the early hours of 6 June '44, off the Normandy coast.—N.B.]

the *Wunderwaffen*? You know, all those rockets and missiles that were supposed to make fossils of old men such's me?

The Reichsmarschall ought to be shot. I mean, if the Luftwaffe could but find London, I wouldn't need to rake my son over the coals. Yes for each Wednesday you see I arrive: first, Peenemünde, then, Nordhausen;[393] and what now Peenemünde again. And Jackie knows that, each time I size up his production, I do so with a noose firmly ensconced about my neck.

By force of a *Führerbefehl* I demand that monstrosity enter mass-production. Yet all I get's a pack of lies: 'The problems of science, Herr General.' Pah—devil take it! Why I've been fobbed; I've been fooled; I've been tricked. Oh, why couldn't I have paid more attention in school? Oh, *why couldn't I have been more like Jack?*[394]

Then again, I've always been rather impressionable; you know, eager to be led for a ride. What with their numbers; their graphs; their poppycock. Oh, it's either, 'We're on it, Ha-bay', or 'Wait till you see her minus the kinks!"

Oh, but ach; *I should have known...*

The Führer's Study: June or July 1944[395]

The Führer is horrified when I make my report: "One hundred sixty-seven changes?" he blurts, what once calm features now turned sour.

"*Jawohl,*" I flinch, flush with embarrassment. "You see, there's this problem with the rudder, and, and I—"

---

393 ['Nordhausen': *i.e.*, the Mittelwerke. Nordhausen is the town right outside.—N.B.]

394 ['Jack': *i.e.*, Mother's fiance, and Hossbach's friend of eld.—N.B.]

395 [Probably at the Wolf's Lair, in East Prussia. He is also known to have visited the Berghof, during the period in question.—N.B.]

"*Silence*," he mocks, affecting a Britisher accent. His mimicries really are quite good, once he has it in for a fellow. Oh, but ach, he's gone off completely half-cocked, upbraiding the desk with his fist; papers they fly.

"Here," he shouts, shuffling me one at random.

I behold a Luftwaffe study.

"One hundred pages," he mocks. "One hundred pages of pictures, diagrams, maps—thirty-seven even in different colors!"

Ach, for the Fat One you see's always boasting of his dread Lufwaffe's 'productivity', even as our cities are being laid to waste; *Göring truly is our misfortune...*[396]

"Now see here," he stews, as if continuing the thought. "The Luftwaffe's productivity exists on paper—*and on paper alone.*"[397]

I wilt under his malefic gaze; as usual, though, he's right.

Still I seem to be harboring some sort of smile, the which it must needs be wiped. For he beholds me what with this malignant grin: "The Army's no better!"

I make a go defending my fellows, which gets as far as a raised fist.[398]

---

396 [It was an old saw of Nazi propaganda, *viz.*, that 'The Jews are our misfortune.' In the early days of the war, Göring had even boasted that, 'If the British are ever to bomb Berlin,' then the people could call him 'Meyer,' *i.e.*, a Jew.—N.B.]

397 [Herr Hitler was wrong. By this point, Speer had instituted measures which, as Hossbach himself has been forced to admit, had boosted productivity to levels previously unimagined: Even with all the bombing. The *Luftwaffe*, specifically the fighter arm, had rapidly begun to reap the benefit of the toil of this technocratic marvel.—N.B.]

398 [This is one of those things that, at first, appeared to be balderdash: Yet it seems such things really did occur. The transgressor, usually a general, often received little worse than the withdrawal of Hitler's favor; or, at worse, dismissal. The testimony of Herr Halder, Guderian, and Manstein argue in favor of Hossbach's asseveration, even if his character does not.—N.B.]

Instant he switches to the subject of technics. "*Nincompoops*," he swears, by which I take it he must mean the engineers. "They'll never get anywhere!"

How dare he. I mean, the Führer may be the Führer but, still, Jack and von Braun are far from ignorant men.

"Now see here," he repeats, indicating a report I'd commissioned on *A4* production; the which to date has been but precious few.

I squint, eying a plethora of 'artistic reproductions' and unfounded facts; which, like yeast, have been added so's to leaven an anemic confection.

As usual, the Boss puts it all in perspective: "Do you realize, Hossbach, each time one of these ninnies makes a change, they jake it up. They say: 'While we're at it, let's have a go with such and such.' Oh—it makes my blood boil!"

Like a schoolboy I blink: "But, but *mein Führer*... why, they said they just needed to work out some of the kinks."

Then, demanding myself be brave, I turn downright bold: "Or is that not what we already do with our tanks; our guns; our planes?"

"*Dummkopf!* Tanks, you fossil, are just like the piston-engine: everyone knows how one's supposed to work. But this, this rocket, just like the Cherry-stone[399]—and, till now, the jet-engine—no one's ever seen.[400] As such, no one knows what one's supposed to look like once it's up and running; oh, where were you in science?" Again he finishes my thought: "Absent!"

---

399 [*Cherry Stone*: the *Fieseler Fi-103*, i.e. 'V1'.—N.B.]

400 [I'd say Hitler was being a fool. Yet, with his memory, a liar is more likely. The jet engine, far from being 'new,' had long been perfected. The first jet powered fighter made its maiden flight shortly before the onset of hostilities: Only *der Führer*'s boundless stupidity had prevented its mass production, relegating the engine to obscurity until the war was all but lost.—N.B.]

Frantic, the F. he begins to pace. Why, he looks like he's about to rap me one over the knuckles. "Think, Hossbach, think—oh, but why can't my Generals *think*? Von Egghead, and that harebrained son of yours they make twenty changes every time they touch something: which leaves twenty, times nineteen, times eighteen," he rattles all the way down to "times one possibilities whereby a thing might go wrong. Bah, every engineer knows that, when you fix a thing, you do it one part at a time, so's to keep track of what went wrong: *experiment, adapt, adjust.* Oh, but you, you've let these bulbous-brained ninnies run you afoul with their treasonous additions. The weapon is *one*, Hossbach. The task is really quite simple: they are to build rockets; *rockets.* They[401] are to fly from point a to point b, where they shall explode; heaping ruin upon mine enemy. And yet what do I get? Pipe-dreams beyond the wildest imagine!"

Poor Boss. Why, he seems so *ill*; a sip of mineral water appears to restore the situation. Ach, I fear he's emaciated on account of me.

He stares at Friedrich, what this queer be-wigged figure up on the wall reproaching. Thus inspired to impugn, the Führer he resumes: "What these uproarious eggheads fail to understand is, should the Anglo-Americans move in from the West—and, by God, if Ivan should ever set foot in the East—there'll be no 'Space Age', for, there'll be no Germans left to build it. As for the West, they've already begun to form beachheads—and yet, where is the Luftwaffe? Like you—absent!"

He sinks into his chair, drained or, what just put out from all the pacing. "First," he fumes. "The Luftwaffe wouldn't give me the jet-bomber I demanded. And now, now these engineers are off playing *Frau im Mond.*[402] Does

---

401 ['They': One would assume he meant the rocket.—N.B.]

402 [*Frau im Mond*, the 'Woman in the Moon': Fritz Lang film, circa 1927, which popularized the notion of travel through space.—N.B.]

anyone even listen to a word I say? He was your responsibility, Hossbach, your charge..."

Why, I can feel it go numb in the face; *ach, I never should have left them alone.* Oh, but what was I to do? I mean, I can't keep watch the whole time: I'm no Gestapo. Plus I can't hypnotize them: I'm no Führer. Hell, every time I threaten to shoot someone they persuade me what with these maps; and, oh good God, the Führer is right—half in different colors...

Now, being young and being a Hossbach you see don't exactly go hand in hand. Oh, but ach, the boy just had to go shooting off his mouth. From how I hear it, he's even begun telling jokes on the Führer; for which he's been repeatedly warned.

Thus imagining my impending impaling, I sigh as the Messerschmidt—that other 'Wonder Weapon'—comes to mind.[403] "*The swine*," I say. "He's always prattling on and on about some such nonsense's 'being good for the war'." Head down I shrink. "Like these ridiculous Fibi-nazi numbers, or something such. Oh, why doesn't he just—"

"*Wait*," he interrupts: "Do you mean *Fibonacci*?"

"Ja," I say; *pray-tell he doesn't bid me explain...*

"The Fibbonacci series is a sequence, a set. We use it in art, as well as architecture, the love of my life."

"*Actually*," I say, gaining confidence, now the F. can fill in the gaps. "He says he's this idea for a breakthrough, a discovery involving the *Two-six-two*."

"Discovery, breakthrough? Go on."

"Ja, the *Two-six-two*," I wax, mysterious, being this exhausts my knowledge of the matter at hand.

403 [The Cherry Stone, *i.e.*, 'V-1,' was a guidance-assisted missile. As previously mentioned, it was a *Luftwaffe* project. And it was indeed ready before the *A4*: Less than two weeks, in fact, after the Allied invasion. Of course, it never achieved anywhere near the precision, nor the destructive prowess, inherent in even the first, liquid fueled rockets.—N.B.]

"*Ah*," he sways, sweeping a swath of hair in, or is it out of place. "This is it—the high-speed bomber I have prophesied! Yes, I've seen it: *seen it in my dreams...*" And, here, here he grows ten feet tall, what the might of centuries towering before me. "A tactical bomber with which to fend off the second invasion![404] Go to him, Hossbach. Yes yes, tell your son, and that idiot professor, they can have whatever they want—Bormann!"

The Reichsleiter, whom I hadn't noticed on my way in, scoots past, what with ever-present zeal, and almost equally omnipresent notepad ready to hand.

"The *ME-262*," the Führer decrees. "Henceforth has highest priority.[405]" He turns, glowing. "Well, Hossbach, this is it: *the Twilight of the Gods*. No," he nods, apparently addressing a debate within. "Man does not mimic history;

404 [It is difficult to fathom what *der Führer* was trying to say. Somewhere in that addled brain lay the monomaniacal notion that Normandy wasn't the 'real thing,' but a feint: The *real* invasion, the Idiot Corporal averred, was still to come. This was a mortal mistake. A relatively minor incursion *did* occur in August, in the south of France. By then, of course, the fate of Hitlerism had already been sealed.—N.B.]

405 [This was sheer bluster. Hitler had ordered the *ME-262* to receive the highest priority as far back as January '43. Hossbach might be conflating the fact that, in May '44, *der Führer* had stumbled on the notion of converting the revolutionary fighters into *fighter-bombers*. The idea was to sink the troop transports amassing in British harbors, as well as to harass the landing craft during the early hours of any invasion. There may, or may not, be some truth in the assertion that a certain engineer's ingenious acuity had helped to make such a conversion possible. But even if he had, please keep in mind that such hybrid creatures would not be ready until the Allies were already firmly entrenched on the beaches. Further, to 'quote' Hitler, 'as any engineer knows,' such experiments entail a complex, necessarily laborious process. The engineer, indeed if he even exists, should be credited with the saving of countless Allied lives, via diverting the Hitlerites from employing a potentially war winning weapon in the role every reputable expert had prescribed, *viz.*, that of strictly a fighter.—N.B.]

rather, history mimics *him*. Yes, this is the break, this is the break for which we have been waiting. Bah, for once, for once these dreamers have done us some good. And who knows? If their invention wins out, they can call themselves General for all I care—so much the better to mock me in the open!"

Insults aside, the Führer and the rocket-men are on finally the same page. Now, anything's possible. Still he needn't repeat: *they are our last hope.*

Oh—God save the Reich!

Chapter 32: The Spy on Prinz Albrecht Strasse
(Or, A Tale of Two Heines): July 15, 1944

Albrecht, my terrier, wakes me from my study. And, ambling to the spyhole I see: the Mademoiselle, headed for the door; Hell's Bells the Gestapo didn't see her. No, she simply sashays up, and knocks. Clad in a dress I might add which must have been painted.

Honored by the courtesy[406], I unbolt the chain then stick out my trap: "Go away."

Elbowing me askance, smoke assails, shawl unfurled before I can eject her. "Seal it," she says, cigarette-holder already in hand then bids me have seat; huh, serves me right for having opened it.

"I'm calling the—"

"Pipe down," she sneers, tail aflail. "Heine and me? We're old pals."

"Himmler?" I glare. "He *loathes* you. And he'd your head, too, were it not for this spell you've managed to cast on the Chief—you, you fucking witch!"

Ach, for, thanks to this hag, I am no longer in the Boss's confidence; and why I'd give Fatty's left-arm to see her be in such straits...

"No you fool, Müller."

Heinrich Müller: the head of the Gestapo. I duck behind the curtain. No time to inquire, now's only to react. "Were you followed?" I say, peeking about.

"Ah, darling, I cannot control what they do. Ptth," she purrs, unburdening her mink, making herself that much more comfortable. "I doubt you're in very much danger." And, thrusting unladylike, she shimmies me onto the couch, emplacing her well-rounded person ever so near.

---

[406] ['courtesy': I think he means the fact that she knocked.—N.B.]

I, I can't trust myself; *oh, look at yourself—what are you* doing? Scanning I pan her breasts to her face, and so behold her mouth: that obscene, ill-painted mouth; what with lipstick like plaster of Paris. Perfume just like a French—

"Those pigs. They must be gossiping all about us by now."

My eyebrows they arch: "*Us*?"

"Oui," she purrs, stroking my thigh. "You know, you and me: our little fling; the one you're going to tell them all about. For surely you daren't tell them what's really on my mind—the real reason I've come. No my friend, that is for Wolfie's ears, *and Wolfie's ears alone*."

"Don't you dare call him that you—"

"Oh, pipe down," she haws, what this she-devil puffing smoke, the light from her cherry matching the gall in her eyes. "Of course, I'll have to tell him through proxy." She shudders, legs shut. "Would you believe? That empty-headed slut[407] seems to have developed towards me the most implacable distaste."

Gee, I wonder why...

"Ah, *Wind*, if you think you're in Adi's doghouse now, look at me," she says, swinging that arse, eyes and red-lips rekindling the fire. What with the bandana and the tricolors of the Republic. "No, much as it pains to say it—it's up to you."

"Up to what, up to who?"

"Simple," she smiles and, seeing there's something she wants, ashes on the tray rather than my newly-cleaned floor. "You must convince him make up his mind." Then, she turns ice-cold, transfixed by this far-off look in her eyes. And, and I swear, I swear she's a million kilometers away. But for the briefest moment, I'm brought to the brink of despair. For I daren't say what's *really* on my mind.

407 [Eva Braun, who had worked at Hoffman's camera shop, back when the Nazi Führer and she first met: Hence the slur to follow.—N.B.]

Her awareness having returned, the filly lets loose: "The war. The war can no longer be won through any strictly military means. The only choice is to sue for peace. Albie and the Amis have already landed, and Adi of all *people* he surely must know: you cannot fight both East and West."

"Oh, but Stalin. *Stalin*—"

"Stalin won't abide any deal: you know this yourself. Ah, but that's no cause for alarm. Oui, I shall just bring my friends in Washington around. Ah," she chuckles; a forced guffaw. "As you know, I've friends in highest places."

"Ach," I suffer, knocking back a mostly-whiskey-partly-sour. "Why don't you just tell him yourself?"

She kicks off her heels, oh, and then what I damned nearly eye-hump her. Having thus enveloped me in her power, she seethes: "Aren't you listening? It's like I said: he won't *see* me. No, that hussy, that hussy of his won't let him. Believe me Hossbach: I know a thing or two of women."

I doubt that very much...

"Let me tell you," she smiles, glove-less hand caressing my face, whiskey-cum-cock adumbrating her breath. "That little camera slut's kicked me to the curb: to the detriment of our great nations. Ah, but blast—blast this stupid war!" She knocks back a glass of Madeira, the which somehow I seem to've fetched. "Wolfie's a stranger in his very own land, out of touch with what's going on beyond his own narrow ken. Meantime, the likes of Himmler, Himmler and that damned little club-foot[408] , they're ruining everything—everything *I* have built."

Why I ought to slug her. "I see," I say, delaying such gratification. "And this Müller, the head of the 'stapo? *He* is the one I am to conspire with, so's to get the Führer to toe *your* line? We shall see—we shall see about that!"

---

[408] [*i.e.*, Goebbels.—N.B.]

I make's if to put in a call to FHQ; *oh, but really—I'm going to do it.* It's just, my nerves. I drop the receiver before the call can be put; or, perhaps I've merely thought better.

Face-flush she shrieks, "*Goebells*: he means deceive his Führer."

"Away with you," I lunge, grabbing her wrist. "Away with you what with your witcheries."

Her face dissolves into a seething mass of confusion. Then, she breaks down, affecting to cry, saying through simulated tears: "I didn't do it for country, king, or Führer: I did it for the *New Man*."

She begins to pace, tracking mud all over my newly-cleaned floor, chain-smoking black-market cigarettes to boot. Act accomplished, she turns. "And what have you done, hmm? A desk-bound General who conspires in secret: in secret with yours truly. Worse," she stares, sultry tone shifting to rocky-strained staccato. "The rapist can't tell Wolfie's friends from his foes."

Nobody talks to me like that...

To my feet I flail, "And which are you?"

Stunned, she says, "*It's too late*," rolling her eyes, teeth puncturing ever-bloodless lips.

Seizing her I demand, "*What* did you say?"

"Unhand me," she squirms, what damned near taking my arm. "The past is past: *let it be.* Oui, for I know Wolfie's mission's no other. It is my punishment, for, I did not bring him up right. Ah, I was so filled with vengeance, vengeance for you and your kind. Even your rape was but a pittance, a pittance I say to what you did to *him*. He was your best friend, Hossbach. Really, how could you? Ah, but he was too good—he was too good for you all! So, so you shot him, right, cut him down: *and so ends the life of England's best and brightest.* Then, then I met *him*. A real Mordskirl.[409] Early thirties, six years my senior. He showed

409 [*Mordskirl*: lit. 'lady killer'.—N.B.]

me Berlin: and I showed him the world. Of course it didn't hurt I'd an inheritance to run through. *Poor Jack.* He died with nothing. His patents however earned millions, allowing me to place Wolfie to power. For he was the coming man. Everybody said so."

And I am tempted to say a thing or two about the only good Frenchman: but more practical things obtain. "So, what now?"

"Call Berlin. Get Müller: tell him *I* say you are to be taken off the list."

"List, what list?"

The rusted cunt, why, she simply sashays out, escaping from her crimes one more time. Oh, but ach; for the Führer you see's forbidden me act against her. And, after all—who am *I* to op-pose *him*?

***

The Führer isn't speaking to me, owing to this business with Jack. I have my new adjutant run a check on the Mademoiselle's 'friend' in the 'stapo. Oh, if I can only find out what they're up to, he'll have no *choice* but to hear me through. For, in war, the darnedest things oft transpire. The Girl's right: he must *choose*. Ach, for, why things they simply cannot go on. And *I*, unlike that stupid slut, care not whether it's Stalin or the Old Man and the Drunk, but, somehow, *peace it must obtain.*

I rack my mind whom to consult, stifling the terrible certainty welling up within. You know, when it just peers out the corner your mind and says, 'The truth's been before you all along'; and, that is—*we are out of options...*

For, as Reynolds, I believe, reminds me: "These days, one must face the unvarnished truth: only *one man* can get you something on Müller."

And so, taking my life in my hands, I go to see: *Himmler.*

Hohenlychen: July 16, 1944

Hohenlychen's a mansion[410], just like any other: tawdry and grand all the same; *huh, just like Himmler.* His batman's[411] a nice enough sort. We trade barbs at the expense of the War Academy. It's good getting a refresher from one so endowed with youth, yet so proper in bearing.

He leads me through this Olympian gallery, what walkway and wall studded with painting and statuesque. Of Greek Gods, Nordic heroes and Pan nymphs they vie for one's attention amidst all the spacious splendor.

To me, it's clutter—oh, what is it the Führer calls it, an 'overdose of art'. For it bespeaks of poverty of the artistic sense. Lacking any appreciation for quality, Himmler's made up for it via the rubric of sheer number. Oh, but it's all wrong, cobbled together like some peasant's idea of the inscrutable. I keep this to myself, smiling whilst mouthing meaningless affectations: a trick I learned at *OKW.*

Alas I'm led to see Himmler, entering a study as wooden and stuffy as the pedant himself. Refusing the trap of a drink, as per Schmidtie's[412] instructions, I do accept a rather fine cigar. Calm, as though I haven't a care, I relate my suspicions concerning the Mademoiselle, insinuating innuendo whilst making sure to mention nothing too specific. I see fit remind him how she and Bormann'd slipped off to that conference with the Chief, as if someone'd forced him rather at the point of a gun.

410 [I suspect the General of being facetious: Hohenlychen is a sanatorium. Himmler's private dwellings might have been 'tawdry and grand,' but, a mansion? I discount the idea that any objective observer could have considered them anything such.—N.B.]

411 ['batman': Perhaps his adjutant, Grothmann, or Macher.—N.B.]

412 [Or, Reynolds?—N.B.]

He eyes me skeptic. I, I'm not quite sure I'm painting it right. Still, he must see: the Führer's well-being's my main concern.

"That's true," he says upon hearing me out. "I've suspected that Jezebel for quite some time. But, *the Führer*," he cringes. "The Führer won't allow me to act. We've had the same discussion regarding Bormann. The upshot is, *USA*[413] trusts them implicit. Herr General," he drones, drumming his nails into the desk. "I will let you in on a great secret."

Inclining his head the Reichsführer draws near:

"Bormann and the Madmeoiselle are part of this 'radio game',[414] a scheme devised to trick the partisans into their own extermination. But, much to my chagrin, the Führer has ordered me beg off. "

"Then I should like to take part in these 'games' too. After all," I say. "Every spy needs a spy, huh?"

Gaily he smiles; *Himmler's in his element.* "Now you see," he exhales, a weak sister decompressing. "How difficult's *my* job. I will provide you a shadow for your protection. Of course, the whole thing must be done with the Führer's permission; I shall obtain it. Meantime, tell no one, okay, not even the Chief; for secretaries too have ears. Speaking of which, we must keep it from Bormann as well, being he too's under investigation." He smiles, and what I daresay almost looks comely. "I'm having dinner with the Boss tonight: I'll bring it up then." Suddenly he turns, looking at me what with these cold soulless eyes and says, "Have you reason to believe he is in any danger?"

"Yes," I nod. "Yes sir I do."

"Then, go, go await the Gabell girl: I've business with her myself; you can catch up with her later. Meantime,

---

[413] ['USA' *(Oo-es-ah)*: Another name for Shitler, as previously mentioned.—N.B.]

[414] ['Radio Game': My translation for *Funkspiel*, about which little is known, outside Hossbach's allegations regarding Himmler.—N.B.]

I'll petition the Chief to deputize you to take part in these 'radio games'. You know Hossbach, her dossier's *this* thick."

He says this with menacing, oh what almost Asiatic eyes, searching me out for evidence of guilt; and finding the none. Oh, but ach, he probably knows it all anyway. The which can only help, seeing he too wants to keep up the charade.

"It's just, the *Führer*," he—begs? "The Führer won't allow me make use of it. Says her file should be made to just 'disappear'."

I almost forgot: Monique represents Vichy.[415] Her arrest would impede the work of the *LVF*,[416] her creation, desperately slugging it out in the East.

"Um, but *sir*," I probe, stifling this lump in back of my throat. "I was hoping to have a little... talk, a little talk with regard to this 'friend' of the Madmeoiselle: a certain General *Müller*—"

"Tiny,[417] the head of the 'stapo?"

"The very one."

"Now see here," he chides, pupils receding. "You best leave *that* one alone. Trust me: the SS will vet him.[418]

---

415 [*Vichy*: Collaborationist France, under the stewardship of Marshal Petain, hero of the First World War. By late July, Paris had been lost. Currying the favor of Vichy, even at this late hour, was apparently still high on the Nazis' list.—N.B.]

416 [LVF, *Legion of French Volunteers against Bolshevism*: The *LVF* had been amalgamated into the *Charlemagne* division of the Waffen-SS. The former had been due to return to France in a matter of hours, then subsequently found itself attached to the *4th SS Police Division*, in a desperate struggle to stave off the destruction of Army Group Center.—N.B.]

417 [re, 'Tiny': Being every other Jerry's named Heinrich, the moniker was bestowed upon Herr Müller, the diminutive chief of the Gestapo.—N.B.]

418 [One might say, 'Of *course* the SS vetted him: He was Chief of the Gestapo.' But Müller had been throwing Nazis in prison, back when Hitler was still a tramp. It appears he had been 'acquired' more than vetted.—N.B.]

And, should there be any evidence of treason, I will act like lightning." He seems to be considering something, then changes his tune. "In any event *Herr General*, it would be helpful if you were to keep an eye on this Müller. Just a little chat. Then, once you have something—and, and I mean, something I can really *use*, something I can take to the Chief and say, '*Mein Führer*—here Herr Müller's head!'—then, only *then*, you are to report back to me."

***

So, it looks like *I* will be watching *him*; and, someone, in turn, me; *and so on, ad-infinitum*. Pah, policemen! Still, in the good old days, those of battling the Reds in the street, a police state was good for Germany. That it tends to breed an atmosphere of mistrust is one thing, what in the midst of civil war; for, there, one doesn't know whom to trust as is. Only, this, this is a fight for our existence. It's imperative we stick together. Ach, for experience you see's served to show such tactics only serve to mitigate all sense of initiative. Moreover the armed forces become secretive in their dealings with the civilians. Soon, a kangaroo court holds sway over the nation, just like the Summer of 1918. The only thing preventing that is—we've the Führer; would to God nothing should happen to him.

At night, I receive a call from Himmler, authorizing me to proceed.

Prinzalbrecht Strasse
July 17, 1944

I'm on my way to Müller, the imp who cannot be trusted. Even as Schmidtie, or, Reynolds, that is[419], taxis

[419] ['Reynolds' had by this time taken 'Schmidtie' 's place as batman, or aide-de-camp. Hossbach has left us no information with regard to either, probably for their own protection. Suffice it to say, Reynolds was possibly often as not referred to by the moniker.—N.B.]

onto the Albrecht, in my mind's eye I keep seeing that bitter old chap. The Gestapo Chief's no alt-fighter; *ach, I remember him well.* Why he's the swine who bade them open fire, when we marched in to clean up that shithole.[420] Still, he's paid his dues, else the Führer wouldn't have him. Yes, that hall of mirrors really does inspire such types, for it breathes the spirit to life. More disconcerting's the fact Tiny's a line to the enemy the drop of a hat. For his is a game of half-truths and lies, a world where nothing's ever as it seems. It does not appeal to me.

Now, no one ever *wants* to arrive at Gestapo Headquarters. Embarking outside the ridiculous art-deco facade, I soothe myself with the knowledge that I come as an envoy from on-high. Negotiating doors of fine plated glass, I'm dwarfed by the ceiling[421] of this ex-school of arts and crafts. Head held high, a pretty little filly directs me to the anteroom where I am to wait. I'd requested this meeting, ostensibly to go over 'Total War' allocations, in coordination with *OKW.* Of course, my real intention's to sniff his arse, and see if he can be trusted.

Chasing me out from my slumber, the duty-guard relieves me my sidearm—which, dammit, it's my right's an officer to carry—while another begs me walk this-way. We come to a door, the which my companion duly proceeds to open when, once inside, he slams it shut behind. Oh, but ach, my shadow's neglected to tarry. Then it hits me: *someone's pulled a* Schweinerei. The voice in my head continues: 'Himmler and Müller're in cahootz; you will be shot within the hour.'

Rather Herr Müller himself looks up from his desk to greet me.

"Heil, Heil Hitler," I say and rise. Not that I should. Swine's kept me waiting nearly an hour.

---

420 [In March '33, shortly after Hitler first came to power.—N.B.]

421 [re, ceiling: Vaulted.—N.B.]

"Stay, stay. Sit, sit," he huffs in dark, staccato tones; hmm, must be an Austrian. What with the foppish hat. And the eyes, these cold stainless eyes. Why he looks just like some back-alley detective. Shuffling his papers he grins: "Let's get to it. Here is the report you have requested: every-other able-bodied man to be called up. Curfews detailed page twelve. Pensions for widows to be disbursed through the office of the *Reichsbank*, in coordination with Dr. Funk. Questions?" he gazes, grumpy, what the malaise of bureaucracy seeming sapped him of all zest for life.

Rather he's alert as a viper. And, I, sensing this, choose my next words according: "Very well Herr, ach, I mean, *General* Müller. Now we've sunk our teeth in it, things should go a lot smoother rounding up the swine that still lurk in our midst."

"Swine?" he says, as if not comprehending. "What *swine*?"

"Why," I say. "It's all in Goebbels' plan. You know: secure the men for the front, then the undesirables will be dealt with in a later *Aktion*."[422]

"Is that what you think, this is some sort of *Aktion*?" Gestapo Man he smiles, clearly amused. Striking a match, the flame thereof grabs my wandering mind when, violent, he shakes it, leaving naught but the burning embers of sulfur to hang in the air. "*That* my friend's how an *Aktion* is run."

"I see," I say, too much sarcasm. "Good to know."

He laughs, as if I've just scored a point. "Very good, Herr General—very good! *Two can play that game.* Say there exists a certain very powerful man. Now, now this man, this man he wants to defect, say, to the Ivans." His eyes they dart towards mine. The stupefied look on my face proves just the reaction he requires. Satisfied he continues: "Now, this man, this man of necessity would need to be on

[422] [*Aktion*: Operation. In Nazi terms, a roundup or assault, often with sinister implications.—N.B.]

good terms with the Russians. Even the *Maquis*." He glares, a tiger eying its prey. "You see where I'm getting?"

I most certainly do not.

"Good," he responds to the silence, pacing behind his desk. "So, you are not so easily led: that will come in handy in your new line of work."

My face it seems to've lost all sense of color. Still, thank God, he deigns not to take note. Piping smoke, through a well-practiced maneuver he exhales. "*Fascinating*, isn't it?"

"Um, sir?"

"I said, it's fascinating. Fascinating how the Commies really aren't so much unlike us."

Huh?

"For instance, take me. Some poor swine stuck in his desk, missing some excitement in his life. Such a man would be perfectly placed to realize the inefficiencies in our system: in our politics, economics; hell, even decisions being made at the front. The Russian? He's done *away* with all that. Stalin *is* the Party. He *is* the State. And he is Commander in Chief in time of war. Yet what do we have, hmm? A 'war lord' devoid of all power, owing to a bunch of ignoramuses who wish to fight this war by themselves? The Goebbelses, the Görings and Himmlers—are they there, out at the front? Heavens no. They know where their bread's well-buttered!"

His mounting enervation's nearly escaped me. For it takes all I have just to keep from saying, 'Ja—at Horcher's!'[423]

My interlocutor continues: "They know how to feed their fat little faces!"

Amidst the shock, I realize: *'The swine, he hasn't* once *mentioned Bormann; nor the Mademoi—'*

---

[423] [*Horcher*: Berlin restaurant, whose closing had been imminent, due to austerities necessitated by 'Total War.' Göring had it kept open, as a Luftwaffe fief, on his own authority.—N.B.]

"Truly," he says, an excess of perfume overwhelming cheap cigar. "We've much to learn from the Russians. Of course her people are inferior—but so what? Each of us have sought to become free from the yoke of Jewish capital; and, by God, each of us has done just that. *Spiritual Communism*, Hossbach: *Spiritual Communism*'s much to offer. Stalin really is a great man. A man I wouldn't mind working for myself, if things should ever really get rough. Oh—but what was I saying? Surely the *Führer* wants to hear only rosy things from his trusty Hossbach. Oh, but that's right: 'Trusty Hossbach' wasn't so trusty after all. Not since that whole *Güntzler* business."

Oh my God...

"Old man—don't mess with the Gestapo! It is *we* who've saved this country; *we* who've cleaned out the riffraff, locked up the defeatists and Jews. Does not the *Führer* not trust my every word? Isn't it getting rather late? And hadn't you best be getting back to Himmler so you can make your report?"

Rising I rasp, "*Good day*," omitting the Heil Hitler. The swine; for, he doesn't deserve to hear it.

Chapter 33: Highjinks and High Theatre at MHQ

July 18, 1944[424]

"*Raid*," spat the sentry, at Monique's, what some rundown ramshackle on an abandoned lake, previously owned by the Ministry for Public Works. Her 'hut', the which surely she considers of anything shy of a mansion is, in reality but a well-fortified, secretly-prospective FHQ. A place 'her Hitler' can tough it out, if things should ever really get rough; her peculiar form of loyalty to the Chief who, in a fit of sentiment, she'd once likened her protege.

It seems the Boss has no idea the place even exists. Her omission stems from a certain narrow-mindedness concerning the Röhm purge back in 'Thirty-four. Why, rumor has it, Papen'd gone there to hide until the dust had settled; not before his secretary, though, bought it.[425]

Her 'government quarters' was supposed to have been a gift for 'Herr Hitler,' as he was known at the time. Oh, perhaps she was just waiting to tell him; you know, 'waiting just for the right moment'. Ach, the problem you see with people like that is, they think they're always number one. Such nonentities it seems have conspired to say nothing with regard to her little 'hut'.[426] And, now, now her precious France's about to 'liberated', what by a bunch of Limeys and Coons.

---

[424] This chapter has been cobbled from carefully compiled memoranda, recorded during the relevant portions of the trial.[—W.H.] [*i.e.*, Seidl lent him his copy.—N.B.]

[425] ['secretary': Doctor Jung, a hired gun in the employ of Weimar. Two other secretaries likewise 'bought it,' during the Röhm Purge in '34. Papen, their master, survived. The latter, who gave Hitler the keys to the kingdom, has been included, along with the rest of the 'war criminals,' currently awaiting the results of their trial.—N.B.]

[426] But *I* intend to change all that.[—W.H.] [The 19th, *i.e.*, the very next day, appears to have marked Hossbach's first acquaintance with 'MHQ'. Whether he ever told Hitler is anybody's guess. Nonetheless the episode seems to have permeated his subconscious. Indeed, the defendant is so deep in trance that, vicariously reliving the scene, he has made it a priority to tell *der Führer* about its hitherto undetected existence. Of course, Shitler's been dead for over a year.—N.B.]

Head-band on she stormed, springing from the sparring-room to the tele-funken, “I'm coming up,” whispered then, cape on, what with the one-piece and that lipstick rouge, attended her mascara in Bunker Number Three.

This being done she entered the lift. Fiendishly working the last bit her cigarette she rose, then came to a stop about twenty meters from the living room in the east.[427] Extinguishing her accomplice[428], she approached the outermost door. Chrome-stemmed valves, three side by side, were unscrewed by her 'seamen'; or, at least, that's how she'd adumbrated them.

The decompression chamber it roared, scurrying them through the chute. With angst she awaited her guard to overtake her, so's to lead her to the hatch. Exiting which they entered upon a bucket of rusty nails and smell of the auto-pool; alas the garage. With wireless[429] her seamen then opened the outermost door.

“Keys,” the older, a swarthy looking chap he uttered, then ushered her to the Peugot. Breakneck they raced for the gate when, a flash of light; windows they flared; a Mercedes came crashing, flashing government plates as though they were the last thing still untouched by this war.

Alas a tint coming off the sun revealed one Walter Schellenberg when, behind him, dogs they barked, flashlights they blared: the *Reichsführer-SS* approached; what his Schellenberg obediently in toe.

Scarcely they'd managed gain Gate One, than the black Peugot arrived. Out backseat she strut, hair all bunned-up sauntering out in nothing but bra and panties. It

---

427 A jet-lift had been installed by a member of the *Polytech*.[—W.H.] [No comment.—N.B.]

428 [He meant cigarette.—N.B.]

429 [He means 'wireless switch.'—N.B.]

must've been a quick strip; clearly, precautions they *do* come in hand.

Now, Himmler he took but one look at this well-preserved twat then, fixed Schellenberg a glance. The puritanical Reichsführer sheepishly gazed, seeking avert her form when, scratching his head, he mumbled, "*Madame*, I am so sorry, so sorry to *bother* you but, I, that is, *we...*" He fidgeted, ratcheting overly-manicured nails; then, after a torturous interminable, shrieked: *"The Spaniard!"*

The Mademoiselle she massaged her neck, freeing-up tensions whilst her whole body resolved into one amorphous spasm. Why, her fully-formed arse assaulted the very air, lilting hips in vilest embrace. With her eyes she rebuked him, what with the most shameless distaste. Then, thrusting, she unleashed her locks, plucked with ever-titillating precision and, pursing those hips, lascivious of intent, Monique released her scent.

Alas the energy-field into which Himmler the High Priest stared presented its challenge; he said nothing.

Schellenberg he raged, "We know all about your little partner—or, should I say—your little Gonz!"

Himmler he aped, "Ja—your little Gonz!" attempting affect modernity, so the better mock her licentiousness.

"Ech," she sneered. "Blow it out your hind. You daren't arrest me: Adi'd never allow it."

"No," Himmler he hummed, bored by the temerity of her capture and so taken to filing his nails. "That's true: I would never do that; I'm afraid however Herr Schellenberg here hasn't the slightest compunction. Bah, it seems he hasn't the scruples that I've."

The barrel-chested lout in horned-rims stepped forth. Seizing the Mademoiselle, he lead her to the bedroom. The Reichsführer he sheepishly stood by, listening. The guards they positioned themselves around the perimeter. A roadblock consisting of empty SD cars

Himmler'd had commandeered surrounded them, blocking the most obvious means of escape.

Schellenberg he looked her over. "*Nice legs*," he rasped, then belted her just for good measure.

Himmler had heard the outpouring of wrath, and so'd judged it to be authentic.

She fixed Schellenberg what with those insolent impudent eyes and said, "The Führer will have your head, you ignorant, impotent man. You've no idea *why* you've so many intelligence agencies now, do you? To investigate each other! *Oui*; that's how Wolfie and I thought of it." The viper, she smiled.

Schellenberg he must've been dying, what to just keep from going to stitches; for, he knew he had to keep up the charade. A real gut-buster, though, it makes but just one sound. The which proved revolting to Himmler who, progressively nauseated, inched farther away from the door.

Falling to her knees, the accursed Frenchie regurgitated all over Schellenberg's newly-shined shoes.[430] Quiet, through puke-bespattered lips, she spake: "*Tell him Gonz's been turned; it'll buy us much-needed time.*" Then, revealing her blood-stained bicuspid, she said, *"Please,"* collapsing to the floor.

Upon receiving the all-clear strode Himmler, for once having mustered some courage—albeit the 'among-an-unconscious-dame' sort—before, alas, the shrinking violet he turned to bay. The poor sot; why, he must've realized he had to help Schellenberg carry the body.

"Is she, um... you know?"

"*Nein*," the General he boasted, what with such equable calm; the opposite of Himmler. Toothish he grinned, "Quite cooperative, really." Now, this sort of thing simply plays havoc with poor Himmler's stomach; and Herr Schellenberg knows it. "Says Gonz's been turned, 'one

---

430 The swine: he should've been wearing boots instead.[—W.H.]

of the Abwehr's best assets'. Swears Canaris will vouch for her."

"*Canaris?*" the Reichsführer he seized, seized like a snake, upon the which has just been stepped. "Quickly. Take the Mademoiselle to Hohenlychen. Get Grabitz, then set her up in hospital." Then he began to stutter, suffering from some nameless fear. "Watch her—yes yes, watch her and, by Zeus—*Canaris!* Yes, I've had my eye on him for quite some time. But, but what if," he fidgeted. "What if something should ever go wrong?" He stared, tufts of light bouncing off the queerest of gaze. Why it's simply impossible to read Himmler's eyes, clouded as they are beneath that stupid pince-nez; which, come to think of it, perhaps isn't so stupid at all. "Schellenberg," he persisted in his panic. "If something should happen to the Mademoiselle—*it will be your funeral.* Of course, I'd let you escape; say, Zuerich. But, but first, first you must take her to Hohenlychen. Oh and—and get Grabitz!" He kept repeating himself, fishing for something to say. "Now, not one word. Not one word till the girl's made a complete recovery."

The driver he took them to Hohenlychen, the 'rest clinic' where Himmler's built his own fucking castle what like some medieval knight, simply to rival his Chief. Hours they passed, the whole while wondering whether she was going to make it; alas, the stupid slut, she finally pulled through.

The General[431] advised that now would be a good time to get her to talk.

"Too much exertion," Grabitz warned. "Could prove fatal."

Gathering the good doctor in his slippery grasp, Himmler he marched off, leaving Schellenberg to 'interrogate' the prisoner; which, of course, gave them time to corroborate their stories.

---

431 ['The General': Apparently, Schellenberg.—N.B.]

Still, the Mademoiselle'd lost a good deal of blood. Her cheeks swollen, with what could only be a dull, lifeless pain, somewhere, somewhere in back her mind, Monique must have been conscious as to her plan. Ach, for, the stupid slut it seems she always has one; the difficulty lay rather in working one out.

***

Oh, how she must yearn for revenge on the man who, it seems, had clearly exceeded the bounds of their agreement. Yes, whether via the Maquis[432], or, her tendrils in the Gestapo, why one thing's for sure: *Monique is going to get even...*

---

[432] [re, 'the Maquis'] Indiscriminate murderers of both soldier *and* civilian.[—W.H.] [Today they are known as freedom fighters, *i.e.*, the 'French Resistance.' I should also point out that, by the last paragraph, Hossbach appears to have put down his notes, and gone back into trance: Hence the resumption of the present tense.—N.B.]

PART III
VALKYRIE

Chapter 34: Bombshell

Recovery Wing at Hohenlychen: July 19, 1944[433]

The doctors were baffled. Next, confused. Then, alas overjoyed upon her 'miraculous recovery' pursuant upon Schellenberg's brutal beating. So much in fact she chanced lure some poor swine into recovery. All it took was a bit of undress. Then this frenzied, frenetic—cheer?[434]

She had lain prostrate, compressing those buxom bulbous boobs into her mouth. "So *sore,*" she'd oozed, shiny bracelets dangling from tumescent skin. Then, Abercrombie, beguiled by the scent—that veiled, voluptuous scent—could hold himself back no more; instant he fell upon her.

"*Whore*," he raved, after going to Milan, moistening her mons what with his beastly maw.

She laughed.

"Jezebel!"

She smiled; no, *dared* him.

Perhaps it was then he realized: 'Hmm... must be a Frenchie.'

The Sergeant had once been reprimanded for having run an unlicensed brothel. Just a few girls. Very good breeding. Only, Himmler you see he wasn't getting his cut; for, it had not the imprimatur of the *SS*.

---

433 [Instruction to the editor] What transpired prior to my coming on the scene became a matter of record during the course of the trial; Seidl wants you to make this more clear.[—W.H.] [Done, via the use of sectional headings, three asterisks, *&c.*—N.B.]

434 [re, 'cheer': Apparently, arising from the rest of recovery. Or so at least claims the 'investigation' the Gestapo had mounted.—N.B.]

Once, he had been part of an elite unit which, like a pelican, in having shed its blood, hath used it to save the Germanic people. Now, he was in gaol—*in gaol with the Mademoiselle...*

"But, a man has needs—"

"*Back,*" she warned, pitchforks in her eyes.

But it was no use.

Instant he shushed, "*It'll all be over soon,*" jacking her knickers then sliding inside her war-weary twat...

***[435]

Proudly Himmler he gives me a tour his fief. Hmm, seems Hohenlychen's a hospital its own; the which we're about to enter.

Now, hospitals you see they give me the creeps, what since that whole Foerster business; *ach, the Müller Question will just have to wait.* Yes, for, there's simply too many people. Besides, knowing Himmler,[436] some invalid in his bed's probably but one more tool of the 'stapo.

Ambulating through the infirmary, we reach the gaol wing of the hospital. The smell of bleach assaults when, smug, he thrusts the door askance, making a sweeping gesture; when we come upon the scene: what some pimple-faced subaltern—climbing all over the Mademoiselle.

"*What is this?*" he rasps, in what passes for the Reichsführer as rage.

"I—but, sir!" he froths, rising to greet his superior, yet struggling to keep his pants up just the same. "Sir I, I am so *sorry* she, *she tricked me*; tricked me and tried seduce me."

Himmler he comports himself as the tenderly father; the which himself he surely must see. You know, the

---

435 [Here is where he 'comes upon the scene.' See note above.—N.B.]

436 [Himmler was technically Müller's superior. On occasion they were forced to collaborate. Hence Hossbach's reticence in bringing the latter to 'Old Four Eyes' ' attention.—N.B.]

Prussian—hell, could be a farmer were it not for this war; and, raising a hand, stings: "*Silence*."

Why, one could but hear the drop of a pin.

"Trust me," he says, turning to that thing, that foul odious thing; by which I mean the Mademoiselle: "*Everything is going to be alright.*" He hands her his kerchief, so's to wipe away the tears. "Answer me honest, I swear: I swear no harm will come. Now—did you willingly have relations with this man?"

She stabs the Sergeant a look; oh, but ach, her tears are manufactured. The fact this filly doesn't spit in his face, just means he's become target for her malice; *and I fear for that man...*

Himmler, however, does not. "*Feldwebel*,"[437] he returns. "Being you're Army I've no jurisdiction. Were you SS, I'd liquidate you myself."

"*Reichsführer*," I say, trying to stay strong; for, *duty calls.* "Reichsführer," I repeat, and why I don't know what's come over me. "This swine here's no Army. I know him myself: *one of Goebbels' men.* Ach, I bet that uniform isn't even real."

Himmler seems miffed. "Someone, please: *take out the trash*."

Arms a-flail, the poor sot's led off; followed by a report a few moments later. Of course, it goes without saying: why, I've never seen the sonofabitch in my whole life...

"You may leave," adds Himmler, what like some priest pronouncing benediction upon the startled Mademoiselle. Yes for, it seems, she's no longer needed for questioning; or, for that matter, any medical reason soever. "Should you have need of anything, anything that is, you've only get in touch with Herr Hossbach."

Like a lizard he darts those squeamish black dots called eyes; then, comporting himself towards the

[437] [*Feldwebel*: Staff Sergeant.—N.B.]

Mademoiselle, smiles: "We Germans really are a *good* sort. It's a shame this had to befall you. My dear, the Aryan's no savage, rather, but a rational, purpose-driven man. That we can be barbaric only speaks to our virtue: for one must have courage to dare. But *this*... this is simply outrageous."

***

The Reichsführer's commissioned me provide her with funds, from an account already marked for such purposes. Of course, Monique's more money than God. I don't think it's bribery so much as a gesture.

"Another passenger, Schmidtie," I inform my batman, whose name I believe's Reynolds; he grants me the indulgence. Therefore we sit, Monique and I in back[438] my Mercedes[439] and say: *nothing.*

Still, as ever with a slit, the silence doesn't last; a quarrel thus ensues. "I can't believe you are friends with, with that *man.*"

"Huh? Why he just saved you from a brute. Really, you ought to show a little respect."

"We'*spect*?" she chides, angling out *my* window, like a factory puffing smoke. "Is that what you call it, grinding us under your Nazi boot?"

"But—but you live in a mansion!"[440]

"Well," she ashes; as though this were an answer. Then, locking eyes, she begs: "Ah, *Wind*, I need this, um, *favor*..."

Now, ordinarily you see, I'd act on the wisdom of ages, and shut my ears the instant she opened her trap; yet *this* order comes from on-high. "No problem," I blanch. "The Reichsführer insists I should see to your every need."

---

[438] I did not chance take my usual seat up front. Indeed, for, I gathered: 'This slut's probably pretty good with a garrotte.'[—W.H.]

[439] Note to any would-be auditors, re, my Mercedes: a personal gift from the Chief.[—W.H.]

[440] [her 'government quarters': Dilapidated on the outside, a fortress within.—N.B.]

What like some reciprocating fucking engine, again she exhales: “It's about Jack...”

Oh—*donnerwetter, nochmal!*

She stretches those stork-like legs, annexing my partition in back. In so doing she heaves a great big sigh; probably a ploy to reveal more cleavage. “I simply *must* see him.”

Escaping the confines my harness, I remain firm; I mean, I've seen it all before. “You *know* I can’t do that.”

“*Ptth*,” she sneers, shifting tactics, as well with her bra. “You don't have to: here, just give him this from me.”

She hands me an envelope; oh, but ach—I can feel the noose approach. Uncomprehending I stare. I mean it would be ungentlemanly to open it. Well, then so be it—*I* shall be a brigand for the Führer!

She makes a mock-effort so to stop me. Why, it's almost as if, with each step, I'm falling deeper and deeper into her trap. I can see myself doing it; only, can't quite get myself to stop. With one arm I hold her back; while, with the other, retrieve my service light. Then, then I behold but one word: *Valkyrie*.

Why, I can feel it go weak in the knees; *thank God I'm in back.* My shoulders they droop, what my head along with them. I try not to shake, affecting rather elicit some semblance of speech, midst the myriad ravings inflicting my desperate mind: “*How long?*”

“Three years,” she stares, gazing out the window, what through the smoke. “For surely you did not think *I* would betray *my* country.”

“But what, but what about the Führer? Really, after all he’s done for us—”

“Us?”

"For, *for Germany.*[441] Why you yourself once worked for the day when the Messiah himself would appear; thence to lead the Germanic peoples. And, in the Führer, you found the one who embodies this."

"Used to. Look around," she nods, as we drive past what used to be a development. "What do you see?"

My head it droops: "Destroyed; completely and utterly, destroyed..."

"Pfft," she sneers. "*That* is only a symptom: *I* see what's behind. Policemen like Himmler; scoundrels such as Goebbels; morphia-fiends like Göring. Not to mention Bormann, the toad."

"So, you know all the gang—what are you sleeping with them, too?"

It's too late to prevent her claws from claiming my skin; morose I thrust her askance. "Pah, Schmidtie—ach, Reynolds—drive!"

Rounding on the Mademoiselle, I speak: "That was quite low of me. Still—*you would betray the Führer?* No, this time—this time, you've gone too far! I shall show this letter, this treason, to Himmler. Only, I shall say, 'I found it lying in the street'. But, but first, first you must tell me what this 'Valkyrie' means—oh, don't play dumb with me! Why, I've seen it some place before; and I don't mean the opera.[442] Yes, I've even made inquiries myself. And it must be something huge, seeing no one's ever gotten back to me. Well, what is it? What are you and your cowardly compatriots planning? Little worker's revolt, hmm? Act of sabotage, yes? Well then—out with it!"

---

441 ['Germany': The German here reads *Germania*. Being the latter is either meaningless, or, in my experience, given to the grossest speculation among the English speaking peoples, I have rendered it as such. Its provenance has been reduced to this note. This ought to rule out all but the most perspicacious, for whom alone such clarification indeed is intended.—N.B.]

442 [re, 'opera': *The Flight of the Valkyries*, by Richard Wagner.—N.B.]

"*It's over*; why kill any more innocents, just to stave off the inevitable?"

"I said the word!"

Silence.

"Reynolds," I scream, attempting out-do his revving the engine. "There's been a change in plan: take us to the *Albrecht*. Yes, for I've a hundred pound package: *just for the Gestapo.*"

She snorts, what with a sultry, defiant tone: "Just do it."

"Scratch that," I say, indicating a corner of the Tiergarten. "Idle there."

Being she's called my bluff, to the Mademoiselle I return. "You may be under the protection of the Reichsführer but, so help me, you vile slut, you, if word should ever get back—I mean it! If one word should ever get back that this word, this word means something untoward then, then I shall have no choice but to turn you in to the—I said stop! Okay, this is it—this is your last chance: *explain to me this word.* Why, I swear, I swear I'll try to find some way for you to see our boy."

I'm bluffing, of course. Only, when I said it, I really did mean it; *huh, seems the Mademoiselle's rubbing off.*

But she says: "I have no clue: it was given me by a stranger. *Oui*," she stretches and, from what I can tell, begins playing footsies with Schmidtie. "He tracked me down on the Wilhelmstrasse, coming out of the Embassy. He must have put two and two together, and thus figured I was in the know. It was theatrical, really. Plus, plus I was hoping Jack might know a thing or two about it. So, *oui*, the opera—oh, oh how he loved it when he was a boy!"[443] She begins to sob. "I *so* just wanted to be a good mum. The word? I couldn't care less. I just want, I just need—ah, I simply *must* see him!"

---

[443] [The opera, re, my 'loving it': She would have been the last to have had any clue.—N.B.]

I don't believe it. Still, emotion tinged with doubt conspires so's to disable my judgment; like an engineer an army its defenses. "I shall check with the Reichsführer. But, please, let it be nothing bad—else you shall have to answer to the Gestapo."

Monique's Villa, on the Outskirts of the City

Rerouting Good Reynolds, we return to 'The Hut'. Where, upon entering, I whisper something in his ear. He sets off, leaving me alone with the disreputable debutante; we engage in idle chat.

He arrives some twenty minutes later, accompanied by two guards: Leutnants Gabriel, and Coyle, on loan from the *Polizei*.[444] I have their colleagues placed around the perimeter. Truth is, I jokingly refer to the place as 'MHQ'; i.e., *Mademoiselle's Headquarters*. By such disposition however I intend to prove who's really in charge.

Now, I've business to attend at *OKW*.[445] For, despite what they say at *OKH*,[446] we've been desperately trying to

---

444 [*Polizei*: Police.—N.B.]

445 [OKW ('Oh Ka Vay'): Unfortunately, I must reiterate, being the whole course of the trial has been marred by confusion with regard to the term: *OKW*, or Armed Forces High Command, was Hitler's very own monster. Its arena of authority encompassed almost the entire western theater; the army, that of the east. Yet, as previously mentioned, the division of duties was not nearly so clear cut. For instance, Hossbach found himself acting as gopher between the high commands, and indeed, Hitler himself, while frequenting the various *FHQ*s. Perhaps this explains why he has 'misremembered' things as such. For, the big lights of *OKW*, from the Summer of '41 to late '44, were quartered in two outer security zones, at the 'Wolf's Lair,' *i.e.*, FHQ. Hossbach's 'half caste' status, with regard to the competing high commands, probably found him spending much of his time with OK*H*: i.e., 'under Zossen.' See note below.—N.B.]

446 [*OKH*, 'Oh Ka Ha': Army High Command. Composed chiefly of monarchists and reactionaries, Hitler's dilettantism could not but have clashed with this clique. *OKH*'s arena of authority encompassed the eastern, *i.e.*, most important, theater.—N.B.]

re-route supplies to Model, who, at the moment, is conducting a historic defense of the East. Thus, having secured MHQ, I return to my post beneath Zossen.

'OKW' 's Underground HQ

Hours they pass, what telephone and telegraph exhausted; or, is it just me? It's hard to say, seeing we've become but one and the same. Tired and disconsolate, seeing there's nothing more to be done, I decide this Monique business can be put off no more; thus do I put a call to Himmler.

Informed of my discovery, he turns apoplectic, what damned near shushing me off the line. Why, I've never *heard* him like this. Swearing me to secrecy, why I've no clue, he weasels the facts out from me; pah, he's already guessed as much. Suffice it to say—*I've been bamboozled.*

Back at MHQ

Thus do I return, criminal-police in tow and warrant in hand; only to find Coyle's throat slit, and Gabriel altogether missing; along with that godforsaken woman...

A quick search reveals curtains haphazardly unfurled. Eschewing the window, I race for the door. Denuded branches lead to tattered trousers, alongside a patch bearing the runes of the *SS*, buried beneath bootprints in the soil.

Scowling past a clod of photographers and detectives, I muscle my way inside, then put a call to Himmler.

The Reichsführer he preens: "Do you mean to say, the girl's gone, Coyle dead, Gabriel missing?" Why, it almost seems he's *enjoying* it. "It's obvious," he says. "This Gabriel's her accomplice."

Now, no matter the levity in his voice, the fact I picked Gabriel bodes ill for me. Thus I seek to deflect it. "We've uncovered a leak in the officers corps," I say. "Gabriel? Sonofawhore's straight from the General Staff. Oh," I laugh, as though it's all quite beneath me. "This is *priceless*. Yes, uncovering this hornets' nest should prove just the tonic we need, so's to spur us to the Final Victory."

Of course, the instant I say it, I know it's only so much *quatsch*. This Gabriel's a man's any other, and so's probably allowed himself be seduced what by her witcheries. Like game am I trapped. As such do I beg Himmler his forgiveness; expecting the none in return: "I take full responsibility for having posted the detail. Coyle was a hero. Nonetheless, I failed to sniff this Gabriel out. And, for that, for that I am prepared to pay: *for my loyalty too is my honor.*"[447]

Now, Himmler you see must've known Monique and I'd been lovers;[448] and so's put two and two together. "Really," he probes. "Investigating the General Staff? Come, *Herr General...*"

Why, I'm surprised; I mean, *how even-handed*. Still, with Himmler, one never knows when he's about to pounce. I mouth something noncommittal, seeing that's the way he seems to like it.

The Reichsführer is not amused. "I have been doing some investigating myself: such as your *relation* to the girl."

---

447 ['*My loyalty is my honor*': Motto of the *SS*.—N.B.]

448 ['had been lovers': The German here is cryptic, and could be taken to imply Hossbach believed his feelings for Mum had been reciprocated. There is room for interpretation as to whether these 'feelings' were indeed physical, psychological, or simply fantastic. Nonetheless, I believe that, on occasion, they took solace in a passion fueled by mutual hate. As such do I append this note: As a compromise between my duty as translator, on the one hand; and, out of respect for the General on the other, with regard to his preference for keeping such things *sub rosa*.—N.B.]

He said 'relation'; not 'relation-ship'. I swallow. For, at the moment you see, Himmler he holds my life in his hands. I press the accursed woman's phone so hard against my face, why almost it's one with my ear. The longest minute of my life it now plays out.

Alas he says: "You shall presently cease badgering the General Staff. The responsibility for this… matter rests firmly with you."

"But, but *sir*. I didn't want her to escape. It's just—"

"It's just you never intended she should be caught."

"Um, *sir*? But, the girl. The girl, she's—"

"I know exactly who, and what, the girl is, General. As for you—"

Oh boy, here it comes...

"I think you've learned your lesson."

I—*huh?* "Um, sir? But, the paper— "

"*Fuck* the paper."

Something strange's going on. I mean, I've never *heard* Himmler use such words; and why it's cut me to the very quick.

At length he goes on, what this booming, yet, somehow, still whiny tone: "We know what the word means, General. And, as for the boy, I am not interested—for now. *Tsk*," he reflects. "You owe me your life, Hossbach; and, should you have any honor, you will devote what's left of it to defending Eternal Germany." Changing gears, he adds, "I will be out of town, and so I'm afraid shan't be able to make it to the Wolfsschanze tomorrow.[449] Moreover my representative it seems has taken quite ill: thus do I charge you to stand in his stead."

"And do?" I say, regretting the instant I've said it; for, my question you see's completely out of form.

---

449 [*Wolfsschanze* ('The Wolf's Lair'): *FHQ* for East Prussia. Again, where Hossbach *would have* been stationed, had he had a more 'normal' role within *OKW*.—N.B.]

"And *do* that which you do best: keep close to the Führer, and make sure no harm comes. To this end I deputize you an honorary member of the Begleit Kommand.[450] Report to me in exactly one week. Heil Hitler."

It's all I can do but to just click my heels, and boast with a manly pride: "*Heil Hitler!*"

Suddenly, the thought occurs, what the contrast in our salutations: his wan, mechanic; mine—*from the heart.*

[450] ['Begleit Kommand' (*Führerbegleitkommando*): Part of the security apparatus revolving around the 'Wolf's Lair'.—N.B.]

Chapter 35: Bomb

Wolfsschanze, East Prussia: July 20, 1944

Himmler's detailed me here, what to this mosquito-infested hell, the Wolfsschanze up in East Prussia. All my training; yet, now, now I'm but some glorified guard.

A terrible bout of nerves threatens come midday, just before the conference is slated to begin. Ach, for Himmler's words they still ring fertile in my mind; like a hangover after the night before. But these are just random things floating through my head; I pay them no heed.

The war conference's running late, on hold till Stauffenberg[451] gets here. Lack of punctuality's one sure way to end up in the Führer's doghouse. Still it seems the Colonel's lost an eye, and part of a hand; everyone knows the Führer will make an exception.

The Colonel arrives a few minutes late. Like Old Ferris at the *Four Seasons*, I stand like a stiff and open the door. Sweeping past he apologizes for his tardiness. I tarry just long enough to hear Schmundt[452] begin reading the Order of Battle, then shut the door behind.

I take my post outside the ornery hut, ostensibly so's to prevent any intruders, ear to the door; for, I've simply got to keep abreast of what's transpired. I mean, the Boss might invite me for discussion to follow. He knows I'm versed in armor.[453] Only, now we're on the defensive, I so rarely get to make use of it. Why I was up all night, immersing

---

451 [*Colonel* Stauffenberg, Claus Schenk *von*: Colonel-General Fromm's Chief of Staff.—N.B.]

452 [*General of Infantry* Schmundt, Rudolf: Lead Führer Adjutant, chief of army personnel.—N.B.]

453 [The original reads 'armour.' A small percentage of the manuscript is in English, a carryover from the days of his youth. As a rule, I have altered such Anglicisms, for the benefit of the American reader.—N.B.]

myself in *Attacks!*[454], in case such opportunity should arise. Pah, this bodyguard stuff's beneath me. A waste of my talent; a detriment to both Führer and Reich.

Actually, it's not half bad. Why, I even get to smoke, which in my wildest dreams I should never have imagined. The only reason the luxury's allotted's because they're using this makeshift hut. Yes, the Reichsführer you see's having the war-bunker reinforced against enemy bombardment. Ach, it must be the first time in twenty years I've been anywhere even near the Chief with a smoke. I bask in the rarity of it all; and, just in case, start rehearsing my Rommel...

Lost in the surreality of it all, almost I don't notice Stauffenberg sweeping past, bidding me out his way.

Cursing under my breath, I squash my cigarette so's to lead him to the exchange, seeing he's an urgent call; *problems with Model up at the front.*

Duty thus fulfilled, I return to my post at the door.

Stauffenberg! Why I could kill the swine; ach, for, *that was my last cigarette...*

The monotonous drone of the Führer's chief adjutant it plods, still reciting the order of battle; when the walls they seem to remove themselves. Doors they fly; a stab; and I'm down. Why, shrapnel it pierces my side. My ears they ring, ring what with deafening roar. Scouring a hole in the sky, I see: the aftermath of explosion. *What, no planes, no roof?* And, cursing midst the pain, I turn myself about, frantically searching for *him...*

I come across the F. midst the remnants of the dilapidated hut, obviously shaken; but, more important, *unharmed.*

"Seal the gates," he shouts. "I said seal them!"

---

[454] [*Attacks!* by Erwin Rommel: The field marshal's influential screed on tactics for tanks and armored formations.—N.B.]

Why he's screaming. Really, it's not his fault; for, it seems, the poor chap can't quite hear.[455]

I round up all the Begleit Kommand I can find, positioning them round the exits with the watchword: "No one in—*or out*."

Time it begins to pass; there is much confusion. Whereupon I essay an investigation. Oh, but it's no use. That is, until the gate-keeper's found. Under my blandishments, he admits having let a certain one-eyed chap leave after the explosion. Yes, a certain Colonel it seems'd come along and threatened him with the firing-squad, if he should disobey at a time such as this...

Stauffenberg!

Immediately I phone Himmler; only, for some reason it seems I can't quite get through. Thus I've no choice but to reach out to Dr. Goebbels. For, something you see it tells me: *the Boss will be safe in his hands.*

***

The Little Doctor responds heroic, what nearly single-handedly crushing the entire coup. Stauffenberg is shot; the Führer, thank God, lives.

Still, we pay a stiff price: Schmundt, the Head Führer Adjutant, lay in hospital, more than likely mortally wounded.[456] And, as if that weren't enough, Korten, Göring's right-hand man, seems himself to be suddenly slipping off. Oh—this is the blackest day in history!

But for all that, the Führer is ecstatic. Why, it's as if a miracle has finally occurred at the front. The Boss himself

---

455 [Actually, his ear drums had burst. Hitler's hearing, never fully lost, eventually made a complete recovery.—N.B.]

456 [The General appears to be conflating his chronology in this rapid retelling of events. For instance, Stauffenberg was not shot till nearly Sixteen hundred, by which time Mussolini had already arrived. Further, Schmundt's injuries had not initially appeared so dire. Two months later, however, gangrene put an end to his abortive recovery.—N.B.]

is almost completely unharmed. I fetch Morell,[457] insisting he give him a sedative so's to calm him.

The portly plumper he looks at me's though I'm an imbecile. "His blood pressure," he chides. "Is completely normal. Yes, the Führer is an example to us all. Would you believe, he still insists seeing the Duce? Nothing I say can dissuade him from this course."

Chaos rapidly unfolds. Alas, amidst the euphoria, the accusations they fly. Someone says, "What about the construction workers?" Dutifully Bormann has them placed under arrest.

Meantime I ring up Müller. Oh I know, I know; but daren't think it. Besides—who am I *supposed* to call?

He sends his best interrogator. The delicate question is put, concerning the whereabouts of Fromm; after all, that's the swine who sent him...[458]

The Führer bids me accompany him meet the Duce. Only, Morell has forbidden the most powerful man leave the premises.[459] Therefore I stand, patient at his side, attempting not assess the gravity of what has just transpired.

***

Gradually the pieces they start to fall into place; that is, in the eyes of the Chief. Yes, this is the scenario to which he is committed: assassins, disguised as construction workers, parachuted in, seeking do to him what they did to poor Heydrich.

"I am *convinced*," the Führer he booms, though we're standing side by side. "No *German* could have done such a thing."

"The Führer is right," I second.

---

457 [Morell, Theo, *M.D.*: Hitler's personal physician.—N.B.]

458 ['him': *i.e.*, Staufenberg.—N.B.]

459 [This is pure bunk. I cannot find even one source willing to corroborate it. Odds are, the threat of a coup would have kept Shitler bound to the 'secure environs' attendant upon *FHQ*.—N.B.]

But then, I recall what I'd learned regarding this one-eyed bloke who, against orders, has already been executed.

For once, at least, it's not the Jews; for, *thank God*, we've already lanced that troublesome abscess.[460]

***

The evidence infallibly begins to mount, contradicting the Führer's own assessment. The conclusion's inescapable: not the Jews, rather, but something far, far worse: *the Army*; all the way to the General Staff...

Yet the Führer will hear nothing of it. Ach, he still insists seeing the Duce. Why he scoffs at the very notion that, as he puts it, "Some one-eyed miscreant's going to stand in the way of running the war. I must see him, I say; oh, oh yes yes yes, see him I must," he pouts to portly Morell, proceeding to make swift sport of the doctor's entreaties that he should not. "Besides," he shrugs. "What would people say?"

***

The Duce's aghast, what visibly shaken upon inspecting the bombed-out remnants of the hut at FHQ. As if the Führer's singed scalp, and ashen-stained clothes aren't enough, Mussolini becomes violently ill upon viewing the scene; where, just a few hours before, *USA* himself had stood. Horrified, he evinces yet a profound sense of admiration for the Chief who, caught in the moment, begins re-enacting the thing.

God, it's as if he were reciting a lecture, rather than recounting this cowardly attempt on his life. No, for the F., a greater miracle could scarcely have occurred. It's as if a real breakthrough'd finally been achieved at the front. He revels recounting the genesis of it all to a now-captive audience.

---

[460] I meant, since they were already in protective custody.[—W.H.] [He means camps.—N.B.]

Still, it strikes me's odd his arm's no longer shaking; what for the first time since Stalingrad. My impression—and, Morell confirms it—is that the blast seems to've eliminated his rather ubiquitous tremor.

Yes, events have come full-circle. For, as Dietrich Eckart, the Führer's mentor used to say, in choosing the Messiah for the German people: "All they really need's someone to scare the shit out of them..."

September '44

Why, nothing is spared him. Come September, the tremors they return; only, now, with a vengeance. For, Himmler's investigation you see's finally complete; the results of which've somehow made their way to FHQ.

The conspiracy, which the Boss'd adduced to Popeye, i.e., Stauffenberg, 'plus a few ninnies at most', was really nothing of the sort; rather the tip of the ice-berg, yielding a whole network of army and aristocrat clad hand-in-glove.

And almost overnight, the Führer's become but a bitter old man. What all bent and shaken, yesterday's sprightly hair turned sallow; *God forbid that he should not live.* Not from any injuries, rather, than the cruelest blow of all: *that of a broken heart...*

Chapter 36: A Second Dunkirk

September '44: Production Works at Peenemünde

'Work smart, not hard,' Grandpa Hossbach always used to say. Still, it cuts me to the quick to hear that Jack, of all people, has been complaining about production quotas 'beyond the ken of reason'. Oh, but I'll put a stop to all that: for genius you see's a disease; for it disturbs brain-function. Such men do not lead, rather, but must take orders from someone on-high. Whether to balance their checkbook; or make good keeping their big traps shut...

I made the mistake of having Schmidtie[461] call ahead. "Ha-bay," he says, helping me into my (the which he forgot to shine) boots. "The boy thinks we shouldn't come, says they suffered a really big raid just the other day."

"So?" I rail. "I lost my Mercedes! Ah, Betsy—"

"*Old Faithful.*"

I give him a look. I mean, just because he drives, that gives him no right to rename her; especially *post-mortem*. "We've survived a dozen such raids. The eggheads? Pah, they're lucky to have had only two. Fetch me my gloves."

He does as he is told, then we're off. Why, the rickety little Volkswagen's a disgrace. I'm tempted to, once we've left it at shore, requisition something better upon our return.[462] Still, like what's-his-name, the swine[463] it seems has grown on me. I'll be more than happy if we make it back to the city.

Peenemünde's more or less the same. "A few demolitions," I chide. "Never hurt anyone." But seriously, how many bombardments will it take, before these

---

461 [He means Reynolds.—N.B.]

462 ['return': To the mainland, after having taken the ferry to and from the island.—N.B.]

463 ['What's his name,' must be Reynolds; 'the swine,' his car.—N.B.]

yellowbellies realize they are at war? For, no sooner have we disembarked, than I catch them making these fixes—in the midst of production!

I grill the lad for over an hour what like some fucking Gestapo; von Braun, too. Yet *still* these encephalitic eggheads have no clue how many parts go into an A4.[464] Why I put the fear of Himmler into them. "I'm so sorry," I say to the disconsolate Professor. "But, from now on, you must deliver the weapon *as is*."

Almost I collapse once he explains nearly a *third* explode premature; still, it can't be helped. "Faulty or no," I say. "The Führer has decreed: *nothing* must be allowed to stop production. Yes, this is the price; *this* is the price we must pay, if ever we are to turn this infernal drain upon our resources into a viable weapon. Use of the Wunderwaffen," I proceed, taking care to rally their slumbering morale. "Is strictly forbidden. That is, until such time's we have enough so's to launch a colossal assault. He says he wants 'annihilating effect'."

An explosion forces me dive for cover. "Oh," Braun says, lifting me to my feet. "Must be the oxygenation works; you know... smoothing out the kinks."

Hands in greatcoat, I fly, what almost neglecting to take Good Reynolds with; then, like a bat out of hell, double-time back to the ferry.

A flat-tire later, owing to the increasingly cratered roads which line the approach to the ill-beleaguered city, we return to the Getaway Place. I call it that for a reason; for no *way* am I going to report to the Chief, without having exhausted a goodly part my cellar.[465]

The body demanding sleep, yet the spirit in need of Brahms, I make a go at the map-room; forced for once to turn my attentions to the West...

---

[464] ['A4': *i.e.*, the liquid fueled rocket.—N.B.]

[465] [Wine, or, more likely, booze.—N.B.]

The cock it crows; a knock avenges itself on the 'do not disturb' implicit on my door. *Swoosh*, the Beobachter appears, the which Good Reynolds duly proffers, via a slit, onto the floor.

Sprawling off the sofa, it doesn't take much to low-crawl it to the door. Paper in hand, blurry of bifocals I read:

'Panic in Britain!'

Ah—Peenemünde has[466] delivered at last! Yes, for the *A4*, re-christened 'V2',[467] is presently wreaking havoc. Why its very existence you see is currently being withheld from the British people, who're thus at a concomitant loss to explain they're being given a thrashing; *hah, just like the Luftwaffe used to bring...*

A Few Days Hence

For the Führer, the effect is that of a tonic administered by the very Gods. To call such advent timely would be understatement. Why just last week, the Boss, devastated by the treachery attendant upon Twenty July, had simply lain in bed for days on end; the war'd just mindlessly petered on.

'Good Heavens', people said. 'What if he should not *live*?' I did what I could to put an end to such rumors; to me, though, he spoke of taking his life.

But, now, as if on cue, the rocket-assault's begun. Yea, for the first time in history, man-made objects have left the confines of Earth's protective carapace[468]; alas, the *Wunderwaffen* are real.

This fact emboldens him. So much in fact the Führer's genius has been unleashed once more. For, no

[466] [The date was September 8, 1944. Moreover one mustn't forget Nordhausen, and the countless manufacturers and distributors disbursed throughout the rapidly retreating Reich.—N.B.]

[467] [Again, the 'V1', or *Fi-103*, was a pilotless missile, developed by the Luftwaffe at *Peenemünde West*.—N.B.]

[468] [*i.e.*, have entered outer space, some eighty kilometers high.—N.B.]

sooner had he heard the good news, than he has devised the master plan: one last push, whereby we shall flush the Amis into the sea—turning thus the tide of the war!

Its genius rests in its simplicity: Roosevelt'll be up for election come November when, out the Ardennes[469], scene our greatest triumph, the Panzers shall roll the Amis[470] all the way to Antwerp.[471] Then, we'll cut the Meuse, dividing Eisenhauer's[472] Army[473] in twain. Which port is simultaneously to suffer bombardment by the *A4*, cutting their line of supply. Whereupon we shall affect an encirclement. Why, the Führer has it—it shall be a second Dunkirk!

Moreover, according to Ribbentrop, any ensuing fallout'll force the Amis, possibly the English too from the war; *then so at last, peace shall reign among the European peoples.* Upon which the *real* Westwall can be built: the reconquest of our air-space through the threat of retaliatory rocket-attack, each behemoth capable of plunging the plutocrats into a heap of smoldering ruin!

This being done, our star shall shine once more. With one irresistible push, we shall send our armies East; crushing the Ivans once and for all.

But, if not, then Europe shall fall prey to the Asiatic horde; Man will regress to the barbarous state; civilization shall be no more. No, what we need's *time*; time for the *Wunderwaffen* to come into effect. Indeed, for, as Bormann of all people has it:

"*On dagger's edge the world now stands...*"

---

469 [Belgian forest, key to the invasion of France in May 1940.—N.B.]

470 [*Ami*: American.—N.B.]

471 [Antwerp: Belgian port. The Anglo-Americans main line of supply. —N.B.]

472 [*sic.*—N.B.]

473 [Actually, army *group*.—N.B.]

October *sans* Fest[474]

The loss of France—or, so say the defeatists—is the beginning of the end; such people, thank God, are currently being strung up; or, if lucky, shot. And it serves them right, too; *for such maggots you see clearly constitute the enemy within.* I mean, we've already thrown them out once;[475] well —why not again?

It would be bad form to contemplate the alternative. For no longer is it a matter of maintaining a Greater German Reich, rather, but a struggle for existence. Yes, for France has become an aircraft carrier; *aimed at the heart of the Reich.* Daily does our airspace play host to this deadly armada. Screams accompany their flight. And not just the bombers. Ach, for the fighters you see accompanying them take shots at sundry women and men. Daily do these terrorists reek vengeance on our ancient cities.

In the East, our prospects are even worse. A series of offensives, begun on the third anniversary of Barbarossa no less, has proceeded to roll up the entire front, all the way from the Arctic to the Ukraine; culminating in the destruction of Army Group Center.[476] Part of Poland has been lost. The rumor-mongers even began caviling about some place called 'Majdanek'[477], where we're supposed to have simply bumped off a million Jews in these 'gas-ovens'; or, as the Russians call them, 'The Devil's Furnace'.

The fact such nonsense stems from the Ivans's proof enough its absurdity. I repeated this *mot* during an air-raid why just the other day. Now, Old Goebbels you see's gone and picked it up. The slogan's a key part of our defense

---

[474] [Due to meteorological constraints, the offensive could not begin till mid December.—N.B.]

[475] ['thrown them out once': *i.e.*, from France in Spring 1940.—N.B.]

[476] [It was subsequently reconstituted, albeit in truncated form.—N.B.]

[477] [The allegations were made by the Russians, a few days after the *Attentat* of 20 July.—N.B.]

against enemy propaganda. Really, I'm glad to've thought of it—even if unacknowledged.

November

Oh—donnerwetter, nochmal! The swine's taken the fight to East Prussia. Alas, even the Führer must see: the stakes they couldn't be higher. Thus have I won back my right to command; in the field, not some godforsaken desk.

Counting on the wisdom of the old-hands, whilst tapping the enthusiasm of many an untried youth, we manage to retake a town near Goldap.[478] Why, we showed those devils a real stand's still possible.

Only, nothing could've prepared us for what we've found: corpses, liberally lining the streets; babies nailed to doors. The Russian, the swine, simply raped anything with a hole. Entire refugee column—steamrolled *en masse*. The Devil? Why—the very Devil himself!

December

Last month, the *A4* managed to damage enough shipping[479] so's to halt the Anglo-Amis in the West.[480] Time

---

[478] [*Goldap*: Village in the heartland of East Prussia. The defendant's cousin, Friedrich, retook it around this time, only to observe similar atrocities upon reentry. Both Hossbachs were subsequently sacked, due to disobeying *der Führer*'s batty orders.—N.B.]

[479] [*i.e.*, in Antwerp harbor. A goodly number were fired at Britain, too. In this connection I should note the passing of Colonel Gabell, which is said to have occurred around this time. I have consulted the records for every *A-4* impact in and around London, and can therefore lay to rest any rumors blaming the rocket for his demise. It appears he had suffered a heart attack or a stroke. Gossip persists that *some* sort of raid *might* have prevented emergency vehicles from getting through: In my opinion, this is apocryphal. He died at home, at the ripe old age of 89. His papers were thoroughly searched: Nothing regarding the 'life energy,' subsequent to The Great War, has ever been found.—N.B.]

[480] [This is absolute bunk: The *A4* sunk all of one ship in port, damaging sixteen more.—N.B.]

has finally been bought; the which the Führer's always prophesied. At last, I beseech him bid word to the people; the people who so patiently suffer.

"Patience," he says. "Just a few more weeks—then the world will hold its breath!"

The Battle of the Ardennes[481]

On 16 December our offensive, as that of any engagement, begins with the greatest of hopes. By Christmas, the 6th Army, under Sepp Dietrich—and, less so the 7th under Model—have made impressive gains.

Yes, another Wednesday has passed, and I've seen nor hide nor hair of Jack. Ach, for the *A4* you see's currently pummeling Antwerp into both earth and sea. Alas —the advent of the West Wall is finally at hand!

481 [Or, as the Allies call it, the 'Battle of the Bulge.'—N.B.]

Chapter 37: *Siegwaffen*—or Death

January 1945

The rest of the battle may better be described by a meteorologist than a soldier. Yes, the first week found both fog and rain to keep the enemy air-force at bay. Oh, but ach; the sun made its reappearance all too soon, escorting the Anglo-Amis with it to the sky. Meantime, the Luftwaffe, like its boss, was nowhere to be found; stalemate thus ensued. The Panzers were consumed; and, with them, the last of our reserves.

No sooner has the Führer called the battle off, than the Russians have launched a colossal assault.[482] Warsaw has fallen; why Berlin itself is now in danger. Our only hope lay rather in Jack and von Braun delivering this 'Victory Weapon'; that is, if such thing even exists...[483]

Why the whole notion of a 'West Wall' rests hand and glove with that of the *Siegwaffen*. The people? Let them believe what they will. It's just, dammit, if I am to advise the Chief, then I must have access to certain basic facts.

But, alas, my clearance it seems has been revoked. No, no more Wednesday sojourns for me; no, from now on, Peenemünde and Nordhausen alike are off-limits.

---

482 [Beginning January 12.—N.B.]

483 ['Secret weapons' and 'wonder weapons' had begun to be used interchangeably, along with *Siegwaffen* ('Victory weapons.') Confusion had arisen due to Goebbels' propaganda. It was a fraud, a hoax, perpetrated on Axis and Ally alike. Apologetics concerning atomics, and even more exotic fantasies, which the Censor has thankfully forbidden me allude, are really nothing but air. The suicide of Hitler, in addition to the presence of the Red Army in Berlin, are proof enough the bankruptcy of such claims.—N.B.]

I have cabled Himmler, so's to register a complaint; oh, but it's no use. He's leading his own Army now,[484] supposed to be saving us from encirclement.

It's obscene, what some amateur my superior? Imagine, a fucking civilian—entrusted with saving the Reich!

Thus that I might avoid my Kampfgruppe's[485] complete destruction, on my own authority I've ordered them fall back; back to the interior of the Reich.

Being this is contrary to the Führer's instructions, he's sacked me right on the spot; disgracing me thus in front of my fellows.

And, now, now he's retiring me what like some two-bit whore...

***

I continue to show up at Maibach.[486] Returning from chow, I find my office locked; leading Müller's minions lend me an unsavory ride off the premises.

Thus have I petitioned to die's a soldier; as the great *von Fritsch*.[487]

---

484 [re, 'Himmler's Army': Army *group*.—N.B.]

485 [*Kampfgruppe,* 'Battle Group': Chiefly comprised of irregular, ad hoc units, of varying quality, often designated by the name of its commander: Hence 'Kampfgruppe Hossbach,' which originally might have consisted upwards of some 8,000 men; in addition to, if they were lucky, perhaps a couple dozen tanks. Previously an undersized division, by now such conglomerate could have passed for a small panzer corps.—N.B.]

486 [HQ, *by this point*, for OKW; as well as, for years, that of OKH. 'The Wolf's Lair' was abandoned in late '44: Hence 'Maibach II,' which, like its namesake, was indeed 'underneath Zossen'.—N.B.]

487 [*Colonel-General* Fritsch, Werner *von*: Commander in Chief of the German armed forces. Hero and mentor to a young Windemeer Hossbach. In 1937, the latter's cousin, Friedrich, took notes at a conference alleged to have hatched a conspiracy to wage aggressive war. Unfortunately, elements of the two cousins' careers appear to have become conflated, much to our memoirist's dismay. Which is understandable, being each Hossbach had, at one time or another, been equally beholden to Fritsch. The latter, as it were, had been

To my eternal shame, my petition is denied.

February

The Führer had the prescience to foresee Stalin's offensive for what it really is: a strategic envelopment, targeting our weak flanks in both Hungary and East Prussia; i.e., *not Berlin.* Oh, but ach—OKH[488] knew better! Now, thanks to them, Berlin really *is* being threatened.

Once more, the Russian rapes anything that moves: women as old as eighty; girls as young as eight; all, all defiled by the thousands. And, what's worse, Hungary has fallen[489]; taking her precious grain with.

"Have faith!" read the broadsheets; yet one cannot feed an army on faith.

"God forbid, if the end should ever be nye," I write P'pa, seeing this might be our last communication. "One must take solace in the fact that the Fatherland's become a battlefield for just the second time in two world-wars; I find this a remarkable achievement."[490]

---

vociferously against Hitler's plan for war, placing the cousins in an untenable light. Yet neither was to suffer as did von Fritsch. Forced to resign, following trumped up charges of immorality, he vindicated himself before a court martial. Hitler refused to reinstate him. Nonetheless, the extraordinary esteem in which the Colonel-General had been held, forced Hitler to grant his request to be sent to the front, at the start of the Polish campaign. Accepting the scandalous demotion to 'Honorary Colonel,' Fritsch met a hero's end near Warsaw, 22 September, 1939.—N.B.]

488 [*OKH*: Army high command, responsible for the ever shrinking eastern theater, as opposed to the Hitler sycophants in *OKW*.—N.B.]

489 [Hungary fell February 13, 1945, the same day Dresden was (partially) destroyed.—N.B.]

490 [*The Battle of Tannenberg*, in the first world war, saw the Russians invade, only to be precipitately thrown out of, East Prussia. This is generally considered the first such breach of German soil. Nonetheless it should be noted that, during the Great War, fighting also erupted in the disputed Alsace.—N.B.]

Truth is, we fear for the safety of our families, even more than that of the men at the front. Ach, for the air-war you see's reached unimaginable heights; or, rather, depths. *Dresden has been completely destroyed.* Hamburg, Essen, Frankfurt, and God knows Berlin take their turn time and again; victims of the holocaust now descending. A new phenomena, the 'firestorm', daily's being created; as a *deliberate tool* of Allied policy. Why what better proof could we provide the German people, that Jewry really means exterminate us?

But we know what we must do to prevent it.[491]

March

In Hungary, the *Leibstandarte* has attempted to restore the situation. Despite their heroic efforts, the land of the Magyars must be left to its Bolshevik fate.

As for the West, the Amis have captured the last bridge leading over the Rhine. What's more, Finland, under threat from the Ivans, hasn't just thrown in the towel, rather, but's actually had the audacity to declare war.

Now we face the threat of an unlimited multitude inhabiting German soil, hemmed in what from east and west; alas the indignity of a two-front war.

I speak not of Italy, seeing no one takes *that* serious. Oh—if only they'd switched sides long ago!

Even our *own* propaganda no longer speaks of the 'Final Victory', rather, than the 'Just Peace' which surely must come.

On the other hand, Speer—who, after all, really ought to know—thinks this 'Victory Weapon''s not only real, rather, but ought to be ready 'any day'. Meantime, he has it, we 'simply must stay put'.

---

[491] I simply meant their incarceration as potential enemies of the state; a goal which, thank God, we had already gone a long way towards attaining.[—W.H.]

I put to him point blank the rumor concerning an 'atomic weapon', laughing so's to make sport of it.

Why, he says, a payload the size of a grapefruit can lay waste an entire city; *preposterous.* Nonetheless, I listen; *and hope.*[492]

As for this 'Victory Weapon', my source in the Air Ministry claims the *Wunderwaffen* to have fallen from Himmler's grasp. Nearly I exhaust my wine-cellar greasing the palms of those in the know.

Alas Speer's sent word: if such things *do* exist, they'd be under Scarface.

Kammler? Oh—God save Jack![493]

Early April

Only, now, these last days of panic,[494] the Führer's allowed me to form my own regiment. We're a formidable bunch; though, at present, we seem to be suffering the increasing indignity of existing only on paper.[495]

---

492 [Lack of direct quotations falls under 'editor's license,' in addition to the strident representations of Herr Speer's attorney.—N.B.]

493 ['Scarface': Likewise the moniker of *Obersturmbannführer* Otto Skorzeny, whereabouts currently unknown.—N.B.]

494 ['last days of panic': It's hard to tell exactly when he might mean, due to the rapid reliving of events in his mind. Court records indicate he retook 'a place near Goldap' in November '44. His *own* account has this some two months later, the ostensible reason for his having been 'sacked.' In any event, come April we find him recruiting *Volkssturm*. As such, he probably received this commission, his last, in late March, or early April, 1945.—N.B.]

495 [The chief difficulties were logistics and armament. His tanks *might* have had gas: Indeed, it helps to have been supply officer at *OKW*. Just as surely however they would have been lacking any reserves. Following the destruction of the transportation system, the powers that be were no longer capable of ferrying stockpiles of munitions, food, and fuel: Everything had to be ad-libbed. From these conditions were primitive weapons, such as the 'Panzerfaust,' as opposed to any alleged *Siegwaffen*, born. As for his precious tanks, Hossbach must have realized that his 'Panzers' were bound to be but glorified infantry: *i.e.*, 'Grenadiers'.—N.B.]

Time begins to pass. Everyone knows Ivan's gearing up for the final assault; the which could come any day.

Fevered imagination, and whispered watchword alike, seeks in the *Siegwaffen*, even at this ungodly hour, miraculous means, with which to turn the war around.

A Few Days Later?[496]

Alas, such eggheaded tomfoolery's amounted to naught. Whether from sabotage of our weapons; or, worse, that of our *hope*.

---

[496] [Supposition based on the sudden loss of morale, prior to the events of 12 April to come.—N.B.]

PART IV
GÖTTERDÄMMERUNG

Chapter 38: The Battle for Outer Space[497]

Peenemünde: Feb. 17, 1945

[“] The Prof had grown tired of all the delays.

“Bureaucracy,” he'd quipped. “The SS is as bad as the army. Really, my spaceship's no fantasy: it can, no, it *must* be built. Yet, these fools, imbeciles who care only for the biggest, heaviest guns. Cretins like Hitler, who think the *A4*'s just another piece of heavy artillery.”

I cringed. “But, where are you going?”

We'd just finished the morning test fire, when Braunie walked out. So, I followed. He marched past the barracks, all the way to the football field, where Doctor Dornberger was overseeing some drills.

Not a good sign, I'd thought. *If Old Four Eyes has it we are to take up weapons, then this is only the start.*

“Braun,” I'd heard the old man shout. Dornie was irate. Or, at least, as irate one can be with a fellow such as that. “Please, state your business.”

“Sir, this won’t take long: I see you've already much business to attend. And yet, if I am not allowed to do my job... which, may I remind you, is conceiving[498] weapons to

---

[497] It's necessary to go back to February, and so relate what had been going on on the Egghead Front. Thus do I insert this account here, written by Jack and obtained by counsel, concerning the former's activities some two months before; I'm sure he will vouch for it. Verily, I *breathe* verity into it. In trance, I write; even as, vicarious, I live. In a sense, I'm more alive these pages here, than the dead man who currently rots in his cell.[—W.H.] [I will vouch for no such thing.—N.B.]

[498] [When a layman goes putting words in one's mouth, alarming one's fellows, one really ought to take a stand. We did not 'conceive' any such thing: Not this late in the act. If this 'document' were legit, the word should be 'develop,' being we were merely fine tuning designs conceived long since. Sorry to disappoint the fantasists but, by this point, the only 'conception' going on at Peenemünde lay in our table talk, our dreams: *Not* back in the lab.—N.B.]

prosecute the war... then, perhaps you'd best find someone else." The message was clear.

Dornberger warmed. "Braun my good man, please, have seat."

Mulling I crept within earshot, pretending to be working on some equations, under the proviso of following the Prof, in order that he might double check me when I was done. Of course, that was all a bunch of malarkey. Nonetheless I thought: *Dornie won't mind.*

That he did not: My presence was neither remarked upon nor ignored, so much as taken for granted. He motioned B. have seat on a log, while I remained standing. Smiling perpetual benevolence, Dornie cut straight to the chase: "Braun my good man, they mean liquidate us: you, me, the whole lot. It's simple, really: By no means may we be allowed to fall into the hands of the Russians."

They nursed their brandy, which the boss[499] had illicitly procured. Me? I wanted to just go in a hole and hide.

Never in a situation he could not master, by his looks or by his charm, Braunie grinned, "So—what now?"

Dornie glanced at his war ravaged nails, shunting them into the light, noting each imperfection. Really I don't think he was looking at anything in particular. Then he fell on bended knee: "Help me, Braun... you've got to help! Find Kammler. Find Kammler and convince him: He's better off us alive."

Braunie gulped, "*Kammler?*"

"Aye," Dornie reflected, "*Kammler,*" failing conceal his fright. "With him, we still stand half a chance. Just please good god, keep well away from Himmler! You must feign you couldn't care less whether the Ivans are coming or no. In short, you must give the performance of your life. Because, one thing's clear: It's already two minutes to midnight."

---

[499] [*i.e.*, Dornberger.—N.B.]

Braunie had heard whispers regarding Doctor Kammler, the new Big Cheese ever since Himmler stripped Dornberger of any real power. Personally, I'd dismissed the more ugly yarns, such as the one saying he'd built extermination facilities somewhere in Poland. Still, I wouldn't want to cross swords with him: Unlike the boss is asking Braunie to do now. But, you know what they say: *Where there's smoke...*

I'd already gathered one could not help but feel unsettled in the presence of a man such as Kammler: For I'd seen a photo of him in *Die Wehrmacht* that made my skin just crawl. Plus, I'd remembered Braunie having said that the man has a coolth which stifles the very air: That it became hard to breathe in his presence.

Perhaps it was but the blindness of youth: Still, Braunie swore he wasn't the slightest intimidated, convinced as ever the world would open up, if only it could see him smile.

Chalk Mine on the Isle of Rügen

The Prof met Kammler in the tunnels, a makeshift mineshaft he'd recalled from years back, while negotiating a contract for the rocket society.[500] All around there arose a great big heat, permeating the infernal cavern. It's not *good* to go into the earth.

Braunie approached the shifty eyed man in his forties. The latter, standing tall, buried his arms in a foppish coat. He wore the diamonds. Not as in the highest decoration, which he did not have. But, those which grace a gold plated watch, which he did. Then, like a viper he struck: “Speak!”

---

[500] ['rocket society': The *Raketenflugplatz*, where Doctor von Braun was progressively ridiculed, validated, then forcibly absorbed into army ordnance.—N.B.]

"Well," Braunie began, clad in the SS uni he so despised for just the second time in his life, "it's like this: We've an opportunity to make a lasting contribution: For the benefit of all mankind. When we are gone, man will have known but two ages: That attendant upon the discovery of fire: And *ours*, suffused with the conquest of space."

Kammler appeared unimpressed.

Braun, inveterate salesman that he is, pressed, "The men to run the new space agency, are destined to inherit the earth." It was a bribe, a hint implying that, in his bid for power, we would be indispensable. "Last," he concluded, as if finishing a lecture, "people are beginning to panic. Men show up late... or not at all."

This last was sheer bluster. But yet, Braunie had said it with such conviction, it *had* to be true.

Kammler's eyes probably expressed a certain sort of ruthlessness under ordinary conditions. Now they fixed their gaze on the generous chin of his opponent. Waving, as if no more need be said, he gazed from under one eye, then delivered his decision, "Assemble the men at Seventeen-hundred: Tell them they are to submit for inspection. Have Gross and Hentschel fetch two cattle cars, then fill them with hay. Hentschel... used to be a farmhand, huh? Have him sequester a horse: By any means. Bring it here, then have it destroyed. The three of you will drag it into the truck: Wait. On second thought, get two horses: One for each truck. Got it? Good. Hide beneath the hay, along with the rest of your team. Bury yourselves under the rotting husk: One per truck. Oh, and you might want to hang on: It's going to be a bumpy ride." He smiled, producing muscular movements indicative of laughter, resembling something akin to a sense of humor.

Braunie enjoined, "What about Himmler, and all his goons?" I would not have believed it, had it not come straight from the horse's mouth. But, according to Braunie, by this point, he was shaking.

Kammler laughed, "Himmler? He'll be driving one of the trucks!"

Back at Peenemünde

Four Eyes had met Kammler at the appointed hour. The former should have been with his army group, directing an attack against Zhukov's flank. Just one day in, and already Himmler had given up.

Perhaps Scarface had lured him with insinuations as to the island's strategic import. More likely, Kammler had suggested the rendezvous with an eye to indicating where the 'bodies'—i.e., wonder weapons—were buried. Clearly, absconding with such leverage must have been in the forefront of each man's mind.

Meantime, I sequestered myself in one of the cattle cars, buried beneath the stinking rot. Like bodies in a grave, Magnus, Zannsen, and perhaps a dozen others joined me on the floor in back. Rees and Klein were in the other car, probably similarly packed.

Sans Braun. For we had insisted, even more so than he, that he be allowed a more dignified means of escape. As such, he flew, flew like a bird in his own private plane. Yet, given the sorry state in the air, I doubt he very much enjoyed it.

Dornie too was absent. Indignant, he'd said he had to stay put with the rest of his team, and that 'The Captain must always go down with the ship.' Which would explain why half the engineers were still at Peenemünde.

The truck was cramped: That much is true. Yet there was room for perhaps a half dozen more. Probably the other car, too. Oh, I don't know how he'd managed to weasel out of it. It's not as if Peenemünde was exactly lying low. The power station had been up and running the whole time. As for the design team, Dornie had refused to release a single one: A great deception. The things a man will do to keep from losing his lunch![501]

Speaking of which, the stench soon became overwhelming. For a time it appeared regurgitation simply would not cease. Eventually the retching came to a halt. Packed like bodies in a ditch, drowning in our own fluids, somebody screamed, '*This is the stench of Hell!*'

For me it was even worse, being I was in the corner, banging my head against the wall every time we hit a bump. Which, given the state of the roads, I would say was quite a bit.

I did however have one advantage: Through a hole in back, I could see outside. That's how I found Himmler, peeping through a magnifying glass just inches away from my eyes. Kammler, wearing a shit eating grin, lurked nearby, trying to hurry him on. They were debating something: A letter.

Shaking his head, Four Eyes pounced, "I detect an anomaly, old boy: Here, upper left corner."

Discarding Himmler's letter, Kammler thrust the envelope to the light. "I see, *Herr* Reichsführer. Believe me: No one will bother. They've bigger fish to fry!"[502]

Himmler appeared to be anxious: Even more so than usual. What I did *not* know is that he happened to be guarding some contraband of his own, stashed away in the glove. An explosive more shattering than any rocket had

---

501 [Dornberger *did* eventually leave Peenemünde, in far grander style than being surrounded by his own vomit beneath a decaying horse: The chauffeur took him to the ferry. Whereupon, having reached the mainland, the latter took him to a hotel.—N.B.]

502 [I cannot chime in as to the authenticity of the account as hereby presented. Nonetheless, it elucidates a powerful, revolutionary form of treason, in which Himmler is now known to have been engaged at this time. The process concerns the miniaturization of data, whereupon a message, via magnification, is thereby revealed. According to the above, Himmler was concerned, lest his camouflage, probably a 'postage stamp,' not be up to snuff.—N.B.]

ever yet borne: Papers for his man in Switzerland... *treason to the Reich.*[503]

Himmler, we now know, had sought out his conscience long since, and come to the most dire conclusion: 'The war can no longer be won through any strictly military means: Therefore, it must be brought it to a stop, before Germany is completely destroyed.' *No matter the cost.*

The new method of intelligence, whereby a message is miniaturized and embedded in something as small as a stamp, had been used before. Still, the novelty must have been threatening. Holding his breath, like a schoolgirl Himmler scanned the envelope. He looked like he would just die, if what he were looking for happened to appear.

And then, it did. The name of his contact in Switzerland: Allen Dulles, Office of Strategic Services. *Eisenhower's right-hand man.*[504]

"Let me decode it," spat Kammler, trying to gather a look.

"Mind your business," hissed Four Eyes, sticking the envelope in his vest. He appeared to be trying to settle himself, using the calming breath Kersten must have taught him. Really, he'd been under so much pressure of late. Nonplussed, Himmler returned, "*Obergruppenführer*: Please, state your business."

Kammler had all but guessed what was already on Himmler's mind: And in his pocket. "*Herr* Reichsführer," he began, spreading his feathers. "There's a problem with

---

503 [If there is any truth to any of this, the 'stamp' could have contained instructions from Himmler's man in Switzerland, or perhaps Count Bernadotte of Sweden. The papers in the glove might have been official documents, and therefore could *not* have been miniaturized; *i.e.*, political dynamite.—N.B.]

504 [One amusing anecdote did *not* come to light during the course of the trial: Dulles's involvement with this shadowy figure has since been confirmed by ______.—N.B.] {The Censor has permitted publication of this note, *sans* ID.—G.W. Pub.}

one of the men: The driver, Shultze... shot up by the Amis heading into town. He's in hospital now. I'm afraid neither he, nor your truck, are in any condition to make it to Berlin."

"But... but I simply must be there by six!"

"I've only two cars to spare. Ech... how do I put it? The men. The men they simply refuse to drive. Call it superstition."

Himmler glowered, "Super what? Oh, what the devil are you driving at?"

"*Come*," commanded Kammler, then someone opened the door behind.

My face was within inches. Even though, by now, we'd become inured to the scent, the chance addition of air brought on the nausea all over. The smell is what hit you first, emigrating out holes such as mine, souvenirs from Allied fighters. "*Here*," he intoned, as if clamping his nose, probably pointing to the nightmare felled before him.

Himmler wretched. For, under his nose, and above mine, lay the rotting remnants of decomposed flesh, which just a few hours before had been a living breathing thing.

Use your damned kerchief, I'd thought, even as it oozed under the falsified-'floor' in back, seeping all over my face. Nearly I swallowed the sickly green spew.

Kammler slammed the door behind. "Terrorists," he thundered, "must be one of the men. *Unless*," he quavered, "the partisans are already in the woods."

"*Partisans!*"

Suppressing the urge to vomit, I imagined his pupils bouncing beneath that stupid pince-nez. This worked so well, in fact, nearly I bit through my lip, in order to keep from laughing. *Partisans.* They were his one fear, the advanced guard of panic and revenge, which currently threatened to ruin all his plans. I'll bet, on hearing the very word,[505] he envisioned his new home: *In Switzerland.*

[505] ['the very word': *i.e.*, partisans.—N.B.]

"In which case," Kammler returned. "You can have these.[506] You'll need to stop at Luentchen's along the way. I know time's a factor. But, please, take any help I can give. I'll have Luentchen ferry you to the mainland, set you up with some gas, then send you on to Berlin. I shall take a page from the Reichsmarschall and divert a squadron for your protection. Ech, don't worry, Luentchen's very thorough: He'll make shrift of the corpses in no time. I should know: built the crematoria myself. Highest quality."

Four Eyes must have turned green, having to stomach such details, which, though easy to order, are harder still having to hear. For, it interfered with his good conscience. That, and his ability to maintain the illusion of a carefree, bourgeois existence. Plus, his betrayal of that Idiot Corporal[507] had forced him to fear his 'good conscience' all the more. He set Kersten fetch him a new set of clothes. And, more important, to refill his canteen. A coughing fit later, Himmler winced, "You expect *me* to drive *this*?"

Kammler reassured him, "I'll have my men seal up the vents. Trust me: No vapors shall escape. Take these nose plugs, if you don't believe me. Oh come! You'll be fine. There's room for four. Unless," he chided, apparently indicating the horse, "you'd like to join them?"

Himmler didn't find this sort of thing very funny, and had started to shout. "*Kersten*," he rasped to the batty masseuse, who, for some reason, had accompanied him. "Get two guards, then bring them. We shall have to send for the rest later. Felix: Grab Grossman. Pittkowitz... it looks like you're with me. Well, men: It looks like we're in for a bumpy ride." Feigning calm, he proceeded to ask Kammler for directions.

---

506 [*i.e.*, cattle cars. These would have been driven to the docks, then towed, via ferry, to the mainland. In reverse order would Himmler have arrived in the first place, *i.e.*, via his truck.—N.B.]

507 ['that Idiot Corporal': Obviously, Hitler.—N.B.]

The latter obliged, “Follow me.”

“Very well. Oh and, by the way,” Four Eyes squirreled, attempting to salvage some semblance of his rapidly declining authority, “*Obergruppenführer*: The conditions in your camp are disgusting: Completely unacceptable. You shall receive my report in the morning. Meantime, impose the strictest curfew. Shoot anyone out after dark. Set a watch on the scientists. Oh and, and one more thing: Get me back my truck!” [”]

Hossbach's Cell:
September 24, 1946

Thus, despite that cantankerous whore's having lain tunnels beneath Nordhausen, the escape of Jack and the engineers had issued from Peenemünde instead; several hundred kilometers to the north.

As for the score or so of designers so needlessly left behind, why who could've known they'd be the safest men in all the Reich? For Peenemünde you see was not to fall for another three months; outlasting the Führer by nearly one week.[508]

---

[508] [It is true that the Russians did not take possession of Peenemünde until 4 May '45. Nonetheless, as regards the chaos of war, it is better to be safe than sorry: Hence the headlong panic which accompanied our flight, some two and a half months before.—N.B.]

Chapter 39: Death of a Tyrant

The Führer Bunker: April 12 or 13, 1945

So much the Moon! Alas, the other shoe's finally dropped: rocket attacks have ceased, owing to the fixed firing-sites having been overrun. At least the swine've failed nab their prey: Jackie left the Mittelwerke, having fled just in time[509]; ach, for, two days ago it fell to the Amis.

And yet, am I to believe a pig's alive, just because, when I kick it, it makes a sound? Sequestered 'safe' in Oberammergau, the rocket men are said to be at work on this 'Victory Weapon' which, the Führer has it, 'shall wrest victory from the jaws of defeat'.

"Some time ago," he says. "We succeeded in solving the problem of fission. Weapons are being prepared—explosives capable of destroying all life within a three-kilometer radius!"

Still, I wonder—which comes first, the 'Victory Weapon'? Or the extermination of the men intended to build it? For, if the Russians don't get them—*the SS will...*

Oh—donnerwetter, nochmal! Why I've simply *got* to get in touch with that impossible woman. The firing squad—later. Now, now I need her ascertain if this Victory Weapon's for real; or but one more of the Führer's fancies. And, if the latter, then, dammit, *we've got to get Jackie out.* Oh, oh yes yes yes—*we* shall save him; and, then, then I shall put a bullet through my brain...

The war is lost. Ach, for surely the Führer must see: at some point, sheer number must eventually come into effect. Why, just look at the Russian! That colossus can no longer be held at bay through any conventional means. In this racial war, this struggle to the death, men shall

509 [Nonetheless, Dornberger and the design team were able to hold on at Peenemünde, almost until the very end. The fact that the *A4* had long ceased to be operational, in no way mitigates their achievement.—N.B.]

reproach us a thousand years hence, for having succumbed to the mindless automatons from the East.

"Oh, where did it all go wrong?" the Führer he rasps, demanding of Bormann a question he cannot answer.

Yes, the Reichsleiter's been through thick and thin. His oversized paw on the Boss's arm, he grins: "There's still hope, right, mein Führer—there's always hope!"

Upon the which Dr. Goebbels bursts in. Pah, the sight of this dwarf in military gear's too much to bear; that he's hyperventilating's all I can do not to bust a gasket.

The F. he jests: "It looks like our Good Doctor here's finally lost it."

"*Nein*," the little one says. "*It is not so.*"

Then, amidst the dizziness of his frenetic entry, I realize he's holding something: a 'San Francisco Chronicle'.

"*Mein Führer*," he says. "It's *February Twelfth*."

"Our Good Doctor's lost it indeed," I say, too much glee in the eye. I mean, I know he's been trying to quit smoking; but this is ridiculous. "You've your months wrong, old boy. Why it's April: April Twelfth."

The Doctor he scowls; then, addressing himself to the Chief, whispers: "But it *is* February Twelfth: *1762...*"

The Führer he flares, retrieving something from that photographic mind. "The *Miracle of the House of Brandenburg*—but, but what's that got to do with it?"

The Good Doctor he bears his paper on high:

"*FDR*—DEAD!"

The Führer he smiles, patting his obedient hound.

"*February Twelfth*," the Doctor goes on. "One hundred eighty-three years, two months to the day[510], the death of the Czarina *saved* Prussia: *three days* before

[510] ['to the day': Probably counting the day before, *i.e.*, April 12, the date of Roosevelt's death. Goebbels' paper was *most likely* the early edition of April 13. There exists a *slight* possibility that he'd gotten hold of the late night edition for April 12. Yet, given Jerry's some five hours ahead, it was almost certainly already April 13 in the land of the Huns.—N.B.]

Friedrich'd sworn commit suicide. Then, with Russia in turmoil—just like the last war—Ivan dropped out; leaving Prussia a free hand. Friedrich he rallied his troops, and so become victor—not vanquished—of the Seven Years War!"

Now, the seventh year of *this* war won't come till 1946; *if only we can hold out a little bit more.* America, in chaos what since Roosevelt's death, will pull out—prophecy fulfilled! Yes, 1946 shall see the use this 'Victory Weapon', upon which Jack and von Braun have been working so hard. Perhaps it's not in vain; if one *believes...*

"Bormann," the Führer quips. "Champagne for the staff; and sweets for me." Hiding a gesticulating paw, he adds, "Gentlemen—we feast! Then, tomorrow—we *fight*!"

Now, I must admit being a bit confused: I mean, it just doesn't add up. So Roosevelt's dead—what does that have to do with any 'Victory Weapon'? Oh, what difference does it make? Either it does not exist; or, if it does—well, then where the hell is it?

At length the Boss he pulls me aside, shunting me into the anteroom, imparting something that, coming from any other quarter, would be punishable by death: "Oh, Hossbach, don't go getting your knickers all in a bunch." Fist-shaking, he trembles: "I know the war is lost."

Why, I can feel it go weak in the knees; I, I simply must sit; oh yes yes, sit.

"The *people*," he raves, feigning no longer hide his spasmodic hand. "The people they need it; let them have their little fancy. No," he adds, what leathery face turned sour. "The German people shall cease to exist." He writhes, fiddling helpless with his hand. "And there's not a damned thing you, or anybody can do about it!"

Ach, for once you see *I* must give the hypnotic treatment. "But, but *mein Führer*," I say, straining so's to believe it myself: "*It is not so.*"

"What do you want, hmm? You've seen it yourself—nobody listens to a thing I say. No," he sighs, resigned to the refrain, repeated amidst the deathly calm. "There will be nothing left." Then, he brightens. "Cheer up old boy: there's still time for you to get out. As for me," he scowls, what those dark subterranean eyes suddenly sprung to life one more time. "I've thought it all through."

An aurora of possibilities, brightens the darksome din my mind. Yes, for an idea you see it's popped into his head. I've seen it a hundred times. Only—could it be? *The brainstorm for which all Europe's been waiting.* I pause upon bended knee, awaiting the grand pronouncement...

But he says: "I shall wait till the last minute, then put a bullet through my brain. It's simple, really: they weren't ready; *the German people were not ready.* And, now, as our Good Doctor likes to say: they're going to get their little throats cut. But, the *betrayal*," downright he screams. "Stinks to high heaven!" One hand held hostage to the other, he begins to pace.

The light it shifts for a fraction of a second, and I'm horrified by what I find: why, his gait is that of an eighty year old man. But then I remember: *Friedrich too returned from his wars a broken man...*

I'm not paying attention; he's talking what a lot of nonsense. With a deep breath, I perk up my ears and listen:

"... even the loyal ones, such as Goebbels and Himmler, have run off to play war: the one, fit for Corporal; the other—sick-bay!"[511]

---

[511] [Goebbels, unlike Himmler, and an increasing number of fair weather fiends, was far from having just 'run off.' Quite the contrary. The little doctor was about to move his family into the Vor Bunker. His performance as *gauleiter* however had proved to be that of an overzealous would be general, whose fidelity to his *gau* had put the overall war effort at risk. A lapdog gone mad, the minister had diverted an unconscionable amount of resources to the hopelessly inept *Volkssturm*, in order to save 'his' Berlin. The allocation of vital arms, ammunition, and equipment, into the hands of wide eyed children and rickety old men, was tantamount to delivering them into the arms of the enemy.—N.B.]

Pah, such ill-humor it gives me the chills; as such do I pull out all the stops. As with faith, where one harps on something one knows cannot possibly be true, in order to make it so, I say: "*There is still time.* We'll take you to the Obersalzberg, the Obersalzberg, and—"[512]

"*Nein*," he growls, striking the desk, what with trembling hands, indicating our interview's at an end.

Anger; good. For surely you see such man will not just simply lay down and die. Yes, *this* is the man we respect; *this* is the Führer we fear. Anticipating the onset of thunder, I await his very next word...

"*Hoss-bach*," he hisses. "Would you be so kind, seeing no one listens to a thing I say, and send in Traudl[513] when you're done; for there's something she must type."

I do as he commands.

Fifteen minutes later, I happen to be strolling past his door, when I chance spot Goebbels go in. I linger just long enough to hear the Good Doctor's wily machinations:

"*Liebling*, come to my quarters when you're done. No, my pet, don't let Magda scare you: this is bigger than us all. And oh yes—I shall need you to take *diktat*. Please, bring the Führer's typewriter with."[514]

---

512 [Hitler had evacuated most of his staff to the 'alpine fortress' a few days prior. It was taken as 'a matter of course' that he was to follow. —N.B.]

513 [Tradul Junge, *née* Humps: Hitler's youngest secretary.—N.B.]

514 [Equipped with oversized keys, intended for *der Führer*'s batty eyes. There exists a certain 'political testament,' attributed to Doctor Goebells, that has since surfaced, along with similar memoranda bequeathed by Hitler. Most witnesses date their composition circa April 29. One may feel sorry for poor Traudl's having been passed about like a showgirl, yet only three secretaries by this point remained. Moreover it's possible Goebbels was no longer on speaking terms with his wife, for reasons that will soon become clear. Otherwise, she could have told him a spare typewriter had already been found. Imagine, poor Traudl, dragging Hitler's typewriter all by herself. What reception, if any, she received from Frau Goebbels, must be left to the reader's own ingenium.—N.B.]

Chapter 40: Into the Bunker

Under Berlin: April 23, 1945

"*Hoss-bach,*" the Mademoiselle she chides, what chin-strapped and helmeted, clad in this lithe little one-piece. Her voice it echoes off the ambient explosions filling the night.

We're humping it back to the city on foot, on the heels of a recruiting mission for the *Volkssturm*.[515] Just a few kilometers now, until we reach center-city. Oh, but I don't see how we're going to make it. And not just the snipers. Nor the artillery, rather; but the fact that all I see's but fire and rubble...

Ach, for Goebbels in his infinite wisdom's seen fit send me here, what with that reprehensible woman and senile ex-General: "Recruit the reserves," he'd said, bidding us round-up the final remnant evading the Gestapo.

But the Russians, who attacked April 16, moved too quick. Our men fought brave, destroying ninety tanks my sector alone[516]; yet still, they keep coming, what this inexhaustible procession of beast-men from the steppe. Army Group Weichsel[517] was completely overwhelmed; then collapsed following a brief, yet futile struggle.

---

515 [*Volkssturm,* 'People's Army': Shitler's last recruits.—N.B.]

516 [The Russians fell upon the Oder, the last barrier before Berlin. Hossbach depicts neither the whence nor where of his unit's 'feats,' other than the vaguest impression. I have been unable to verify any of it, save to say Jerry enjoyed his greatest success April 16. Within two days, though, the Red Army was able to cross wherever it had need.—N.B.]

517 [Army Group Weichsel, *i.e.*, Army Group Vistula: Himmler's charge, which he all but abandoned, before being replaced by Gotthard Heinrici.—N.B.]

The F. put everything we had into defending that river. Now it's been breached, there's nothing but children and old men between us. Guderian's been charged with helping recruit such dregs. Meantime, the Mademoiselle delights in her task of teaching women how to fire upon men. Of course, none of it's going to do any good; for, we simply haven't the weapons.

Guderian leads us through the bomb-laden pasture. Our plan's to stick to the byways and underbrush, lest the Russians simply steamroll us to the street.[518]

We've been traveling for days, covering just five kilometers the last twenty-four hours; no sleep, too. Alas the old boy feels ill. We take the opportunity to find cover, then relieve our basic bodily functions.

This being done, a bout of relaxation ensues. Withering wheat bespeaks the lack of manpower left for harvest. Still, the stalks provide enough obstruction, so's to provide for cover.

"*The best years of our life*," she says from her little patch of hay, what ever-present cigarette-holder ready to hand. "And for what? For *this*," she points, indicating the mighty be-swasticked eagle, once a symbol of power; lying in a gutter in the street.

"The problem," I say. "Was not with the Führer: but *ourselves*. Yes, it's *we* who've failed him. No, let there be

---

[518] [The intricacies of a creature so unwieldy as the International Military Tribunal must be plumbed to its depth, in order to establish the *political* context, within which took place the events of the trial. For instance, Hossbach's spell in the 'punishment bunker' appears to have stemmed from his having told a reporter that the Russians had 'simply steamrolled entire columns of civilians en masse.' Scrawled atop the sheaf, he left the following note.] "Göring sees no harm in this: but *I* most harshly condemn it. 'The men,' Fatty said, what just the other day. 'Must be allowed their little fling. For the old-timer, it keeps him honest; and, the boy... well, the boy—*it makes him a man.*' "[—W.H.] [He's purporting to be quoting Göring.—N.B.]

no mistake: history shall judge us harsh. To think, some cretin even tried assassinate—"

Oh—Gott in Himmel![519] Did not the Mademoiselle *herself* once mention the possibility his removal; hell, *before* Twenty July? Fiend—told me in the Führer's own kitchen! I, I must have blocked it, I, must have forgot; for, so much you see already has transpired.

I glare, what murder in my eyes. Only one thing, only one thing's keeping my sidearm at bay; and, that is, without her—*without her, we would be lost.* Guderian? He's a fool. *Me?* I'm not so sprightly's I used to be. The firing squad—later. *Now?* Pah, devil take it—*Monique's the best man we've got...*

"Something wrong?"

Guderian; the swine. He's his own reasons keeping quiet, regarding the events Twenty July. Lying supine, in the 'prone semi-supported'—that is, piles of hay in place of sandbags—he rolls me this bottle: "Here: this'll wet your whistle."

"Really, *Herr Generaloberst*," I say, with exaggerated ernst, what the obsequiousness simply dripping off my throat; *I'm a bit tipsy.* Yes, for I've my own flask; and, well, what now this bottle, too. "Herr *Colonel-General*," I repeat, after a swig. "Why you *yourself* once had a taste such glory—victories to last a thousand years: the riches of the Ukraine; field after field just flowing with Rumanian oil; the paradise of the Crimea; and space—I assure you, Herr Colonel-General—plenty of space!"

He bounds his patch to mine, seizing me by the wrist: "It's *over.* It has been a long time—*and you and I know it.*"

With ease I shove him off; and, why who could've known, somehow make it onto my feet. "I bet that stupid slut put such ideas into your head," I say, circling about, smashing his bottle and thus turning it into a weapon...

---

519 ['God in heaven.'—N.B.]

"Knock it off!"

Why, the Mademoiselle: she's left her post's lookout come reprimand us. "You're behaving like children. Now stop it, the both of you. We know our goose's cooked: let each man find the best way to sum up his life."

"Why, you rusted cunt you—I'll strangle you this instant!" I lunge; pah, I'm so drunk, I can barely move. "Come here you, piece of arse; piece of arse, hah—piece of shit! You, you vile slut you—*you tried to assassinate him.*" And, eying her what with death, I drop my bottle out of some well-won instinct.

"Ptth," she sneers. "Listen to Attilla: the 'Lion of Liechtenstein'—some moralist! It takes courage, Hossbach: *courage*; the one thing you don't have. No, not 'courage' to go shouting hurrah; or march under fire on some godforsaken field. Such may pass for courage among the race of men. Yet, as any woman could tell you: *men are fools.* No, what I call *courage* requires the willingness to essay the outrageous; to attempt the unthinkable. *Oui*, I daresay it even took *courage* to try what that one-eyed Bosche once did..."

Stauffenberg? Why—she's talking about Stauffenberg!

I twist my toe into this twig, long since festering in my boot, that the pain thereof might stifle this murderous scream from within. I think it over for a space, then decide to let her have it; you know, *really have it once and for all...*

'Ach, mein *Führer*', I'll say, beaming with pride; then hand him her head on a plate. By my silence however I bid her continue.

"As I was *saying*," she says, as if *she* were the one to've planted this twig in the first place. "Ah, don't you *see*: we have been playing with the wrong toys all along. Oui—*for I have seen the future.*" She darts, bouncing from her haystack to mine. Artfully posing her cigarette, what like a model or fucking t-square, her eyes they meet mine: "I saw it when I went into the earth: I saw it at—" She stops; then, apparently thinking better, inhales.

All I can think of's this hay catching fire; the which those fighters'll lock in on like a shark for blood...

"Our *destiny*," she says, pointing skyward. "Resides with the Prof; and our boy. That's alright—*I know Guderian knows.*"

"Leave me out you foal," he rasps in the dark, confrontational tones of three-year old scotch.[520] Steeling himself, his color it returns, what with a calmness which puts me quite to shame. The Generaloberst he takes stock: "Fact is, it looks like we're stuck the next few minutes; like it or no. And yet you—yes, you, Hossbach—you would quibble over things past? 'But, the *Führer*'," he prances, peeking about; seeing someone's got to keep watch. "He's a madman—there, you can tell him I said it—say it to his fat bloated face! No," he jeers, taking a flask from his ruck, seeing I've already made short-shrift the whiskey. He demurs, anticipating the Madmeoiselle's response: "I haven't begun to drink. Now, shut up the both of you—*and listen*: today, today we shall report to FHQ for the very last time. Then, the Mademoiselle and I shall head west—say, why don't you join us? Yes, you simply *must* get out while you can!"

I flail, what fit to be tied by this treasonous twain: "*You* would abandon the Führer?"

Limply he says, "I tried to get him to leave. Being a typical Austrian: won't listen to a word I say."

The Mademoiselle she butts in; and, somehow, ends up taking command. "What *I* think," she exhales, eying the next wave of fighters coming in out-of-the-sun. "Is that we go down: deep in the earth."

[520] [re, scotch: If three years old, it would have been bottled in either '41 or '42, *i.e.*, probably black market. Hence, one may gather, the 'impurities which so darken.'—N.B.]

"The *sewer*?" Guderian and I say, locked in synchronized distress.

"*Oui*," she snipes, hands on thighs. "I hear Berlin has the loveliest underground in Europe.[521] Besides," she soothes, teasing us what with those luscious locks: "Jean Valjean has nothing on you."

Guderian he blushes; but *I* am not amused.

Monique she continues: "First, we issue somewhere safe. Next, try to reach Baur.[522] Then—we'll just have to take our chances up in the air."

I rasp, a bit loud for our attempt at cover and concealment—but, then again, I trust we've already put paid to that: "I will not abandon the Führer!"

Guderian he blusters: "Don't be a fool. Really, holing up with Hitler? It's suicide."

"All the same," I say; unsure if it really is so.

"*I'm staying.*"

But—*the Mademoiselle?*

"I, I don't understand," Guderian says, what thinking he'd the hussy all to himself.

"I do," I say, stealing a drag from the snatch then sizing her up. Smiling I glance at the Colonel-General, the only one back in the prone. "Monique's the one man—no, not man, mind you—the *one man* still capable of telling him the truth. Oh, I know, I know: I've told him myself. I said, 'But, but *mein Führer...* we've made a fortress of the Obersalzberg; yea, a *fortress* capable of holding out for weeks on end.' Oh, but ach; Goebbels just had to go putting a flea in his ear regarding the *Götterdämmerung*.[523] The swine; it's as if he were staging an opera. I tried to warn him[524], really I did. Oh, but he's *changed*," I stomp,

[521] [Balderdash. Everyone knows Warsaw's is tops.—N.B.]

[522] [*Gruppenführer* Baur, Hans: Hitler's personal pilot.—N.B.]

[523] [*Götterdämmerung* ('Twilight of the Gods'): Apocalyptic opera by Richard Wagner.—N.B.]

[524] ['him': *i.e.*, Hitler.—N.B.]

stanching my cherry, heedless of any smoke which might thus ensue; then, pivoting, rail upon the Mademoiselle. "He's *changed*; changed since last he beheld those siren eyes. So help me," I flail, what fighters be damned. "You noxious slit. If you so much's bat an eye then, I shall be there, Mauser in hand; prepared to erase the sexiest arse ever to grace the confines of the Reich."

She smiles: "You've quite a way with the ladies."

And, somehow it seems, I'm back in her good graces.

But she says, "You've come a long way for a rapist."

"So help me you, you malicious slut you, I'll—"

"You'll what?" she laughs, mocking me open. "Have Himmler take care of me? My dear, Heini won't lift a finger. Not since that scoundrel—for which, by the way, I've been meaning to thank you—violated me; *pffft*, now I can play him for years. Simply capital! Really, I'm so glad that I thought of it."

Stifling my contempt, I concede, thus acceding to a deal with the Devil: "I shall take you to see him." Then, almost under my breath, add, "Under *my* protective custody."

"Oh *Wind*," she laughs, aiming that fraudulent smile, what like a dagger straight for the heart. Only, I won't budge. Yet still she persists, stroking me what with those calloused ancient hands. Her act worn thin, her patience runs low. "You know, Hossbach, someone once tried pointing that thing—the very one you're thinking right now—at me, and lived; that is, until he got to the infirmary."

"Thanks for the tip."

"Don't mention it," she says, flashing the smile for which men have killed.

"You realize," I say so's to caution her. "There's every chance we won't make it." I mean, Monique might be a vicious slut but, after all, she *is* a woman...

Her mind somewhere else, she gasps, "*I was there from the start*," what the coldness having gone from her eyes; and, something almost akin to human warmth slumbering therein. But she says, "If Wolfie's bent on shooting himself, we're already dead."

Why, I could have her head; ach, for 'Wolf' you see's a name used by us *Old Fighters*. Yet still she persists: "It cannot *be*," screaming, shoulders convulsing—those scandalous, sensuous shoulders—pummeling her fists into her face. Then, then she does something the likes of which I did not think her capable: just a tear. A small, genuine tear, followed by a veritable flood awash upon her war-weary face; wiping away the war-paint which hides the tale of years. Then, alas, through it all she shrieks: "I am his *creator*!"

Oh good God; *Monique's beginning to scare me...*

"Monsieur," she repeats: *over and over*, as if there were something funny; what the enemy set to return any minute. Why, I don't think she knows quite just where she is. A drag of her cigarette seems to restore the situation when, dangerous, she smiles: "*I* will usher him out."

"Who—Jack?"

She sneers, not so much's batting an eye: "No—*Wolf*."

"Is that a threat?" I snipe, veins to burst.

Instant she shushes: "*Men*; you're so emotional." Trying to change the subject; huh, Monique 101. "Ah, don't you see? There's only one of me to go round; still, a girl must do what a girl must do. The Prof—looks like *I* must free him, too. And who knows? Perhaps even our son."

"You, you cantankerous slut you, why—"

"*Stop!*" comes this manly, caustic voice.

Why, Guderian—pink's a jellyfish a few moments ago—has transformed back to his old bickering self; hah, back to a *Colonel-General* once more. Peering about he screams: "*Run!*"

I leap, then roll. Tumbling downhill, heading for the wheat-field I crawl in the prone unsupported, what all the way to the street. On the way down, I swear having passed a perfectly good Panther[525], all dug in, seemingly abandoned.

I am the last to arrive, about a hundred meters hence, seeing I've been scanning for fighters: blue, nothing but blue. They must've gone home; only, *they never go home.* No, more likely, they're after some other poor swine.

Guderian he senses this. "Now," he says. "Into the tunnels," meaning the sewer. He turns to me: "You've your flashlight, yes? Torch?"

"I've my service light," I say, trying to prevent the words escaping my mouth; only, like so many things, far too late: "*In the jeep.*"

"Never mind—looks like we're flying blind!"

"Ptth," she puffs, grimacing towards Guderian. And, wetting those lips, those obscene lips, she coos, "Wolfie was right; really, turning tail after the first few hiccoughs..."

The nerve; I mean, after all these cockroaches have done to redefine the meaning the words 'turning tail'.

She lights another smoke, then eyes me up and down. "Hoss-bach," she purrs, as though I were her servant. "Take this rag, then siphon that Panther. You must soak it, *really really well.*" And, extending her be-gloved fingers, she demonstrates. "You must roll it *really really tight*; oui, *all the way in-side.*" With an impolitic gesture,

---

[525] ['Panther': German 'super tank,' which suffered more than its share of teething.—N.B.]

she hands me her canteen, the likes of which I have never seen. "Asbestos," she smiles. "See—instant torch!"[526]

Receiving her rag, I repeat my effort at sprint and concealment, the which I have already concluded: *I am far too old.* Unfortunately, like most of the 'soldiers' we've managed corral,[527] we've no ammo for cover.

Breathless I make it to the tank, then soak the rag 'really really well'. On a whim, though I know we haven't the time, I pop the hatch and peek; then instantly wish that I had not. The driver's dead; as for the rest, I shudder to think. Yes, somewhere there probably lies an unmarked grave, bearing their naked remains; and, but what could be anywhere, *Ivans*, dressed as Panzers—*headed for Berlin...*

I sprint, then crawl's before, in case the Russkies should chance be snipers. Retrieving her rag, she dips it in the lip her canteen; then, doing the honors, sets it to torch. A fiery halo thus ensues, illuminating our passage-way through night.

"That'll help orient us," Guderian concedes. "Nothing more. Well, we'd best hurry," he winces, eyes towards the sky. "For this torch's liable to bring our friends back."

She sneers, "No: it'll buy me time to radio Gonz to come get us."

The Spaniard? Oh good God...

"Come get us?" Pathetic I watch the old man cringe. Yes, poor Guderian's growing more agitated by the minute. It doesn't help the sound of artillery's getting louder.

---

526 ['see': Figuratively, of course, until he had actually drenched the rag in the Panther. Then, via the application of fire, the canteen would have provided a chassis for their 'torch.'—N.B.]

527 [It is not known from whence such 'dregs' were supposed to have been culled. It is entirely possible that they had simply selected a cadre, then moved on, after having taxed the recruits with the responsibility for rounding up the final remnant.—N.B.]

"Never mind," she says. "When I give the signal, make a beeline. Head two blocks east, then meet up. Ready? Now!"

Leaving no time so's to consider the wisdom as to her plan, we're off.

We meet at the Friedrichstrasse; alas, it's time to go in. "And take us where?" I demand, delaying our descent into the subterranean dark.

"But, the Führerbunker," she ordains; usurpation's her approach as ever. "Gonz has, how do we say, gotten into the Two-two-three[528] business: imagine, a plane, which needs no runway, capable of both landing, and take-off—*vertically*. Then, poof—you're up in the air!"

---

[528] [The *223-C* was the first combat ready 'copter. I must however hasten to question whether the designation as given is correct. For one must never forget that the go-between with regard to this record revolves around that ever litigative species, defense attorney, *sui generis*. As such it is not prudent for me to cast aspersions on the 'facts' alleged therein, insofar as even the most miniscule chance of their being proven correct might obtain: Or, so at least my own attorney has advised, after consultation with the Censor. All this as preface to say that, to whit, a *C-223* could neither have accommodated four occupants, nor obtained speeds in excess of 183 kilometers per hour. Moreover, it is highly unlikely that such craft could ever have borne three passengers, let alone have evaded the Red fighters, while maneuvering through the woods. The former could be explained with reference to a variant of greater capacity, adumbrated by a different letter. The last, sequentially speaking, the *223-F*, does not quite fit the bill. Perhaps further variants existed, of which I am not aware. A more remote possibility postulates the existence of some hitherto unknown type of VTOL (Vertical Take Off and Landing), which, in addition to extra capacity, could have been capable of speeds, and even maneuverability, vastly superior to the sitting duck with which we have been presented. Of course, it need not be stipulated, I have no knowledge of the existence of any such animal. Further, it must be repeated, I have only had occasion to fiddle with the manuscript where cases of the utmost exigency required.—N.B.]

"Now I've heard it all," Guderian he groans, looking to me's if to say, 'So—*how does it feel?*' But he says nothing; therefore, he too acquiesces in her plan.

The Mademoiselle she springs open the hatch, then bids us go inside; *why, it's the Führerbunker all over.* I let the spell of claustrophobia pass, wading through all the filth and debris; dead bodies, air-raid victims, abound.

"Here," she grunts, climbing down, somehow summoning the strength to drop the Colonel-General his ruck.

From which he unearths this transmitter, barking at me the whole while to set the damned thing up. The grouse; why I'd no *idea* he'd been humping it all this while. No wonder he's been gruff.

This being done, she radios for help; *now* I see why she lied about Baur. Ach, for, in Monique's twisted mind you see the Boss must view our arrival's something fortuitous; not some desperate scheme endangering the life of his pilot. Besides, for Baur to evade air-supremacy would be seen as something common. What some Spaniard? A minor miracle.

Having conveyed our coordinates, she impresses upon me to close the hatch; thereby removing the last of the light. We traverse through the deleterious muck, our re-lit torch scarcely illuminating [three meters] in front. Now the cat, or transmitter's out the bag, Guderian rejoices my having to shoulder his burden. The swine must make do leading the way; what the witch barking directions from behind.

Following an inordinate procession of false turns, interspersed midst various do's and dont's, we issue out this manhole into what seems to be a park. Fighters they strafe in the distance; oh, but ach, memories are evoked by the strangest of things. Alas I recall: *burying Cindy Williams in the sand...*

"Take off your jacket."

"Huh?"

"Schnell!"

'But, my medals,' I wish to say; only, seeing Fast Heinz surrender his own, shames me thus to simply just follow. And then it clicks: we waste no time dressing our transmitter in the most highly decorated *Daunenjacke*[529] ever to be surrendered without so much as a fight. "*E-tool*," I bark, nodding to the Mademoiselle, all the while digging with my claws what just like a cat; burying Cindy—er, our transmitter—in this childish pen.

"Enough," Guderian barks; quickly we scamper before the fighters return.

The Girl, who had been standing guard, leads us to the basement of a gutted-out apartment; where, through a hole in the masonry, anxious we scan the sky. Minutes they seem eternal. My mind it begins to drift; that my body, drool. Worse, my flask it seems to be empty.

No sooner do I nod off, than a sound like the Devil himself wakes me out from my slumber. Cursing the absurdity this strange vertical-lifter, not to mention the Mademoiselle's outrageous idea, it hovers before me. I am shunted in back, whence the whooshing summons me alert; pah—infernal contraption! Yes, we Hossbachs have been good Protestants now for centuries, dating to the time of Luther; nonetheless, '*Our Father, who art in Heaven...*'

Still, this Gonz proves to be an excellent pilot. We've no trouble at all, until reaching the outskirts of center-city,[530] where a few *Sturmoviks*[531] chance appear. They chase us over the trees, down into the woods. Madly we dash, almost one with the earth; then, hover. Alas it seems we've finally lost them.

---

529 ['Daunenjacke': Jacket. They had not time to bury the whole transmitter: Hence the jacket for cover.—N.B.]

530 ['center city': The manuscript reads 'Berlin-Mitte,' *i.e.*, the middle of Berlin.—N.B.]

531 [*Sturmovik*: Soviet ground-attack aircraft, whose chief merit lay in its copious armor.—N.B.]

We emerge out over the ruins of the Reichs Chancellery. Why, the devastation's appalling. To think, the Führer actually *lives* beneath, what like those beasts I saw under Nordhausen. Luckily, Goebells has had the Tiergarten[532] converted into a runway; upon the which this Gonz seamlessly lands.

Whereupon I'm thrown for quite a shock. "Why—what's *he* doing?" I say, indicating our pilot climbing out, adjusting my volume as the din of the engines dies down. "But he can't possibly—"

"You've got to be joking," the hussy intervenes, hands on thighs, what cigarette-holder already in hand. I mean it can't possibly have stayed lit during the entire flight; and yet, there she is: smoking like a fucking chimney. "Wolfie and Gonz? *They're old pals.* Back to the days of the civil war," she coos, by which I take it she must mean Spanish.

I cannot tell if she is bluffing.

Before I can consider, the Spaniard he smarts, "I cannot *leave*," but in the harsh, guttural tones of the Castilian, imperiled by a bad German-pidgin.

I say to myself, 'She fancies *this* over me?' But then I realize: 'He is on the verge of tears.'

"My ship," he sighs, lamenting 'his' wounded Two-two-three. "My beautiful beautiful ship: she's taken a hit to the engines; she shan't fly again."

"Underground now—all of you!" Guderian says. "To the silo: Hossbach, show them the—"

"I know the way," the Mademoiselle she struts, leading Gonz by the arm, what damned near straddling him.

---

532 [*Tiergarten*: A lovely little park in central Berlin. Of course, a 'copter... or, for that matter, any VTOL capable craft, can land most anywhere. Nonetheless, it had to have helped to have had a stable surface, devoid of civilians, in order for the pilot to land.—N.B.]

Swarthy old swine! Pah, she's doing it just to spite me; *why, I've half-a-mind...*

I try to put it out my head, accompanying them through the tunnel for the burial this strange vertical-lifter.

***

Monique leads us to what appears to be an airplane graveyard. We're underground now, not far from the Führerbunker, in what must be an extension of the Berlin Subway. Gas-laden wreckage accrues, interspersed with unrecognizable parts scattered all about. A false door; oh, then ach, the other side, a sight for sore eyes: a *Fieseler Storch*, almost alone intact midst a heap of abandoned ruin. So, this is what the Spanish have been hiding—under our noses the whole time! The implications are staggering, bringing sundry things to mind. Still, as ever with that woman, there's simply no time to inquire.

We squander precious minutes waiting for Gonz and Guderian to make the tumultuous trek to ground. An eternity later they reappear, having siphoned enough fuel from the Two-two-three. Dutifully the Mademoiselle and I help them feed it to the Storch; which latter's usually a one-seater. This one's a training module: just enough room for pilot and Hitler; that is, if she can get him to come round...

Guderian and I stare, eagle-eyed. He's no love-lost for the Chief. Still, a soldier's a soldier; thus is he consigned to his fate. Of course, I insist upon staying, thus that the Boss might presently break out.

But, what about the Mademoiselle? Why surely she didn't come all this way simply to die. Well, what's she going to do? Ach, for I know that woman: she's always got something up her sleeve. Besides, Francois[533] won't exactly be pleased to see her. Nonetheless we escort her through

533 ['Francois': *i.e.*, the French, suddenly anti Nazi. Before 'D Day,' however, collaborationists, such as Mother, were by no means in the minority. As we will see, such congruence led to the most fanatical French holing up with Hitler, to the very last.—N.B.]

this jungle of concrete, past the winding halls into the Führerbunker what like some Goddess, who currently holds our fate in her hands.

Up above, sirens they wail; yet I no longer care. Yes bombs they may fall but, to me, that's all a lifetime away. Now, ours is but to protect the Mademoiselle, what like some queen fucking bee: but with Gonz, Guderian and I her drones; and why I bet she's just waiting for somebody to sting.

Ushering her down the secret stairs, we pass the supply hut—ah, the cage! And again I find myself carried away to another place, another place in time; *ach, when I was in charge of one of these contraptions...*

Now, the Boss's needs are the supplies that I must tend. And it'll probably be the death of me; pah, then so be it. After all, a soldier cannot abandon his post. Yea, the Reaper hath scythed the fields of Europe one end to the next. And from such sacrifice shall be renewed the glory of Magyar & Hun; of Angle & of Saxon; yea, of all our tribes who so people the Earth.

And the Earth is going to need it. That is, if Man's to stand a chance against the barbarians from the East; ach, for Stalin he simply will not stop at the borders of the Reich.

Let the rest of the world take note.

The Vor Bunker

As children were we taught that the vanquished too are worthy of honor. For Nature is pleased that so many be tested; that, somewhere, something better might obtain; *indeed, war is the father of all.*[534]

[534] ['War is the father of all things.': Saying attributed to Heraclitus, yet echoed by Bismarck, Teddy Roosevelt, Churchill, Hitler, Stalin, and just about every world leader since.—N.B.]

Only, now, now the Reich is being destroyed, why what hope can there be, for a world which knows honor not? Yes we have stood behind our Führer, and shall do so until the very end. Ach for, as Goebbels himself's convinced me, without his name, and what the prestige that goes with it, it would be the end of our existence. Why his whole *life* bears testament to the fact that, under the Jew, the Earth would pass through space a dull, lifeless sphere; *this*, this is that against which we must fight. And so as thanks—you *bomb* us?

It takes moral turpitude you see to resist swaying from one's path at the very last moment. As long as the Hitler name's still ripe upon peoples' lips, all is not lost. It's just, if he can't save us, *no one can*; whoso alone understands this understands our German Revolution...

I tell myself these things, even's I wait to be ushered into his presence. In need of sleep, any sleep, rather, I pass into this fugue-like state. Oh, if we can just make it to the other side the hall, then everything will be set to right. Why there's scarcely any room's we stumble past this sea of refugees currently clogging the Vor Bunker.[535]

Gonz, ever vigilant, insists it's his duty inform us we've precious time to get out. "There is one more ship," he says, by dint of which he must mean a Storch; or, rather, Two-two-three. "Hitler," he adds, biting. "Is impermeable to reason. If we leave now—and I mean right now—I can still get *one* of you out."

Setting his previous canard—i.e., that he 'could not leave'—aside, as well's my desire to uncover this stash of flying-machines[536] he seems to've suddenly recalled, I pay him no heed. Ach, for, this swine's no German, rather. So

535 [*Vor Bunker* (pr. 'For Bunker'): Bunker 'before,' *i.e.*, on top of, the Führer Bunker. Like the subway, it too had attempted to house and feed an ever increasing number of refugees.—N.B.]

536 For, where there's one, there's more—lessons of a Supply Officer! [—W.H.]

he can't possibly understand that, without the Chief, perhaps it's best if we should just die.

Guderian's paying him closest of mind. Still, the corridor's so dark and crowded, if he were to make a dash, six of one to half a dozen the other that we'd ever find him.

Rather the Mademoiselle turns to her Spaniard, seizing him what with those dark courtesan eyes and says: "*Sit.*"

And, he, as any man, obeys.

Vor Bunker, Security HQ[537]

Pah, that rusted cunt you see's taken it on herself to convince the Boss there's still time to get out; I demand that I should go with.

Deeming my sally of such inconsequence, she deignsn't even argue; breathless I follow.

But alas, I fear: *the fate of the Reich's about to devolve upon the ministrations of that devilish woman...*

537 [*i.e.,* Hossbach's quarters.—N.B.]

Chapter 41: Cyanide

Under Berlin: April 23, 1945, approx. 05.00

"Out my way," I say, stealing past the sentry, yielding Guderian so's to gain entry. We're in the Vor Bunker, where the Goebbels children, and most of the staff, currently reside.

Guderian's presence here acts like a tonic. The men are stricken with a holy, almost superstitious dread: *he*, Hero of Smolensk; *he*, Chief of the General Staff. Yet little do they know: *he is but yesterday's news.*

The SS we come across see him's he is: that is a defeated, argumentative old man. Why, a man so unhinged's to engage in verbal fisticuffs with the Führer; for which he was summarily dismissed.

That was just a few weeks back.[538] Therefore it's incumbent on me to bring in the heavy artillery, introducing myself and so staking claim for entry.[539] Surely the swine must recognize me; for some reason though I seem to be having some trouble.

Alas Monique she simply sashays up, making small talk what with the men. One of the guards it seems he knows her; pah, Himmler's stud—bedeviled by a woman! He lets us through. Gonz's treated as an orderly, and plays the part according.

So's not to cause the Boss's blood-pressure to skyrocket, I leave Gonz and Guderian with some refugees from the 'Women's Auxiliary to the Hitler Youth'.[540] Whereupon, upon the accursed Frenchie I turn, making an impassioned plea that I should be the one to see him first; she startles me by proffering no objection.

---

538 [Guderian was dismissed March 28, 1945.—N.B.]

539 ['entry': *i.e.*, to the Führer Bunker below.—N.B.]

540 ['Women's Auxiliary to the Hitler Youth': I am unaware of any such thing.—N.B.]

Oh, now I see: I am to soften him up for her peace-offensive; which latter's punishable by death. Yes, I am to just casually let slide that the Mademoiselle happens to be here.

Descending to the Führerbunker, I can hear Guderian say: "Godspeed!"

Too late I realize: *mine's a fool's errand...*

The Führer Bunker

The Boss is at his desk—a pitiful sight: arms behind the back, what hands fiddling nervous. Sheepish his scalp snow-white it sinks; sinks's though his neck were no longer able support it. Worse, this darksome, unholy gloom; ach, *mein Gott*, he is more dead than alive.

Save for the eyes, those penetrating eyes; which presently seek reason for my imposition.

I feel's if I should comfort him; only, do I *dare*? Oh —what difference does it make? Yes, I know, I know: I know he could have me shot; *huh, that'd just save Ivan the trouble...*

I proffer belated greetings,[541] presenting a gold-watch inscribed with the date of the Party's founding. Oh, I know he's an infinitude such trifles; still, the sentiment's duly noted. Now—business. "Our um, *friend*," I say. "Thinks she can get Eisenhower to the table—"

"Or to her bed!"

"*Whence*," I continue. "A cease-fire might be arranged, along the Western Front, yielding defensive—"

He rails, brushing that unruly mop; only to find it precipitately fall back: "Everybody's always telling me about these glorious 'defensive positions'. And, *now*? Now he's in the heart of Reich—some defensive position! *Eisenhower*? That Yid's[542] just biding his time; much, I might add, as we."

541 ['belated greetings': Hitler's birthday was three days before.—N.B.]

He smiles, seemingly his old-self once more. Still, like an engine past it's prime, the vital spark it seems has faded; faded along with the tale of years. But again, the eyes; those deep, penetrating eyes...

"No," he adds. "I don't like it; I don't like it one bit. Tell the Mademoiselle from me I *forbid* negotiations, save to buy time to allow the *Victory Weapons* to come into effect. There—recite it like an order you have received: say, 'This is a *Führerorder*'. There—let them put that in their pipe and smoke it!"

His words may sound the same but, in truth, they're hollow; ach, for, *war you see it changes a man.* Previous it was his hands. Now, now his whole body it shakes, stricken with some nameless fear; why, it's as if the very Fates have conspired.

I know who's behind it, too: *the Luftwaffe.* Their incompetence is simply criminal; our cities but one heap of ruin. And, now, now Ivan he stands on German soil; ach, *mein Gott*—I know a thing or two of which the Russian is capable...

Thank God Bremen still holds. Last I heard, P'pa was going to try to make it to Holland, seeing that 'That's where the Kaiser went when things got rough'.

'It's been almost thirty years,' I'd written, by way of response; God knows if he ever got it. '*Things change.* Especially seeing what sport civilians seem to make for enemy tail-gunners.' Desperate I begged him reconsider.

I try to push it out my mind; and, bracing myself, turn to face the Chief. "There's still Ribbentrop."

"I don't give a damn for your Ribbentrop!" he rasps, what this vacuous look in his eyes, impersonating our Foreign Minister.

Really, so *ungentlemanly*; not very becoming. Still, he's right: Ribbentrop's a fool. Only, fool or no, I've given

542 [Certain Nazis remained convinced that Eisenhower was somehow a 'secret Jew.'—N.B.]

my word to brief Hitler of his plan to get Stalin to the table, so as to preserve a modicum of our existence.[543]

"Stalin's aims," the Boss resumes. "Are essentially the same as mine," mouthing the most irreconcilable *quatsch* anybody's ever conceived. "Only, whereas I've thousands of holders of the *Knight's Cross*, the cream of the nation behind me, the Georgian can call on a hundred-million ridiculous Slavs, that neither can read nor write: *but know how to kill Germans.* Plus, once the Georgian is gone, what's to stop these kikes from sicking those apes on us? And it will be the end of all existence: as the beginning, the Earth shall pass through space a dull, lifeless sphere..."

Well, that just hangs it: I make the most momentous decision in my life. "Come," I say, hands together so's to keep warm. "We shall go down in a blaze of glory!" And, clicking my heels, promontory to the Hitler salute, he stops me, returning the German one instead; you know, like we did in the Kaiser's Army so long ago. Against my better judgment, I can hear myself say, "But, the girl. But what about the girl?" I mean, I know I just said it; still, deep down, really I'm thinking of Jack.[544]

"Who? The what?" Why, he seems perplexed, as though we were no longer speaking of the same thing. Gazing through the shadows, I gasp as a glimmer of light it silhouettes his face; alas comprehension it dawns. "Oh, I'm not worried about her sneaking out: I'm concerned lest she might get *in*."

So, I take it he means Monique for all her crimes to simply just disappear. Still, he's right to fear her reappearance. I mean, it's just not right, what getting his hopes up the way she always does; not this late in the act.

[543] [Ribbentrop had made a similar offer in '43, with this difference: Once he had lured Stalin to the table, he, Ribbentrop, would personally gun him down. The plot soon foundered upon Hitler's refusal to sanction it, saying it would be, 'Asking for trouble from Providence.'—N.B.]

[544] [Bullshit.—N.B.]

Ach, for he knows she'll only quote some ridiculous specification concerning some new weapon; you know, the kind of numerics for which his statistophile brain goes ape. Then, then she'll launch into some languid discourse concerning the exploits of such-and-such pilot, who may, or may not, ever have existed; oh, why did I *bring* her?

He tells me straight-faced that Jack and von Braun are about to turn the tide of the war; oh, but ach, I've heard it all before: the 'Victory Weapon' clap-trap, upon the which he is always harping. Why, he told me himself, what just the other day: it's only so much *quatsch*. Only, now, now it seems he's become victim of his fancy; and so unable to distinguish lie from truth. Still, it's not *my* place to find fault; I mean, how could anyone hold up under such conditions? Oh, but he must play the politician: the 'Victory Weapons' are all he has to dangle. Thus he clings to them; clings to them like a drowning man the proverbial straw...

Somehow, I've got to keep the Girl from heaping kerosene on his illusory hopes. But then I realize: *it's already far too late.* Ach, for, the sentry must've seen her. Yes, even's I'm butting heads in here, Monique's presence must be spreading like wildfire. As usual, the Boss is the last to know; oh, but how do I *tell* him?

"All I need's one more victory," he says, pacing; or, hobbling, rather, pointing to the map, suddenly become warlord once more.

My heart it begins to pound. Concussions they spread, what from the artillery, colliding with God knows what above, leveling apartments; utilities; why entire city blocks. Plus who's to say the concrete'll hold up for long? They don't call them 'bunker-busters' for nothing...

My chest it begins to quake; oh, but ach, I can feel the nausea welling up within. Yes, a suicide-psychosis it seems's taken hold of the Führerbunker; to which even *I* am not immune. On my way down, two SS toughs were busy discussing the merits of various forms of suicide:

apparently the topic of choice. Eyes closed, I see: *my heart, ripped by my own hand, presented to the Chief; alongside that of the Mademoi—*

With almost religious awe, I come to; and behold the genius of *him*: the 'Victory Weapons', and all such *quatsch*, are strictly for domestic consumption; *thus that we might die like men.* Yes, it's just as he told me some two weeks ago.

He smiles, in silent affirmation of the thought; my heart it skips with quiet relief.[545] "Then," he says. "And only then can there be any talk of peace: with either side for all I care." Exhausted he sits. "Only, if Stalin, know you this..."

A crippling chill envelops, both emotional and moral. For, so many good men you see already have died; and why I shudder to think there may be more. "With Stalin," he wisps, what so soft I can barely hear. A glass of water shakes its way to his face, parching more desk than throat. "We shall just have to fight it out again: it's just in my nature. Moreover, when I'm gone, who will have the strength to carry on the struggle? No, there must be no talk of peace: *not while I'm Führer.* You'll see—this time, we shall not give in two minutes to midnight!" The old boy he glares, fixing on me.

He calms down long enough for Morell to waddle in and take his pulse: normal; *absolutely normal.* Ach, all this talk of 'one more victory' is thought by some to be aimed at obtaining better terms. Only, as I've just learned, our 'peace offensive''s a sham. Why, we're just playing for time; time in hope that, as he puts it, "That rot of a son, and that idiot professor, can come up with something so big that, even now, we might obtain a glorious victory..."

Of a sudden he grows larger than life. For a moment, even his color it seems returns. "Speer thinks

---

[545] [Apparently, such silent *sympatico*, which Hossbach alleges to have been real, was worth confirming that the *Siegwaffen* were not.—N.B.]

these atomics might be ready any day. Until then," he adds, what mailed fist. "We must hold out a little more!"

Again, I'd arrived a has-been; and leave feeling a million marks. Why, I revel his strategy, seeing it espouses a mastery of brevity and wit. Yes the only thing that can be said against it is, at present, it bears no relation to the facts...

The Vor Bunker

Instant I pass from his presence, that reality gat hold; and alas my hopes are dashed like that of some victim before some savage Red Man's God. And, losing all hope, I lose all restraint. Flailing my way to the Vor Bunker, I find the Mademoiselle in the midst of several young stallions. Extricating her out from this revolting scene, I pull her off to the side, then demand that I should go with.

Ignoring my plea, she summons the guard, what with her twat and her charm, allowing her exit the Vor Bunker, seeking Hitler below.

Why I hadn't the chance to tell her: *he doesn't even know you're here*; and I'll be damned if I'm going to be upstaged by that disreputable woman.

Thus, leaving Gonz and Guderian up here to hide, I go after, descending the spiral staircase one more time.

The Führer Bunker

Stomping past this swell of human misery, oppressed by the pall of forlorn hope which suffuses it, I head for the study. Oh, but ach; the Siren she's beaten me to it. Bormann, too, what his little note-pad ready to hand, transcribing everything the Boss might say. I turn to the Chief, what the most woeful wince upon my face; *but they are in a world of their own.* Yes an invisible shield it seems surrounds them, outside which Bormann and I are but spectators; *perhaps we always were.*

Oh, we've sacrificed our lives we have just to be here. Still, so far's they're concerned, *we do not exist.* And so at last I recognize my place: forever a spectator to history. Well, it's in God's hands now; or, *the Mademoiselle's...*

"Adi," she says, sashaying up to the desk, unlit cigarette-holder glued to her hand. "You must think of the *big picture*," 'accidentally' touching his thigh.

He makes this face, this face I can't describe; then puts his fist through the wall. Like a seizure, it's over before I can quite think it through. Why, he's never acted this way; at least, not around me. With difficulty he composes himself: "You think you've a better grasp of strategics than *I*? Well then, prove it: oh, *jede Frau*[546]—save us from the Ivans!"

"But, *mon frer*," she sulks, not from any disrespect, rather, than a pendant to her charm. The thought occurs that here are two hypnotists going at it; the effect is rather disturbing. "There exists," she says, batting those courtesan eyes, caressing his snow-white scalp. "The *political* solution..."

She raises her hands, what those vile be-gloved hands and, fondling her cigarette-holder, obscures the last of the light; ach, why it's like a *cave* in here. "I shall just have a little talk with Eisenhower. And *he*—"

"*Nein*," Hitler he roils, fist to the desk, what dark coronal masses ejecting from his eyes. "There shall be no capitulation in this war—not at two minutes to midnight! Yes, for *Providence* sent me—"

"Oh—blow it out your arse."

He grabs his chest, face chalk-white; merciless she continues: "No, Wolfchen—the world will go on without you. Ah, don't you see? Germany's got to get in, while the getting is good."

546 [*jede Frau*: lit. 'every woman.' An epithet, possibly referring to her protean charm.—N.B.]

He nods, color returning to his face, aware less the Mademoiselle rather than some memory within. Then, regaining the thread, the last chain linking them like a latticework of interweaving destiny he says, “When I'm dead, Europe will find out all about the Russians; of course, by then, it will be too late. Bah, you filthy frogs—you and your effeminate English! You've been corrupted through centuries of miscegenation; Christianity; and everything else the Jew has thrown at you. And you've become stupid; stupid as we. The German people should thank its lucky stars they ever found me. And yet, what do I get? Nothing but cowards, hypocrites, betrayers. No, don't talk to me about the German people—the German people will get what's theirs! As for the Russians, they'll rise first in Italy, one-by-one in their Bolshevik cells. Next, the Low Countries. Then, before you know it—*Paris will be next.* And it shall be the Bolshevisation of Europe. The spiritual Judaization of the race; the masses turned to plebs like back when I found them. No, there can be no talk of capitulation. From now on I offer only victory, or—death!”

Oh, but ach; why, everything, everything I've ever held sacred, what just like our cities's being destroyed; the very love of the race itself repudiated by the one man fit to save it.

Monique remains unperturbed; my God... she's *shaking* him: “It's *over*—the Thousand Year Reich is no more!” And, leading him by the hand, she walks the prematurely aged figure to the tapestries, similar to the ones Göring'd once tried to save in lieu of the Reichstag. Tears they make their way down her face, what with the subtlety of a seizure. She points to the painting of Friedrich, thus that he might have something on which to concentrate. “It is our doom, Adi, *our doom*; that is, unless *I* do something about it. Come,” she quips, cupping his face in her hands; those dirty, ancient hands. “Let me take you to the—”

"*Nein,*" he strikes, his target this time the wall. "It's too late: Göring can negotiate when I'm dead." He hobbles past; Bormann and I step out of the way.

Why, I doubt he even *sees* us. Body all hunched, he 'stands' under the portrait of Friedrich, shielding his eyes. Then, a miracle: of a sudden he grows larger than life. And, buried beneath the rubble of our ancient city, he stands as if atop the roof of the world and says: "*One must know how to die.*"

And, that's it, his last piece of wisdom: 'One must know how to die'. I reproach myself, seeing I've told this to the troops a hundred times; yet still, coming from him, I expected something more.

"No," she says, unable to accept the inevitable. "I will not leave Europe to this fate. Forget Eisenhower: I will just have a little talk with Laval. And *he*—"

"Laval?" he croaks, in a voice so hoarse why I can scarcely make out what it is he's trying to say. "He's the most hated man in Europe!"[547]

"A trifle," she adds, side-stepping. "For *he* can get word to Ike; *oui*, I've thought it all through. Gestapo-knows he's passed more than his share to Washington; surely they'll wish repay him. Or don't you think? Just promise me one thing—you won't kill yourself till I get back."

"But, but where are you *going*?"

And, with a wince, she whispers, "*Back to the front.*"

She turns, facing him one more time. Invisible or no, scarcely do I believe my eyes—why, they're holding hands: sexless, bloodlessly holding hands; gazing deep in each other's eyes...

I try not to stare; but this is impossible. And I wonder—do they see what *I* do? Ach, for in Monique's eyes I see this relentless struggle: *a dragon thrashing its tail to the cyclic rhythm of the world...*

---

[547] [Psychologists would call this a clear case of projection.—N.B.]

In Hitler though I'm shocked by what I find: *an abandoned baby, what all pink and gooey*; and yet, healthy and wise, growing into a boy. An ancient villa it comes into view, leading to an enchanted forest high atop some Himalayan hill. There he sits, what like some Buddha ensconced in one final vision. The child, whom one so wants to help, becomes hopelessly lost in the tunnels of existence. Alas the poor sot he can't find his way; for you see the umbilicus has been cut, severing him from the mother which is life.

Now, now he's become but some trembling old man, grown all bent and shaken. In fact, it is no longer he rather but some refugee; a malcontent blinding me what with its malevolence...

Monique must've seen it, too; for presently she turns away. And, before me shakes this crumpled old man. Ach, it pains me to say it but, if I'm thinking it, surely she must be too: *perhaps it's best if he should just die...*

He fiddles, hands shaking, catching the one with the other, then hands her this silver ampoule: “My child, take it; ah, ah yes yes yes, take it and go.”

She places the ampoule in a locket round her chest; then, turning round, faces him one more time: he needn't tell her what it contains.

***

We deposit Bormann in the Vor Bunker, not stopping to gather Gonz and Guderian, then come to ground.

Entering the lobby, I admire the beautiful murals still standing midst the ruins of the Old Chancery. We pass the long, Doric columns, coagulating what with the stench of ruin and death, when Monique she comes to a halt. Assorted tools they lay all about. Demanding me fetch her some pliers, I lead her to what's left of the auto-pool. Upon which she says, “I think you'd better step back.”

Why, I will do nothing of the sort. Ach, for thirty years now I've lived by but one rule: *never trust that impossible woman.*

She pries her trap apart, but almost against herself, as though some invisible force were compelling her that she should not. Then, securing her molar, she fastens tight; *and pulls.*

Searing waves it seems they blast, ebbing and flowing what like some great heat; myopic penetrations burning out from within. Next she takes a needle from God-knows-where. An altered state of consciousness it seems to subsist, whereby naught exists save for needle and eye. And, amidst the pain, somehow she manages thread an almost atomic-eye; then, with a shriek, pinions it in back her mouth. With a hyena howl she jabs, eyes floating back; oh, but how can she *see*? Terrified I watch's she fiddles with the locket round her chest, retrieving a silver ampoule; the which she places beneath her blood-red tongue. And, cursing what under her breath, she locks those lascivious lips at an angle sufficient to cement the ampoule in place, thus that it might take all her strength just to break; once breached, though, death follows within seconds.

Frantic I search for my own 'Führer's Christmas packet'; and, wondering, cannot help but think, 'When the time comes—*will I be half the man's* she*?*'

And, loosing a scream, she estranges me out from these thoughts, thrusting the needle back through her gums; covering herself with a sickly red-spew. The instant she returns, shaken by shock to reality of Earth.

In my arms—how, I do not know, seeing everything's happened so quick—Monique regains consciousness.

The pain of Atlas it taxes my shoulders as she rises then leaves me behind; and, fleeing midst the shells, exits the Reichs Chancellery for what could be the last time.

Chapter 42: Last Cigarette

Ruins of the Reich's Chancellery: April 23, 1945, approx. 06.00

I find myself wandering, what like some rootless Yid, all about the Chancery. I watch as she fades, fades from my vision; and I wonder if I'm ever going to see her again.

I need a drink; and, by God, I am going to get it. I mean, otherwise, I'll end up like him[548]; just some bloodless ghost, trapped in this mortal coil.

Exiting the auto-pool, I come upon Eva in the lobby. Huh, seems she's headed for a smoke; at least *she* respects him.[549] Still, should anyone even be here? True, the bombing's all but stopped—I mean, why destroy what's about to be yours? That said, their fighters take shots at sundry women and men.

"*No one knows I'm here*," she says, as if getting away with something.

Suppressing a smile, I call security, with whose leadership the Boss's entrusted me, from[550] the line in the lobby. Dispensing with the password, I'm put through to Scheldte; pah, how *eerie* to think he is beneath. Instinctive I glance at my feet, so as to facilitate communication. With a gaze of concrete I say, "Tell the Boss our Viennese's with me: *I* shall protect her. Now, no one's to go anywhere without *my* permission; ach, for it's no longer safe to enter center-city.[551] *Hmm?* Oh, oh yes yes yes: *Heil Hitler.*"

---

548 [re, 'him': Hitler, I think.—N.B.]

549 [Shitler had lost his authority to such an extent that people had actually began smoking in the Führer Bunker. It's common knowledge how he abhorred the particular vice: Hence Hossbach's observation, 'At least *she* respects him.'—N.B.]

550 [In Berlin, the telephone system was, incredibly, somehow still able to function.—N.B.]

551 That is, without being made a head shorter.[—W.H.]

Returning to my damsel, I take her by the hand and, whistling, lead her to the Wilhelmstrasse. Any farther would be unthinkable; huh, as if it isn't already.

"Thank you," she says's we stop, fastidiously straightening her skirt.

My, what *breeding*. Why, it's beneath her even to comment on all the fire and rubble. With my lips I light her expertly rolled smoke, exhausting our last working match. Eye to eye, and cherry to cherry, I proceed to fire mine up.

Artillery it screams, what the rot of decomposed flesh assaults the very senses; even's fire envelops the night. By contrast Eva is like some heavenly scent, whose beauty hath wakened some dying chivalry within. Yet there's a baseness in every beatitude. For, it's our 'last cigarette'; the only way we can be together.

We pretend to take survey the city, only caring not wander too far. And yet, every word you see's a mask some passion; each banality but some desperate caress.

Time's up; a stomped-out cherry tells all. And yet, to what've *I* to return? Oh, let them string me up; some other poor swine can take my—*huh*, what's this? Why, she's *gone*, passing into the distance but a silhouette in the night;[552] returning to her tomb like a good little corpse.

Recovering from my revery, I find myself alone; a certain freedom thus ensues. Only, should I turn deserter? I laugh at the absurdity, even's I drift into the city. *'Nein,'* I say to myself. 'I'm just going for one more drink.'[553]

The city's like a mountain that's been put through a blender then exploded out from within. Saddest still's the memorabilia; *you know, signs that speak.* Things that say, 'Someone used to live here'.

---

552 [Sunrise appears to have been obscured by the quotient of fire and smoke in the sky.—N.B.]

553 [While the *Vor Bunker* harbored liquor aplenty, a certain degree of normalcy, or, the illusion thereof, is what Hossbach appears to have sought, during his unauthorized 'stroll.'—N.B.]

And, like a round of Russian Roulette writ-large, here and there some edifice still stands. One chances emit a sound, the likes of which I cannot shake: *signs of life.*

Surveying the anomaly of electric-light in a bombed-out city, why I just have to see what's inside. Then I remember: *Old Man Dannecker.* The morbidity assaults the very senses. Ach, for scarcely do I believe my very own eyes: two old ladies, one of whom's just purchased a bottle of wine, heading for the cinema. It's incomprehensible they should be wandering, what the Ivans already in the suburbs.[554] Moth to the flame, I follow, in search of the lie, that glorious lie, *hope.*

There's supposed to be a motion-picture; yet the screen's blank as it is dumb. Full of wonder I sit, embracing the illusion nothing's amiss. Yes, we drink our little wine. Some chat, whilst others simply cherish a place to sleep. The fact there's electricity's confounding, seeing I can't make hide nor hair of it; *hmm, must be a dynamo somewhere.*

I try to make small talk, laughing when others laugh, chasing my wine what with drink; pah, the sense of security a roof seems to provide. And, it takes me back. Or, within; in to the memories playing the screen my mind...

***

I'm back: back in 'Thirty-three. The Führer's just come to power. That's me, exiting the cinema with a lady hand-in-glove. I try to kiss her; pah, nothing but sour—

***

Grapes? Yes, it seems I've spilled my wine all over. And, it takes me back; back to the impossible now.

Hazy of mind, I take in the theater. The walls they seem to be intact; though there's this gaping whole where a window once stood. Perhaps it's best to just stare at the screen; or, rather, turn to the insides of one's mind;

---

[554] [re, Berlin: The Russians first entered the suburbs between 21st and 23rd April.—N.B.]

anything, anything but behold the darksome din of a world without sun. It's hard to tell, what through the fog, but Dannecker's must be the only roof for blocks; let alone electric. Of course there's no food. And the wine fetches a king's sum; *paradise.*

Poor Dannecker: lost his wife he did during the war[555]; plus, I hear his son had to be left at Stalingrad. Now, he's nowhere to be found. Still, I seem to 'recall' someone having said the old boy's alive. Oh, I don't know whether to *believe* it, but—wait: *somebody's coming...*

I smile, putting on airs: oh good God, *Magda*; Magda Guttenberg, in the front row with her 'son'. I go to her.

The stately Frau's one of the 'Lebensborn'[556]; brood-mares for the master race. Or, was. Ach, for, like an old ship, her body it seems can no longer stand the strain. So, Himmler gives her these: Polacks one and the same, 'so as to recover their Teutonic heritage'.

I know it's a weakness but, still, I shed a tear. For, the policy may be cruel: *but Magda is not.* I look to these Polish, or, German boys awash with guilt. For you see it brings to mind the central conflict: 'Do I stay here, and die with this shell of a man?[557] Or should I try and make it to Bremen; you know, meet my end at the old man's side?'

After a bout of small-talk I am able to ascertain Bremen fell to the Anglo-Amis a few days back.[558] Now, P'pa'll be safe; at last, a great burden is released. Alas I'm free; yea, for the first time, free to do whatever I want...

---

555 [*i.e.*, the first.—N.B.]

556 [*Lebensborn: SS* breeding program.—N.B.]

557 ['shell of a man': Obviously, Hitler.—N.B.]

558 ['Thank God,' he means, it fell to the Anglo-Americans: Not the Russians. Our memoirist appears to have been misinformed: Bremen did not 'fall' till April 26. Only *part* of the city had previously succumbed.—N.B.]

Oh, but who am I kidding; as if I'd actually abscond. No, now I know: *I shall die in Berlin*; the only question being—above, or, beneath?

Hey! *P'pa...*

***

I see you, old goat, staring out the corridor my mind. And, I behold the face, a face more radiant what with every swig; I miss you, old boy...

***

And, I'm lost; lost midst the memories playing the screen my mind. Memories are—*killing me.*

***

There I am, gallivanting what without a care, running barefoot through the heath...

***

I'm at the Inn, watching the old goat seduce yet one more wench. Alas he sends me home—alone; always alone. The wretch. For he just had to stay and get flaming drunk on the way. Eventually, Muti falls asleep; I never.

P'pa's back. Why he's delirious, waking poor M'ma.

"Oh Auggie. *What's it this time, hmm?" she says, piercing him what with those expansive Yorkshire eyes.*

"Went for a stroll," he smarts, removing his vest after one more day for Greenbaum the Jew. "That Yid treats me right," he says, in response to Muti's request that he should seek another line of work. "Why it's a privilege to work so many hours." Then, grave, he turns upon me: "Remember that, Wind; ach, for you too may have a family some day to support."

*Then, humming some off-key Brahms, he collapses upon the couch—*his *couch, what reeking tobacco and booze; why I bet the neighbors can smell him...*

***

"D'ye want a drink?" says the devilish apparition before me; huh, seems we're at the pub.

"Come to P'pa!" he says, paddling her bum.

"Do it again," I say. "Oh, oh Vati Vati Vati—do it again!"

"Bourbon!" he wails, eying her up and down...

"Bourbon!" she flails, storming the—

***

Why, something's exploded outside; pah, a little too close for comfort. I come to, and laugh: laugh like old P'pa; oh, I miss that old goat.

But enough. No, tonight, tonight is for *now*; to truly *live* again. And then, and then you see I shall descend to the Führerbunker, and join the already-dead. Still, I must hurry. For God forbid the Russians should get there first and find me missing; I mean, I wouldn't want them to get the wrong idea.

Nonetheless I linger, what milking the moment for all it's worth. I am enjoying my new-found anonymity when, out the corner my eye, an impossible thing causes me swallow all the air in my lungs: why, the SS—*heading straight for me.* I stand; I stammer; *why, I can feel the firing squad approach.*

A badly-rolled cigarette dangles out an obscenely scarred mouth, illumining my point-of-view. Then, recognition it hits; and almost I ask for one my own. You know, a 'last cigarette'...

I mean, for there he is, admiring himself in the looking-glass when—wait, that's not it; no, that's not it at all: *he's looking for bugs, he is.*

Why, I feel just like a child, keeping goal against boys twice my size: 'Oh, please—don't kick it to me!' Yes, for even Himmler's the fear of God in him, whenever somebody mentions the name: *Kammler...*

Sonofabitch, he walks up, what this energy of oppression washing over: *cold as fucking ice*; nay, the very void. I mean, it's like he's not even here.

As if reading my mind, he proffers a cigarette; the which I duly accept. We smoke a good, long while. He knows I appreciate the extravagance, what having been cooped up with the Chief. Boss says it causes cancer; pah, it helps me relax.

So much, in fact, almost I forget to whom I am speaking. We exchange pleasantries, then he says, "So, Hossbach—*you ever think of the future?*"

The—*huh?* I mean, we're wandering about, only just waiting we die—and *he* can think of the future?

"Yes," he adds, weighing me what with these cold, reptilian eyes. "Soon, there will be ships: a massive fleet surrounding the Earth. Imagine, a vast armada—*heading straight for the Moon.* Then—"

"You shouldn't *say* such things," I prate, reprimanding him from fear for my own. Then, the alarming notion it hits: and, that is, *I've just told an Obergruppenführer*[559] *off.* And not just any Obergruppenführer, rather, but *Kammler*; why, the only thing I fear more's an anonymous civilian...

He chides, "But, *the Führer* won't hear it," elbowing me for agreement, which doesn't bother me; and, impersonating the Chief, which does. "'*Kammler'*," he says. "*'There's a war going on'*," persisting in mimicry what for all the world to hear.

The people they stare; *again, the noose it begins to tighten...*

He smiles, incorporating much his own brand of mockery, finger under the nose, aping the Chief: "Hitler? Man's off his rocker!"

Oh boy...

"You know I was able to sell him some yarn about von Braun winning the war? And let's not forget Himmler," he wails, waking the family next to me. "That one's out for

---

559 [*Obergruppenführer*: lit. 'upper group leader.' One of the highest *SS* ranks, superior, so far as comparison is possible, to Hossbach's army designation, *General der Panzertruppe*.—N.B.]

himself," he smiles, swigging something dark and probably viscous.

Why, I expect the Gestapo any minute...

"'Ja'," he returns, resuming his impersonation of the Chief. "'Kammler old boy, Himmler has important work.' Oh—hot balls and blather! Mark my words, Hossbach—I'll pluck the pigeon-shit straight from *der Führer*'s eyes!"

Oh good God; he's on a drunk, he is. Still I'd rather die than linger. Well, once the Gestapo gets here—looks like I'll get to do both.

"*Hit*-ler?" downright he screams.

But I haven't said a thing; it scarcely matters. All wound-up, he just keeps right on going. "That little sheisster refuses to see treachery under his own Jewish probosces. *Himm*-ler? I'll squash him like a grape!" The Obergruppenführer he exhales, savoring the uproar he's caused.

The theater it empties post-haste: until it's down to just him and me. And, eying me queer, he says, "This um, *boy...*"

Now, I've killed a man before; yet never have I been so wroth.

"A toast," he adds. "To *Güntzler.*"

I seem to have gone numb, seem to have gone numb in the face. What with the horror of emptiness I realize: he's not on a drunk; no, he's not on a drunk at all. Or, I should say, rather he *is*; yet still in complete control. *Sonofawhore*; has me right where he wants...

"Fret not," he chides, ghoulish fingers traversing a chin that looks like someone must've snuck up on it and beat it with a bat. "I'll do what I can for the boy; you have my word. Really," he ashes, fixing on me like a serpent. "I'm not asking for much: just the usual papers, from our um *mutual friend*. Ech—don't play dumb with me! You know her quite well."

Oh good God...

"Now," he pivots, piercing me with basilisk eyes. "Else the girl dies!"

My heart it skips a beat. Without realizing I say, "Please—don't *hurt* her."

"The Mademoiselle will be my hostage; that is, until such time's I can cut a deal with Himmler, soon's old *Grossfaz*[560] bumps himself off. Ech, I know all about it: the ninny plans to do away with himself—he and his floozie!"

By Zeus! Perhaps the air-raids have returned after all; I mean, the Gestapo's sure taking its time. My feet they melt into the floor. Why, I didn't know the man could drink, let alone laugh; pah, I think I liked him better's a robot...

"I shall alert the Führer," I say. "He'll never let you have her!"

The Obergruppenführer he leans in, what nearly stumbling and, balancing one arm, proceeds to spill his drink. Undismayed he returns, "What if—*what if I had her son?*" Maniacal he leers.

Now it's my turn: *a real gut-buster.*[561]

The OGF is not amused: "That, that isn't funny—I said, stop!"

Mocking I clap, what relishing his perplexity. "Obergruppenführer, I've a surprise for you—*you are under arrest.*"

His elongated skull's an easy mark for my Mauser; dutifully I size him up. Debating my next move, I flounder's this fog's unleashed, obscuring my line of site—*gas, gas, gas!*

No, not gas, rather; yet still I cannot see. I lunge; I leap; and, flailing at the void, alas recover my vision.

Of course, by then, he's already gone...

---

560 ['Grossfaz' (pr. 'Grossfahtz'): Acronym for *Grosse Feldmarschall alles Zeite* ('Greatest field marshal of all time.') Originally an homage to Hitler, the epithet eventually conveyed nothing but the most profound contempt.—N.B.]

561 [*i.e.,* he laughed.—N.B.]

Chapter 43: Ragnarok

Berlin: April 23, 1945 continued

I flee the fog-laden cinema, so's to avoid the ministrations of the Gestapo. Of course, given our sorry state, I doubt they'll even come. Still, one mustn't risk it. Moreover the Boss's got to be wondering where I am; for I mean Eva must've returned hours ago.

I make my way to the Chancellery, more mad dash sans cover and concealment than a solitary stroll; whereupon, obtaining the lobby, I reflect. For, even in the best of times you see it's wise to feel him out before thus intruding. As such do I put in a call to Scheldte, 'convincing' him corroborate my story; why I put the fear of Himmler into him.

Belligerent swine—cut me off! "Mohnke[562] says stay put: you are to rendezvous with a commando team on the East-West Axis, commencing Twenty-three hundred."

Well, you know what they say about shit and a hill; at least, now I'll get to have one more 'last cigarette'. Thus do I repeat my maneuver, what like some crazy man scrambling for position midst the burned-out hulks, eventually winning the East-West axis.

Whereupon I wait until midnight, lamenting the uprooted trees that went into making the runway; thank God the Führer insisted on keeping some. Holed up thus in the wood, just like the good old days at *Gymnasium*, I hide midst the trees, nursing my purloined bottle, and wait.

And wait. I mean it's obvious: *nobody's coming.* Yea, one last cigarette; and then, and then you see I shall

---

[562] [*General* Mohnke, Wilhelm: Battle Commandant of Berlin, who, between Hitler's apathy and Hossbach's dereliction, had become saddled with such minutiae.—N.B.]

descend to the Führerbunker while I still can. Only, before I can inhale, an old-fashioned dogfight diverts my attention. Why, I haven't seen a dogfight in years, seeing the Luftwaffe frowns on it.

A white Gustav[563] it soars like the Devil himself, flanked by two Mosquitoes marauding on-high.[564] He runs them through the gauntlet, what with such savage elan: pummel, then dive; roll, twist, contort. Smoke it flares coming in out-of-the-sun, evading Albie's[565] fighters. The co-pilot disperses the Mosquitoes[566], leaving a third, an Ami, to seek battle when, realizing the new proportion of forces, he turns yellow and flees.

Gustav he flashes forth, like a *Feuerball*[567] fastening on the rim of the sun. Instant he aborts his upward gesture and dives; commencing his victory lap.

Wait, that's not it; no, that's not it at all. Rather he's headed for an emergency landing. Only, the wind you see's too high. What with mounting terror I realize: *something's terribly wrong.* A piece of metal, a wing perchance it falls, helpless towards the Lustgarten. The plane it plummets on the Unter den Linden; smoke it assails our violated sky.

Somehow it seems I'm racing towards them, having accosted some *Volkssturm* manning the flak. No 'chutes; therefore we concentrate on civilians; indeed, for, all around, the Lustgarten is on fire.

---

563 [*Gustav*: Variant of the *ME-109*. Technically, a *BF-109 G*, or 'Gustav,' equipped with an extra cannon, mounted under one of the wings. This particular model must have been a 'G-12' of the sub series, *i.e.*, a trainer, with pilot situated *behind* trainee. Her fuel capacity would have been sacrificed, in order to accommodate the extra cockpit. Given Hossbach's point of view, his could have been but an educated guess as to who was actually doing the flying.—N.B.]

564 [*Mosquito*: 'The Wooden Wonder,' a fighter-bomber/reconnaissance extraordinaire.—N.B.]

565 ['Albie's fighters': *i.e.*, Mosquitoes.—N.B.]

566 [*i.e.*, via machine gun fire.—N.B.]

567 {Footnote deleted by Censor.—G.W. Pub.}

And, choking what from all the petrol, midst a sea of flames I watch's our fighter comes careening towards the concrete. Binoculars they wrap themselves about my obsolescent eyes; my breath it comes to a precipitate halt.

At the very last moment he manages nudge his nose just enough so's to collide with the earth intact. Gustav he tumbles and roars; even as the pilot tries to extricate himself from his 'chute.

With a deep breath I summon my expenditure. For, in my mind's eye you see already I'm racing towards them. And, well what do you know? *I am doing just that.*

Speed is of the essence. Ach, for the Amis have by no means missed the spectacle; *they'll be back.*

Alas our pilot he succeeds in extricating himself from his 'chute. His co-pilot though isn't so lucky; *bullet through the cheek.*

A shell it explodes; rending the veracity my vision. Hurling myself into this ditch, so's to avoid being buried beneath the rubble, Gustav he goes up what just like a torch. The pilot's lodged to the fuselage; fusing his back to the still-smoking beast. Why, petrol's everywhere; so much so the very skies seem darken.

Aghast, swallowing what more oil than air, I fear I have drawn my very last. 'A ditch?' I chide myself for having contrived such an unseemly end when, choking, I realize: *it probably just saved your life.*

Oh, but ach, the pilot he wails. I wish to say, 'Stop! Lest you should bring him back'; and, now, now I realize what I must do...

Zigzagging left and right, I make my way to the poor sot. Turning him on the side, I try to pry him off. Oh, but it's no use: his back's fused to the fuselage. And, studying his face, I wonder—*the Mademoiselle?*

"*Hoss-bach,*" she whispers, my attention drawn to this far-off look in her eyes. "The *Victory Weapon*, it's..."

She hefts a finger, as if to accuse the very sky; looks to me; says "Jack"; then is no more.

I flail, instinctively grabbing her face and so focusing on her eyes. "Please, don't *go*." Gentle I try easing her off.

And yet, and yet the whole time you see something is haunting me; taunting me what with these visions. Yes for I can see myself traversing the runway, bearing some kind of torch; blow-torch, I think. Why, I must have gone back to the jeep. Colonel Traylor he must've driven; then, then brought me back. That's how I came upon the pilot; *the pilot...*

I manage pry her off the flaming Gustav; though there's this nasty bit of machinery attached to her spine. And, gathering her in my arms, I run the dead-man's sprint; why the very air's suffused with sulfur.

'Oh, if I can just make it back to the jeep; yes, perhaps she's still—'

The aftershock it comes, as ever it must; explosion thus ensues, thrusting her out my arms, even while visiting me what with concussion. And, in an instant I realize: *I'm never going to see her again...*

Scrambling for the jeep, I get her ignited on the third go, then look all-around: and, I swear, I swear there's no one around. Still, I've *memories*; memories you see of someone driving me—

Why, the Col-onel![568]

Alas this soothing voice: 'Ah, *Wind*: it's going to be alright.' Ah, *Muti*; she's singing my favorite song...

Shivering, what fragments of steel embedded my chest, we reach the *Alt Museum*; then, nothing.

***

A medic, or doctor it seems's asking for my papers.

Do you know who I am? I say; only, the words you see they don't quite seem get out. Doped up what on some

---

[568] [Ger. 'Oberst'—N.B.]

whiskey-morphia confection, three men they pass me to a friendly face.

Ah—Schmidtie!

He deems not recognize me. Rather he mumbles some medical mumbo-jumbo, then summons the stretcher-bearers; the which proceed carry me off.

The light it hits; and, suddenly, suddenly it's dark no more. In anguish I re-enter the world of the flesh. Oh, how I revel being alive! The sunlight it seems confirm this.

Sun? Why, how long have I been out?

My hopes are dashed the instant I'm shunted into the underworld; like Hades forced to inhabit the land of the dead; *indeed, the sunlight is no more.*

***

I open my eyes, like a babe in the womb, what this vague glow enveloping: *Opa... Muti?*

Nein; back in the Führerbunker once more.

Chapter 44: Cocaine

The Vor Bunker: Apr. 25, 1945

My injuries are such that, according to Dr. Schenck, it will take weeks to recover; but we haven't got weeks. Therefore the Boss's set me up with Morell, what with all his magic potions. And, while in health you see I wouldn't let the swine lay a finger on me, as the Führer once said: "I don't keep Morell around for his scent."

And, well now I must admit: *he's nursed me back in no time.* The infection that set in my chest's being treated with the new sulfonamides which, the portly plumper asserts, he was the first to truly exploit. As for the pain, he insists getting me off the morphia.

Helplessly bearing the brunt of it, I curse the swine for the love of God just give me something. Still never, never in a thousand years did I expect to be submitted to such treatment, what cocaine awash in my blood; why I ridicule such tomfoolery. Yet, to tell you the truth—I've never felt better.

Cocaine; the Boss swears by it. Yes, for it makes you feel like a young buck; a million marks. Why it doesn't even enter one's head to take stock of one's own limitations.

Several Hours Hence

Word of disaster increasingly filters through. Worse, the treatment it seems to've worn off; *this* I fear's what's gotten us into trouble. Still, without it, why who knows? He could've wound up an opium-fiend, like Göring.[569]

---

[569] [On April 23, Göring attempted to 'usurp' Hitler from power. Bormann, apparently on Hitler's authority, had the Reich Marshal placed under arrest. There exists a certain passage purporting to relate the incident. The author has asked me to withhold it, pending the results of the trial. 'Göring's betrayal,' Hossbach told me, by way of Doctor Seidl, 'was really nothing of the sort. The Führer had

Still, there's every chance he'd have come to his senses long ago, and realized the futility of this two-front[570] war. An understanding could have been reached—probably with Stalin, in lieu of the Battle of Kursk;[571] *but hindsight is for suckers.*

***

More cocaine; alas, in just two days, it can now be said: his immenseness[572] has already nursed me back.[573] Why I can take on anything. The world? A pittance. Only, now, now that impossible woman's... gone—*who will look out for our son?*

I hector some ninny in the communications bunker let me use of the last line leading out.

---

issued multiple decrees, empowering the Reichsmarschall to take charge, in event the former had lost his freedom of movement.' By April 23, the bunkers had but haphazard contact with the outside, to the point of being forced to rely on enemy proclamations in order to follow the course of the battle. News of Hitler's intent to commit suicide spread like wildfire. So, at least *this* story runs, it was Göring's duty to act as he did. Not so Bormann, who, in turn, related Göring's 'usurpation' in terms such that the former appears to have received authority requisite to order the arrest of his rival. Göring still claims to be acting head of state. Dönitz, as we will see, likewise lays claim to the now farcical title. My father, understandably, perhaps, remains ambivalent as to whom he should so 'honor.'—N.B.]

570 [Again, three, if you count Italy, which Hossbach, of course, does not.—N.B.]

571 [re, 'Kursk': Hitler had not yet undergone cocaine treatment at this time. He *might* have received Vitalmultin injections: With similar results. The *real* second front (as opposed to the 'war' between OKH and OKW) led to the abandonment of the attempt to pinch off the salient at Kursk: The invasion of Sicily in July '43.—N.B.]

572 [Apparently, Doctor Morell: But cf. note below.—N.B.]

573 [Perhaps he meant one of the orderlies, or assistants, acting on Morell's behalf. For Hossbach, as we will shortly see, was at pains to claim the latter had, by this time, taken quite ill.—N.B.]

The Communications Bunker[574]

"Dornberger? Hossbach—listen: we must meet. The tree, the tree at the corner of—"

"Ex-*cuse* me? Does this concern the Professor?"

"*Mm-hmm.*"

"Relax, Herr General. Relax and take heart: *I have taken care of it.* They have been released: strictly on a probationary basis. It's all the bombing—downright relentless! Ech, we've got to save these chaps while we can; and I don't just mean the bombing..."

Save them indeed: *save them from the SS.* I let loose the heaviest sigh. "Really, what *foresight*. Why I was just about to try and convince—"

"There is no need. I've had a talk with the Professor: he and his team are already on board. Oh, don't worry. I assure you, my plan is infinitely better than anything *Old Sour Puss*[575] might have in mind."

"Please; spare me the details. But come, do tell—exactly *who* is being dispersed, and to where? After all," I lie. "We might have need track them later."

"I've no clue. I simply said, 'Evacuate everyone essential'."

There's no *way* he's going to say anything over the line. Nonetheless I redouble my efforts, attempting somewhat more circumspection, blunted though it might be what from all the cocaine; really I'm not sure what I'm saying...

He gasps, "You'll have to take it up with Kammler; only, I don't think you should."

"General?" I wince, hoping I haven't quite heard him aright.

"*Kammler,*" he repeats, causing me bite my tongue. "One of Himmler's," he adds, heedless.

574 ['Communications Bunker': Pendent to the Führer Bunker.—N.B.]
575 [*i.e.*, Himmler.—N.B.]

Why, I can't tell if it's the stress; or whether he's stark-raving mad. Still, this Dornberger's all I've got. Plus, even what with all the cocaine, I know one doesn't work *on* Himmler, rather, but *through*; at least, that's what the Mademoiselle would have said...

Like a suicide he proceeds: “Perhaps I am mistaken: it may be the other way round.”

“The devil you mean?” *Ach, I reprimand myself the instant I've said it...*

“Simply Old Sour Puss may be Kammler's after all.” The line crackles; the electricity it threatens go out. Instant he adds: “*I shudder to think.*”

This Dornberger must think he's on borrowed time; and, so's coveting the firing squad instead. That, or, he's on one hell of a drunk. Like a nightmare he proceeds. “I for one cannot say. Oh, don’t worry: I won’t let *anyone* lay a hand on the Professor.”

The Professor?

“Yes,” I say. “The Professor. Now see here: you simply *must* tell me where they are. Yes for I've a *very* important message; the which I simply *must* deliver in person.”

Oh, how do I *say* it? I mean, it's none of his *business* who's just up and died. I am *beside* myself; can't *think* straight. And yet, somehow, somehow, beneath the haze, one thing is clear: *Jack he simply must know.* Yes it's clear as day: *now, nothing else matters.*

On a whim I say, “Consider it a *Führerorder.*”

Now, I know this Dornberger's a scientist, and that that species doesn't put much stock in a *Führerorder* these days; as if they ever did. Still, he wouldn't *dare* contradict one—*I think...*

He doesn't buy it a second: “Why stick your neck out old boy? It's already two minutes to midnight.”

He speaks not of the time, rather, than the end we all know must surely be nigh. Still all I can think is, 'That's how he wishes go down?' Worse, I'm ill at ease with what he just called me: 'Old Boy'? Why the swine's older than I.

"Did Himmler put you up to this?" he says, paranoia adding to his tally of indiscretions.

Oh God; this is the last call I will ever make. "Himmler? *God no.* Now see here: these men simply *cannot* be allowed to fall into the hands of the Russians. Still, to turn them in to the Gestapo? Why, what at a waste! No, the future, the future our people demands that we should spirit them out." Alas more from paternal love what than all the cocaine I say, "Oh, dammit—we must get them to American lines."

"Is this a *Führerorder* too?"

He's got you there, 'Old Boy'. "Now see here," I repeat. "Do me this favor, this one favor, and I shall be forever grateful."

"Humph," he snorts, pausing an eternity then adds, "Leave it be. The men are safe. Should anything change, you will be the first to know." And, I swear, I swear he's almost laughing's the next words they fall: "*Heil Hitler.*"

And, alas, alas with this slogan—the which, these days, so many mouth, yet so few believe—my part in saving Jack has come to a precipitate end. 'Oh Monique,' I say, say whilst trying convince her; not finding it the least bit odd to be talking to the dead. 'Our boy's just going to have to figure it out for himself—*just like everyone else.*'

As for the Chief, he's already made up his mind simply to die; therefore am I relieved of any moral compulsion to report back to him. Besides, the rocket-men really are in good hands with this Dornberger—*I think...*

Upon reflection, I don't believe it a second; or—*am I lying even now?*

The Vor Bunker

Back to the Vor Bunker, where I run into Speer. Oh, I don't know how it got started. But, somehow, somehow the discussion it turns to the possibility of kidnapping him —Hitler—before the Ivans get here. Yes to 'spirit him to the Obersalzberg', an impressive, if not quite impregnable redoubt, capable of holding out for weeks: just enough time to launch this 'Victory Weapon', the which Speer himself seems more than adequately informed.

The Minister,[576] who's more than his share of confinement to hospital, suggests we operate via Morell. Together we approach the quarters of the slovenly physician.

"Come," the latter he coughs from his cot, still nursing a head-cold.

We make small talk, in between a bout or two of drink, amidst many a frivolous toast; you know, to the 'good times of eld'.

Oh, but ach, despite Speer's elbow constantly striking my ribs, the cat it seems's gotten my tongue. Therefore he takes it on himself to ask if it would be ethical —'hypothetically, of course'—to subdue a patient, 'if said patient's life depended on it'.

"Are you mad?" Morell he chafes, flopping off his cot, backing into the corner thrusting up his palms: "I will not betray my Chief!" The portly old prig turns plucky, uprooting what hair he has. "Do you know how many times I've tried to get him to rest? 'That,' he'd always says. '*That* is simply impossible.' Therefore it's fallen on me to keep him alive. *Alive,*" he underscores. "Beyond any human capacity." He says this with no small amount of pride.

"But, the Boss," I say. "The Boss is not well"; and God knows I could just box him by the ears...

'You're *killing* him,' Speer he suddenly screams, arching those bushy brows. 'Herr Doktor, I shall hold *you* personally responsible, if anything were to befall him.'[577]

---

[576] ['Minister': *i.e.*, Speer.—N.B.]

[577] {Speer is paraphrased, never quoted.—Legal Dept., G.W. Pub.}

Huh; about as incensed's a bureaucrat can get.[578]

"No," the doctor retorts, hefting a fat bloated finger. "'The Captain too must go down with his ship'—*that* is what the Boss would always say," the portly old prig, pink's a sow, feels compelled explain.

The swine; why, he's never seen a day of battle in all his life. "So, that's it," I say, caving to the God of Necessity. "The *Thousand Year Reich* is no more." My body it begins to shake. I bite my nails, a habit which, all these years, I have been unable to break; now, it all seems so inconsequential.

"Oh, you must have *faith*," the doctor he sighs. "Any day now we're going to launch the *Victory Weapon*: and thus pluck victory from the jaws of—"

"Quatsch!" I say. "Why, it's all a bunch of malarkey. 'Victory Weapon'—pah, there's no such thing: a mirage, a mirage I say the Boss has concocted; thus that the people might not lose their spleen."

I can't believe, can't believe I *said* it; but just this morning I'd have strung up the sonofabitch who had...

Speer he just hangs his head; ach, for, we both know the outcome to this scheme.

Still I try to save it: "Morell, you breathe one word —one word!" And, here, here I make a gesture, the likes of which I am not proud; still, I mean, the Boss's *life* is at stake...

18.00

The swine, why he went straight to the Chief; I expect to be arrested any minute.

---

[578] The swine now claims to've returned to the Führerbunker, so's to've put poison-gas in the vents; huh, what a way of going at it.[—W.H] [Speer 'confessed' to the 'poison gas plot,' during the course of the trial: Any minute now, we'll see if anyone believed him.—N.B.]

19.30

The Boss has called me in to his study, what Goebbells standing there smug's his shadow; *huh, I guess Bormann's too drunk to play it.*

I deny any such complicity; oh, but it's no use. Goebbels does most of the talking. Speer receives a verbal lashing. Then, the Chief, the Chief he just stops, stops what almost mid-sentence and bids us take leave.

Speer he slips off, probably to hide[579] in the Vor Bunker. Meantime I sulk in the commons,[580] pretending to entertain various rumors. All anyone cares about is, 'Where's Wenck?' [581]

Morell he waddles in, on the way to giving the Boss his evening injection.[582] And, though the ceiling's supposedly bomb-proof, the walls are only all-too thin. Why I can hear Hitler say, “How do I know you're not trying to poison me? Kidnap me and take me to the Obersalzberg! That, or, make me just disappear...”

Ach, mein Gott*: the Boss has completely lost it.*

Morell he can't get a word in. Uncomprehending he pleas, “But, mein Chef, *it is not so*,” whining what just like a broken man; *or record.*

---

579 Actually, he started running, and did not stop, until he chanced find himself the apple the prosecution's eye.[—W.H.] [It should be noted that Speer too has been charged with the most heinous of crimes.—N.B.]

580 ['the commons': A bench, plus some chairs, outside Hitler's room, in the hallway of the Führer Bunker.—N.B.]

581 [*General der Panzertruppe* Wenck, Walther: Head of the *12th Army*, whose spearheads were supposed to be racing from the west, in order to save Berlin.—N.B.]

582 [Hossbach alleges the good doctor to have failed to appear for two days prior, *i.e.*, the same period he *previously* claimed to have been under Morell's care. Whether the allegation is intended as payback for the latter's having 'breathed one word' to Hitler, or meant to convey genuine relief at the 'Reich Injection Minister' 's reappearance, one cannot quite be sure.—N.B.]

Hitler he shrieks for his Goebbels; the latter now duly appears. Ignoring us, he heads for the study. All I can make out's but a few manic whispers.

The latter he returns, then orders me summon Scheldte; with which I duly comply. I watch almost mechanical, as the act[583] is finally played out. And, unceremoniously, the 'second most powerful man in the Reich' is led up and out.

And, there he goes, to be whisked off, Goebbels confides, in the last plane still capable of taking off[584]; and, with it, the last chance of saving Hitler's life.

---

583 ['the act': The ejection of Morell from the environs of the bunker complex. Others date this to April 21, *i.e.*, four days previous. The latter is more in keeping with what is known of Herr Speer's movements.]

584 [This is incorrect. The very next day, Hanna Reitsch returned to Berlin, along with Colonel-General Ritter von Greim, crash landing on the east-west axis. The latter was promoted to field marshal, and anointed Goering's successor, as head of the (now nominal) Luftwaffe. Hitler rejected the lovers' entreaty to die with him in the bunker. Two days later, they took off from the same improvised strip, allegedly in order to arrest, of all people, Himmler.—N.B.]

Chapter 45: The Death of Adolf Hitler

The Führer Bunker: April 30, 1945

The Boss hasn't been himself these days, a tragedy not only for Germany, rather: but all civilized people. Indeed, history shall judge us harsh for having done nothing but sit around, bidding him weave his magic wand one last time...

And, now, now the other shoe has finally dropped: Chief says the war's lost, wants to shoot himself; falling to my knees, I beg him reconsider.

Embarrassed he walks out.

After Lunch, in the Commons

These thoughts parade uninterrupted in my mind, even's my human self, the one they call Hossbach, is dealing a round of cards with his mates. Daily do we abscond from this our impossible reality, for the pleasure of the immediacy of the moment. Yes we live underground in this our city of the dead, juxtaposing false hope with the desire for sleep in mimicry of death; hey, it helps one to cope.

Yet my mind is scarcely on the rails; let alone this stupid game. Why it's Hitler: he's pacing, pacing behind this stupid wall. Ach, how it gladdens me I can but hear; yea, hear and no longer see. For, these days, his whole body it shakes; pah, the sight of him's more than I can take. Now, he can't even sit without someone to put a chair under him —is that it, is that why he's pacing? He wants to sit, you see; only, his adjutants[585] are off playing games with the secretaries. Oh, perhaps he'll just shoot himself even now; you know, *make an end of it.*

[585] [As previously stated, while stationed at *FHQ,* in this case the Führer Bunker, Hossbach often had to revert to his old *rôle* as Führer adjutant. Here he also appears to have been saddled with that of chief of security, a detail which, given the hopelessness of the situation, he doesn't seem to have taken very serious.—N.B.]

I glance at my cards—a five, a seven, two nines and an ace—and think: 'What does a Führer adjutant do with no Führer? And, does he know that, in taking his life, he's taking ours with?' Up till now, I'd no reason to doubt him—even when his reasoning rebelled against all common sense. For he could always muster the one indomitable argument: *he'd always been right before.* Only, now, what the defections, the betrayals, why—the fools!

I'm a bit tipsy. It's just, I can't believe, can't believe she's *gone*; ach, mein Gott—*I am going to die alone...*

A message arrives. Why it's Wenck: his attack it failed ere it ever got started; as usual, I am the last to know. The Chief must've known for some time; thus his insistence that he should just die. I tried, tried to keep in *touch.* Oh, but how was I to know? Communications were lost days ago. Even before, we'd taken to dialing random numbers to find out what was going on in the city. The phone it would ring: *then Russian voices come over the other line.* That's when I knew—*we're all for the high-jump.*

War Conference at 14.00[586]

Some feckless ninny he blurts in the Boss's ear about some rabbi who's just placed a curse on him and Göring.[587]

"Bah," he flares. "The Jews!" then storms off.

Well, there's no point continuing without him[588]; thus I return to the commons.

---

586 [Conducted in a small room, roughly equidistant from Hitler's quarters and the 'commons.'—N.B.]

587 [Actually, according to the *New York Times*, on Goebbels and Himmler, too.—N.B.]

588 [Here Hossbach must be mistaken. For independent testimony, established during the trial, maintains that, by this point, Hitler had ceased to take part in the daily war conference. That he had 'resigned himself to leading a domestic life.' An understandable concatenation.—N.B.]

The Commons

Eva's perfume it comes wafting over so's to greet me. Oh, how I would but to just part those lips; then, weld her tongue to the back my throat...

"*Hoss-bach,*" she smiles, putting on airs, what lifting my chin with her glances. But she says: "*I'm staying.*"

Ach, mein Gott: *all that is good has died...*

"Me and the Boss,"[589] she goes on. "Intend upon shooting ourselves as soon as the Russians get here." Then, as if for my sake, she brightens. "Oh, don't worry: I've no fear of death."

As a soldier, I understand, have to; it's just, *I cannot join them's yet.* Ach, for someone you see has to stay and look after his final disposition.

Yes, one last bout of sleep; ah, *sleep*, the best friend Man ever had. Besides, I have to be ready when the Russians get here; after all, *a man must know how to die.* But, inside, I'm shaking; *powerless.*

"Gin," Eva cries, good-natured.

How are they still awake? Oh, how I long for one last cigarette; but I must hold my piece. Yes, for it's the one thing Hitler simply will not suffer. Plus, it's too dangerous to venture outside; not just for me, rather, but everyone involved.

As I'm thinking this, the most appalling of scenes's taking place: for it's Eva, Traudl, and Bormann, smoking—*in the Führerbunker.*

The implications are in such bad taste, why I wish to run them all through with the sword; *the voices they return.*[590] Only, *now*, I pay them no heed.

At last—*alone.*

---

[589] [I had to scratch my head, thinking this to be some sort of error. But then I recalled the words of Hanna Reitsch, alleging Eva to have used the appellation in referring to her beau.—N.B.]

15.00

Times like these, even the most hardened sonofabitch's inevitably driven to the brink of despair. Why one cannot help but marvel the dignity our weaker sex. The Führer'd ordered them out days ago; back when there was still time to get out of the city. But they behaved in scandalous fashion, disobeying a direct Führerorder.

The F. he didn't flinch. His face a mask, what the paternal quality simply oozing off his throat he said, "You realize, girls: *it's suicide.*"

But they were not to be moved. And, he, sensing this, begrudgingly gave way. Touched by this display of loyalty he'd crowed, "If only my Generals had the courage of you ladies!"

Now, scarcely a week has passed. Yet still, the smile has long exhausted itself on that emaciated face. And that's it. That's all that's left, what this burned-out husk of the man that I once knew; *hah, let them smoke.*

And of course I cannot leave. For, I have sworn the oath[591]; and shall defend Eternal Germany till my dying breath.

Ach, it's so *stale*; must get air or go... *mad.*

---

590 [Given the defendant's state of mind, it is hard to ascertain the 'voices' to which he is referring. Eyewitnesses have testified regarding a 'bunker psychosis.' If this is the case, the voices probably appeared during the days following his operation. Of course, Hossbach now alleges to have suffered such hallucinations during the Great War. In my opinion, the latter are a conflation, stemming from the peculiarity of his compositional process: Not so those in the Vor Bunker, where his sleeping quarters would have obtained.—N.B.]

591 [The oath of personal fealty to Hitler, supplanting that of loyalty to the state.—N.B.]

Skulking in the Vor Bunker

The Goebells family's here, too; though no one wants to talk about it. Yes for, once the Boss is dead you see Magda plans on simply snuffing out the lives of their six little children; then, she and the Good Doctor shall shoot themselves.

Oh, what difference does it make? So many have died already; as a rule, the very best. And yet cowards—men who surrender entire cities without a fight—*they* live. The German people have failed him; *we* have failed him. Why I feel just like some dirty Yid, whose Messiah has just offered himself up for the cross; and the last hope dies within.

We sit upon a vast, rapidly expanding abyss. And all one can do at a time like this is to but clench their teeth and wait for release; even in death. The tension in here is pregnant with fear; our odds insurmountable. Every thought it seems must inevitably fall prey to some chimera, a phantom leading to the precipice of sanity. Should one fail to maintain their clarity then all bets are off.

Thank God for the Goebbels children, and their unquenchable faith in their 'Uncle Führer'. I mean, no one wants to admit it, but, *they have been a boon to us all.*

And yet for all that we are doomed. Oh, but I don't believe what Frau Goebbels said what just the other day. That a 'life without the Führer is a life not worth living'; *but maybe she's right.*

Time has lost all meaning; sleep but one more thing to do without. Did you realize that, why just last week, one could count the distance of the Russians in kilometers? Now they're over our heads! And any minute now they'll realize we've been under their noses all along...

An explosion it rocks the above, riveting my attention to the fact that Berlin is being destroyed.

The Goebells children are caroling down the hall. But how such Jewish twaddle[592] ever infiltrated the Führerbunker's beyond me; for, one cannot guard against ideas. On and on they drone, echoing down the corridor, bouncing off the wall like a punch in the face; *no wonder if the Russian can hear them.*

Still these little angels haven't the slightest that, at this very moment, their own mother is plotting their death.

Meantime the shadow of the Good Doctor it slumps past my door, the which I've no longer the strength to close. And, in an instant it's clear: *the swine*; why, he has it worse than me. For, just the other day, he was the Boss's successor.[593] Only, now, now the ingrate's gone and defied him; and so shall be following his master to the grave. What, you think I don't envy him? Still, a *soldier* must obey; *civilians.*

Ach, for poor Goebbels you see's but an emaciated ragbag, whose hideous eyes betray the long-lasting lack of spiritual sustenance. The maniacal grin now a dull lifeless stare; the scowl of a madman become the smile of an idiot. As Dietrich Eckhart, the Führer's mentor used to say, 'The *soul* of such an one has left its body'.

Now, naught but a shadow remains, haunting the halls of the Führerbunker. What with the eternal pacing, the incomprehensible muttering at no one in particular—oh God, is that what Fate has for me? *I'd rather have Russians...*

Poor Goebbels's caught me staring. Two beady little eyes they flash forth, as the Good Doctor he springs to life one last time. Then, beating his womanly fists in the air he howls, "If only we knew more to *hate*."[594]

---

592 [It was a fundamental tenet of Naziism that Christianity was a Jewish conspiracy, aimed at the overthrow of the pagan world.—N.B.]

593 ['The Führer's successor': *i.e.*, as chancellor.—N.B.]

594 [Again, a possible conflation. For another eyewitness attributes the words to Hitler.—N.B.]

And like that, he vanishes, off to his own private death-chamber; and the whole Führerbunker it breathes a sigh of relief.

Why, I'm being a cad. I mean, for all his faults, Goebbels still loves *him*; and well that ought to count for something.

Back to the Führer Bunker

I make my way to the commons, so's to share one last round with my mates; then, perchance, a little harmless flirtation with the ladies.

Oh good God, *Eva*. The sight of the Boss's girlfriend's thrown me for a loop; and, alas, I cannot help but think—

"Cards?"

"M—*Eva.*"

I mean, I *see* Eva, yet cannot help but think 'the Mademoiselle'.

"Sure." After all, who am *I* to refuse a lady? Besides —*it's her last request.* Scarcely have I begun to even banter, when Günsche steps in to ruin the mood. The big blonde beast he kicks his chair out from under, then throws his cards in a huff. His deep iron voice it rings out, what with the impress of steel: "I am not in the mood. *Ladies*," he bows, then, turning those deep-blues on me, says, "Duty calls—*as you well know.*"

My instinct is to slap him. Of course he's right. Still it irks me some mere Major dare address me in such fashion. Oh, I suppose it's a sign of the times; yet even manners it seems they can't save us now...

The Vor Bunker

Back to my quarters, I try to obtain some semblance of sleep. Oh, but ach, I keep coming to: simply too many memories...

***

Ah, Paris, where the women are fast; and the men run even faster. We're at the Opera House. The Führer is giving an impromptu tour, from blueprints he's committed to mind. Today, today I bare an especial pride. Ach, for I know for a fact he's never set foot here in all his life. At heart you see he's really an architect.

***

A tunnel it opens, swallowing malformed images. The Führer he dissolves; and, in his stead—the Mademoiselle. We embrace; and yet, and yet the whole time you see I'm wondering from where she's going to draw the knife. Her surprise it comes from another quarter entirely when she says, "He is your son*."*

***

England, nineteen and having the time of me life. Yes, the Jacker and I's sneaking through the lab when, shush—*we've just flooded every single toilet in university...*

***

Artillery it pounds me out from my senses, even's the warm smell of cunt it comes wafting into the room. Monique's swollen mons it gyrates up against my face, familiarizing me what with the essence of her twang. Thunder hard I pound, and I strike. Her senses beyond repair, she melts into a myriad of coruscating forms. Yea, astride my lance the cockroach bitch she writhes; even's I pierce to the knighthood of her cunt. On, Tallyho, ride; on, Valkyrie, wail! Nature implodes; we lie insensate.

***

I stare at my hands, what dimly aware this relentless hum coming from the bunker filtration. Oh, but where'd she *go*?

And, re-sealing my eyes, I try to find her; try to recall...

***

Bodies; surrounded by bodies. There is a report. Men marching; or, rather, were. The Feldhernhalle; Göring goes 'oof'; and then Ludendorff speeds off into the night...

***

No, that's all past. In truth I see: the 'Daily Mail'. Ach, salacious sights of that malicious cunt gallivanting through the 'Twenties. 'The Mademoiselle,' it reads. 'Bedding with kings—and, sometimes, queens—shuffling her sex the way a man deals arms...'

***

The veil of fog is lifted, and from the page I turn to something more definite: yes, that *was the dream;* this, this *is the now. I am in prison. The Führer is with me; yet still I dream of that forbidden cunt. Yea, she who fashioned her twat as a rostrum, from which speak to the people. Ach, for in Monique's twisted mind you see she bethought Hitler her mouthpiece; a thing of beauty, if not genius...*

***

A draft it rushes past my door; pah, I should have asked the dwarf to shut it. Oh, but where *was* I? Oh yes: *then there was the time—*

***

The walls they reverberate with a mad patter, thrusting me out of the vision; *pitter-patter; pitter-pat-pat; pitter-pat.*

'Hossbach old boy, now's no time to go skittish. Why it's just a bit of heavy artillery.' Still I can feel the barometer dip in my soul; even's this relentless force it unleashes itself in the very core of my being. And my attention is drawn to the roar of the bunker filtration. Yes, that's where I am: *back in the Führerbunker once more...*

Günsche he bursts into the room: "*It's time.*"

We race for Hitler's study.

Linge he meets us outside. The Little Lion he's shaking. With averted face, he motions us towards the door.

We enter the death chamber, and I'm wracked by the swooshies. There's blood, everywhere; why, *it is the Boss's blood.* And yet, there he is, slumped in his chair like I've found him after many a night.

Eva she lay beside him, embalmed in bliss on the couch. What so calm and quiescent, almost I apologize for having wakened her; *and yet, the blue on her lips speaks of cyanide instead...*

I grab his head so's to comfort him; only, there's nothing left to comfort. I reach around, seeking the exit wound. My hands are mummified with flesh; *it is the Boss's flesh.* It captivates even while it repels me; only, now's no time for a mystical experience.

Günsche he sticks his humongous head out the door, giving the all-clear. Linge, who's been guarding it the whole time, rushes in to help gather the bodies. Günsche and I take Hitler; Linge, Eva.

Oh, but ach; *the wound is bad.* With a towel I cover his face, lest such image not burn itself into anyone's mind.[595]

On the way out, the Devil himself appears: *Bormann.* He wishes to help carry Eva's body.

Linge he shoots him a look, the likes of which even a man such as Bormann can have seen but a few times and lived; for, it is the face of a desperate man.

The Reichsleiter he scurries like a mouse before the proverbial cat. For Eva she *loathed* him; and Linge is right in so protecting her honor. Still, we have to hurry. For the Russians are shelling near the garden, where we are to bury the bodies.

We bear our burden up from the bunker and out into the ruins of the Reich. Like a wheel-barrow we hump it,

---

[595] [Günsche and Linge were unlucky enough to end up behind Soviet lines. Rumor has it, they have been repeatedly tortured, in an effort to uncover Shitler's 'true whereabouts,' largely due to Hossbach's having covered that idiot's head with that ridiculous towel.—N.B.]

escorting our parcel out to the garden; the Little Lion close-in from behind. We toss our bodies in a ditch, whereupon, Kempka, as per instructions, sets them to torch.

A piercing white hue irradiates the sky, unleashing a concussive force. Phosphorus it tears into my brain; why, the very earth it recedes. And then I realize: *I'm flying...*

I scream; a good sign, I like to tell the casualties. For, it means you're *alive*; helter-skelter we race for the Chancery.[596]

Only, Goebells you see's still standing, saluting his fallen idol. He's risking his life, he is; we pester him come inside. Oh, but what does he care? It's his last hurrah; let him enjoy it. Ach, for, in a matter of hours, he and his family will be joining them; and then we'll have to go through this barbaric rite all over...

Still, nature is nature: Bormann and I continue to heckle him. The Little Doctor he hobbles back, then we seal up the entrance.

Frantically scampering midst the ruins of the Chancery, we come at last to 'safety' below. As if by unspoken agreement, we keep running till reaching the Vor Bunker; whereupon collapse immediately ensues.

The silence it jars me back to our unspeakable reality; and, that is, *Hitler is no more...*

---

[596] [*i.e.*, the old one. As for the deceased, the reader might wonder why no mention has been made of their now infamous wedding, less than forty-eight hours before. Seidl informs me that his client has no first hand knowledge of any such undertaking, 'having had more pressing matters with which to attend.' An offended silence met my imputation that the more likely explanation is that the General had quite simply not been invited. As it stands, all the eyewitnesses to the much ballyhooed nuptials are either dead, or missing.—N.B.]

Chapter 46: The Mother's Way

Vor Bunker: May 1, 1945

It was Magda's idea to do this. You know, to bring the children; and, now, the inevitable denouement must fall upon her. Ach, for Magda's whole *life* you see revolved around *him*. Why, some swine even say, 'Helmut belongs to the Führer'. But I assure you: the boy's the Good Doctor down to the cheekbones. Anyone saying otherwise ought to be shot.

Magda. What beauty. Such severe beauty, punctuated by a raw, what almost animal essence. Alas everyone—joking, at first, but soon with the utmost respect—called her 'The First Lady of the Reich'; now, she has nothing.

A knock it jolts me out from my reverie, delivering a thundering blow; oh, why couldn't they've soundproofed the door?

"General, have you seen this circular Bormann's been passing?"

Ah, Günsche: "*Come.*"

Entering he hands me this sheet, the which at a glance I can tell's been typed on the Boss's oversized keys: alright... *really?* Why, he's gone and named Dönitz his successor. *Dönitz?* Pah—at least it didn't go to Göring! Still, *Dönitz?* I mean I was sure Bormann was after the succession. Only, now he gets his chance and—*Dönitz?*

It goes on, apparently a will of some sort, regarding which Hitler saw fit to just leave me in the dark. Huh, seems Goebbels was supposed to join a new cabinet, including the Admiral. Only, seeing where the Good Doctor's about to be a few hours from now, Dönitz has assumed dictatorial powers. Worse, he's gone so far's to declare himself Führer. As if there could be more than one! The whole thing's simply preposterous.

Ach, I feel so *alone*. Even the Vor Bunker's now but an empty shell. For the spirit you see which informed it is gone; now, nary a soul remains.

It could be worse. This I realize upon negotiating the crowded passages of the Vor Bunker. It's simply seething with refugees[597]; a veritable city of the damned, poised on the edge of the abyss. We skirt our way through, attempting to prevent rumor from leading to headlong panic. But this is impossible. Every effort had been made to seal off a section, so as to smuggle the bodies. Still, like a hive that's just lost its queen, somehow—*they know.*

Every now and then some SS, usually a Frenchie, is giving himself the *coup de grace.* Pressing on, lest such splatter spackle my greatcoat I muse: *is suicide the only way out?* Ach, for some of the SS you see've sworn an oath to destroy themselves upon the death of the Führer. And I wonder, 'Am I supposed to join them?[598] Or does my duty lie in making a stand with bunker security'; *that is, if such thing even exists...*

Hossbach's Quarters

Frau Junge is outside my door. With courage born of naivete she says, "We're attempting a breakout tonight. Would you like to go with?"

I turn it over a few minutes in my mind, savoring the relative solitude of quarters when, whether from apathy

---

597 [How could 'nary a soul' remain, yet the whole place be clogged with refugees? Either such simpletons didn't count, or, for Hossbach, such things as 'souls' had quite simply ceased to exist, upon the 'apotheosis' of Hitler.—N.B.]

598 Dr. Seidl has expressly—and, so far's I'm concerned, successfully—demonstrated I was *not* in the SS. Rather my 'membership' was strictly honorary; hence my conundrum. For there exists simply no precedent for weighing such informality. Still, the Boss being gone, I realized my loyalty lay with the Army that, for some thirty-odd years, I had so dutifully served.[—W.H.]

or cowardice, I agree to go with. Of course, I'm only doing it for the ladies; ach, for I've seen what the Ivans can do. Besides—*better be shot trying to escape, than fall into the hands of the Russians...*

Meantime, Goebbells it seems's slipped off with his wife. No sooner do I realize this, than two gunshots they ring out.[599]

In the Garden

Günsche and Linge dispose of the children, who, in their sleep, have already been poisoned. I grab Magda, then double-back to get the Good Doctor.

Kempka repeats his *róle* as per the petrol. Their bodies they burn in a makeshift grave, just a few meters from the Chief; and the wench with whom he has chosen to so tie his fate.

Back to the Vor Bunker

Footsteps outside my door. Ach, for perhaps the last time in my life, a woman has come to my room: why, it's Traudl; *huh, seems the little filly she can't get enough...*

"Bormann is at the zoo."

Pah, how patently unromantic.

"In a tank," she returns, nixing any hopes of *carpe maedchen.* "Beneath the lions' cages. We are to meet him there, then head for American lines. The Reichsleiter carries a message, intended to get Eisenhower's attention. But we must leave, *now*. Oh and, by the way—*this is a* Führerorder."

Oh good God, I've said it a hundred times. Yet only some frivolous kitchen-slut could ever preface it with 'By the way'. Really, have I been so put out by the Boss's death that the last mission of the Reich's been entrusted to some perfectly ridiculous woman? Why the very idea of piling in

599 [From the courtyard, as later depositions were to prove.—N.B.]

some tank, what with the Russians all about's simply preposterous.

In the commons, our 'Battle Group' assembles. The swine, they sit, sipping their tea.[600] Taking command, I assume the voice of reason: "We'd do better to pass ourselves off as civilians." But I am overruled; huh, seems rank doesn't mean what it used to.

Oh, what does it matter? *The zoo's as good a place to die as any...*

***

Why, what *happened*?

I remember turning off the Voss Strasse, when a shell it went off, thrusting me into this rotting husk of lumber; I'm a little worse the wear, but, *alive.*

What half-blind and hunched, I set to searching for my companions. Ach, we must have become separated, even before the explosion. For, I'm alone; bleeding, and, *alone...*

***

Oh thank God: I have been spotted by a detachment of the Hitler Youth; it is to them that I owe my life.

We make a suicide-run on the bombed-out craters which used to be roads leading out of the city, then head north.

Where, if successful, we are to link up with Admiral Dönitz for the final defense of the Reich.

600 [Or, one would imagine, something a tad bit stronger.—N.B.]

Chapter 47: Flensburg

May 1, 1945[601]: appr. 21.00

Requisitioning a couple of Red Cross trucks at gun-point, we hightail it to Flensburg, where the Admiral's set up command at the Naval Academy. My task here's to defend the palatial establishment against any incursion across the fjord; whereby layeth the land of the Danes. Imagine, me, a Panzer General: playing at guard; I mean, it's like I'm back in the fucking SA.

The castle's been occupied by the Admiral, so's to provide *de-facto* FHQ; or, as the Allies have it, 'Office of the Head of State'. Really it's something more. Yea, for the first-time since Stalingrad, that accursed malaprop intended to honor the Dwarvish Tsar[602], camaraderie it springs like sulphur, steaming our way off the fjord. Ach, for this slender strip on the Baltic's become but our last bastion of *blut und sohl.*[603]

The view is grand; especially seeing's I get to smoke. No, nothing like fleeing the moment, escaping one's cares so's to appreciate the bounty of nature. Oh, how it fills one with ardor, being this's the *Heimat*[604] for which we must fight.

---

601 [Hossbach had written '1 Mai,' in a scarcely legible aside. This was indeed the date of the breakout. The seat of *government* however did not relocate to Flensburg until the 3rd. In between, Dönitz set up shop in Ploen. The Grossadmiral's broadcast, at which Hossbach has Himmler being present, actually took place there. Himmler *did* however visit Flensburg, as early as 3rd May. The author appears to have conflated the incidents. This need not diminish the veracity of his account, provided one take cognizance of the facts I have hitherto mentioned.—N.B.]

602 [Obviously, Stalin.—N.B.]

603 ['*Blut und Sohl*': 'Blood and soil.'—N.B.]

604 ['Heimat': Homeland.—N.B.]

Memories they intervene: I recall the Führer saying he'd never negotiate; and that 'Göring can do it for me when I'm dead!' Well, now the moment has come to pass[605]: I am given a rifle, and told to take shifts with the rest of the men; huh, looks like I'm a sniper now, too.

Chatting up the rank-and-file, I learn some disturbing things: Himmler it seems's weaseled his way past the guards sent to arrest him.[606] And what now Bormann, who was supposed to effect his liquidation, has simply disappeared.[607] Why just last week, I considered the Reichsleiter but one more traitor; a parasite eating into the heart of the nation. Only, now the end is here, Bormann it seems was truest of all; *unlike Göring and Himmler.* But the whole *world's* upside down; *maybe Magda was right...*

At length I gather the reasons behind this detail: *Himmler's on the way here to take power.* With just one bullet, I can put an end to it all; pah—let him come!

Sonofawhore, Dönitz won't have it. Says Himmler cannot be made into a martyr; *a martyr for* whom*?*

I stand atop my little turret, what finger just itching to fire, taking in the verdant scene overlooking the firth. The Anglo-Amis are just a few kilometers off. Ach, the fjord it seems's become a second Channel. Imagine—the Germans a sea-faring people! And yet one bomber still could lay waste to us all. After that, anarchy; or, worse—*Himmler'll take power...*

---

605 ['negotiation': *i.e.*, with Dönitz: *Not* Göring.—N.B.]

606 [On April 29, Reuters published word of Himmler's 'peace offensive' through Switzerland. Hitler (again via Bormann) is said to have telegraphed the order for his paladin's arrest. The same day, Mussolini and his mistress were found murdered in a square in Milan. As with Göring, Hossbach left a chapter detailing the incident. Being they consist of nothing but the most vainglorious gloating I have excised them: To the benefit of all concerned. In the General's defense, one should take cognizance of the most shameful conditions which his captivity must have engendered.—N.B.]

607 [Allegedly killed on the Weidendammer bridge: He has been tried *in absentia.*—N.B.]

Hour after hour we wait. Why I'm beginning to doubt he's even en-route. Worse still's the torture; the time to *think*. To think, that is, of *him*.[608] And, to grieve; to grieve, alas, for *her*. Plus, my boy—oh, but where is my *boy*?

The dogs they filter out, running amok. Spotlights they flood a clearing in the woods; *Himmler himself approaches...*

Ah, I can see him, see him beneath the trees. And, casting my scope aside, I signal the Admiral he's come: "Two, perhaps three guards; perhaps a hundred meters." And, fingering my weapon, an abandoned Tokarev,[609] I hiss: "*Sir*: I think I can take him. Take him from—"

"*Stand down!*"

Now, obedience you see's a tough nut to crack. Thus with a tear in my eye I allow this betrayer of the German people pass unhindered; *why, it's the hardest thing I've ever had to do in my life...*

"Let him through," the Admiral he radios the gate. "Hossbach," he says. "Don't let them in the castle just yet. Devise a ruse so's to separate him from his team: *I'll take care of the rest.* And don't let them leave; at least, not till I've figured out what to do with them. Oh, don't prevent them doing their job—provided, of course, any contact with the outside's strictly forbidden. Got it?"

"*Verstehen,*"[610] I say, albeit still somewhat unsure.

Now, there's six men to my squad. Our task is to cover the upper-left quadrant.[611] Behind this column I lean, my person emplanted firm on the patio.

---

608 ['him': Obviously, *der Führer.*—N.B.]

609 [*Tokarev*: A Russian made, semi automatic rifle.—N.B.]

610 [*Verstehen*: 'Understood.'—N.B.]

611 [Presumably, of the castle.—N.B.]

The *former* Reichsführer[612] is shocked to find me barring him entrance to Mürwik.[613] "Hossbach, place yourself under arrest with one of my men."

"Sir," I beg, having him on. "If I can *just* see your permission—"

"The Reichsführer does not need permission!"

"I am so sorry: but the Führer has ordered your arrest."

He bolts to the alert, searching the meaning my eyes.

"The order originates with Hitler," the Admiral elaborates, stepping forth, two men at each side. "As you can see, we're all under arrest of sorts, owing to the enemy across the bay. Himmler, you are free to do as you please, provided you follow but one rule: give me your *word* you'll refrain from making contact with the outside. Should you attempt to leave, I shan't try to stop you. But you would be doing so at your very own risk: I wouldn't recommend it."

"But—but I am the Reichsführer!" he pouts, what his feelings evidently hurt.

"And that you are—or, *were*: Himmler, your actions are treasonous; and, therefore, punishable by death. But, being I'm in charge here,[614] I trust you'll find I can be quite magnanimous: so long as you keep within *my* rules. No doubt I could use a cool-head such's you; especially in the days to come. So, are you with me?"

"*Ja*," the old RF he mouths, in half-muted tones, what fully feeling the helplessness of the situation.

---

612 ['The *former* Reichsführer': Himmler's arrest was ordered April 29. He was succeeded by *Gauleiter* Karl Hanke, defender of Breslau, and lover of Maga Goebbels.—N.B.]

613 [*Mürwik*: The castle, previously Naval HQ, used to house the Dönitz regime.—N.B.]

614 ['in charge here': Ostensibly, North Germany: Of this much Himmler was aware. Yet Dönitz was about to recast the phrase in an entirely different light.—N.B.]

"Oh," the Admiral soothes. "It will all be over soon. We will surrender to the Amis: at least *they* fought with honor. But the Russian? He's not human! No, there can no capitulation to *him*; not so long's there's refugees trying to flee."

"I daresay," Himmler he says, leaning against the balcony, slowly retrieving a map from his pocket. "*Here*," he stabs, adjusting that ridiculous pince-nez, clutching for the power he so recently held: "*Berchtesgaden*: we make our stand here." He struts, whether from habit, or, seeking a cleft into the castle. "That will buy us some time: time for the enemy to come to finally blows. By Zeus! Once the world sees how those beasts behaved on German soil, they'll have second thoughts about sicking them on Europe."

"Sure," Dönitz he chides, blocking the entrance as though he were the last line of defense. "And that'll make great pulp for idiots like Ley[615] who'll believe it. But *I* know you'd only use such time to cut a deal with your friends in Switzerland. Tell me: do you think *Ivan* would allow a simple thing such as Swiss neutrality get in the way? Would *you*?"

"But," he stammers. "The Law, the Law of *History* proves the enemy alliance to be so... *unnatural*, a breakup is bound to occur." He fidgets, distracted by the waves; or, more likely, the sounds of artillery just across the fjord. "Otherwise, history can have no meaning."

"You're *hoping*. Now, if you'll excuse me—*I've a people to save.* You of all people ought to understand: that used to be the virtue of the SS."

I heave a great sigh, sensing a reconciliation is at hand.

---

615 [Ley, Robert, *Ph.D.*: Head of the monolithic *Labor Front*. Fanatical Nazi, and inveterate drunk, Ley hung himself within days of having been indicted: A relief to his fellows then facing trial.—N.B.]

"The *Lebensborn*," Dönitz concedes, what giving the devil his due. "In them you have preserved a healthy stock, from which to rebuild our people. And, trust me—*the German people are going to need it.* But, these Generals..." And, here, here he eyes him with what can only be called the most profound contempt. "The SS has produced not one General worthy of an Army—let alone Führer of the Reich!" Why, Dönitz is *beside* himself; they stand face to face.

Himmler is aghast, apoplectic. "Sir, I—*I* challenge *you...*"

The Admiral he hefts up a hand, then steps off to the side.

An unshaven NCO issues out the door. He's missing an arm, he is, his presence here merely meant to show Himmler his true position.

"That'll be all, Sedgwick. Now, as for *you*," Dönitz he turns, inhaling the scent carried by a breeze coming off the shore; the better so to stomach the odiousness of his adversary. "I'll make you a deal: just stay within these walls," he motions, indicating the imposing fortress to which Sedgwick has returned. "On your own recognizance. Otherwise I shall have no choice but to throw you in brig with the rest of your men; *and I don't think you'd like that...*"

Himmler he glares, what murder in his eyes. Still that doesn't change things one bit. The Reichsführer[616] he takes some time to compose himself then says, "Presently we shall stay. However, you still haven't answered my question."

"A *duel*? Nonsense: the Führer's strictly forbidden it."

And, with these words, I see: Hitler's death is still being kept from the German people; and, apparently, from Himmler himself...

616 [*Former* Reichsführer, as previously mentioned.—N.B.]

"You shall be well-treated," the Admiral resumes. "However, dispel any illusions you might have: *I* am in charge. Your word no longer carries any weight around here. Oh, sure, one of your goons might bump me off in the middle of the night. But I am surrounded by *Kriegsmarine*[617], men who'd gladly exchange their lives in order to purchase mine. And yet you, what have you done, hmm? Gone and plotted treason behind the Führer's back—that's what! *I* on the other hand must negotiate the surrender of all North Germany. Plus there's still this little matter of the *V-weapons*[618] with which to attend."

Why, I daren't breathe...

"Himmler," he goes on, fingers a-tap, what air more reticent than regal. "I've seen to it your order to liquidate von Braun and his team will not be carried out. No," he paces, mindful to keep an eye on Himmler, 'and all his goons': "Germany is going to have need of them yet. Yes, we must get them out, get them out while we can. Oh—we must send them to the *U.S.A.*[619]"

Why I can hardly contain myself; what a *Mordskirl.*[620] In fact, far more flexible than ever I've given him credit.

"Should you exit this door," the Admiral proceeds, indicating the whence Himmler's trying to gain entry. "Once hostilities end, I shan't try to stop you. But, first,

---

617 [Kriegsmarine: German Navy.—N.B.]

618 ['V Weapons': 'Vengeance Weapons' (*Vergeltungswaffen*), Gocbbels' misleading moniker for the rocket (*A4*, or 'V2'), plus the Luftwaffe's primitive pilotless missile, the Fi-103 (*i.e.*, 'V1.') The press has proliferated a plethora of pulp purporting 'V' to have stood for 'Victory Weapons,' *i.e.*, atomics. In which case they should have been known as 'S Weapons,' as in *sieg*; or 'A,' as in *angst*. Moreover, as everybody knows, it was sheer American ingenuity, which ever produced anything of the sort.—N.B.]

619 ['der U.S.A.' in the original. It need hardly be noted that, by this point, 'U.S.A.' no longer meant Hitler.—N.B.]

620 [*Mordskirl* ('lady killer', *i.e.*, 'stud'): Its use here is derogatory to Himmler.—N.B.]

first you must do something for me. Now—*where's Kammler?*"

"Kammler?" Himmler he writhes, what palpable the look of terror in his eyes. "*He's come for me...*"

"No you fool, not *for* you: *I* however am come for him!" The Admiral he preens, putting on a front. "We must get these boys to America; that is before Ivan snatches them up."

Himmler's eyes they bulge—slowly, at first, then retreat, recalculating possibilities. "Admiral," he preens, apparently just as adamant about not calling him Führer. "I can deliver Kammler: *for a price.* Of course I shall require my own team, in addition to the release of my men. Find me Kersten; bring me Bach[621]; and, most important—get me Sepp Dietrich!"[622]

The Admiral he simply says: "*No.*"

"Then let me go, and I'll find them myself: *then* you can have Kammler."

The Admiral he stares a good, long while then says: "I am so sorry; but I cannot help you."

Now, Himmler's team, three-men strong, each thrust a left-foot forth, finger on the trigger; and everything's at an impasse.

I tense up, haven't the stones; ach, for the Führer you see was the vital spark which informed us; *without him truly we are nothing...*

"Stand down," Dönitz ordains, his first act as 'Führer'.

---

621 [*General* Bach-Zelewski, Erich, *von dem*: Like Kammler, an *Obergruppenführer*, or General of the SS. Though implicated in sundry crimes, he has managed to escape prosecution, via the novel device of testifying against his superiors.—N.B.]

622 [*General* Dietrich, Joseph 'Sepp': Hitler's favorite soldier. The *Oberst-Gruppenführer* (SS) held the highest rank after Himmler. Considered a father to all his men. The Allies however have not been so filial, sentencing him to life for his purported role in the massacre at Malmédy.—N.B.]

We retreat from the aim to the ready; actually, I never quite made it to the former. Only, now, now I've no choice but to make my stand as one of Karl die Kleine's men.[623]

"I have changed my mind," the Admiral returns; words the *real* Führer never would have uttered. "You are free to leave: you've only enter *that* door," he points, indicating a blockhouse leading to the woods.

Shells they scamper across the fjord, painting the sky with the luminance of light. It's hard to say, but—*it looks like the enemy's drawing near...*

Himmler he turns deathly pale. "Then you have won: at present we shall stay. And I wish I could tell you where Kammler is, really I do. But, quite frankly, I have no idea. Now, snap out old man—I say snap to! Oh, this is all your fault: you should have liquidated Braun while you still had the chance. Really, how *senile*, countermanding a direct—"

And, realizing he's overextended himself, Himmler retreats to the safety of a subordinate silence.

This is our cue. Neurath[624] and I set up a transmitter in back of the truck. He mans the controls, then I return to the patio so's to join the Admiral.

Ach, for Himmler you see's about to become privy to a stunt the likes of which he can scarcely conceive...

***

We erect a platform at the bottom of the patio. Following which, I take my stand next to Himmler two-steps behind. We are arrayed in triadic fashion, what silver and bronze flanking gold.[625] Of course, Himmler he's no

---

623 [*Karl*, Dönitz's Christian name; *die*, article denoting femininity; *kleine*, small. The unspoken reference is to Charlemagne, a 'giant,' known to Jerry as 'Karl *der* Grosse,' *i.e.*, great.—N.B.]

624 [*Kapitainleutnant* (Lieutenant) Ludde-Neurath, Walter: Dönitz's adjutant.—N.B.]

625 ['silver and bronze flanking gold': The reference is to the Olympics. —N.B.]

idea what's about to transpire; still, sensing the import, why he wouldn't miss it for the world.

The Admiral approaches the mike and says: "Citizens of the Greater German Reich! Our beloved Führer and Reichs Chancellor Adolf Hitler has fallen while defending Fortress Berlin. This is Admiral Dönitz: the Führer appointed me his successor. Let the world know it is my unshakeable will to continue the fight on the Eastern Front: and on the Eastern Front alone. The German people have no quarrel with the armies of the West. We will not interfere with their continued operations; *quite the contrary.* In fact I promise them passage—*all the way to Berlin*. Should however they continue to harass us then we shall defend ourselves to the very last. Long live the Greater German Reich!"

I turn to Neurath in his truck; ach, but he just shakes his head. It's some time before he realizes the Admiral's actually done. It's fitting, really, seeing there's nearly a minute of nothing but air. I signal an unmistakable hint. Belated he puts on a march, babbling incoherent when it is done.

Alas the Admiral is ready: a technician is called; the microphone it screams; what Himmler and I damned near butt heads just shielding our ears; the Admiral at the mike he downright nearly joins us. Which latter shoots Neurath a look, inducing him thus to button his trap.

A second address, intended for commanders in the field, is set to be broadcast on secret Wehrmacht frequencies. Old Dönitz he takes a step back, such that now he's nearly on top of us; then, bracing, falls upon the mike:

"Soldiers of the West: cancel all offensive operations, save to secure lines of retreat. Orders to follow, re: which units to be employed. General effect to be that of disengagement followed by rapid redeployment via railway out east. Stragglers and remnants of decimated units to follow, individual or in groups, via undefended lines.

Deserters to be shot. Northernmost troops to be ferried to the Baltic in order to save refugees, in concert with the *Kriegsmarine*. Last I have contacted the Red Cross and, as a gesture of good will, have arranged for the transfer of all *POW*s and camps."[626]

"But, you can't *do* that," Himmler he flails, unsuccessfully trying to grab the mike. "You must liquidate, I say—liquidate them all!" He lunges, flush with derangement in his eyes.

And, unseemly though it might be, I am forced to tackle the most dangerous man in the Reich; once restrained, though, he lay like an angel complicit.

The Admiral he finishes his communication; then, turning to the *former* head of the SS, snaps, "Himmler my dear—you were in cahoots with the enemy! Really, selling Jews for trucks?[627] And, now, now you wish to simply just bump them all off? There's Aryans in those camps, too. And besides: *we've lost much blood already.*"

"Then I have failed," he says, much to my surprise.

Progressive you see I've allowed the swine squirm out from under, once it'd become clear he entertained no more such impulsive notions.

"The camps," Himmler says. "It's true: the Führer always said we should liquidate everything we might find, in case an insurrection should ever occur, so as to deprive it of its leadership. For, apart from being a leader, the Jew is a carrier of typhus; so we *can't* just let them be. Not to mention the whole refugee crisis. Oh, Herr Admiral, I exhort you—expunge this pungent excrescence!"

---

626 [*i.e.*, concentration camps. The German reads, 'KZs.'—N.B.]

627 [Himmler and a Zionist named Brand flirted with a (failed) scheme during the last few months of the war. A thousand Jews were actually released, with the promise of more to come. Jerry was to receive trucks, 'only for use in the east.' Hossbach claims Hitler knew nothing of anything Himmler 'and that crony Eichmann' might have had 'in store for those Jews.'—N.B.]

"We need chips my boy," the latter he says, refilling his pipe. "But these creatures in your camps—how am I supposed to cut a deal with *that*? Trust me: these Yids are no threat to anyone; ech, you've seen to that. Like these marches I keep hearing about. Men dropping like flies. Oh —look at the mess you've made!"

"One hears quite a bit of exaggeration," is all the RF can muster, insomuch as offer a reply.

"You've some stones, Himmler; *some stones.* Hossbach," the Admiral screams. "Draft the appropriate papers."

Well well well—looks like I'm an adjutant once more...

"Jawohl," I say, "Herr Chancellor," employing his civilian title—for, is not the *Red Cross* a civilian organization? Besides, I'd rather *die* than call him Führer.

In an aside, or rather, bid to win the Admiral's acclaim, I maneuver Himmler onto the patio. Hushed of breath I speak: "We need the engineers alive. Be a good chap now, will you, and draft an order to Kammler stating as much; the Admiral would be forever grateful."

Himmler he sneers, knowing what full-well my motive. Still, having heard it straight from the Admiral's mouth, he knows it comes from the top. "*Fine*," he says then, bidding me find the necessary implements, condescends so's to oblige.

Into the Castle

After conferring with Neurath, I ensure the drafting will be done on the *q.t.*[628], alleging the Admiral demands silence so's to go over some papers. This being done, the former he leads us inside; the RF and his guard cautiously follow. Assembling to an ante-room, Neurath produces

[628] [re, 'on the q.t.': An anglicism, adorning the original, meaning 'on the quiet.'—N.B.]

some cigars which, more than anything, seems to put them more at ease; then, he disappears behind the door.

An eternity goes by, shamming converse with two toughs, while Himmler he gives me the Evil Eye. Eventually the adjutant returns, informing us the 'drafting room'[629] is ready, and bids us please presently follow.

Retiring to one of the guest-rooms, equipped with full felt-rug yet service-issue cot, I manage to steal a few moments' sleep.[630] Alas Good Neurath appears, presenting an envelope which, he assures me, contains Himmler's written plea. I accompany him to the Admiral, so's to hand it to the old sot myself.

"*Sir,*" a Leutnant he shouts, once we've been packed into the Admiral's obstreperous lair. "The lines are down."

Crackling it fills the very air; the electricity it precipitately go out. We flood the room with our service-lights.

Himmler is fetched, thus that we might keep an eye on him. The poor girl; why, he seems so *scared...*

And, rising above the deafening din, what with countless secretaries and subalterns, the Admiral he says, "Gentlemen—it looks like we're in a ride. Still, I offer no choice: *for millions of lives are at stake.* Oh—God save the Greater German Reich!"

He struts off, gathering his bodyguard and light-bearing adjutants; which, apparently, does not include me.

From habit I follow, leaving Himmler alone[631] with his mates; who, quiet, slip out into the merciless cold...[632]

---

629 [Given the chaotic conditions, I doubt Mürwik had any such thing. The delay was probably spent fabricating a facsimile of the stamp and letterhead of the 'Reichsführer SS.'—N.B.]

630 [Apparently 'hide and go sleep' trumped the order to 'separate Himmler from his guard.'—N.B.]

631 ['alone': *i.e.*, free of any guard, save the (apparently oblivious) 'countless secretaries and subalterns.'—N.B.]

632 [re, Hossbach's allowing Himmler to slip off: This was unintentional. The defendant is merely relating a fact which, much to his embarrassment, he was to realize all too soon.—N.B.]

Chapter 48: Kammler

Waiting in a wheat field, somewhere south of Flensburg: May 5, 1945

Daily hath our cities paid the price for Göring's criminal malfeasance. Only, now, there's nothing left to bomb; *yea, our blood is on his hands.* And yet, but just like the Luftwaffe, the Reichsmarschall is nowhere to be found.[633] Yes for the paradox of all military training is, in order to get a man to take a hill, he must be willing to die. Which, inculcates a certain sense of superiority over the masses he is intended to lead. Why such man feels he can take on most anything. Therefore the Army must be kept in the field at all costs; at least, until they get their fill of the fling. For the entire history of Rome is but testament to the danger of allowing one's soldiers return premature. Ach, for the chain of command you see it breaks down; such nation must end in civil war.

Which calamity almost overtook us Twenty July, when the swine they tried to assassinate him. Had they succeeded, there could have been no talk of us fighting anyone but ourselves come 1945. Of course the Boss is dead; Göring, however, is not. Yet still, is our would-be Caesar, what this red-rouged pompadour, champing to cross the Rubicon—or even the Rhine? Pah, Göring—some successor!

'What's this?' you say. 'Dönitz has the succession. See, it's right there—the Führer named him in his will.'

Fool; if he were a man, he'd come claim it; so much the rot in that sybarite's soul...

You think it's better across the pond? Oh, our enemies like to paint themselves as some moral, upright force, pitted against us 'evil Huns'. In fact, this impossible

---

633 [The same day would find Göring released from Luftwaffe 'confinement' (essentially, house arrest.) He subsequently sought captivity behind American lines.—N.B.]

wedding of Capitalist and Communist's the result of inferior beings having set themselves up as Führer.[634] For there's an order implicit in nature; and why such triflers have no idea the harm they've caused. The instant the blood runs thin, some idiot declares himself king, or president; thusly have the Teutonic peoples become despoiled.

The extermination of my people's an historical inevitability, what since the swastika ceased to fly. Only, where Genghis Khan once failed—*Stalin shall succeed.* Pah, this naval sheisster's the audacity to command; just thank God Hitler didn't live to—[635]

Kammler!

There he is, traipsing through the field like some modern legionnaire. I envy him his chin; his abandonment; his lack of care and concealment.

He turns, fixing on me: "*Howdy.*"

And, alas, I see no Roman, rather, but a cowboy from the American West: the hat; the forehead; the irascible leer; the devolved head what with a face that only a mother could love.

Hand on holster he sneers: "*You?*"

And, oh good God, I can see death in his eyes. The mammoth jaw, but so slack and sinister; *Kammler, the man with the leer.* I try not to stare at his disjowled face when, gazing into blackest of pits I see: *nothing*. With a deep breath I remind myself say from whence I have come: "I have come straight from the Führer."

"The *Führer*?" he scowls, bloodless, white.

"Oh, not *the* Führer," I say, what relishing his confusion. For I simply *must* maintain the illusion of strength. Yes for I'd called in this favor, and so'd sent a

---

634 ['Führer': I remind the reader that, in German, the term means 'leader'.—N.B.]

635 [This is yet one more passage at which, as editor, I have had to just throw up my hands. Everybody knows Hitler, via Bormann, had himself appointed Dönitz president. Yet, as the *muzhiks* used to say, 'If the Tsar only *knew.*'—N.B.]

telex, *seeming* to've come from FHQ[636], dictating where we should meet. His interest piqued I add, "I meant, *Admiral.* Or haven't you heard?"

"Ech," he sneers. "I am no fool. Now, the Führer—*where is he?* What have you done with him?"

I laugh; *gallows humor.* "Hitler is quite dead, I assure you. Before he died, he named Dönitz President. Goebbels was supposed to assume the Chancellorship[637], but decided to kill himself instead. The Admiral has combined both offices, and set himself up as 'Führer'."

The Leery One is not impressed. "What does any of this have to do with me?" he lilts, motioning towards his pocket.

The swine, he'd only agreed to meet me, so's to find out 'what really happened', i.e., to the Chief. Yes you see for I'd pulled a fast one, so's to make him think something was really up; it was the only way. Now, disappointed to learn the truth, he senses the trap.

And I realize: 'Ha-bay, you're swimming with the sharks. Why just one wrong move, you'll sink; sink what just like a rock.'

"Now now," I say. "*Obergruppenführer*: no need shoot the messenger." My voice it trails in panic; quickly I recover. "I'll be honest: we need Braun and his team alive."

"This is not the Reichsführer's wish," he smiles, clearly back in his element.

"Oh, but it is," I say, thrashing some wheat, then hand him the envelope bequeathed me by Himmler.

He leers, what this stupid smirk on his face. Like lightning he proceeds to pry the letter out. Scowling he eyes it by the light of the moon. "Oh, that's Himmler

---

636 [re, '*seeming* to've come from FHQ': The only reading that makes any sense is that, by 'FHQ,' he means 'The Führer Bunker.' In which case the plot was intended to make Kammler believe Hitler was still alive, sewing confusion and doubt accordingly.—N.B.]

637 ['assume the Chancellorship': *i.e.*, become Prime Minister.—N.B.]

alright. Well he—he can just go to the devil!" There follows a perfunctory shrug, perquisite to a sneer. "I guess they're somebody else's problem."

Why, I'm amazed he's taking it so well; my charm you see it must have rubbed off.[638]

His face a mask, an ephemera, he tucks the letter in his pocket and says: "If you are lying you will be shot," then stamps into the cold, oppressive night.[639]

Dönitz's Office

Back at Mürwik, the Admiral debriefs me. "So—where's Kammler?"

I'll be dammed if I know...

"Sir," I say, in that simple language that's the virtue us sons of the soil. "The Obergruppenführer's given his word. Besides, he saw the signature. An old forger like that[640] must know it really is Himmler's writing."

"Fool—he did nothing of the sort!" Why, I never; ach, for the *real* Führer never stooped to insulting me in such fashion. His fingers they beat time on the desk. "Do you have the letter?"

"Ja," I say, seeing Neurath was good enough to make me a copy.

---

638 [He was taking 'it' so well, because there was nothing to take. Braunie, via Dornberger, had already reached a deal with Kammler. As such the latter's meeting with Hossbach outside Flensburg appears highly suspect. Some think the *Obergruppenführer* was already dead. One may even doubt it was he with whom Hossbach had met. All I can say is, such conflicting accounts *might* have abetted Kammler's escape, amidst the very confusion they tended to engender. I fancy he is either dead, or, less likely, has reinvented himself as one of the most powerful men in the world.—N.B.]

639 [By all accounts, never to be seen again.—N.B.]

640 [One may ask why, if Hossbach's characterization is correct, Kammler would have needed help procuring any such papers. The Reich had been undergoing air raids for months. Given the collapse of the transportation system, perhaps the *Obergruppenführer* no longer had access to the 'tools of the trade.'—N.B.]

"*Amateurs*," he says, what more than a hint of haughtiness in his throat. "This Kammler's in cahootz with Himmler; I'll bet he's left a code here somewhere—Neurath!"

And, dodging the feverish activity which constitutes the chaos of Dönitz's den[641], not to mention his entire regime, Good Neurath retrieves my carbon-copy.

"Get Krylock," the Admiral he huffs, then irritably storms off.

Neurath obediently accompanies him; and, shrugging, bids me I should follow.

The Grossadmiral's Quarters

Leading us to a spartan billet, but so at odds with the rest of the place, the Admiral he resumes, "Neurath here knows a man in the *Forschungsamt*[642]; perhaps he can decode what Himmler has hidden."

Bidding me have seat, Dönitz allows Neurath use of his own private line. I try to make small-talk, while the latter he waits for the operator to connect him. But he just stares, eagle-eyed, absorbed in his adjutant's task.

"He's sending Lorentz," he rasps, upon finally obtaining a connection.

My he's piqued, obviously envious the brandy that we've been sipping; the which he was not proffered.

I open my trap, and get as far this anecdote[643] when, smiling, I realize the punch-line's far from having sunk in.

Rather the old-boy he eyes his adjutant and says, "Neurath, I wanted you here for a reason: no one outside

641 [It is clear from the context of that which has preceded, as well as that which is to follow, that by 'den' he means 'office.' I have chosen to retain the term, in addition to employing this note, in lieu of mucking with the translation any more than I already have.—N.B.]

642 [*Forschungsamt*: Wiretapping service, under the auspice of Göring. —N.B.]

643 [As to the substance of which, luckily we have been spared.—N.B.]

this door," he adds, with the slightest nod towards me. "Must know the whence, nor why, regarding which you have been sent." He finishes his drink, then sends his adjutant to ascertain the fate of my son; even's I, a *real* Führer Adjutant, can but sit and wait.

"Listen," Dönitz he pants, once Good Neurath has left.

Oh, I suppose words are issuing out his mouth; still, none of it seems much use. Rather I employ my eyes, so's to take in the 'ambience' of the place. It's not very big: about the size of a barracks[644], save the transmitter, telegraph, and telegraphy in lieu of beds.

The Admiral he begins to pace. "*Kammler,*" he says and, with that, my ears they perk. "Thinks Himmler's our prisoner; that we acquired his signature under duress."

"But," I say. "He is... and we did."

He beholds me an abnormal while. Head down, hands behind the back, he shrugs. "I have told Himmler he is free to go."

"You *huh*?" I demand, in a voice why I'd never use with the Führer.

"*Someone* it seems let him slip off."

Oh...

"That's alright: Neurath caught him and his cronies sneaking around the pier. That's when I decided: things have gone on long enough. They left an hour ago. Why," he adds, mocking. "Did you need to see them?"

Why, I could just box his ears—oh, I'd give him a thrashing! Rather I stare.

He whispers: "*Lao Tsu.*"

---

644 ['barracks': Further consultation (with one of my colleagues at Fort Bliss) corroborates my assumption that, by 'barracks,' he means 'quarters.' The German had left me somewhat uncertain. In such instances I have, as a rule, deferred to the advice of native speakers.—N.B.]

"How-who?" Pah, these naval sheissters; ach, they're always picking up these foreign customs. The Führer he frowned on it.

"Lao Tsu," he says. "A Chinaman, wrote the *Art of War*; which really you should read." He pauses, searching for comprehension and, finding the none, continues. "If your enemy's enemy's your enemy, then—set the cat among the pigeons!"

"But," I jest, stuck in this chinky red chair,[645] what trying free myself from this infernal contraption: "*Who*'s the pigeon?"

"It does not matter. Put two thugs like that together and, I assure you—soon, they'll be seeing enemies everywhere. Let them chase their own tail!"

Why, I think I'm beginning to get the drift...

"Kammler'll be so busy trying to keep one step ahead of Himmler—and, vice versa—neither *one* will ever make it to Oberammergau; where, by the way, the engineers have been sequestered."

My lucky stars!

"Sorry I had to send you on such a fool's errand; but, then again—*that's why I'm Führer.* Once Dornberger'd sent word that they had arrived, I had to find some means of convincing Kammler that they were under threat of bombardment.[646] You should be *proud*; for, you've bought them much-needed time. Besides, the Führer didn't *really* mean to have them liquidated."

Huh? The Führer'd fought the rocket-men all along; only these last few months did he seem content to just leave them be. I stammer, "They were arrested, arrested by—"

---

645 ['chinky': He means Japanese.—N.B.]

646 [Imagine the look on Dönitz's face if, some day in reading this, he learns Kammler had forged the Dornberger deal in the first place. The Grossadmiral is likewise awaiting the verdict to his trial.—N.B.]

"By the SS; Hitler never signed off. Oh, I know it must be hard, given your proximity to Hitler but, what we had here was really a two-party state: the *NSDAP*,[647] under Bormann; and the SS under Himmler. And, now that Hitler's dead, Himmler's goons are off bribing the Gauleiters[648] to come work for him. And why not? The SS still holds all the 'marks. Of course they're fabricated; still, it's possible people will accept them. In fact a little birdie even told me you *yourself*'d once been charged with your own son's liquidation, 'if the Russians should ever get near.' Oh, why do you think he gave you cyanide?" The swine; *he laughs.* "Times have changed old boy. Hitler was hoping for a miracle: we all were. Only, now it hasn't come off, do you think *I'm* going to go down as the one who lost *space* to the Russians?" Grousing he upbraids his desk.

I half-listen, half-gaze out the porthole, entranced by the mist steaming off the shore...

"Even if we were to bump off every scientist that we might find, surely we'd never catch them all; then, Ivan would have the only ones. In which case, nothing could stop him. The war it would have been in vain; oh—it all would have been in vain! No, we must be *proud* of their achievement. Ech, for the sake of the German people we must do everything possible in order to protect it. To this end I have opened negotiations with the Amis, for the express purpose of the scientists' preservation."[649]

"Sir," I say, stating the obvious. "Aren't you afraid Himmler will come after you? With more than four men this time, too, now he knows the score?"

---

647 ['NSDAP' (*Nationalsozialistische Arbeiterpartei)*: National Socialist German Worker's Party, *i.e.*, 'Nazis.'—N.B.]

648 [*Gauleiters* (District Leaders): *NSDAP* members who, in the end, had become responsible for their respective fiefs.—N.B.]

649 [In just one page, we find both Kammler *and* the Americans playing Dönitz the fool. It was sheer brilliance on the part of the Americans that, having already reached a deal with Kammler, they were able to elicit concessions which Dönitz had no need to make.—N.B.]

"No," he huffs. "He won't. Himmler, for all his faults, is still a gentleman; and a gentleman keeps his word. Besides, the West knows they'll have to fight Ivan sooner or later. And, they're going to need a buffer zone in order to do it: *here, right here in Germany*; just like we had with Poland. Save that Ivan's gone and moved his border *west*; like a dagger piercing Europe to the bone. As such, if we are to eke out even a modicum of an existence, then this demands that the German people still live; *this* is why we are fighting. We must save our soldiers, our refugees out in the east. My whole *policy* consists of surrender to the Anglo-Amis with our honor still intact. *This* is the solution which for too long has been denied the German people—and I won't stand for it: *not while I'm Führer.*"

"In which case then, *Grossadmiral*,"[650] I strain, stressing the title. "I request leave, so's to visit my son."

"It's like I told Himmler—go! If you can. For, *there*," he adds, pointing out the porthole towards the land of the Danes. "*There* is the front."

I nod, acknowledging the danger. He confers his blessing with a shake of the hands, decommissioning me from the service; thus putting an end to a journey some thirty-odd years in the making.

I depart with a hollow feeling in the pit of my stomach. Now, they say it isn't soldierly to cry but, dammit, some things just cannot be helped; for, the Admiral's order means the emasculation of my people.

And, with it, the end of the Thousand-Year Reich...[651]

---

650 [*Grossadmiral* (Grand Admiral): Since 1943, Dönitz's actual rank. Hossbach has employed his old rank, probably more from familiarity than any intended slight. Yet, to his face, we find the defendant using the actual term: In lieu, of course, of 'stooping to calling him Führer.'—N.B.]

651 [His math is a bit off: It lasted scarcely more than twelve.—N.B.]

Chapter 49: Verdict

Oct. 1, 1946:[652] Hossbach's Cell

I had to hide my toilet paper, upon the which I have been writing, seeing somebody was coming; *oh thank God, it was only Seidl.* We exchanged pleasantries. Of a sudden he made a most solemn gesture then whispered, "*The verdict is about to come through.*"

Seidl, you fox; must've bribed one of the guards. For he'd this bottle. "You know: *to help see you through.*"

I rasped, "You should've brought cyanide instead!"

***

Why, I feel sorry for the old chap; really, it's not his fault. Or perhaps I realize this only now; you know, after the whiskey. Oh, but where'd he *go*? I mean, he was *right here*. How long's it been—days? *The voices they return*; ach, I thought I'd rid them long ago...

Wait—something's taped to this bottle. Seidl, you fox, he *was* here: a letter; or, series of missives from Jack. Either he couldn't send them; or, more likely, the Gestapo at some point'd gotten hold. Somehow, devil knows, my attorney'd managed obtain them. Perhaps it's better, what the delay. For surely I should have met my end several times over trying to find him; now, I suppose the Tribunal will see to that.

I haven't time to copy them: I'll keep them here, along with this record, in hope some sympathetic gaoler may some day preserve it.

---

652 [The only reminiscing left involves letters *supposedly* written by me. As such have I decided to cease use of italics in differentiating Hossbach's present, *i.e.*, prison house narration, from his heretofore exhausted recollections. Lest there be any confusion, 'my' letters, concealed in Hossbach's manuscript, have been reproduced, in bold faced italic.—N.B.]

[Note: Here follow 'my' purported letters.—N.B.]

[“] *April 3, 1945*

Father,[653]

The Russians are coming.

Every day, more and more orders pile up, one contradicting the other. Himmler says, “Stay put.”[654] ***Meantime Kammler's train is at the ready, prepared to take us to his own private camp. Then there's the army: They insist we take our billeting to Bleicherode, not far from Nordhausen. Last, the Grossadmiral insists, by hook or by crook, that we make it to the Baltic: Whence he swears the Kriegsmarine will evacuate us to Holland.***[655]

Oh—bother them all!

*****[656]

That B. Really, he is so grand. As ever, he had a plan: Dressed in impeccable SS gear (impeccable since he's scarcely ever made use of it), he commandeered some trucks. We loaded them with priceless equipment, then hightailed it before anyone was the wiser.

Until we got to the bridge. An imbroglio ensued trying to cross. The guard said we should do no such thing. B. got out to argue, but was told to wait along with the rest: To 'wait for word,' **i.e.,** ***from Himmler.***

---

[653] Through two world wars, this is the *one word* truly that breaks my heart.[—W.H.] [This note was scribbled atop one of 'my' purported letters.—N.B.]

[654] ['stay put': Judging from the date, apparently at the Mittelwerke.—N.B.]

[655] [For Holland read 'Flensburg.' Either a blind, or, whoever wrote it didn't know their Dutch from their Danes.—N.B.]

[656] [re, '***': Date unknown, possibly on, or just after, April 3. I have appended three asterisks, due to a change at this juncture in the purported letter's ink. This, I take it, is intended to indicate a new entry; and, possibly, date.—N.B.]

B. stormed, "There is no time! Really, how **dare** *you get in the way of the* SS?*" He screamed, expletives at the top of his lungs, pointing to the forbidding letters atop our column. Frankly, I'd no idea what he might mean. The trucks were supposed to read, 'BzbV Heer,'* **i.e.,** *'Working Staff of the Army.'*[657] *Somebody must have screwed up, for they actually read, 'VzbV,' which means, well, nothing.*

Thanks to B., it now means, 'Project for Special Disposition.'[658] *Just innocuous enough to fill the guard with superstitious dread, twisting his mind with terror untold. B. strolled off, flashing that irresistible smile, every now and then threatening some poor bloke with the most medieval torture.*

The guard was driven to panic, disclaiming all responsibility. He even included, free of charge, a foulmouthed diatribe aimed at his superiors. Needless to say, he let us through.

We hadn't the slightest where we were going. B. said he used to know the place, back when he was seeing this bird. Yet his memory's not much these days, thanks to the havoc you and your Nazi bigwigs have caused.

There came a moment of indecision: Z. thought we should make for Kammler's, but B. ruled this out in no uncertain terms. And yet, where could we go? Then I recalled this wonderful castle, a hotel I'd read about when I was in England. It was a tough call: We made for my little villa.

And, though I can't say where, I will add our quarters are relatively safe. Plus we've all the amenities one could possibly imagine: And, by amenities, I mean we're almost completely surrounded by the Amis down in the valley.

Then so at last: **The end is almost here.**

---

657 [*i.e.*, Dornberger's group.—N.B.]

658 [*VZBV*: 'Vorhaben Zur Besondern Verwendung'—N.B.]

May 2

Weeks of waiting have nearly driven us batty: Until last night, when finally we heard the good news. After a hearty breakfast, we sent B.'s brother M. off on a bicycle, in search of the Amis below. He speaks better English than the rest of these Jerries. Plus they did not... or, I should say,* I *did not... exactly enjoy the prospect of what might transpire if I had been chosen to accompany him. As for M., he is to reveal our existence, then offer our peaceable surrender.

Meantime we've taken shelter in an abandoned hotel, somewhat less exotic than advertised. Rumors have been put about regarding these 'rampaging Moroccans' and assorted negroes from the French possessions. As such does the most important drinking party in history begin.

Pity the poor women in the valley: For there's simply no* way *that we'll ever be able to drink it all.

Eveningtime,

M. has returned, albeit alarmingly late, and given the good news: Our offer has been accepted. Even as I write, we are on our way behind American lines, hoping for a [—"]

***

I had to put the letter down, seeing a light'd come on just outside my cell. Well, guess I'll keep reading; no point hiding anything now...

But *wait*: ach, the sirens they *wail*—an air-raid? Only, could it *be*—the Führer was right: the Allies have come to blows at last!

***

No: *it's Göring.* Andrus, the swine, feared he might kill himself in his cell.[659] Of course, it turned out to be just a bunch of hot air—pah, just like the Reichsmarschall! Yet now we must pay for Fatty's crime, real or imagined: our belts and utensils have all been confiscated—not my crayons, thank God, nor this record; neither the illicit missives which they happen to conceal.[660]

I skim the letters's fast's I can, in case I should not live to finish.[661] Seems he's some place called El Paso—Texas, I think; or, perhaps the United States.[662] Well, at least one of us's going to make it. As for me, they must still be deliberating; well, it won't be long now...

Screams from the long-buried past erupt in my mind when, pounding the bars, I wail, "Stalin will have you all!"

Shivering, my body yet it burns; ach, how I wish I could but crawl, crawl outside my skin. And yet I cannot leave, trapped in this mortal coil. Why I accuse the very air —*but what have you done with the Führer?* My temples they scream; and my heart, my heart it begins to pound; must be a heart attack, or a stroke. Almost I rejoice; for, *now*, now you see there's no going back...

Bile it sluices out the side my tongue, up from beneath what like I'm on some sort of a drunk; the whiskey didn't help, either. The guards? They pay me no heed;

[659] [re, Göring's flirting with suicide: The incident, and the punishment allegedly inflicted, has been denied by the warden, as well as his chief of staff. Nonetheless, I wouldn't put it past them to keep it under wraps: Especially being the verdicts are expected any minute. —N.B.]

[660] ['crayons': Unfortunately, to this much I may attest: The implement Hossbach used, while composing the bulk of this record.—N.B.]

[661] [There appears to be some pages missing, *i.e.*, from among the documents I have received. Otherwise I would have transcribed the remainder of 'my' purported letters. Nonetheless Hossbach has summarized what he avers to have been my supposed movements: These I can neither confirm nor deny.—N.B.]

[662] [This is really very funny: I repeated it to all the gang.—N.B.]

swine, they laugh. And, alas, alas the thin veneer of a gentleman I've managed to construct it begins to unwind; *the voices they return.* And, like a fetus in the womb, I find myself traversing the various stages of life; or, as the Jew Freud would say—*I've gone stark-raving mad.*

Digging through my toiletries, I clasp the cyanide I've managed to conceal:[663] *in a minute, it will all be over...*

'Wait,' cries a voice, demanding me confront the hysteria building up within. 'There's still the verdict.'

I say this whilst stroking my phial, what like some Visigothic chief blessing his arms for battle. And, though I hesitate commit it to writing, let my contempt be my amends—*save it for the Russians!*[664]

'Get a grip,' I say; ach, for, the voices, the voices are starting to overwhelm. And I behold the face; *the face of P'pa floating above.* Oh, that's him alright: the gray bearded plume, what the comic insolence of disrepair. And the eyes —those cold, defeated eyes, upon the which M'ma would say, '*Ech*—that's him, alright.'

Oh, why are they taking so *long*? Frank, who used to be a sheisster, once told me the Amis, by whose rules this fiasco's being conducted, like to employ something called 'due process'. Which means we must wait for the Jew-lawyers to wipe the blood from the paperwork, so's to ease their good conscience. What with imaginative

---

663 ['cyanide': As the General has previously attested, the cyanide had been confiscated, when first he arrived at Mondorf. Here, he must be grasping at straws. Unless his previous statement, made with a clearer head, was an outright lie, in case his manuscript were discovered. In which case, the cyanide, *i.e.* the 'second phial' is, in actual fact, quite real.—N.B.]

664 [The defendant's fear is that, even if he should happen to survive any sentence the court might impose, still he might be turned over to the Russians. Therefore, it is out of character for him to have written as such. He must be beside himself. Moreover, writing everything down had become a habit, a way of maintaining his sanity, while awaiting the results of the trial.—N.B.]

letterheads, and fancy gobbledygook of all sorts; *huh, dotting their I's while crossing their t's...*

Nuremberg Court:
October 1, 1946

There was an eruption just outside my cell: the bars they'd flung open, ejecting a mass of guards; upon the which I was caught up. “Wait,” I'd said. “My notes,” purporting need them for my defense.

One of the guards—an Englishman, thank God—piped, “I fancy you's long done wif your defense; but then again I's no barrister.”

Whereupon I grabbed hold this record. Thence they marched me out of my cell, and dragged me here into court.

I am made to stand facing my accusers: one judge for each nation. The Cockroach has a heckuva head; why, his encephalitic index's off the charts. My, what good race; *he'll be sympathetic.* Besides, look at all the French who served with the Waffen-SS; not to mention Vichy. Yes, it's like I've always said: I am rather fond of the French. Surely they'll reciprocate.

Ah, the English. Yes I've tried to charm them's best I can, seeing we've a thousand years of history between us; but one pure race of Angles and Saxons. Only, their judge he wears a mask, what skin all blotchy albeit light.

Oh, but ach, the Yids you see've corrupted them what with their Wall Street; just as they did the ancient pagan world. With Christianity, the Jew exterminated countless Teutonic peoples, confabulating an unholy confection of pacifism laced with Jewish Law. And, now, now he's come for us: he's come for the better, higher man; *and, now, the rest of the world shall soon share our fate...*

Seidl, seeking cheer me up, hands me this note: “Churchill's buyer's remorse!” Yes, for the ex-PM you see's supposed to have said, 'Looks like we slaughtered the wrong pig!'[665] I hope his judge agrees.

The Russian, *the swine.* Why he thinks the firing squad too good, and wishes us all that we should just hang. His neck is set on the head of a peasant, what with all the fashion-sense of a Yid to boot; *I know his vote.*

Alas the Ami: head broad, skin smooth; though the earlobes they don't quite mesh. And I wonder, 'Does *he* have German blood?' Well, one thing's clear: *he* shall decide my fate; oh, God have mercy on his—

"The International Military Tribunal is now in session," Judge Lawrence he drones. "I shall read a brief statement, followed by the charges proffered against you, accompanied by the Tribunal's decision as to each."

I want to say no, to refuse; but obedience you see's a hard nut to crack. Originally, I'd planned no defense at all, as Fatty himself'd once boasted. Only, seeing him relent and make a real stand, inspired us to think such a thing's still possible. I am confident I have left nothing of consequence out of this record, whose final chapter I write on court-appointed paper, even as the Justice he mumbles the preamble; why, at this rate, I'll die of old-age before he gets to it.

A thought it comes to mind: before all the judges, what on bended knee I shall cast a glance and say, 'Goetz von Berlichingen!'[666] The courtroom shall erupt in a sea of guffaws; three pounces on the gavel shall cause them to cease...

I come to, aware of Judge Lawrence's prattling—even while, without realizing it, listening to his every word; and, equally sans thought, stretch my mind to recall, and so transcribe, everything he said:

---

665 ['Looks like we slaughtered the wrong pig.': Saying attributed to Mr. Churchill, meaning, 'We should have fought Stalin instead.'—N.B.]

666 [*Goetz von Berlichingen*: fig., 'lick my arse!'—N.B.]

"Under Article 27 of the Charter, the *International Military Tribunal* charges one Colonel, later General of Panzer Troops *Windemeer Hossbach*, with four counts: one, conspiracy to wage aggressive war; two, crimes against the peace; three, war crimes; and, four, crimes against humanity. The Tribunal has examined all the evidence and come to a decision with regard to each of the charges proffered against you: we, the International Military Tribunal, find you..."

THE END

www.ingramcontent.com/pod-product-compliance
Lightning Source LLC
Chambersburg PA
CBHW030826310726
48980CB00006B/661/J

* 9 7 8 0 6 9 2 6 7 2 0 5 1 *